**Praise for the**

...citing Western loaded with intrigue, suspense, and ...plot twists. One of Estleman's best, a smart, tightly ...d story."

—*Publishers Weekly* on *The Book of Murdock*

"Estleman is best known for his mysteries, but he's equally adept at Westerns, as he demonstrates again here. His novels—regardless of type—are peppered with humor, irony, and melancholy, and as a narrator, Murdock delivers all three. A clever plot and a satisfying conclusion round out a very enjoyable read."

—*Booklist* on *The Book of Murdock*

"Estleman rivals the finest American novelists with his gritty vision and keen ear."

—*The Washington Post Book Review* on *White Desert*

"Prose as picturesque as the Painted Desert. When Page Murdock shuffles the words, deal me in."

—*The New York Times Book Review*

"A historical Western in mirror-smooth mahogany prose . . . Louis L'Amour looks down with envy."

—*Kirkus Reviews* on *Port Hazard*

"A wildly entertaining read with great period atmosphere and dialogue." —*Booklist* on *Port Hazard*

# THE
# HIGH
# ROCKS

# STAMPING
# GROUND

· LOREN D. ESTLEMAN ·

A TOM DOHERTY ASSOCIATES BOOK / NEW YORK

This is a work of fiction. All of the characters, organizations, and events portrayed in these novels are either products of the author's imagination or are used fictitiously.

THE HIGH ROCKS AND STAMPING GROUND

*The High Rocks* copyright © 1979 by Loren D. Estleman

*Stamping Ground* copyright © 1980 by Loren D. Estleman

A Forge Book
Published by Tom Doherty Associates, LLC
175 Fifth Avenue
New York, NY 10010

www.tor-forge.com

Forge® is a registered trademark of Tom Doherty Associates, LLC.

ISBN 978-0-7653-8242-9

Our books may be purchased in bulk for promotional, educational, or business use. Please contact your local bookseller or the Macmillan Corporate and Premium Sales Department at (800) 221-7945, extension 5442, or by e-mail at MacmillanSpecialMarkets@macmillan.com.

First Edition: October 2015

Printed in the United States of America

0  9  8  7  6  5  4  3  2  1

# CONTENTS

# THE
# HIGH
# ROCKS

*To my mother and father,*
*once again and with feeling.*

# CHAPTER 1

For three years running, the north central section of Montana's Bitterroot Mountain range was struck by a series of harsh winters that paralyzed transportation and left the old-timers with nothing to talk about in the way of worse winters gone by. During one ninety-day period, temperatures plummeted from a record one hundred and five degrees in late August to minus forty-two on Thanksgiving Day. Winds blasting straight down from the North Pole swept snow clouds before them in an incessant stream, smothering the jagged landscape beneath shrouds of snow which in March of the third year obliterated all but the roofs and the church steeple in Staghorn, the one settlement that had managed to survive the ruthless climate of the Bitterroot.

Most of the damage, however, remained undiscovered until the final spring thaw, when the snows receded and landowners were able to gaze for the first time upon the winter's legacy. Cattle were found frozen stiff in huddles of up to a dozen. Barns and corncribs were crushed flat beneath tons of snow or smashed to splinters by the avalanches that heralded the onslaught of warm weather. Great trees that had stood for centuries jammed narrow mountain passes where they had fallen after being uprooted by the tremendous pressure of the glaciers sliding down from the peaks. Corn and

silage, deprived of its shelter, had been taken up by the
heavy winds and strewn all over the countryside, leaving
without food what little livestock remained. Everyone had
his work cut out for him in the spring of that third year.

But whatever their troubles, no matter how large a task
they had ahead of them, the people of Staghorn and its en-
virons could take comfort in knowing that there was one
who was worse off than they. Somewhere in that sprawling
wilderness, far above the level they considered safe in any
season, there existed a man who had elected to brave the
winter's perils alone and unprotected. Of all the mountaineers, he alone had not come down from the high country at
the first sign of blizzard. And when the flood waters had
subsided and the time had come to see about gathering together the fragments of their lives, the farmers paused in
the midst of rebuilding their barns and laying new sod on
the roofs of their houses to look up at the hostile mountains
and ask:

"I wonder how Bear made out?"

Bear Anderson was as much a part of the lore of that wild
region as the Flathead Indians, who still took time out occasionally to cross the mountains in order to do battle with
the nomadic tribes over the game-rich plains that flanked
the foothills, or the marauding packs of wolves that terror-
ized farmer and cattleman alike when the snows were deep
and game scarce. To children he was the Bogey Man, a figure of towering menace who would swoop down from the
mountains and devour them at a gulp if they neglected their
chores or failed to say their prayers before retiring. The
name given to him by the Indians was unprintable in any
language, but in moments of charity they called him Mountain That Walks, a force more to be avoided than reckoned
with. To everyone he was a presence, a thing seldom seen

but nonetheless there, like the great pines that grew high on the snow-capped peaks and were seen close up only by mountain goats and soaring eagles.

He was the son of a Norwegian logger and his Swedish wife who had come there early in the 1830s, lured by tales of virgin timber and the riches that awaited the man who could carry his weight in the lumber camps. Those who had known Thor Anderson said that he was nearly six and a half feet tall and capable of felling a white pine in fifteen fewer strokes than it took his closest rival. His wife, Greta, bore him six sons, four of whom died in infancy. Of the fifth, Olaf, little was known except that he marched off to fight for the Union in 1861 and never returned. That left Bear.

If that was his true Christian name, or if it had been bestowed upon him because of his size, no one knew. Bear he had always been, and Bear he would always be. It was a name that suited him like the sun in the sky. Of the two surviving sons, it was he who most took after his father, both in build and disposition. At the age of twelve he was six-foot-two and still growing; by his twenty-first birthday it was said that he had surpassed his father, with arms like pork barrels and shoulders so broad he had to swivel them to get through a doorway, like a deliveryman carrying a kitchen stove. There was no denying that at his maturity he was the biggest man in Staghorn. That he grew to be larger than his father could not be proved, however, because by that time Thor Anderson was dead, and so was his wife, Greta.

In the 1860s the Bitterroot range served as a buffer zone between no fewer than four Indian nations. To the northwest lived the Kootenays, avid hunters who nevertheless avoided tracking game into the mountains for fear of coming into contact with their mortal enemies, the fierce Blackfeet who

made their home along the upper Missouri River. Eastward
lay the territory of the Crows, the boundaries of which remained fluid as they moved with the migratory bison, a
year-round source of food, clothing, shelter and fuel. In the
mountains themselves existed the Flatheads, or Salish. Of
all the savage tribes, these were the most feared, as they
were known to cross the mountains in search of a fight, and
it mattered little whether their victims were Crows or white
settlers, for they lived only to spill blood. Long periods of
uneasy peace laced with sporadic outbursts of violence had
made the prospect of living in the mountains an unsettling
one for all but the Flatheads. It was only by a cautiously
maintained system of trade and tribute that any white was
allowed to remain above the level of the plains, and there
were times when even that was not enough, as the Andersons learned early in 1862.

The War Between the States was not a year old when
Bear returned from an overnight hunting trip into the mountains, a buck deer slung across his saddle, and discovered
his parents' cabin burned to the ground. The snow that had
not melted before the heat of the blaze was trampled with
moccasin prints and the tracks of unshod horses. Inside, he
found his parents—what was left of them—huddled together beneath the charred debris of the bedroom as if
Thor with his last act had tried to shield his wife from
the Indians' attack. Near the bodies lay the double-bitted axe
which Bear had seen his father use every day of his life; the
blade was clotted with blood and hair, singed and blackened
by the fire. That meant that one brave at least had paid for
this slaughter, probably with his life. There was not a scrap
of food or a usable good to be found anywhere in the wreckage of the cabin, and the horses were missing from the
lean-to stable out back. The motive for the slayings, then,

was clear; the Andersons had been guilty of having more than the savages.

It took a fire almost as large as that which had consumed the cabin to thaw out the ground enough for Bear to bury his mother and father. When that was finished he left and, according to all accounts, never returned to the site. He took along only his horse, the supplies he had with him, and his gun, a Spencer carbine. There was nothing else to take.

That, at least, was how the people of Staghorn put it together from the evidence and from the tales told by the occasional friendly Blackfoot who came to town to trade for meat and corn. He was not heard from for months, and then only secondhand, in the pidgin English of those same Indians. The story they had to tell spread swiftly throughout the settlement and provided the basis for the legend that was to come. Mountain That Walks, they reported, had begun to take Flathead scalps.

His first victim was a boy less than sixteen years old. Armed with only a knife, the youth had been sent alone into the wilderness as part of the traditional test of manhood. His failure to return to camp at the end of the allotted period prompted a search, at which time his corpse was discovered lying wedged between two boulders at the bottom of a steep ravine. At first the braves thought he'd fallen, but upon climbing down they found that his throat had been cut and his hair lifted. Nearby they came across the boy's knife, thick with blood. He had been killed with his own weapon.

Infuriated, Two Sisters, the Flathead chief, dispatched a party of braves to track down and apprehend the killer. They never returned. After three days a second party was sent out to find out what had happened to them; they came back with the corpses draped over the backs of their horses. Every member of the original group had been shot and scalped. The dead braves were buried in full state, after which, upon the advice of the medicine man, no more parties were sent out.

That had been fifteen years ago, and in the time between then and the end of that third deadly winter Bear Anderson had not been seen more than a dozen times, and then only for a few minutes at a stretch by the Indians with whom he traded. Each time, they swore, he had fresh scalps swinging from his belt. The trade completed, he would depart, vanishing among the tall stands of pine toward no one knew where. How he knew that the Flatheads had been responsible for his parents' deaths remained uncertain, but most believed that he had followed the telltale tracks from the burned-out cabin to the Flathead camp. In any case, they were the only Indians he killed.

More than once he had been thought dead. But each spring brought new tales down from the high country, tales of raids on small Flathead encampments and warriors following tracks that led nowhere. It was said that in some camps the women appealed to the Great Spirit to rid them of this evil shade that struck and vanished, only to strike again many miles away within minutes. And the squaws were not alone in their concern. At night the mountaineers would sometimes look up and see reflected in the low-hanging clouds the fires of great war councils convened for the sole purpose of plotting one man's destruction. Their plots bore no fruit; he remained as elusive as the spirit the women believed him to be.

But this time it was different. The three successive winters that had lashed the Montana section of the Great Divide had been the worst in the territory's history. If wild game could not survive them—and there was plenty of evidence, once the snow was gone and the forests began to stink of death, that much of it had not—what chance stood a man? As the weeks crept by, and spring hardened into summer with no sign in the settlement of the beautifully cured furs that Bear used for trade with the non-Flathead savages who remained friendly to him, it became apparent that at last the legend had met its master. Conversations around cracker barrels swung slowly away from the subject of the scalp hunter to the new administration in Washington and the market price of grain. It was at about this time that Staghorn's complacency was shattered by the most sensational story yet to come down from the lofty peaks.

When the story came to be told, it was appropriate that it was White Mane who told it. A tall brave whose sinew had long since shriveled to dry flesh stretched over bare bone, this Blackfoot was well past the age at which his fellows were usually abandoned by tribal custom to the Indians' death spirit. It was believed that he was allowed to live only because his stubborn independence prevented him from becoming a burden to the rest of his tribe. Once a year he came down out of the mountains, laden with furs from animals he had trapped and skinned, to bargain with Bart Goddard at the mercantile for whiskey. Although it was against the law, Bart always gave him what he wanted in return for the pelts, partly out of greed and partly because he knew that the old man drank the whiskey himself and kept it hidden from the young braves in whose systems the spirits were as dangerous as a fire in a dynamite shack. Besides, White Mane was a consummate storyteller when his tongue was loosened by strong drink, and nobody loved a good tale more than Bart Goddard.

It seemed that three weeks previously, the old warrior had been on his way to the river to check his traps when he stumbled across a scene of carnage such as he hadn't witnessed since the last war with the Flathead nation. Flathead braves lay about the glen in every position, most of them shot, two stabbed, one with his throat and face slashed beyond recognition. All were missing their scalps. Near the edge of the clearing, White Mane discovered a warrior who was still breathing, despite the fact that he had been stabbed and his hair also lifted. The brave lived just long enough to tell him what had happened.

The Indians had been part of a hunting party on the trail of a grizzly one of them had wounded. When they stopped to water their horses at the river, it was discovered that four of their number were missing. Since these four had been riding at the rear of the detachment, and Mountain That Walks was known to pick off stragglers, a great deal of excitement ensued when the absent braves did not respond to calling. Like the people of Staghorn, however, the Flatheads had been of the opinion that Bear had perished during the winter, and so they were quickly mollified when the head of the party dispatched two warriors to look for the miscreants. It seemed likely that the four had found something the others had missed and were off on their own trail in pursuit of the grizzly.

When at the end of an hour the searchers had not returned, the party doubled back to find out what had gone wrong. They hadn't traveled over a mile when a sharp-eyed buck spotted something in a clearing several hundred paces to the north. The party rode in that direction—and came to an abrupt halt when they saw what that something was.

They were standing in the center of a circle of tall poles, from the tops of which dangled six bloody scalps.

The leader had barely enough time to raise a cry of retreat when the first shot rang out and he fell from his horse dead. Six more shots sounded, as fast as a rifle could be cocked and fired, and when the last one echoed over the mountaintop only two braves remained on horseback. One of them bolted for the surrounding forest. The other—he it was who told the story—watched in horror as a huge creature which he at first thought was the grizzly they had been tracking dived headlong from the branches of a nearby pine, collided with the rider, and carried him to the ground. A knife flashed, followed by a bloodcurdling scream. Then the beast rose to its feet and stood looking down at the still form which a moment before had been a hot-blooded brave with thirty scalps to his credit. It was only at that moment that the remaining Indian recognized the beast as a man.

Snatching up his rifle, the Flathead gave vent to a war cry and charged the killer. The latter looked up sharply as if he had forgotten about him, and leaped aside just as the Indian fired. The bullet missed him and shattered a limb on a nearby tree. As the brave pounded past, the man on foot reached up with one enormous hand and wrenched the rifle out of his grip. In the next instant the rifle swung around and the butt came crunching up against the Indian's temple. The Flathead felt a bursting pain in his chest as he fell. After that he remembered nothing until he awoke with his bloody head being supported by the old Blackfoot's hand. Moments later he died.

The story grew in the retelling, and by the time it reached the newspapers back East it was reported that Bear Anderson had slaughtered thirty braves with his bare hands and skinned them to make a coat. In no time at all he was a figure of national renown. Articles about him, which bore no resemblance to the facts, began to appear in newspapers from New York to Oregon. Lurid paperbound novels describing his supposed adventures filtered westward from the great publishing empires along the East Coast. In July a correspondent came to Staghorn all the way from Chicago, spent some days talking with the citizens and asking questions, then left; two months later he published a book in which he claimed to have spent six weeks with Bear Anderson up in the Bitterroot, where the scalp-hunter related his life story exclusively for the journalist. By the fall of 1877 Thor Anderson's boy rivaled Wild Bill Hickok and Buffalo Bill Cody for reader interest in places where Indians were things unknown and a gun was something worn by a policeman.

The interest was not confined to the East, however, and that's where I come in.

# CHAPTER 2

**A**rthur's Castle was the somewhat exotic name for the four-story hotel that stood at the north end of Staghorn's main street, but it fit; operated by an Englishman who insisted upon being addressed as Sir Andrew Southerly, it was the only place I knew of in the Northwest where the towels were as thick as rugs and there was a bath to every floor. The fact that there was only one attendant, who could haul buckets of steaming water to only one bath at a time, was immaterial; in an area where bathtubs of any kind were scarce as passenger pigeons, the presence of four in one building was a luxury almost unheard of. They were the hotel's main attraction. If you're wondering why I bother to go into so much detail concerning bathtubs, it's merely to explain why, when first encountered in this narrative, I am naked.

I had been sent out from the U.S. marshal's office in Helena to bring back a wife-murderer named Brainard who had been picked up on a drunk and disorderly charge in Staghorn, where the sheriff had identified him from his description on a wanted dodger. Now, it was a rule of Judge Harlan Blackthorne's court that each of his deputies check in with the local peace officer immediately upon reaching his destination, but it was a rule of my own not to let any rules hinder me. I figured that if Brainard had waited during the week's ride it had taken me to get there, he'd wait a little longer while I freshened up at the Castle. What I hadn't figured on was the impatience of the local peace officer.

I was immersed to my chin in nearly scalding water when the doorknob began to turn. My gun, a .45 caliber Deane-Adams English five-shot revolver, was hanging in its holster on a chair beside the tub. I palmed it and drew a bead on the door between my bare feet, which I had braced against the tub's cast-iron lip. I cocked it just as the door swung inward.

The steam rising from the tub was so thick I could barely make out the dark smudge of a man's form standing in the doorway, but that was enough. In my profession, when someone comes in on you without knocking first, you've got to figure he isn't there on a friendly visit. I'd learned that the hard way; the same thing had happened to me twice before and two men were dead because they hadn't taken that extra second to brush the door with their knuckles. My finger tightened on the trigger.

"You still carrying that dandy's gun, Page?" drawled a deep voice with a faint trace of Mississippi around the r's.

I held onto the gun. Boot Hill is full of those who put their weapons away when they heard a voice they recognized.

"It's this way, Henry," I said. "Only two men in the West ever carried a gun like this one. The other was Bill Hickok. You figure it out."

He laughed then, and I knew it was going to be all right. Even so, I didn't relax my grip on the revolver until he came farther into the room and I could see that his gun was safely in its holster. I let the hammer down gently and leathered the five-shot.

Henry Goodnight hadn't changed much since I'd seen

him last, which was going on three years ago. Hatless, he wore his auburn hair shoulder-length, the way some of them still do up in the mountains, and he dressed like a banker, complete with Prince Albert coat and shiny beaverskin vest with a gold watch chain glittering across the front. The effect was somewhat marred by the silver star he had pinned to his belt. His gun was ivory-handled and rode waist-high in a cut-down holster designed to carve seconds off his draw. He had moist brown eyes, kind of gentle and slow-looking, that had fooled more than one self-styled fast draw into thinking he could take him. To date, none had. He had been elected sheriff of this isolated community of trappers, farmers and cattlemen eight years before and there had not been an election since. The locals recognized a good thing when they had one.

"You've changed some," he said, grinning behind his moustache. "Back on Ford Harper's spread you wouldn't take a bath but once a month, and then only when it rained."

I grinned back. I'd almost forgotten those days when we made our way from one cattle camp to another with one rope between us and a pair of backsides like buffalo skins. "What makes you think this isn't my first this month?"

"From the looks of the water, I'd say it was."

"There's a lot of dust between here and Helena." I extended a soapy hand, which he took in a grip usually reserved for the butt of his six-gun. "What's on your mind, Henry? You know I would have showed up at your office sooner or later."

"More likely later." He swung a black-booted foot up onto the seat of the chair and leaned forward with his forearms resting upon his thigh. This made him look casual but alert. It was one of a half-dozen or so poses he had practiced to the degree that he could go into any one of them without looking as if he were affecting it, which he was. Henry was vain as a bride. "Hobie Botts told me he saw you ride in half an hour ago. I need your help."

"Don't tell me your prisoner got away."

His teeth glittered behind the reddish fringe along his upper lip. "You know me better than that, Page. When was the last time I let a prisoner escape?"

I shrugged, soaping the back of my neck. "I haven't seen you in three years, Henry."

"I suppose I deserved that," he said. "What I've got is a drunk and disorderly over at Goddard's who's a mite more drunk than I can ignore and a damned sight more disorderly than I can tolerate. If you listen close you can hear the glass breaking clear over here. He's got friends with him who are behaving themselves, more or less, but I can't say I trust them if it comes down to me or him. The town doesn't give me a deputy. How'd you like a part-time job? Say, fifteen minutes at the outside?"

"Indian or white?"

"Half-breed. His name's Ira Longbow, and he's hell with any weapon you put in his hand. Some folks say he's the son of old Two Sisters himself, but no one knows for sure. He acts like he believes it. Can I count on you?"

I sighed. "Hand me that towel."

Dressing, I ignored the change of clothing I'd laid out and put on the outfit I'd worn during the ride from the capital, stiff with dust and sweat. I didn't want to get any blood on my fresh linen. I put on my holster without bothering to tie it down—my gun was going to be in my hand all the time anyway—and together we left the hotel and crossed the street in the direction of the mercantile, a long low building constructed of logs that served a dual purpose as general store and saloon, with a thin partition in between. Henry hadn't exaggerated; the sounds of breaking glass and splintering wood were audible all over town.

Something big fell apart with a tremendous crash as we neared the building. I winced. "Goddard won't be happy with you for taking so long to investigate."

"Bart's been acting lately like he owns me and everything else in town," he said. "It won't hurt him to be taken down a notch or two. Here he is now."

A beefy old man who had been pacing the boardwalk in front of the log building came storming over to meet us, pushing his way through a crowd of onlookers. He had thick white eyebrows and a great shock of hair of the same color which had a habit of tumbling over his forehead like an avalanche of fresh snow. It had been white as long as I'd known him, and I'd been born and raised in Staghorn. "Where the hell you been?" he demanded of the sheriff in a voice just short of a bellow. "That son-of-a-bitch breed is running me out of business!"

"Hello, Bart," I said.

He glared at me in a preoccupied manner from beneath the shelves of his eyebrows. "Page Murdock," he said. "I heard you grabbed a badge up at the capital." Without waiting for an answer, he returned his attention to my companion. "What about it, Sheriff? Are you going to do something about that maniac, or do I go get my shotgun?"

"Hold onto your hat, Bart," drawled the other. "What got him started this time?"

"How the hell should I know? I ain't no injun. He come in falling-down drunk, and I refused to serve him. That could of been it." Something struck a wall inside the building hard enough to knock the chinking loose from between a couple of logs. He jumped at the noise. "You going to stop him while I still got a place of business?"

"Where'd he get drunk, if not here?" asked Henry.

"What is this, for chrissake? Everything I own is being smashed to bits and you act like I'm the bastard that's do-ing it. There's a dozen families run stills up in them moun-tains that don't care who they sell to; why else you think I got to operate a mercantile? The competition here is worse than in Virginia City!"

The sheriff looked thoughtful. "I sure hope you're tell-ing the truth, Bart. I warned you last time if I ever caught you serving liquor to Indians, I'd close you down."

"You won't have to. Two more minutes and Ira Longbow'll do it for you!"

We left him fuming in the street and stepped up onto the boardwalk. The crowd parted respectfully for the dashing figure of the sheriff, taking little notice of the dusty saddle tramp at his side. My gun was in my hand. Henry's remained in his holster, but with him that was as good as holding it. With his left hand he gave the bat-wing doors on the saloon side a shove and stood back while they swung shut. When no bullets followed he cautiously led the way inside.

It was a long room with a low ceiling, half again the length of a railroad car and several feet wider, leaving less than a third of the building for the mercantile on the other side of the partition. Red- and green-striped Indian rugs decorated the bare logs that made up the walls. A number of hooded kerosene lamps swung from the ceiling. The glass had been broken out of two of them, which explained the oily tang that accompanied the normal saloon smells of cheap whiskey, stale sawdust, and sweat. Smashed tables, bottles, chairs and glasses formed a pile against the walls and bar. The big mirror on the wall behind the bar was a web of jagged cracks forking outward from a triangu-lar hole in the center where something had struck it, giving me a fly's eye view of the rest of the room and its contents.

A trio of youths stood behind the bar, two of them drinking quietly while a third poured himself a tumbler full of amber liquid from a brown bottle in his left hand. They wore leather vests that had never touched cactus and narrow hats with cocked brims that had never held a horse's fill of water. They dressed alike, looked alike, even wore their cartridge belts at the same low-slung level in imitation of a gunfighter in a dime novel. Kids. I treated them as I would any nest of baby rattlesnakes that blocked my way out of a cougar's lair; I kept them covered. The fourth youth was Henry's worry.

Standing in the center of a cleared section, he was a scarecrow, bones and sinew covered by skin the dusky red shade of old barn siding. Dull black hair hung in lifeless wings on either side of his forehead from the part in the middle. The whites of his eyes, though bloodshot, were dazzling against the lackluster copper of his complexion, in the centers of which the irises were as black as his hair and as shiny as the buttons on an old maid's shoe. His nose was fleshy, his lips thick and flat. Wisps of downy black beard clung like spun sugar to his cheeks and chin. His clothes were homespun and faded, his boots run down at the heels. He wore no gun belt. His hat, a black Spanish affair with a low flat crown, hung between his shoulder blades from a thong knotted at his throat.

He stood with his legs spread apart and the upper half of his body bent forward at the waist, swaying slightly, as if the weight of the Dance six-shooter he held in his left hand was slowly pulling him over onto his face. The barrel showed a tendency to drift as well, but it remained pointed in the general direction of the sheriff.

Somewhere along the line, Henry's own gun, a Colt Peacemaker with the front sight filed off and the hammer shaved to ease the trigger pull, had leaped into his right hand. I hadn't seen him draw, so he must have done it as we were entering and my attention was claimed by the three at the bar. Not that I would have seen it in any case. Eight men had died who hadn't. He covered the half-breed.

I could see that the boy with the bottle was going to go for his gun before he made a move. They get a special look on their faces when they're thinking about it, kind of sly and frightened at the same time. I fired, there was a crash, and he was holding the neck of the bottle and nothing else.

"Don't," I advised him. He took it in the right spirit. He raised his hands.

"There's two ways we can do this, Ira." Henry spoke in his professionally tough voice. "I can take you to jail and you can sober up in a cell that's not too dirty, or I can turn you over to Josh Booker. Your choice."

That meant something only to those who knew their way around Staghorn. Josh Booker was the local undertaker. If it meant anything to Ira Longbow, however, he didn't show it. He maintained his unsteady stance, his gun barrel-to-barrel with Henry Goodnight's.

I decided to toss my own two bits into the pot. "You boys had better talk some sense into your partner," I told the three at the bar. "If that Dance goes off, you're next."

"You can't shoot all of us," muttered the youth at the far end. His tone was petulant, scarcely audible, like that of a boy talking back to his mother, but who wasn't sure he wanted to be heard.

"Why not? This gun holds five cartridges, and I've only fired one. That gives me one to play with." None of them seemed to have an answer for that.

Henry took control of the conversation. "What's it going to be, Ira? I'm being paid by the month."

Ira seemed to be having trouble making up his mind. His black eyes shifted, glittering unnaturally in the light seeping in through the grimy front window past the blurred white faces pressed against the panes. "Go away, Sheriff," he said at last. His voice was pitched low for his age, muddied slightly by his condition. "This ain't your business. Me and my friends are just having some fun."

"At whose expense? Give me the gun before someone gets hurt." Henry held out a steady left hand to receive the weapon.

The boy at the far end of the bar snatched at the butt of his gun and I shot him. The bullet struck his left shoulder just below the collarbone, spun him around, and slammed him into the cracked mirror, bringing a cascade of glittering shards showering down around him. His revolver somersaulted from his grip and glided along the polished surface of the bar until it reached the edge, from where it dropped to the plank floor with a thud. In the same instant I recocked the Deane-Adams and brought it to bear on his two companions. They threw up their hands, shaking their heads frantically. The one closest to me still held the neck of the bottle my first bullet had shattered in one hand.

The wounded youth stood with his back against the wreckage of the mirror, his right hand gripping his left shoulder, blood oozing between his fingers. His face was dead white.

"Three left," I told him, unnecessarily. His gun was beyond his reach and all the fight was gone from him.

I glanced in Henry's direction and was surprised to see that he was standing there alone. At his feet sprawled Ira Longbow, a purple bruise swelling on his left temple where the sheriff had brought the barrel of his six-shooter smashing against the half-breed's skull. The youth's gun lay two yards away where it had landed after leaving his hand. Henry wasn't paying any attention to him. He was busy sighting down the muzzle of his Peacemaker and scowling.

"Bent the barrel, damn it," he growled.

"You should've used the butt," I told him. "Indians got hard heads."

Now that the danger was past, the room began to fill with people. The sheriff showed them his gun and they backed off, leaving a clearing around the scene of destruction. He fished a shining coin from his coat pocket and tossed it to a young boy dressed in threadbare homespun, who caught it in one hand. "Go fetch Ezra Wilson," Henry directed him. "Tell him we got a wounded man here. Hurry!" The boy took off at a run, his leather worksoles clapping on bare wood.

"What happened to Doc Bernstein?" I asked.

The lawman regarded me dully for a moment, as if he'd forgotten all about me. "He's dead. A small raiding party led by Two Sisters hit his place last year and burned it to the ground. They found Doc in the front yard and skewered him with a war lance. His wife and boy were in the cabin when they put the torch to it."

"Oh."

Ezra Wilson was a gray little man whose features, once out of sight, were impossible to recall. They were crowded in the middle of a face that seemed to grow straight out of his detachable collar with no neck in between, broader at the top than at the bottom and crowned by a head of washed-out red hair parted in the middle and pomaded to the extent that it looked as if he hadn't grown it at all, just painted it on with a thick brush. He walked like a crab and carried a cylindrical black bag like a doctor's. He was Staghorn's barber.

"See what you can do for him, Ez," said Henry, indicating the young man with the hole in his shoulder.

I watched as the barber directed the youth to take a seat in one of the few unbroken chairs and removed his vest and shirt. The wound was as large as a baby's fist and glistened with blood, but no bone had been touched that I could see, there being no chips visible.

"Passed clear through," piped Ezra, reaching into his bag and withdrawing a bottle of alcohol and a roll of gauze, items most likely appropriated from the late Doc Bernstein's effects. He proceeded to clean and dress the wound, not too gently. The young man whimpered and bit his lip a lot.

"Why'd you do it?" I asked the patient. I had collected the guns from all the parties involved and heaped them on what was left of the table in front of me.

"I recognized you suddenly." The petulance was still in his tone, tempered by pain. His breath came in gasps. He probably thought he was dying. I would too, after a quarter of an ounce of lead had slammed through me.

"So what?"

"You're Page Murdock. Everyone says you're fast. I wanted to see how fast."

"The hell with fast," I said. "I already had my gun out. Anyway, Henry Goodnight's faster than I am; why didn't you try to take him?"

"I wasn't out to commit suicide."

"So instead you collected a bullet in your shoulder."

He shrugged, then regretted it. "I'm still alive, ain't I?"

"You're damn lucky. I was aiming for your belly."

The barber finished dressing the wound and stood back, wiping alcohol off his hands with a broad white handkerchief. "What you want done with him now?" he asked Henry.

The sheriff looked at me. "You pressing charges?"

"If I do, does it mean I have to stick around for the trial?"

"You know it does. You're wearing a badge. Carrying one, anyway," he corrected, noticing that I wasn't sporting one of the tin targets Judge Blackthorne handed out.

"Forget it," I said. "Chalk it up to high spirits and let him go. Without his gun, of course."

"Of course." There was a sneer in Henry's tone.

"You might as well turn the others loose too, if you've a mind. They haven't done anything but watch anyway."

The lawman holstered his damaged weapon. Taking this as a cue, the two youths who had emerged unscathed from the shoot-out helped their wounded companion to his feet and left, supporting him between them.

"You'll get paid, Ezra," Henry told Wilson. "I know the boy's parents."

Bart Goddard came loping into the room, head down, barrel torso tilted forward, nearly bowling over the barber, who was on his way out. The face beneath the mop of dry white hair was crimson. He took in the damage with a sweeping glance. "Who's gonna pay for all this?" he demanded.

Henry shrugged. The fate of his six-shooter had put him in a sour mood. "You'll have to talk to Ira about that after he sobers up." He caught my eye. "Give me a hand getting him over to the jail."

That wasn't as easy as it sounded. The half-breed couldn't have weighed over a hundred and twenty, but it was all dead weight and raising him to his feet was the most physical labor I'd engaged in for some time. When at last we had him supported between us, Goddard glowered at him from beneath the heavy mantel of his brows.

"There ain't enough wampum in this old man's whole tribe to take care of what he done today," he said.

Henry said something to him that for reasons of delicacy I will leave out of this narrative, and together we trundled our burden across the street to the jail.

The warmth put out by the little iron stove hissing away in a corner of the sheriff's office was a welcome change from the damp chill of the street. It was still September, and already the first icy blasts of winter were making their presence felt at that high altitude. Old-timers whose sole purpose in life was to predict the weather were laying odds that the region was in for yet another severe winter, perhaps the harshest yet.

The jailhouse was the second that had been built on that spot since Staghorn's founding fifty years before. The first, a log affair with a sod roof and no foundation, had perished within two years of its construction when a prisoner set fire to his mattress during an escape attempt and the flames spread to the walls, eventually engulfing the entire structure and killing the arsonist. In its place rose a stone building with steel bars on the windows and thick wooden shutters with gun ports in the centers which could be swung shut and locked in the event of a siege from outside. The office, a rectangular enclosure separated from the four cells in back by a flyblown wall, was furnished with two straight chairs and a desk with a scaly finish created by too many layers of cheap varnish. Its top was a litter of dog-eared wanted circulars and telegram blanks, many of which were soiled with coffee rings. A chipped enamel coffee pot, once white, now blackened at the base and up one side, gurgled insistently atop the stove and boiled over, its contents sizzling upon the iron stove top. The smell this made was harsher than burning hides but not as acrid as spent gunpowder. In any case, it was not an appetizing aroma.

We went through a thick oaken door at the back of the office and deposited Ira Longbow in the cell nearest the door. The one opposite was already occupied. I studied the face and form of the man stretched out on the cot through the bars and checked them against the description on the wanted circular I'd been carrying in my hip pocket. Short, squat, black hair thinning, prominent jaw, incongruous button of a nose permanently reddened by a lifetime spent chugging cheap whiskey. Pointed ears. Mean little eyes. Forearms as big around as my calves. It was a perfect match. Leslie Brainard, the Helena teamster who had strangled his wife to death in an argument over money.

"That him?" asked Henry.

I nodded. "I'll grab a good night's rest over at the Castle and pick him up in the morning. I've earned that much."

"Just so you get him the hell out of my jail. He's the most unaccommodating prisoner I've ever had."

"What's this situation with the Flatheads?" I asked him, when the connecting door was shut and we were back in the office.

He unbuckled his gun belt and draped it over a wooden peg beside the front door. "It's Bear Anderson again," he said. "Every time he takes a scalp, Two Sisters uses it as an excuse to go on another raid. Usually he confines himself to horse-thieving and looting. Doc Bernstein and his family were the first white casualties in years. It's coming to a head fast. The army's trying to get the Flatheads to sign a treaty, but they aren't going to get anywhere as long as Anderson's still up there."

"Which means they won't ever," I said.

Henry eyed me curiously. "You know him, don't you? I forgot."

"I grew up with him. I'll bet Bear and I explored every cave and crag in those mountains as kids. To get him down, they're going to have to find him first. Then they've got to take him. That's a job I wouldn't hand out to my worst enemy."

"Funny you should say that."

The voice wasn't Henry's. It was thin as a razor and marked by a high Ozark twang, something like a bullet ricocheting off a rock. My back was toward the front door. I turned.

The voice's owner was as thin as the voice itself, and short enough to walk under my outstretched arm without ducking. Even so, the outsized hat he wore, together with a yellow ankle-length duster, made him seem even smaller than he was. His face was ordinary except for a crossed right eye that even when it was looking straight at you appeared to be focused on something beyond your shoulder. His nose was prominent but not gross, his hair, what I could see of it beneath the broad brim of his sweat-darkened hat, the color of wet sand and long enough in back to brush his collar. Sandy whiskers, some twelve or thirteen days old, blurred the lines of his chin and emaciated cheeks.

He had two men with him, who looked enough alike and had enough years separating them to be father and son. Both wore their hair long, the old man's dirty gray compared to the younger man's brown, and their clothes, neutral in color beneath a skin of dust, were trail-worn and frayed at the cuffs, collars, knees and seats. Their eyes were small and close-set above huge hooked noses, beneath which their faces fell away to scrawny necks with hardly any chins to interrupt the sweeping lines. They were clean-shaven, or had been until about two weeks before. The young man wore steel-rimmed spectacles and had a long-barreled percussion cap pistol stuck in his belt. The old-timer carried no weapon that I could see. Saddle tramps, both of them, with just enough of a furtive look about them to be wanted for something.

"Who are you?" I asked the man in the duster.

"Name's Church." When he spoke, he had a habit of grinning quickly with all of his white, even teeth, but it was more of a nervous habit than an expression of emotion, as nothing he said seemed humorous. "These here are Homer Strakey, Senior and Junior." He tilted his hat brim in the direction of his companions. "Which one of you is Sheriff Henry Goodnight?"

"I'm Goodnight," said Henry, cautiously. He edged nearer his six-shooter hanging on the wall. "What's your business?"

"They told us over at the saloon you got a breed name of Longbow locked up in jail. I'd like to bail him out."

"What for?"

"I need a guide. Folks around town say this Longbow knows them mountains like nobody else. What about it? I got the money."

"Mister, I wouldn't send a yellow dog up into those mountains this time of year," said Henry. "What do you want up there that won't wait till spring?"

Church unfolded a sheet of paper he'd had in a pocket of his duster and handed it to him. I read it over his shoulder. It was a warrant for Bear Anderson's arrest, and it was signed by President Ulysses S. Grant.

# CHAPTER 3

"Would you mind explaining this?" asked the sheriff, handing back the shopworn scrap of paper at the bottom of which the presidential seal was a gray smudge.

"I don't see why I got to, but if it'll spring the breed I don't suppose it'd hurt." Church refolded the warrant and returned it to his pocket. He had strong hands, callused on the insides of his thumbs and forefingers and strung with tendons as taut as telegraph wires. "Chief Two Sisters has refused to talk peace with the army till Bear Anderson is gone from the Bitterroot. General Clifton met with Grant last April to get permission to send in troops, but the President didn't want to give the injuns the idea he was making war, so he signed this here warrant and ordered Clifton to hire a civilian to do the job. Well, it so happens the general remembered the good job I done for him a couple of years back when he sent me into Canada after a bunch of deserters, so he wired me to come see him. I get twenty a week and expenses, with five thousand waiting for me when I bring in Anderson, dead or alive." His eyes slid in the Strakeys' direction. "We're splitting that, of course."

Junior giggled then, a high, keening neigh far back in his nose. The effect on me was the same as if a rat had just scrambled over the toe of my boot.

"Well, Grant's not President any more, but I suppose his signature's still good," said Henry.

"Church," I said, after a moment's reflection. "I knew I'd heard that name before. The way the story was told to me, none of those deserters made it back to the fort alive."

The man in the duster swung his attention back to me, or so I thought. With that crossed eye it was hard to tell. "Who are you?" he demanded.

I told him. The grin fluttered across his face like bat's wings. "Hell," he said, "you're a fine one to talk. You've kilt your share."

"I'm not above killing," I said. "Back or front, it makes no difference to me, as long as it had to be done. That's where we disagree. You just kill. I don't even think you like it, particularly; you just don't feel anything about it, one way or the other. That's what scares me. You don't care."

"You're breaking my heart." He returned to business. "What about it, Sheriff? Do I get the breed or don't I?"

"In the morning. Let him sober up first." Protecting his left hand by wrapping his linen handkerchief around it, Henry lifted the coffee pot and poured a stream of steaming liquid into a yellowed china mug he had retrieved from atop the clutter on his desk. At no time had he strayed more than two steps away from the gun in his discarded holster, and he kept his right hand free; Church and his two friends made that kind of impression. "I'll talk to Bart Goddard tonight and get an estimate of the damages. If you can pay that, I guess you can have Longbow. If he doesn't object."

"We was figuring on leaving tonight." The bounty hunter's tone was mildly insistent.

"Then you're lucky he's in jail. Nobody travels in the mountains at night. Not the Flatheads, not Bear Anderson. Nobody. It's a good way to get dead."

"Why? What's up there?"

"Wolves, for one thing." Henry studied the steam rising from his mug. "There's not much game left after last winter, so they're traveling in packs of a hundred and more. They'll attack anything that moves. Also, there's a chance your horse will step in a chuckhole in the dark or lose its footing while you're feeling your way along one of those narrow ledges that wind around the mountains, and nobody'll find your body till spring. And if you get past all that, you've still got grizzlies to worry about." He leered behind his moustache. "Outside of that, it's a waltz."

Church stared at him for a moment with that peculiar detached gaze. At length he shrugged, his duster rustling with the movement. "I guess we got no choice any way you look at it," he said. "Where can we get a room for the night?"

The sheriff directed him to Arthur's Castle.

"We'll be back first thing tomorrow." Church left, followed by the younger Strakey. The old man hesitated a moment, ruminating absently on what appeared to be a plug of tobacco distorting his right cheek, but could just as well have been a rotten tooth. Then he, too, withdrew. He walked with a strange, rocking limp, putting me in mind of a trail cook I once knew whose right leg was an inch shorter than its mate. When he was out of sight, Henry took a big swallow of his scalding coffee, as if to get rid of a bad taste in his mouth.

"If that's what the army is hiring these days, I'm glad I got out while I was still a corporal," he said.

"Don't underestimate Church," I told him. "All the stories I've heard about him end the same way; he gets his man and collects his bounty."

"If he does it this time, he'll have earned it. What about

those characters he has with him? Bent or not, I'd bet my six-gun they're wanted somewhere."

"That's your worry." I stepped toward the door. "Take good care of my prisoner, will you? I'd hate to have to explain to Judge Blackthorne how you managed to poison him with that coffee of yours."

"Where are you going now?"

I leered. "Charlene McGrath still in business?"

"You're too late. She pulled out for Deer Lodge last week. Won't be back till April."

"I can't wait that long." I scowled. "Guess I'll just pick up a bottle and get quietly drunk in my room."

"Make sure it stays quiet. I've got too many drunk and disorderlies locked up now." His eyes twinkled over the rim of his china mug.

I collected my key from Sir Andrew at the hotel desk and went up the carpeted stairs toward my room on the second floor. On the landing I met Church, who was on his way down. He had discarded his hat and duster and was wearing a striped shirt without a collar and a pair of pants, fuzzy at the knees, which had once belonged to a gray suit. The bone handle of what looked like a Navy Colt protruded above his holster, curved forward for a left-handed draw. His sandy hair was beginning to thin in front, a condition he attempted to conceal by combing it forward over his forehead, Napoleon-style. He stopped when he saw me.

"Me and the boys been in the saddle quite a spell," he said. "You know where we can find us some female companionship?"

I told him the sad news about Charlene McGrath. He cursed and continued on his way, leaving behind a smell of leather, sweat and dust. The bounty hunter seemed to be one customer who wasn't attracted by the Castle's many baths.

He stopped at the desk, where I heard him ask Sir Andrew what any single man asks the hotel clerk his first night in a strange town. The answer he got was the same one I'd already given him, so maybe now he believed me.

I didn't sleep well that night. Maybe it was because, after seven nights of sleeping on the ground. I couldn't get used to the acre of featherbed with which the Englishman provided each of his guests, but I didn't think so. My mind kept wandering back to the thought of Bear Anderson alone in the mountains with a bird dog like Church on his scent. That the mountain man could take care of himself was something he had proved again and again throughout the decade and a half that had elapsed since the murder of his parents, but the bounty hunter had spent at least that much time proving the same about himself. Why I cared at all was another mystery. It had been a long time since Bear and I had seen each other, and I doubted that he'd even recognize me. Growing up together didn't mean we were friends; he'd never saved my life or anything like that, nor I his, and no matter how hard I tried I was unable to remember a scrap of conversation that passed between us during all the time we spent together hunting and exploring in the Bitterroot. At length I gave up trying to puzzle it out and went to sleep just as false dawn was beginning to dilute the blackness outside my window.

My first stop after rising some two hours later was the barbershop. After a shave, I went over to Goddard's mercantile, where I ordered supplies for the trip back to Helena from the owner's hawk-faced wife, Hilda. The prices there were twice as high as any I'd encountered during the trip across the territory. I secured a receipt from her after paying and stashed it away in my coat pocket among the others to be used as proof when I presented my list of expenses to

Judge Blackthorne. Leaving the stuff there for the time being, I then went to the livery stable.

The man at the stable was new, but only in the sense that
he hadn't been there on my last trip to Staghorn. He was an
old jasper in a greasy slouch hat with a square yellow pen-
cil stuck in the band and a face like a peach pit. As I
approached he squinted up at me from his seat beside a
pot-bellied stove in the livery office and rose creakily to his
feet when I asked him for my horse.

After he led it out of its stall—it was a big buckskin I'd
had five years, fresh from a rubdown and a night's sleep—I
inquired about Leslie Brainard's horse. The old man stared
at me, blinking in confusion.

"It's all right," I said, showing him my badge, which I
kept in my breast pocket. "He's my prisoner."

"It ain't all right." His voice reminded me of two tree
trunks rubbing together in the wind. "He ain't got no horse."

"He didn't walk from Helena," I pointed out, patiently,
I thought, under the circumstances.

"Oh, he had a horse, but that was before he lost it over
the poker table to a pair of treys." The old man laughed
noiselessly, opening his mouth to display a toothless cav-
ern and heaving his chest in and out like a skinny bellows.
"Reckon that's what made him disorderly."

"No wonder the territory's in debt," I grumbled, and
asked him to show me what horses he had for sale.

He sold me a chestnut mare that had seen its good days,
but none of them since Appomattox. The saddle and bridle
were twelve dollars extra. I collected a receipt for that, too, as
well as for the horse and my own animal's care, knowing
all the time that the judge was going to argue the validity
of the dirty scrap of paper with the old man's mark at the

bottom, and after returning to Goddard's and loading the supplies onto my horse's back, I led the animals over to the sheriff's office.

I found Henry seated at his desk over a mug of hot coffee which, from the smell of it, might have been the same one he'd been sipping the night before. Mingled with the burnt-grain odor was the unmistakable scent of Bay Rum.

"You've been to the barber already," I reflected.

His slow brown eyes looked me over from head to foot, taking in my clean clothes and freshly shaven face. "Look who's talking," he growled. He was one of those who aren't to be trifled with until after they've had their second swallow of coffee. "That cross-eyed son of a bitch got me up at five o'clock this morning to turn over his precious half-breed. There's nothing to do in this town at five o'clock but get a shave, and I had to get Wilson out of bed to do that. I enjoyed that part," he added, smiling maliciously.

"That explains his mood when he shaved me." I fingered the strip of gauze covering the nick at the corner of my chin. "Did Church go the damages?"

"Eventually. At first he tried to pay it off in army scrip. When I told him what he could do with that, he dug out a purse full of double eagles heavy enough to break your toe and counted out what I'd told him. I'm thinking of going into the bounty-hunting business; it pays better."

"Where's my prisoner?"

He sat staring at me until I realized what he was waiting for and drew out the warrant signed by Judge Blackthorne. When it was on his desk he left it there without glancing at it, slid open the top drawer, and handed me a ring of keys. "You want a pair of handcuffs?"

I shook my head and showed him my own, a pair I'd had

forged especially for me in Butte. On the other side of the connecting door, I handed them between the bars to Brainard and told him to put them on. He glared at me murderously with his mean little eyes, but he did as directed, sliding the manacles over his huge teamster's wrists and snapping them shut with a grating noise that made me wonder if I should have cleaned them after accidently dropping them into the Beaverhead River last spring.

"He got a hat and coat?" I asked Henry on the way out.

The sheriff jerked his head in the direction of the peg beside the front door, where hung a black-and-red-checked woolen jacket with patches on the elbows and a shapeless brown hat. I retrieved them and handed the hat to Brainard. "Put it on."

"What about the coat?" His tone was a belligerent snarl.

"Those cuffs stay on," I told him. "If it turns cold you can slide it over your shoulders like a cape. Maybe it'll keep you from getting any ideas."

He pulled on his hat with a savage thrust.

I shifted my drawn gun to my left hand and offered Henry my right. "Take care, Henry. I'll see you next trip."

He accepted it. "Keep an eye on him. He's craftier than he looks."

"I wasn't planning on inviting him to bundle with my sister."

We left town at a walk, headed south and east in the direction of the Clark Fork River. The air smelled of rain, or possibly snow; there was a metallic sharpness about it that set my facial muscles to tingling. The buckskin's breath was visible in gray jets of vapor. Two miles out, Brainard, riding several yards ahead of me, got out his coat and wrestled it onto his shoulders. By nightfall we were within sight of the Clark Fork. The sky was overcast and leaden.

I dismounted first, then drew my gun and pointed it at the teamster. "Off." When he was standing, I directed him to lie on his stomach while I removed my horse's saddle. He did so, cursing when he scraped the side of his face against a bull thistle and squirming to get away from it.

There's something about making a stupid mistake that, no matter how it finally turns out, haunts you for the rest of your life. Since that moment I've come up with a dozen ways to handle the same situation without risk, and I've used just about all of them. That day I didn't.

I was undoing the cinch of my saddle when the buckskin shrugged its powerful shoulders. The buckle shot out of my hand and the saddle slithered away from me and fell to the ground on the other side, blanket and all. I muttered a curse and ducked under the horse's belly to retrieve it. In that moment my prisoner hurtled to his feet and brained me with a rock he'd picked up from where he'd been lying. I swam to the ground through a red swirl.

# CHAPTER 4

Either it was dark when I awoke or I was blind; for a long time I wasn't sure which was the case. I was lying on my back where I'd fallen, which meant that I'd turned over or had been turned over by someone else. That was convenient, as I was able to turn my head and retch without drowning myself. Not that it made me feel any better. At the bottom of the hill, the rush and gurgle of the river competed with the pounding inside my skull, and the pounding won. I wanted desperately to slip back into unconsciousness, to experience sweet oblivion, but at the same time I sensed that if I did I would never come out. With a superhuman effort I heaved myself up onto my knees and staggered to my feet. Twice I nearly fell, but at last I managed to place a steadying hand against a slightly yielding surface that turned out to be the flank of the chestnut, which was busy munching at the tall grass that carpeted the slope, and got rid of what was left in my stomach. That left me feeling more human, but just a little.

Gingerly, I raised a hand to the back of my head—and took it away as if I'd touched a hot stove. There was a soft spot the size of a half dollar beneath the damp and matted hair. A little more effort on Brainard's part, and I wouldn't have gotten up at all.

My gun belt was, of course, missing, as was the key to the handcuffs. I took advantage of the light cast by the three-quarter moon to search for the cuffs themselves and found them a little farther down the slope with the key still in the lock. My horse was gone as well, which spoke well for the teamster's taste, along with my saddle and the saddlebags filled with supplies. I found my hat where I'd fallen and put it on, tilting it to avoid the injured area, then mounted the mare on the second try and turned it in the direction of town.

It couldn't have taken me longer if I'd crawled the distance. Long before the mare's hoofs struck the washboard surface of Main Street, the sun, a pale glow behind the cloud cover, had floated clear of the distant peaks and the streets had begun to fill with early-morning shoppers and merchants on their way to roll up the blinds in their windows. Snowflakes the size of wood shavings danced and swirled about in the air. It wasn't cold enough for them to stick, however, and so they vanished as soon as they touched the ground.

I dismounted before the sheriff's office, nearly folding when my weight came down on my legs, and caught Henry just as he was locking up before going over to the Castle for breakfast. Today he was wearing his hat, charcoal gray with a low crown, a wide, sweeping brim, and set off by a gold band—the style of headgear favored by gamblers who preferred not to store their derringers in plain sight. The brim wasn't wide enough to conceal his look of surprise when he saw me swaying before him.

"I need a fresh horse and supplies," I told him. "Get them for me, will you, Henry?" Then I fell into a heap at his feet.

The room in which I came around smelled strongly of

carbolic and something else almost as pungent. Summon-
ing all my strength, I forced open my eyelids, which evidently someone had sewn shut. Ezra Wilson's gourd-shaped
face swam into focus, dissolved, then came back and stayed.
I noticed that the pomade had begun to lose its grip on his
hair, allowing a band of pink scalp to peep between the
loosened locks near his crown. His starched collar, missing now, had left its mark in the form of two horizontal red
welts at his throat. His features seemed even more pinched
than normal. Beyond his head, a water-stain shaped like a
buzzard with a broken wing adorned the yellowing plaster
of the ceiling.

The mattress beneath me was not one of Sir Andrew's
featherbeds. A little thicker than a poorly constructed quilt,
it was stuffed with straw and studded with metal buttons
that dug into my back like pebbles. I could feel the slats
beneath it. There were four of them running sideways, not
enough to support my one hundred and eighty pounds. As
a result I lay bent in the middle like a sprung bow.

I had started to raise myself onto my elbows when a mule
kicked me in the back of the head and I fell back, blinking
at the fireflies swarming around my face. For a moment
the pain was blinding, but as I lay motionless it ebbed into
a sea of blissful warmth that drew me, as it had hours before, toward the brink of unconsciousness. The pounding
returned (if indeed it had ever left), but now it seemed muted
and distant, like a blacksmith's hammer striking an anvil
wrapped in cotton. The effect was mesmeric. This time I
didn't fight it. I slept.

The barber was still there when I awoke a second time,
or maybe he was back. He was dozing in a paint-spattered
wooden chair near the foot of the bed with his legs stretched
out in front of him and his hands folded upon the swell of

his belly. A kerosene lamp stood on the cracked veneer of the bedside table, hissing and sputtering and casting a liquid glow over the bed and onto the ceiling, where the buzzard still crouched with its injured wing thrust out to the side.

I avoided the temptation to sit up, remembering what had happened the last time. Instead, I unstuck my tongue from the roof of my mouth, rolled it around a little to see if it still worked, and called out Wilson's name. He shifted in his chair, crossed one ankle over the other, and went on sleeping. I tried again.

"Wilson!"

He came awake with a snort, nearly pitching headlong over onto his face when he drew his legs under him and his ankles became tangled with each other. He blinked about, bewildered, and then his eyes fell to me and comprehension dawned in his expression. He grunted like an old dog that had been kicked out of its master's favorite armchair.

"You're alive," he noted morosely. "Thought sure you'd be stone cold by now."

"Sorry to disappoint you."

He smoothed a careful hand over his thinning hair. The band of pink disappeared, then eased back into view as the locks separated again. He eyed me as if he didn't know what to do next. "Suppose you want to eat."

I hadn't thought about it, but as he said it I remembered that as far as I knew I hadn't eaten since breakfast at Arthur's Castle the morning I'd left with my prisoner, and God knew how long ago that had been. I nodded. The movement made me aware of the pounding in my head and I placed a hand against it. It was encircled just below the hairline by a bandage like an Indian headband.

Outside, I heard a wagon rattling past, followed by the

grinding sigh of hinges as a large door was swung open or shut nearby. I decided that I was in the back of the barbershop, which was next to the livery stable. No wonder Wilson was so surly, I thought; I was lying in his bed. Carefully I eased myself into a sitting position with my back supported by the brass bedstead. My head weighed fifty pounds.

The barber had left his chair and been swallowed up by the blackness beyond the globe of light thrown by the lamp on the table. Dishes rattled, something wet splattered into something dry, and then he came back bearing a soup plate full of steaming something which he balanced in one hand while he drew his chair up to the bed and sat down. He lifted out a spoonful of liquid, blew on it, and slid it underneath my nose.

"What is it?" I studied the contents suspiciously. It smelled like boiled rags.

"Venison broth," said the other. "Been cooking all day. Shot it last year and all I got left is jerky. Eat it. Worst it can do is make you heave."

I opened my mouth and he inserted the spoon. It tasted pretty good, but then the judgment of a man half-starved is not to be trusted. I held out my hands for the bowl. He handed it to me and I finished the broth in silence.

"How long was I out?" I handed back the empty vessel and wiped my lips with the graying linen napkin he had given me.

He shrugged and set the bowl and spoon on the table next to the lamp. "Nineteen, twenty hours. When the sheriff brought you in I told him you wouldn't last till sundown. Yours is only the second fractured skull I ever saw. Man who had the first one died two hours after it happened. His didn't look near as bad as yours. What was it, a rock?"

I started to nod, then thought better of it and said, "Yeah."

"How's it feel?"

"Hurts like hell."

"I got something that'll fix that." He got up and walked back into the gloom, this time in a different direction, probably toward the front where the barbershop was. He had no shirt on over his long-handled underwear and his suspenders flapped loose around his knees. A moment later he returned, this time carrying a tall square bottle in one hand and a shot glass in the other. He sat down and poured a thin stream of pale brownish liquid into the glass. The sickly sweet scent it gave off was overpowering, like that of too many flowers in a room where a corpse lay in state. When the glass was nearly full he thrust it toward me with the same nonchalance with which he had offered me the venison broth. I was suspicious of the human race today. I asked him what it was.

"Laudanum. Take some; it'll ease that ache." He pushed the glass closer. The fumes filled my nostrils and made me drowsy.

I turned my head away. "Pour it back."

"Don't be stubborn." He slid the medicine around toward my lips. "It's the best cure there is."

"I once knew a cowhand who felt that way," I said, looking at him. "He got stomped by a bronc and the doctors fed him that stuff for a solid week to ease the pain, then released him and told him he was good as new. Know what he was doing the last time I saw him? Screaming his lungs out in an insane asylum. The attendants had refused to give him any more of that good medicine. No, thanks. I'd rather have the pain."

"Suit yourself," he said, and drank the stuff himself. I stared at him, but I don't think he was aware of it. His pupils clouded and his pale lips were turned upward at the corners in a half-smile. It was the expression of a married man who had returned to a favorite mistress. I made a mental note to do my own shaving the next time I came to Staghorn.

Somewhere off in the gloom a doorknob rattled. "Ezra?" The voice belong to Henry Goodnight, calling from in front of the shop. "Ezra, you asleep? Open up."

That broke the mood. The barber shoved the stopper back into the bottle and shot me a stern look, as if swearing me to secrecy.

"He won't hear it from me," I assured him. "It's not against the law anyway."

That didn't have any effect on him at all. He went out to let Henry in. A bolt squeaked back, there was a muttered conversation, and then the sheriff came striding into the lamp light. He had traded his Prince Albert and fancy vest for a hip-length brown canvas coat with fur at the collar and cuffs and bone buttons that dangled loosely from the threads that held them, and his hat now was a Stetson. He walked as if this was the first time he had used his legs all night. There were dark circles under his eyes and his smile was weary.

"You must have a cast-iron skull," he said. He pulled off a pair of brown leather gloves and stood massaging his right hand with his left. "I had you buried hours ago."

"Where have you been?" I wasn't in the mood for saloon stage banter.

"To the Clark Fork River and back, tracking your prisoner." He swung the paint-spattered chair around and straddled it, folding his arms atop the back. Exhausted or not, he hadn't forgotten to pose. "I don't think you'll have to worry about him any more, because he's as good as dead."

"You shot him?" I started to get up, then remembered the mule waiting to kick my brains out and settled back.

"Why waste a bullet? I followed his trail north as far as Glacier Pass, where it swung west and headed straight into the mountains. I figure he's on his way to Canada by a route where he won't meet too many people. He'll meet a lot more than he reckoned on once the Flatheads find out there's a white man in their midst. He won't live to see Canada."

I felt a chill, but not from the thought of Brainard's reception at the hands of the Indians. A vapor of cold air had begun to waft from Henry's clothes over to me. The temperature outside must have dropped considerably since I'd returned to Staghorn, as there was a light dusting of snow on the sheriff's hat and coat, now turning to beads of moisture in the heat of the shop's invisible stove. I shivered slightly beneath the thin stuff of my nightshirt. I decided that Henry had helped Wilson undress me and put me to bed; the thought of the little barber attempting it alone was just too ludicrous.

"Is the situation that bad?" I asked Henry.

"Take a good look around you," he said. "There isn't a homesteader in the area who'd step outside his house without a rifle or a gun on his hip. It started after Doc Bernstein got killed, and since last spring when all those braves were scalped in that hunting party, it's been just a matter of when Two Sisters thinks the time is right to strike. That's what I tried to tell that bounty hunter Church, but he wouldn't listen. Likely his scalp is already decorating a pole in some brave's lodge."

There was a moment of silence while he appeared to be searching for something else to say. Absentmindedly he resumed massaging his right hand with his left where they rested on the back of the chair. He saw me watching, looked down at his hands, saw what he was doing, and dropped them to his knees.

"What's the matter with your hand?" I asked him.

"Nothing. I think I sprained my wrist when I pistol-whipped Ira Longbow." He got up. "Anyway, you can stop worrying about Leslie Brainard. He won't be strangling any more wives."

"Tell that to Judge Blackthorne."

His laugh was theatrical, as was everything else about him, but it was genuine and it did me good to hear it. "You'll think of a good excuse," he said. "You always do. Meanwhile, leave your head on that pillow and don't let Ezra get too close to you with a razor in his hand. He really wants that bed." He strode out past the barber. A moment later I heard the front door clap shut.

Wilson came over and returned the chair to its original position at the foot of the bed. "You need anything else?" He seemed gratified when I told him I didn't. "Chamber pot's under the bed," he said. "Holler if you need help." He settled himself into the chair, squirmed around until he found the hollow he wanted, and was asleep again within five minutes.

I waited until I was sure he wouldn't wake up, then, slowly—not so much because of him as because of my head, which had settled into an almost bearable throb—I peeled aside the threadbare counterpane that had been covering me and swung my feet to the floor. The boards felt like ice. For a moment I sat there, preparing myself. Then I took a deep breath and stood up.

A shotgun exploded deep inside my head, spraying the walls of my skull with red-hot pellets that burst in turn behind my eyes and dizzied me so that I had to clutch at the bedstead to keep from falling. My stomach did a slow turn,

like a whale rolling over in deep water. Then, with excruci-
ating slowness, the pain began to subside. At length my vision
returned and I found myself standing with knees bent,
holding onto the bedpost with a kitten's grip. I welcomed
the throbbing inside my head as an old friend.

After a few minutes of searching, I found my clothes in
a heap at the bottom of a scarred wardrobe in which there
was nothing else but Ezra Wilson's shirt drooping from a
wire hanger on the rod. I dressed, easing the hat on last so
that it topped the bandage, and went out through the darkened barbershop. Wilson hadn't stirred.

The snow was an inch deep on the street and still falling. The cold air felt good on my aching head. I spent ten
minutes banging on the door of the mercantile before Bart
Goddard came storming out from the back, wearing his
nightshirt and carrying a double-barreled shotgun, and
another twenty getting him to open up and sell me enough
supplies for a two-week journey. As I was leaving with
the bundles he muttered something that I wouldn't have
stood for had I been in any condition to do something
about it. I pretended I hadn't heard him and headed back
down the street toward the livery stable, where I was in
luck. There was a light on in the office and the old man was
awake.

My cash supply was running low by this time. I'd brought
along a little extra for emergencies, but as I hadn't anticipated any the extra wasn't much. So instead of renting a
better horse I paid the old man for the care he'd given the
chestnut mare, brought in by the sheriff, and asked him to
saddle it and load up the supplies I had brought with me
while I called on Henry. I felt strange going through all
these familiar motions; but for the hour and the way my
head felt, it might have been the day before yesterday.

The door to the sheriff's office was locked, but there was a light on inside. I knocked.

"Just a minute," called Henry's voice.

It seemed longer before the door was opened. He was hatless and in his shirtsleeves, and he had either just put his gun belt back on or had been in the process of removing it when I knocked; the thong with which he usually tied down his holster was hanging loose down the seam of his pants leg. He was surprised to see me.

"No lectures, Henry," I said, when his expression became disapproving. I went past him into the office.

His desk was bare except for a pan of hot water standing on top of it. Next to it was a folded towel—a thick one, most likely stolen from Arthur's Castle. I dipped a couple of fingers into the steaming water and put them to my mouth. They tasted of salt.

"How's the wrist feel now that you've soaked it?" I asked the sheriff.

"Better." He closed the door. "What are you doing out of bed?"

"I came to borrow a revolver and a rifle. Got any to spare?"

"You're not going after Brainard."

"No," I said acidly, "I just thought I'd do a little rabbit hunting up in the mountains. It'll be good for my head. Of course I'm going after him. That's what Blackthorne pays me for."

"He's dead, Page. You'd just be wasting your time."

"If he's dead I've got to see his body. The judge won't settle for anything less and neither will I. Do I get the guns or not?"

He got his key ring out of the desk, went over to the gun rack, and unlocked a padlock securing the chain that held his half-dozen rifles and one shotgun in place. "Which do you want?" he growled.

"I'll take the Henry, if that's the best you've got."

He tossed me the carbine, a slightly battered piece with a triangular chunk missing from the stock. From a drawer in the bottom of the rack he took a box of shells. I accepted it and loaded the rifle. "What about a revolver and gun belt?" I reminded him.

"This is the only other one I have," he said, handing me a gun and holster he'd taken from the drawer. "This means I can't get mine fixed until you come back. If you come back."

I slid the revolver from its holster. It was a Peacemaker like his other one, but unlike his other one the butt was plain wood without a trace of ivory. I freed the cylinder and thumbed it around. It was loaded. I strapped on the belt. "Care to come with me?"

He laughed shortly. "I'm not paid to commit suicide," he said. "Besides, that's out of my jurisdiction."

"That never stopped you before."

"No, thanks."

I nodded, eyeing him thoughtfully. Suddenly I whipped the Colt out of its holster and pointed it at him.

His reflexes were sharp. No sooner had I made the move than his right hand swung down and scooped up his own gun. Then it spun from his grip and clattered loudly to the floor.

For a long moment we stood staring at each other, me over the barrel of the gun he had given me, Henry with his right arm crooked and not a weapon within reach. The ticking of the clock on the wall behind his head sounded like pistol reports in the silence.

I holstered the Colt. "Rheumatism, right?"

"It comes and goes." He sank to his heels and retrieved his gun. His right hand reminded me of a gardener's claw, it was that bent. "How'd you guess?" he asked, when he was standing again and the gun was in its holster.

"You were too quick to say no when I asked you to come with me," I explained. "You like action too much to give me that answer that soon. And when I asked you about your wrist, you changed the subject. How long have you had it?"

"A year and a half, maybe longer. Lately it's been getting worse. If it wasn't for my reputation, I suppose I'd have been dead long ago."

"You can't get by on your reputation forever."

"I know it." There was annoyance in his tone. "What else can I do? I'm too old to punch cattle. The only other thing I know how to do is use a gun, and now I'm losing even that. Where do I go, to the Old Sheriffs' Home? There aren't enough old sheriffs around to make a thing like that worthwhile. We don't live that long."

"Who else knows?"

"No one. Doc Bernstein knew—he guessed it, just like you—but there was nothing he could do for it, except prescribe laudanum when the pain got too bad. I tried it once, and it put me out for twelve hours. I haven't had any since. I'll take my chances with the rheumatism."

I let it drop. "Watch your back, Henry," I said. "Tell Wilson I'll be back to pay him." I slung the Henry under my arm and headed for the door.

"That's what you think," he retorted.

Tracking was impossible after the snowfall, but if what Henry had told me was true, there was only one way Brainard could have gone. West of the Clark Fork, a couple of hundred thousand years before even the Indians came, glaciers had carved a wedge five hundred feet wide through the

Bitterroot Mountains. From the point where the ice had emerged, the pass took a ragged turn north toward Canada, narrowing as it progressed until there was barely enough room for a man on horseback to squeeze between the encroaching pillars of rock. In another million years it would close up tight. For now, however, it was the shortest available route through the range in the direction Brainard was heading, and it was more than a safe bet that he would choose to take it rather than attempt to push my buckskin over the nearly vertical mountains. I reached the opening shortly before noon and dismounted to take a look around. That's when I found the fresh tracks.

There were a lot of them near the northern edge of the opening, churning the snow into dull piles and exposing the brown earth beneath. They represented six or seven horses, none of them shod. A hunting party, I judged, returning with its game from a trip into the plains. Flatheads, or they would have avoided the mountains entirely. The tracks were only a few hours old. While studying them, I felt a crawling sensation between my shoulder blades and wondered if I was being watched. I stood up and scanned the peaks, but they were the same color as the sky, and the outline of a human head would have been impossible to see against the wood-ash gray of the clouds. I decided that if someone was watching it was too late to do anything about it. I mounted up and steered the chestnut into the pass, taking what advantage I could of the narrow strip of shadow left by the pale glimmer of the sun directly above my head.

It was late afternoon when I found them. The horse smelled them first and shied, tossing its head and chortling through its nostrils. Then I caught a whiff. A musty smell, like you get when you split a deer carcass down the middle and spread its ribs. My stomach, empty now of the venison broth I'd had that morning, began to work. I breathed through my mouth and coaxed the mare forward into a stand of low pines up ahead.

Leslie Brainard, what was left of him, hung naked by his wrists from a buckhide thong wound around the trunk of a pine six feet above the ground. His legs had been pulled back so that he straddled the trunk, his ankles lashed tight behind it. Ragged stripes of purple glistened from his collarbone to his pelvis where the flesh had been torn in strips from his body. His eyes started from their sockets farther than I had thought they could without actually popping out onto his cheeks. His mouth was wide open as if he had been screaming, but his screams had been incoherent because his tongue had been cut out. A hole the size of a fifty-dollar gold piece showed black and empty between his breasts. He would have welcomed it.

His tormentors hadn't outlived him by more than a few minutes. Five of the seven Indians lay where they had fallen; the other two had managed to crawl several yards through the snow before expiring. Behind them, the trails they had left were streaked with red. None of the corpses had been stripped of furs or buckskins, which would have been the case had the attackers been their own kind. Four still had weapons in their hands. All they were missing was their scalps.

I swung out of my saddle, holding onto the reins to keep the mare from galloping away in its panic. The snow was trampled with footprints. One, a blurred oval such as a fur boot might leave, was nearly large enough for me to stand in with both feet. At first I thought it was a normal print that had grown with the melting of the snow around it, but then I found more of them and I remembered.

I tethered the horse to a juniper bush, pulled off a glove,

and squatted to feel for a pulse at the throat of the Indian lying nearest me. The snow was no colder than his flesh. In his abdomen he sported a hole identical to the one in Brainard's chest. I inspected the others. Same story, although the holes weren't always in the same place. One of the Indians, a crawler, had a second wound in the back of his head, puckered with powder burns, as if his killer had walked right up to him and placed the muzzle against his skull before pulling the trigger. This time Mountain That Walks had left no one to tell the tale.

My first intimation that I wasn't alone with the corpses came when I heard a squeaking footfall in the snow behind me. I swung around, drawing my gun.

"A mistake, white skin." The words were grunted rather than spoken, as though torn from a throat that had not used the language in years.

The way out of the pines was sealed off by a semicircle of mottled horses, astride the bare backs of which sat a dozen fur-clad riders whose features looked oddly alike within the frames of their shaggy head pieces. Their hair was long and black and arranged in braids hanging down onto their chests, their eyes black slits in the glare of the minimal sunlight coming off the fresh snow. They were the corpses on the ground around me come to life. The only difference was that each of them was armed with a carbine, and that every one was trained on me. Almost every one.

The one that wasn't was slung over the shoulder of the Indian in the center, the one who had spoken. This one had a moon face, fleshy for a brave, in which not a crease or a wrinkle showed, making it look like a child's India rubber balloon with features painted on it. The impression of lifelessness was carried further by the fact that the face wore no expression at all. His mouth was bland, his eyes like doll's eyes and without brows. They watched me unblinkingly. For all its emptiness, though, the face carried more of a threat than the scowling visages of his companions with weathered rifle stocks pressed against their cheeks and index fingers poised around the triggers.

I returned the Colt to its holster. I needed no more convincing to know that I'd wandered into a trap set by Rocking Wolf, nephew of Two Sisters and next chief of the Flathead nation.

# CHAPTER 5

For two beats after I put away the gun, no one moved. We might have been snow sculptures in that lonely glade. Then, at a signal from Rocking Wolf, the brave mounted at his right lowered his gun and trotted over to me, where he sat looking down at me with an expectant scowl.

"You will surrender your weapons," directed the Indian in command. His English was ponderous but correct.

Thinking that it was becoming increasingly difficult for me to hold onto a firearm, I unbuckled my gun belt and handed it up to the brave. There was another long silence while his eyes searched me from head to foot. At length they settled upon the hilt of the knife protruding above the top of my right boot. The scowl became ominous. I stopped, drew the knife from its sheath, and gave it to him, handle first.

While the brave had been engaged in disarming me, Rocking Wolf had nodded again, this time to a savage at his left, who swung past my skitterish mount and hooked the Henry out of its scabbard, then tossed it to his superior. Rocking Wolf caught it in one hand and examined it perfunctorily. With a shrug he handed it to another brave.

"I do not applaud your preference in firearms," he told me. "What is your name, and what have you to do with the thing that has happened here this day?"

I told him my name. "As for the rest," I added, "I prefer to talk it over with Two Sisters. Where is your chief?"

Rocking Wolf barked something in Salish. Immediately the brave who had relieved me of my revolver and knife reached down and snatched a handful of my collar, thrusting the point of the latter weapon against my jugular as he did so. His hands smelled of rancid bear grease.

"Perhaps opening your throat will show us the way to your tongue," said the chief's nephew.

The bite of the knife acted as a spur to my already racing thoughts. "Killing me will gain you nothing, Rocking Wolf," I said hoarsely. "Whereas allowing me to live may lead you to the hiding place of Mountain That Walks."

The forbidden name brought a reaction from all who understood the language, even Rocking Wolf. Again there was a long silence. I felt a drop of blood trickle down my throat and into my collar.

"How is it that you know my name, white skin?"

I hesitated, allowing my eyes to slide toward the Indian holding the knife. At a nod from his superior the brave withdrew the blade and relinquished his grip on my collar.

"I used to run into you and your brother, Yellow Horn, in the mountains when you were hunting." I rubbed my throat, smearing the blood. "That was many years ago. Few words passed between us at those times."

"I do not remember you."

"It's likely you didn't notice me. I was always with Bear Anderson, him who you call Mountain That Walks."

For an instant, Rocking Wolf let slip his mask, revealing the naked hatred that writhed beneath. Nine rifles were poised to fire; there was a beat during which I was one harsh syllable away from death. Then he retreated behind the India rubber facade once again.

"You are either very brave or very foolish to tell me that," he said. "I have not yet decided which is the case."

"Do we have a bargain?"

"What makes you think I value your knowledge? The murderer of my people has left a clear trail to follow, and we are expert trackers."

"Now who's being foolish? Nightfall is less than two hours away. Even Salish can't track a man in the dark. By tomorrow the snow will have returned to cover the trail. I grew up with Anderson, remember; I know how he thinks. I alone can lead you to his lair."

He studied me in silence. His thoughts were impossible to read. After an eternity he looked to the brave with the knife and gave him a curt order. Reluctantly, the brave backed his horse away from me.

"Mount your horse," Rocking Wolf directed. "You will get your meeting with the chief."

I waited until all weapons were put away, then stepped forward to untie the chestnut.

It was the work of five minutes for the braves to gather up their dead and sling them over the backs of their horses. When that was done, Leslie Brainard was left alone to decorate the tree where he had met his merciful end. By morning the wolves and coyotes would finish the job that had been started by the Indians.

"Where is Yellow Horn?" I asked Rocking Wolf, once I was in the saddle. "I don't see him in your party."

"My brother is dead," he said. "Killed last winter by Mountain That Walks." He gave his horse a kick and led the way north.

The pass inclined steadily upward to about six thousand feet, where it leveled out, yielding what would have been a spectacular view of the sunset over the Bitterroot had it not been for the thickening veil of clouds that reduced the violent reds and purples to a vague rust on the horizon. Soon even that was gone, and from then on we felt our way forward with only the aid of the snow's own mysterious source of illumination. An hour after sundown it began to snow again, this time in large wet flakes that slithered down our faces and made sizzling noises when they struck the ground. I dug my chin into my chest for warmth. Around me, the Indians rode straight as andirons; in their bearskins they remained as warm as if they hadn't left their fire-lit lodges.

The Flathead camp was laid out across a broad spot in the pass, between two cliffs of sheer rock. Only the tops of the temporary animal-hide structures were visible above the snow. Here and there a torch burned, its flame flaring and faltering beneath the snow's untiring assault. A hundred yards before we reached the camp we were stopped by a rifle-toting sentry atop the east cliff, who addressed our leader in rapid Salish.

Rocking Wolf answered him in the same tongue, gesticulating in my direction and snarling a string of words that didn't sound much like compliments. The sentry lowered his weapon and waved us on.

"You're late getting out of the mountains this year," I remarked as we entered camp.

"That is because Two Sisters cannot be moved." Rocking Wolf kept his eyes trained straight ahead of him. "Ten suns ago he was thrown by his horse. His injuries have yet to heal."

A scruffy dog of uncertain ancestry came bouncing out from behind one of the lodges and announced our arrival in raucous barks. It was joined by another, and soon we were surrounded by mongrels of every size and description, snapping at our heels and raising enough racket to bestir the corpses on the backs of the party's mounts. Here and there a flap was pulled aside and a half-naked brave stepped out of his lodge to stare at us with suspicious eyes.

The chief's lodge, a squat cone made of buffalo hide and bearskin sewn together and stretched over six stout poles bound together at the top by a strip of uncured leather, was no grander than those that surrounded it. A colorless haze of heat drifted out through the opening in the top, causing the crossed ends of the poles to shimmer like sunken pilings at the bottom of a shallow pond. Rocking Wolf dismounted before the lodge and, out of habit, landed a glancing blow with the sole of his right moccasin boot alongside the head of a black-muzzled mutt that had gotten too close. The dog shrieked and drew its upper lip back over its yellowed fangs, but it shrank away. The Indian exchanged a few low words with the fur-clad brave guarding the entrance, who ducked inside for a moment, then returned and nodded curtly. Rocking Wolf told me to stay where I was and entered the lodge through the low flap.

News that a white man had been brought in alive along with the corpses of the missing hunting party had spread quickly throughout the camp. Everywhere I looked I met a hostile face, leaving me with little doubt about who they believed was responsible. I thought of Leslie Brainard's fate and wondered if they could have anything worse in store for me.

The wails of the women were conspicuous by their absence; I came to realize after a moment that there were few, if any, squaws in camp. Probably they were waiting for their men back at the permanent village west of the Bitterroot. That was proof enough that the prospect of crossing the mountains was no longer a casual one now that they were part of Bear Anderson's domain. The thought didn't gratify me. A savage afraid, like an animal cornered, was a thing best left alone.

The quickening snow had put out the last of the torches by the time the chief's nephew emerged from the lodge and signaled for me to enter. I dismounted amid a chorus of threatening growls and elbowed my way through the throng, expecting any time to feel the burning pain of a knife blade being shoved between my ribs.

But the aura of command that surrounded the chief's lodge was too great, and presently I found myself blinking in the light of the fire that burned in the center of the cone. After the dimness of the snow-covered landscape outside, it was some moments before my eyes could discern anything in the gloom that surrounded that crackling brightness. Meanwhile, I occupied myself by listening to the voice that addressed me as soon as I entered.

"You're far from home, Page Murdock." It was a dry voice; something that had been left too close to the fire so that all the moisture had been allowed to bake away, leaving only the brittle shell. It handled English with less difficulty than Rocking Wolf, which was no surprise. During his fifty-odd years, Chief Two Sisters had learned to speak three languages fluently.

"Farther than you think, Chief," I said after a moment. I fished my badge out of my breast pocket and held it up in the firelight. "I'm a deputy U.S. marshal operating out of Helena. The man your braves were torturing when they were surprised by Mountain That Walks was my prisoner. He's the reason I'm here."

The fire hissed and belched while Two Sisters digested the information I'd given him. Gradually, I was able to make out the lines and finally the details of a lean figure sitting up on a straw pallet on the other side of the flames, his back supported against one of the sturdy poles and a buffalo robe drawn up to his chest. His eyes were black hollows beneath a high, square brow. The shifting firelight threw his equally square chin and sharp cheekbones into relief against the corrugated parchment of the rest of his face. He had a wide, firm mouth and a nose with a crushed bridge, as if at some time in the distant past it had come up hard against the flat of an enemy tomahawk. His hair was shoulder-length but unbraided, the color of tarnished silver. The term Flathead being a misnomer foisted upon the Montana Salish by the early pioneers, there were no signs of the artificial flattening of the skull practiced by some western tribes. His breathing, loud in the seclusion of the lodge, was even but careful, as I suppose any man's would be after he had broken several ribs falling from his horse.

There was a third party in the lodge, a squat, broad-shouldered brave whose features were impossible to make out as he stood almost completely enveloped in shadow beside his seated chief. His chest was naked and powerful, leathery slabs of muscle glistening beneath the obligatory coating of bear grease. When he moved his head I caught a glimpse of firelight glinting off the buffalo horns of his headdress. That would make him the medicine man. Knowing that, I didn't have to see his face to guess what he thought of my presence in camp. There isn't a medicine man west of Buffalo Bill's show who doesn't view all white men as a threat to his authority.

"This man you say you were hunting," spoke up Two Sisters. "Which of your laws did he break?"

I told him. His scowl carved deep lines from his nostrils to the corners of his mouth.

"A foolish crime. We Salish beat our squaws when they make us angry, but we do not kill them. What's to be gained?" He sighed, easing his breath out between his cracked ribs. "It's a shame that Mountain That Walks arrived when he did to put an end to his suffering. The fate the hunting party had planned for him was far more fitting. He is the one responsible for your injury?"

I put a hand to my head, touching the bandage beneath the brim of my hat. The pounding had become so much a part of me that I'd forgotten I was wearing it. I nodded.

"He had no firearms?"

"He did after he hit me. I saw no sign of them where he was killed. At the time I assumed Bear Anderson had taken them, but they could just as easily have been picked up by Rocking Wolf and his party."

Two Sisters shook his head. "My brother's son says the only weapons he saw were those that had been carried by the dead braves. Their horses were also missing, perhaps frightened off by the shots." He paused. A stick of wood near the heart of the fire separated with a loud report, sending up a geyser of sparks and bathing the chief's face in brief, fiery brilliance. His eyes were sad. "It's a bad thing to have happen," he said. "Tomorrow I will have no choice but to call a council of war."

"Not if I can lead you to the lair of Mountain That Walks."

The flare had died, returning his face to shadowy patchwork. "Rocking Wolf has told me of your boast," he said. "How will you do this?"

"How do you hunt any game? By knowing its habits. I spent a third of my life hunting those mountains with Anderson. His movements are predictable. Depending on the weather and the shifting of the game he lives on, I can place him within a few miles at any given time."

"Remarkable. And where is he now?"

I smiled. "You don't really expect an answer to that."

"I suppose not." He returned the smile, faintly. "I'm curious to know why you are offering your service in this matter."

"I'm always willing to help when the price is right. In this case it's my life."

He thought that over. Outside, the snow settled onto the sides of the lodge with a sound like frying bacon. At last he spoke.

"You're probably lying, but I can't afford to pass up any opportunity to avoid war with the whites at a time when we are so poorly prepared. It has been five of your years since the bulk of my people was moved forcibly to the valley you call the Flathead, two days' ride east of this camp. Our numbers now are small." He swept a hand across his face, as if to erase the memory. It was a neat piece of acting. "You and Rocking Wolf will leave at dawn tomorrow. You have until the next moon to return either with news of where to find Mountain That Walks or with his body slung across a saddle."

"Just Rocking Wolf? You must trust me."

"A party would attract too much attention. As for Rocking Wolf, he is the best of my warriors. I would advise you not to attempt an escape."

"You didn't worry about attracting attention last year, when you headed up the bunch that killed Doc Bernstein outside Staghorn," I reminded him.

"The old white man," he said, after a pause. "I remember the incident. He gave us no choice. We had reason to believe that he was harboring Mountain That Walks after one of our party had wounded him. We asked for permission to search his dwelling. He was going to shoot."

"What about his wife and child? Where they going to shoot?"

He studied me for a moment without speaking. The chief used silence like a weapon. "You're an emotional man, Page Murdock. I didn't realize that before."

"And was Mountain That Walks there?"

"No. Apparently we were mistaken."

I didn't carry it any further. The confrontation had given me a clear idea of the boundaries of his patience, and they weren't as broad as they'd seemed. Nothing about him was as it seemed. I changed the subject.

"I need food and a place to sleep. Can you fix me up?"

"My nephew will see to your needs," he said. "One more question."

I had turned to duck through the flap. I stopped and looked back at him.

"Since you know so much, perhaps you can tell me why a party of four white men was seen two days southwest of here by my scouts the day before yesterday. Is this a new trick on the part of your army to rob my people of their birthright?"

He spoke casually, but I could tell that he had been waiting to ask the question ever since I'd appeared in the lodge. I pretended to give it some thought, though of course I already knew the answer. "Was one of them a small man wearing a big hat and a long yellow coat?"

"The scouts described a small man with a big hat. There was no mention of a coat, yellow or any other color."

"He probably traded it for something warmer. His name is Church, and he has a warrant signed by the President for the arrest of Mountain That Walks. Two of the men with him are his partners. As for all of them being white, your scouts need glasses; the fourth is a half-breed who calls himself Ira Longbow." I hesitated, letting the silence work against the chief for a change. "He claims to be your son."

If I expected any kind of reaction to that last piece of information, I was disappointed. Two Sisters could have given Rocking Wolf poker lessons when he wanted to. Finally he nodded. That could have meant that he believed me, but it could just as well have been a sign of satisfaction at hearing an expected lie. In any case, he didn't return to the subject.

"The next moon," he reminded me. "I can wait no longer. By then the first blizzard will be on its way to block the passes with snow and ice. We must leave the mountains by then or be trapped. When we return in the spring, we will be carrying arms and wearing paint for war with the whites. Much to my regret."

I left, my back tingling beneath the medicine man's hostile scrutiny.

A sour-featured brave escorted me like the prisoner I was to a lodge near the camp's center. There I was handed an earthen dish heaped with chunks of lean, bloody meat by an old squaw whose cracked pumpkin of a face told me she had borne worse dangers than those offered by Bear Anderson's mountains. I ate hungrily, not pausing to wonder which of the dogs that had greeted me earlier was going into my stomach; to a man in my condition it tasted like tenderest sirloin. When it was finished and the dish was taken away, I stretched out fully clothed on a flat straw pallet beside the fire and drew a mildewed blanket up to my chin.

I was prepared to spend the night staring up at the cloud-lathered sky through the opening in the top of the lodge. As it turned out, however, I had little trouble getting to sleep. So great was my exhaustion that nothing could have kept me awake, not even the fact that I didn't have the slightest idea of where to find Bear Anderson or his lair.

# CHAPTER 6

"You are leading me in circles, white skin." Rocking Wolf spoke flatly and seemingly without emotion, but the emotion was there, in his words. They dripped cold fury.

The sun had risen dazzlingly over twelve inches of fresh snow, shining through the spots where the wind had slashed the cloud cover into fibrous shreds and turning the uninterrupted vista of white into a blazing brilliance that hurt the eyes and did little toward relieving my headache. We had followed the pass northward until the flanking cliffs fell away, at which point we had taken a turn to the west and swung lazily in the direction from which we had come. It was midmorning before we stopped at the top of a gentle rise and looked out over the Christmas-painting scenery of crystallized trees and blue-shadowed drifts. I was still stuck with the broken-down chestnut mare, while Rocking Wolf had secured himself a fresh mount that morning from his stable of painted stallions—a situation meant to discourage any plans I might have entertained about escaping. Over his shoulder was slung a Winchester with a shattered and thong-bound stock. In the distance a river etched its way southward through the foothills, its chocolate color startling against the carved whiteness of its banks. To the south, clouds drifting across the mountaintops tore themselves lengthwise along the razor edges of the peaks. The air was brittle.

"No circles," I corrected him. My breath hung in vapor. "We're just taking the easy way south. By now the narrow part of the pass is piled up with drifts three feet high. If you'd rather flounder your way through that, you're welcome to try, but I'll be waiting for you at the other end."

"How do I know you are not leading me into a trap? You have already admitted that Mountain That Walks is your friend."

"Was my friend. I haven't seen him in over fifteen years."

He looked at me, and I got the impression that he was smirking behind the coarse scarf that swathed the lower part of his face, leaving only his eyes visible between it and his bearskin headpiece. "And does the white man find it necessary to see his friends every day to ensure that they remain friends?" he asked.

"Look around," I said. "If I were going to lead you into a trap, would I have chosen this area? From here you can see ten miles in every direction. The pass would have been a far better place for an ambush."

"Where are we going?"

I nodded toward the mountains to the south. "Straight up. If I know Bear, he'll be heading where no Indian in his right mind would follow him. This time of year a mountain goat would have trouble getting around on the high rocks."

"That is a long way to go if we are to return by the next moon."

"You can talk to your uncle about that," I said. "He's the one who set the time limit." I urged the mare forward down the slope.

The wind began to rise about noon, and for the rest of the day it blew in ever-increasing gusts, bringing snow

swirling down from the sides of the mountains and rippling
the wet stuff in the flat spots until they resembled sheets of
corrugated iron. After a while my face grew numb and I
fell into the habit of pinching it from time to time between
gloved fingers to make sure the skin wasn't frostbitten. Steam
rose from the mare's neck and withers.

Night fell without warning, the way it does in the mountains; one minute we were riding along through snow tinted
orange by the wallowing sun, our shadows stretching out a
mile to our left, and the next we were plunged into darkness. We made camp on a slope, using a stand of jack pine
for a windbreak and building a tiny fire with the aid of
boughs from a dead tree, over which we warmed our stiff
fingers. Rocking Wolf watched from a safe distance while
I used a knife borrowed from him to pare off a couple of
slices of bacon from the small slab I had bought in Staghorn. I cut out more than was needed and slipped the extra
slices inside my coat to keep them from freezing. When
I was finished he held out his hand for the weapon. I returned it reluctantly. My skillet having disappeared along
with my horse the day Brainard got away, I strung the slices
on a stick and roasted them over the flame. This done, I offered one to the Indian. He shook his head, holding up a
three-inch length of jerky which he had taken from inside
his bearskin where he had been keeping it warm beneath
his arm.

"Suit yourself," I said, crunching the crisp bacon between
my teeth. "There won't be many more hot meals where
we're going. We can't take the chance of having Bear smell
wood smoke once we hit the mountains."

"White men." Rocking Wolf ground away contemptu-
ously at the tough jerky. "How do you expect to conquer the
Indian when you insist upon taking all the conveniences of

home with you wherever you go? Give a Salish a knife and a piece of jerky, send him out into the wilderness, and he will come back two moons later as healthy as he was when he left."

I let that one slide while I studied the strip of bacon remaining on the stick. "What do you plan to do with Mountain That Walks once you've got him?"

He paused in mid-chew. His browless eyes glittered in the light of the little fire: "That decision belongs to the chief," he said. "When I was a boy, not yet strong enough to draw a bow, I saw the punishment of a white soldier who had been captured in the act of raping a squaw. He was a big man, like you, with big hard hands and a face like cracked leather. I think he was what you would call a sergeant. The braves stripped him and turned him over to the women, who have their own way of dealing with the crime of which he was guilty.

"It is a compliment to his strength and training that he was still alive when it was over. He begged to be killed. The braves did not oblige. They left him lying there until he ceased to beg." He went on chewing. "This was for the crime of rape. I imagine Two Sisters has something much more fitting in mind for the murderer of our people."

"Do your people enjoy seeing suffering that much?"

"We enjoy it no more than the whites. When a man commits a crime among your people, he is usually compelled to hang from a rope by his neck until he chokes his last. Our punishments are neither worse nor better. They are just different." He finished eating and rolled himself up in the buffalo robe he used for a blanket. "Sleep," he said. "We will move again at dawn."

I sat there a moment longer, gazing at the uneaten slice of bacon. In the firelight it took on a reddish glow, as though it were dripping with fresh blood. I thrust it inside my coat and made ready for bed.

Staying awake was harder than I'd anticipated. In many ways, riding a horse all day long is more exhausting than walking for the same length of time, and in spite of the cold and the hardness of the ground I had all I could do to keep my eyelids from falling shut of their own weight. I stuck it out for the better part of an hour, and then I got quietly to my feet and picked up my saddle, holding onto the cinch lest the buckle jingle. Rocking Wolf lay motionless beneath his buffalo robe on the other side of the guttering fire. With the saddle under my arm and the blanket and saddlebags slung over my shoulder I stepped cautiously through the wet snow to where our horses were standing in the shelter of the pines, mine tethered, the Indian's hobbled. I gazed longingly at the painted stallion for a moment, but I was no bareback rider, and saddling it was out of the question as it was unfamiliar with the procedure and would undoubtedly have balked and alerted its master. Besides, I was getting used to the chestnut, which says something for the adaptability of human nature. I saddled the mare.

I had my foot in the stirrup and was about to swing my right leg over when something piled into me from behind and carried me with it to the ground, emptying my lungs upon impact and clapping my jaws shut with a jarring snap. The mare whinnied and tried to rear, pulling taut the reins that held it. Snow sifted down from the pine's shivering boughs. My skull rang. Dazed, I lay on my face in the snow for a long moment, grinding pieces of what had been a perfectly good molar between my teeth. Then I scrambled to my feet and swung around, fists clenched. I stopped when Rocking Wolf placed the muzzle of the Colt I had borrowed from Henry Goodnight against my forehead and drew the hammer back with a sound like a walnut being crushed.

"I wondered what had happened to that," I said finally. I let my hands drop to my sides.

Moonlight drenched the Indian in silver, but it might just as well have been dark for all the expression he wore. His bearskin and leggings were covered with snow from his tackle. "You might have died, white skin," he said. "I would not like to see that happen. Not until we have found Mountain That Walks."

He held the gun on me while I unsaddled the chestnut, and kept me covered all the way back to camp. Then he put the weapon away inside his bearskin and settled down on his side of the glowing ashes as if nothing had happened to disturb him. His seeming carelessness didn't tempt me. It would have pleased him to shoot me in the leg during an escape attempt; I would still be alive to lead him to his quarry and would give him less trouble. Wrapped in my blanket, I lay back and stared at the sky. The moon, shot with clouds like black arteries in a blind man's eye, was full. Tomorrow it would begin to wane, eventually to be replaced by a new moon.

"Don't remind me," I muttered, and drew the blanket over my head. But that was too much like what they do to corpses, so I pulled it down and turned over onto my left side.

When day broke, crisp and cold as the leftover slice of bacon I had for breakfast, we had left the camp far behind and were starting up the grade that wound into the mountains. The wind had died down, but that was only temporary, the lull before the big blow. The air stung my nostrils and the sun was so bright coming off the clean surface of the snow that I was forced to ride with my eyes squeezed shut most of the time to keep from going snowblind. It was because of this that I failed to see the tracks on the northern slope until my horse was right on top of them.

I turned to the Indian, but he had already noticed them. He nodded once, curtly. I obeyed his unspoken command and dismounted for a closer look.

Four horses had trampled the snow into a trail of slush that girded the mountain from east to west.

"Have you ever known Mountain That Walks to travel with companions?" I asked Rocking Wolf.

"Never." He bounded to the ground and squatted for a moment beside the trail. "Nor have I known him to ride a shod horse. You have laid a poor trap, white skin." He drew out the revolver and pointed it at me.

"Put it away," I said, wearily. "I thought you Indians were supposed to have such good eyesight. Can't you see that one of these men is wounded?" I pointed out the spots of blood that peppered the snow.

He spent a long time studying the crimson specks. Finally he returned the gun to the inside of his bearskin and stood up. "We will follow them," he said. "If it is a trick, you are the one who will pay."

We didn't have far to go. Two miles later the Indian reined in and signaled for me to do the same. He sniffed the air. I followed his lead.

"Wood smoke," I said.

He didn't reply, but kicked his horse gently and together we rode forward at a walk around the bend of the mountain. We halted at the top of a rise that fell away before us into a fan-shaped hollow, at the bottom of which three men sat huddled around a fire at the base of a lone pine. A fourth lay wrapped in blankets nearby. Their horses, tethered to the tree, craned their necks to nibble at the needles on the lower branches above their heads.

"White men do not belong in the wilderness," observed Rocking Wolf in a low murmur. "It is a foolish camper who kindles his fire beneath a tree heavy with snow."

"Not if he doesn't want anyone to know he's there," I said. "Those branches do a pretty good job of breaking up the smoke so that it can't be seen from a distance."

"You know them?"

I nodded. "It's Church and his bunch, the Strakeys and Ira Longbow. That's Church, the small one with his back to us. They're the party Two Sisters' scouts reported seeing a few days back."

"Will they give us trouble?"

"They want what we want. Of course they'll give us trouble."

We were picking our way down the slope when one of the tethered horses spotted us and began snorting. Church, who had been facing away from the rise, sprang up and spun on his heel, drawing his gun as he did so. On the other side of the fire, Ira Longbow rose slowly with his Dance in his hand. He wore the black Spanish hat I'd seen earlier, low over his eyes in the manner of a caballero, but it didn't help; he still looked like a half-breed. The third man, Homer Strakey, Sr., watched us from a kneeling position beside his son's prostrate form. As before, I was unable to tell if he was wearing any weapon at all. Which made him the one to watch.

We stopped five yards from camp, and for a space the horses' fidgeting was the only sound for miles. Then Strakey, Jr., began moaning in a low voice and broke the tension.

"Page Murdock." A grin flickered across Church's face,

but it was just his peculiar tic manifesting itself once again. He made no move to holster the gun. He had a gray woolen scarf pulled down over his hat and knotted beneath his chin, and he had discarded his duster in favor of a hip-length sheepskin coat that looked as if it hadn't been cleaned since it was removed from the sheep. "You turn renegade?" His crossed eyes took in the Indian mounted beside me.

I assured him that I hadn't, and introduced Rocking Wolf. The bounty hunter laughed shortly and spoke over his shoulder to the half-breed. "Two Sisters' nephew, Longbow," he said. "I reckon that makes him your cousin. Ain't you going to say howdy?"

Longbow said nothing. He eyed the Indian from beneath the brim of his hat, the whites glistening against the dusky hue of his face.

A gray enamel coffee pot gurgled atop the fire behind Church. "Coffee smells good," I said. "Mind if I have a cup?" I placed my hands on the pommel of my saddle, preparing to dismount. Church raised the gun.

"I'd rather you didn't," he said.

I relaxed my grip on the pommel. On the other side of the fire, Junior gasped and arched his back beneath the blankets that enveloped him, cursing rapidly in a breathless voice. His father placed a gnarled hand against his chest when he tried to sit up and eased him back down. The young man's face shone with sweat in spite of the near-zero weather. There was pink froth on his lips.

I watched him until the convulsions subsided, then returned my attention to the bounty hunter. "Like to tell me what happened?"

"Not especially."

"I'll tell you what happened." The old man spoke without looking up. He was supporting his son's head with his right hand and massaging his chest with the left. His voice was shrill and cracked. "That injun-scalpin' bastard kilt my boy."

"You found him?" Rocking Wolf leaned forward eagerly.

"We found him," said Church, loosening a little. "He was gutting a buck in a stand of pine eight, ten miles east of here." He snorted. "They told me he was big; they didn't say he was huge. His hand just about swallowed up the bowie knife he was using. We rode right up to him, got the drop on him. I told him to stand up. At first he acted like he didn't hear me. I said it again, and that's when he cut loose.

"He had a rifle inside that carcass. He fired twice, blasting a hole through the back and hitting Junior in the belly with the first shot. There was so much blood and meat splattered over him you couldn't tell which was his and which was the deer's. The second shot went wide. I fired back and so did the breed. I think one of us hit him, because he staggered, but in the confusion he got to his horse and hightailed it east."

"You didn't follow him?" I prodded.

"Hell, no. He knows this country better'n anybody. We'd of rid straight into an ambush. Longbow says he'll return to the trail on the other side of the mountain. We'll head him off from this direction after we break camp. We been riding most of the night."

"What about young Strakey?"

"He's done for. I'd of put him out of his misery hours ago, but the old man won't let me." He grinned spasmodically. "I care about the men I ride with."

"Christ, that's touching."

The mirth fled Church's face. "What's your business here, anyway? Sheriff Goodnight said you was taking a prisoner up to the capital. That him?" He flicked his gun barrel toward the Indian.

I told him about Brainard and about how I came to be riding with Rocking Wolf, including the deal I'd made with his uncle. It was surprising how little time it took to recount the story.

"I don't believe it." This time it was Longbow who spoke. "Two Sisters hates the white man. He wouldn't drink out of the same lake." The way he said it left me with few illusions regarding his own sympathies in that direction.

"That sounds strange coming from a half-breed who claims to be his son," I retorted.

"Son of a bitch!" he spat, and fired the Dance straight at my head. But by that time I was already moving, flinging myself sideways off the saddle just as the bullet clipped the brim of my hat. I hit the ground, rolled, and came up on the other side of my horse. Longbow drew down on me again.

"Stop."

Rocking Wolf's command, delivered in a dry monotone, made the half-breed pause. He looked up at the Indian. I did too, turning my head just enough to keep both of them in sight.

The Indian had unslung his Winchester, and now he sat with it trained squarely in the center of Ira Longbow's narrow chest. No one, not even Church, had seen him move.

"Ira, you are so damned dumb." The bounty hunter spoke like a father who had caught his son behind the barn with his neighbor's daughter. "Put the gun away before somebody gets killed."

"Tell that to the Indian. My business is with Murdock." He steadied his revolver at my head. I ducked. To hell with my reputation.

"Homer." Church pronounced the name flatly. It was answered by a metallic click from beyond the fire.

The half-breed cast a wary eye in that direction, where the old man, still crouching over his son, had slid the latter's percussion cap pistol from his belt and was pointing it at Longbow. Strakey's white-stubbled jaws worked ruminatively at a plug of tobacco the size of a crabapple.

"I don't like to get mixed up in family quarrels, Ira," said Church, "but if you don't put that gun where it belongs, I'll have Homer splatter your brains all over this side of the mountain."

Not too far away, a squirrel leaped down from a tree and thumped through the snow to another, stopping once to chatter angrily at the intruders in its midst. It might have been the most important thing there, the way all of us appeared to be listening to it. Finally, Longbow eased the Dance's hammer back into place and returned it to its holster with a brutal thrust.

"Good boy," said Church. He returned his attention to Rocking Wolf. "Your turn, injun."

The nephew of the chief of the Flathead nation didn't have to be told that two guns were better than one. Without removing his eyes from the half-breed, he uncocked the rifle and slung it back over his shoulder. His face remained impassive as ever. I exhaled, only then realizing that I'd been holding my breath.

"I just give you your life, Murdock," said the bounty hunter. "I hope you remember that."

"What makes you so generous?" I reached up and took hold of the chestnut's bridle, stroking its neck with the other hand to calm it down. Unarmed as I was, it seemed a good idea to keep the animal between me and the half-breed as much as possible.

Church holstered his weapon with a dime-novel flourish, proving that there's a little Henry Goodnight in all of us. "I got one rule," he replied. "I never kill law. Not unless it gets in my way so bad I can't go around it."

"I'd say I'm in your way right now. We're both after Bear Anderson. We can't both have him."

"You ain't in my way. Not yet."

"But if I should be later?"

"Like I said, I hope you remember that I give you your life once." He shot a glance over his shoulder at Longbow, who stood glaring at us from his side of the fire. "You'd best ride. I don't know how long I can hold back the breed. If you get kilt, I'll have to kill the injun too, and I'd rather not make an enemy of the Flatheads this early in the hunt."

"I guess that means we don't get any coffee."

"You wouldn't appreciate it anyway. Old Man Strakey can read sign like a Blackfoot, but one thing he can't do is make coffee."

"One warning." I mounted the mare and looked down at him. The scarf gave his narrow face an animal cast, like a cross-eyed fox. "The Flatheads have been trying to get the drop on Anderson for fifteen years, and all they've gotten for their trouble is the biggest burial ground in the Northwest. He didn't get his reputation by running away."

"He ain't been wounded before."

"Ever hunt a wounded bear?"

He shrugged. "I ain't taking no more unnecessary chances. Warrant says dead or alive. I tried it one way. There ain't but one way left."

"Good luck." I gathered up the reins and began backing the horse down the trail. Rocking Wolf followed suit.

"Which way you headed?" called Church.

"East."

"You're the one needs the luck."

Once we were out of effective pistol range we turned around and headed back the way we had come. After we had gone a mile, I cast a sidelong glance at the chief's nephew. "You risked a lot back there," I said.

"I had little to lose." He kept his eyes on the trail.

"All the same, I suppose I should thank you. I can't think why it sticks in my throat."

He met my gaze. "I said before that I am not yet prepared to see you die."

Paralleling the trail left by Church and his men, we reached the point around nightfall where they had shot it out with Anderson. The buck carcass was gone—dragged, judging by the marks in the snow, into a thicker grove of trees a hundred yards to the north. In its place lay a shaggy gray hulk stretched on its side, the hole where its throat had been now empty and black with frozen blood. Its fangs were bared in a death's-head grin. "A pack," observed Rocking Wolf, indicating the paw-prints that overlapped each other and obliterated the tracks left by the bounty hunters' horses. "Fifty, perhaps more. They fought over the kill once and will again. By morning the sound of their further fighting will attract more wolves from the lowlands." He scanned the snow-swept countryside as if searching for the beasts. "Tonight one of us will sleep and the other will stand guard."

"Are you volunteering?"

He looked at me, reading my thoughts. "Not necessarily," he said. "You will remember that I sleep lightly."

The tracks of an unshod horse, a big one, led east around the base of the mountain. Rocking Wolf dismounted to inspect one of the dark spots that mottled the snow around them. They were so similar to those that had marked the bounty hunters' trail that I had paid them little attention, assuming them to have been left by young Strakey. But now I noticed that there were more of them farther on, beyond the point where the opponents had separated. They showed black in the light of the rising moon.

"He has been hit," confirmed the Indian, standing. "Much blood has been lost. He is in trouble."

"More than you think." I pointed to the snow at Rocking Wolf's feet, where the track of a large wolf overlapped one of the big horse's hoofprints.

"Perhaps they have grown tired of venison." He mounted and waved me ahead of him down the trail. "There is much moonlight. We will follow for one hour."

I was glad of the excuse to keep moving. With no clouds for insulation, the entire range was laid bare to the elements, rendering useless our heavy clothing and making the snow squeak beneath our horses' footsteps. I rubbed my face at intervals with my gloves to keep the blood circulating, but as soon as I stopped the numbness would creep back in and I'd be forced to do it again. After a while my arms felt like lead. I kept at it, however, driven on by a boyhood memory of a trapper I had once seen in Doc Bernstein's office, a young man who had been found unconscious in the snow on the outskirts of Staghorn. His face had split from exposure and had begun to ooze blood and raw meat through the cracks. It must have been as painful as it looked, because that night he had made his way to his gun and put a bullet through his brain. I rubbed until the skin felt raw and then I went on rubbing.

The trail led down a steep slope on the windward side of the mountain, an irregular incline swept by the wind in some places to bare rock interrupted in the middle by a crevice some twelve feet wide.

"Devil's Crack," I told Rocking Wolf, once we'd stopped

to view it from a distance of fifty yards. "Two miles long and a hundred feet deep at its shallowest point. We'd save several hours if we jumped it."

"And if we did not make it across?"

"Then I guess we'd save the rest of our lives."

He grunted distrustfully, but a quick glance around seemed to assure him that there was no place nearby to set up an ambush, so he gathered up his reins and, slapping his stallion smartly on the rump, took off down the slope at a gallop. I did the same, but there was no way the mare could hope to catch up to an animal at least six years her junior, and that was why we were several lengths behind Rocking Wolf when I spotted the thong.

It had originally been covered with snow, but the wind, its gusts confined to this side of the mountain, had exposed a two-foot length to glisten wetly in the light of the moon where it had been made fast to an upended tooth of shale. It was taut as a guitar string and raised about a foot and a half above the ground.

I shouted a warning to the Indian and drew back on the reins so hard the chestnut reared onto its haunches and slid on its rump for twenty feet before coming to a stop. I was pitched off and had to grab the thong in both hands to keep from sliding over the edge. I stopped with my boots dangling in mid-air. But it was too late for Rocking Wolf. His horse hit the thong, screamed, and pitched forward onto its chest with an impact that shook the mountain. For a frozen moment, Indian and horse were a tangle of arms and flailing legs, fighting for traction on the icy rock. Then they sailed over the edge of the crevice and into space. The stallion's screams echoed off the walls for an impossible length of time, then ceased abruptly. The wind whistled irreverently in the silence that followed.

It was not a long silence. I was lying stretched out full length on my back, my gloved hands clutching the thong that had just claimed Rocking Wolf's life and saved mine, when I heard a sound like a guitar string being plucked and the thong, weakened when the Indian's horse had struck it, gave away where it had been lashed to the rock. I began sliding.

I was about to go over when a hand grasped my collar, stopping me. Beneath my feet, an outcropping of brittle snow fell apart and sifted down toward the bottom of the crevice. Icy air played over my boots and up inside my pants legs where they hung over the edge. But the grip on my collar held firm and began pulling me backward. Empty space gave way grudgingly to solid ground. In another moment I had gained enough footing to turn over and see my rescuer. In that instant it occurred to me that I might have been better off if I'd fallen, because I found myself staring into the grinning, bearded face of Bear Anderson.

# CHAPTER 7

He was even bigger than I remembered. Crouched though he was, one leg thrust out for balance, its mate drawn up beneath him, a massive hand clutching the jagged rock to which the thong had been tied while he maintained his grip on me with the other, he was nearly seven feet of solid muscle without an ounce of suet anywhere. He was made to look even more ponderous by the bearskin he wore poncho-style over a buckskin shirt and pants tucked into the tops of fur boots the size of snowshoes. The eyes beneath the rim of his fur hood were the clear blue of his Scandinavian ancestors', and his features, despite the leathery grain of his complexion, were even and handsome enough to turn the head of a mining camp's most hardened prostitute. His full beard, like his shoulder-length hair, was reddish and streaked with yellow. The only flaw was a jagged patch near the corner of his jaw on the left side where the whiskers grew sparsely over scar tissue—the remnant, I judged, of an old tomahawk wound. But for that, he hadn't changed in fifteen years.

The mystery of where he had come from so quickly was explained by the snow clinging to his shoulders and the front of his bearskin. Lord knew how many hours he had lain there after setting his trap, covered with snow from head to foot, waiting for his pursuers to come along and blunder into it. He had the patience and ruthless cunning of a tracked cougar. He didn't appear to recognize me, but I don't suppose it would have mattered if he had. I was an intruder in his territory and worse, I had been riding with one of his mortal enemies on his own trail. The grin he wore disturbed me. I had a feeling it was the last thing a lot of Indians had seen this side of the happy hunting ground.

I decided to bluff it out. "Long way down," I said, acknowledging his assistance with a nod.

"Goes all the way to the bottom."

A cracker-barrel answer, flat and noncommittal as a storekeeper agreeing that rain was wet. His voice was gentle and curiously high-pitched for a man his size, but held a harsh edge as if he wasn't used to using it. He watched me through unblinking blue eyes.

"I reckon I would have too, if you hadn't happened along," I ventured.

"Reckon."

The conversation was becoming one-sided. I tried to pull myself farther up the slope, but failed to purchase a grip with my gloves on the smooth wet surface of the rock and gave up. My chest and stomach grew numb where I was lying in the snow. I was painfully aware that the scalp-hunter's fist on my collar was the only thing that stood between me and oblivion, and from the look on his face I gathered that he was debating with himself whether it might be a good idea to let me go. At length he sighed resignedly and pulled me up onto a better footing.

"Thanks," I said, and started to get up.

He didn't reply. Instead he swept a loglike arm around behind me, crushed me to his chest, and with his free hand thrust against my chin began pushing my head backward until my spine quivered like a drawn bow. One of

Ezra Wilson's stitches on the back of my head popped audibly.

"What's your name, injun lover?" Anderson demanded, through his teeth. "What you doing in my mountains?"

I couldn't answer. He was holding me so tightly I couldn't breathe and the pressure on my jaw made it impossible for me to form words. Blood pounded in my head.

"Answer me, injun lover!" He increased the pressure.

My lungs screamed for air. I was like a swimmer going down for the last time within sight of a shore full of people; help was only a cry away, but I was unable to ask for it. My spine creaked where he was bending me backward. I fought to retain consciousness. My eyesight shrank to pinpoints of light in a black shroud. Bear Anderson's contorted features faded into insignificance and I felt myself floating away from my body. Then I felt nothing whatsoever.

Half-formed images chased each other endlessly through my head. Now I was suspended in mid-air, my head, arms, and legs dangling while some unseen force bore me upward over uneven ground to where the air grew thin and sharp as flying thorns. Next I was lifted even higher and transported from pale moonlight to abysmal darkness, where small furry things with membranous wings fluttered about me, brushing my face with feathery strokes. In the next moment I was pitched like a sack of grain to the earth. After that there was a long stretch of nothing until I awoke with heat on my face.

The first thing I saw when I opened my eyes was flame. I drew back in panic, pain shooting through my abused joints, only to find to my relief that I was lying on my side and looking into nothing more dangerous than a campfire, consuming a small pile of wood a foot in front of my face. Around me, the warm light cast by the fire rippled over stone and splashed weird, writhing shadows over walls and ceiling tinted orange by the glow. Beyond the flame was a black void. I was in a cave or tunnel of some sort, and I was not alone.

In the entrance, two eyes glowed eerily green in the reflected light of the fire. As I watched them a chunk of wood rolled off the top of the pile and crashed into the heart of the flames, sending up a spurt of yellow and illuminating the opening. I found myself staring into a narrow face with a coal-black muzzle and mouth parted to reveal two rows of sharp, curving teeth separated by a dripping tongue. Amber eyes with black slits in their centers studied me as if in fascination. One pointed ear, the muscles of which had been torn in some long-forgotten fight, refused to stand up like its mate, and so hung sullenly almost to the corner of the jaw. Beyond this was a bushy neck, a deep chest tapering to a visible ribcage, and two powerfully bowed forelegs covered with matted gray fur. The wolf was in view but an instant, and then the flare died and only the glowing eyes remained.

There was a roar in the cave. Something buzzed past my right ear. I heard a yelp and then the thudding sound of feet fading into the distance. A thin stream of dust, dislodged from the cave's ceiling, settled onto my head and down inside my collar. I rolled over onto my right side. In the gloom at the back of the cave, Bear Anderson sat upon a flat rock with a Spencer in his hands, a plume of white smoke twisting out of the barrel.

"Just nicked him," he said, more to himself than to me. "That won't make the old bastard any easier to handle after this."

"You talk like you know him," I said. My voice sounded strange in the comparative silence that followed the shot's echo.

"Ought to. Two years ago he and his pack cost me the best horse I ever had. We go back a long way together, Old Lop Ear and me." He fished a fresh cartridge out of his pants pocket—he had doffed the bearskin—and reloaded, jacking a shell into the chamber to replace the one he had fired. He grunted with the effort. That's when I noticed the dark stain on his buckskin shirt along his left side.

"How bad is it?" I asked, nodding toward the wound.

"Just a graze." He laid the Spencer on the stone floor by his feet and sat gripping his knees in his enormous hands. "Bullet scraped around the ribs and got stuck in back. Can't reach it, but it ain't doing me no harm. I'm letting it bleed out some before I try to dress it. How you feeling?"

"Sore." I placed a tentative fingertip against the back of my head. It still throbbed, but the cut had ceased to bleed a long time ago. I unwound the bandage and cast it into a dark corner of the cave. Cold air stabbed at the wound. "What I'm wondering about is how come I'm still alive."

He grinned, lighting up his end of the cave. "Not because of anything you did," he said. "You should of said something when I asked who you was, Page. I'd of snapped your spine like a chunk of dry firewood if I didn't recollect you at the last minute."

"What was I supposed to do, knock it out in Morse code on your forehead?"

Behind Bear, my chestnut and a rangy dun that stood a good hand higher than the biggest horse I had ever seen began to snort and nicker, straining at the bonds hobbling their forelegs. They had just caught the wolf's scent. Bear made soothing noises deep in his throat and reached out to stroke the dun's muscular breast. "Easy, Pike." He said something to it in a guttural tongue that sounded like Blackfoot.

"Where are we?" I looked around.

He laughed.

"Don't tell me you don't recognize Spirit Peak! Hell, this is where you and me used to cook our rabbits when we was kids. The injuns think this is where all the evil shades meet to plot their wicked deeds. They won't come nowhere near it."

"You live here?"

"Just part of the time. Mostly I like to be where I can keep an eye on what the Flatheads are up to." He studied me curiously. "You going to tell me how come you was riding with Rocking Wolf?"

"Do I have to?"

"Not if you want some fresh air. It's a ten thousand foot drop from here to the bottom of the mountain."

I told him. He listened in silence.

"Got a badge?" he asked, when I had finished.

I flashed the scrap of metal I carried in my breast pocket. He stared at it a long time, but that was just for show. The Bear Anderson I knew had never learned to read. Finally, he nodded and I put it away.

"So that part's true," he said. "How do I know about the rest? You might be in with that bunch that tried to bushwhack me night before last. Come to think on it, you didn't act very surprised when you seen I was wounded." He reached down and scooped the rifle off the floor with a deft movement of his right arm. "Start talking."

"There's not much to talk about. I met them west of here yesterday, if it was yesterday. How long have I been here?"

"Six hours. Two more from Devil's Crack to here. Keep talking."

"Church—that's the leader of the gang that jumped you—is being paid five thousand dollars by the U.S. gov-

ernment to bring you in, dead or alive. It seems you're standing in the way of a treaty with the Flatheads."

He spat. "A treaty with Two Sisters ain't worth belly
skins. He'll sign it with one hand and lift your scalp with the
other."

"Tell that to Ulysses S. Grant. He's the one who autho-
rized the warrant."

"What business does General Grant have with me?"

"He's not a general any more. He's the President. That is,
he was until recently. At any rate, his signature is still good,
since he signed it before he left office. Right now I'd say
you're just about the most wanted man in the country."

He grimaced suddenly and placed a hand in the area of
his left kidney.

"Why don't you let me take a look at that?" I started
to get up, and found myself staring down the bore of the
Spencer.

"Sit," he said. I sat.

Outside, the wind hooted past the entrance, turning the
entire mountain, which I remembered as a network of caves,
into a gigantic pipe organ. The fire flared and buckled with
the current of air inside our shelter. It was getting colder
outside.

"Hand me that sack," said Bear. He indicated a worn
gunny sack heaped against the cave wall near where I sat.
It was mottled with brownish stains, some old, others fresh
and moist. I hefted it and was surprised to find that it didn't
weigh much, though it bulged with its contents.

"What's in it?" I undid the knot in the top.

"None of your business. Hand it here."

I ignored his warning tone and looked inside. It was full
of scalps.

"Satisfied?" He stretched out an arm as long as my leg

and snatched the bag from my grip. He opened it and began pulling out specimens, which he stretched out on the floor at his feet. The cave filled with the stench of rotting flesh.

When the last of the scalps—there were seven of them—were lying before him, he produced a bowie knife from the sheath at his belt, cut five leather strips from the fringe on his shirt, and knotted them together. This resulted in a thong six feet long, upon which he proceeded to string the scalps.

"What do those do for you?" I was just beginning to get over the shock of that grisly discovery, when I'd been expecting to find food in the sack. Now eating was the farthest thing from my mind.

"You wouldn't understand it." He tied on the last of the scalps and set the knot with his teeth. Then he stood and secured one end of the thong to a jagged crag in the wall nearest him.

"Try me."

"Ammunition." He stepped across to the opposite wall, found a fissure in the granite, and jammed the thong's knotted free end into it. Now the scalps were strung like hideous Christmas cards across the cave. "You'd be surprised what the sight of a dozen or so of them things hanging from your belt will do to a injun when he's all fired up for a fight. I seen them turn tail and run after just one look. Course, they don't get far."

The stench of the bloody relics was getting to the mare, which whinnied shrilly and tossed its head, trying to get its teeth into the hobbles that held it. Bear's dun, however, remained unperturbed; the big horse had found a patch of green moss growing out of a crack in the stone floor and was busy nibbling at it. The scalp-hunter laid a heavy hand on the mare's neck and smoothed back its bristling withers.

Immediately it began to breathe more easily. He had a way with animals.

"You eat recent?" he asked me.

My appetite wasn't what it had been before I'd seen his trophies, but I had no wish to starve to death. I shook my head.

"There's a buckskin pouch under them ashes," he said, nodding toward the fire. "Pull it out."

I seized a stick from the fire and stirred the ashes until I encountered a bulky object and worked it out smoking into the open. Although it had probably been dampened and was still covered with what I supposed had once been wet leaves, the buckskin was now dry beneath a coating of soot. I used the stick to push aside the flap. Immediately the aroma of roasted meat enveloped me. Sclaps or no scalps. I was suddenly ravenous. But I remembered my manners. I offered Bear the first piece, a leg so tender it fell apart in my hand. He shook his head.

"You eat it," he said. "I swallowed enough rabbit in the last few weeks to sprout my own fur. That's about the only thing that's left after them last three winters. I had my taste all set for some venison, but your friend Church spoiled that in good shape."

"He's no friend of mine." I said it through a mouthful of meat so hot it made my eyes well up. Bear saw my predicament and tossed me a patched-up canteen full of water. I gulped it too fast and nearly choked to death. It was the best I'd felt in days.

"You grow your rabbits juicy up here," I commented, once I'd recovered and was finishing off the meat.

"It's the pouch does that. I learned it from the Blackfeet. The buckskin holds in all them juices you'd lose if you staked it out over the fire in the regular way. If I had me some dried wild onion skins to crumble over it, I'd show you a real meal."

I grunted my understanding. After the events of the past few days, it didn't even seem strange that I was sitting there surrounded by drying scalps at the top of a mountain listening to a recipe for cooking rabbit. It seemed to go with the territory. I flipped away the last of the bones and wiped my hands off on the front of my coat. "Why'd you kill Brainard?"

He had been whetting his knife on his buckskin sleeve, stropping it back and forth like a razor. Now he paused. "What makes you think I done it?"

"He was shot with the same rifle that was used to kill the Indians who were torturing him. And don't tell me you didn't kill *them;* those are their scalps drying on that thong."

"I done what I would for any white man in the same situation." He resumed stropping. "Once I come across a white trapper after the injuns was finished with him. He was hanging from a tree, just like this Brainard, only this one was all red and slippery from head to foot like a skinned rabbit, on account of that's just what they done to him. And he was still moving. I done for him too, but by that time he had went through so much that I don't suppose it mattered to him. This time I got there early enough to make it worth something. I hope I can count on somebody doing the same thing for me when it comes my turn."

"You think it'll come to that?"

"Bound to. I'm slowing down now, else I wouldn't of had to shoot none of them injuns more than once." He waved his knife in the direction of the dangling scalps. "Sooner or later, some young buck is going to get in a lucky shot, and then I'll be meat for Old Lop Ear."

"Why don't you quit?"

"A man does what he's good at." Rising, he returned the knife to its sheath and reached for his bearskin. "It's almost light. Can you saddle up, or do you want me to do it for you?"

"Where are we going?" I gathered my legs beneath me. Pain rocketed up my spine.

"Devil's Crack. I got a scalp waiting for me at the bottom, remember? By the time we get there, there ought to be enough light to risk the ride down." He threw the bearskin on over his shoulders.

"Thanks, but I'd just as soon stay here and wait for you."

He reached down and took hold of my left shoulder in one hand, crushing it. "Bet you won't."

"Why not?" I grunted, through clenched teeth. He was cutting off my circulation.

"You know as well as me that you ain't getting out of these mountains till you finish the job Two Sisters sent you out to do. I'd heaps rather have you in front of me than at my back."

"What about afterwards?"

"Afterwards is afterwards." He squeezed harder. "Can I count on your company?"

"Where's my saddle?" The words came out in a gasp.

The wind had unfurled a tarpaulin of dirty gray between mountains and sky, so low that when we led our horses out of the cave we found ourselves in the very midst of the haze. We descended five hundred feet before we came out of it. Beneath the ceiling, the panorama of the Bitterroot spread out dizzyingly before us, tents of white dotted with black stands of pine, with here and there a shallow depression to mark the frozen surface of a lake. It had just begun to snow again; I watched as the first wave of flakes emerged from the clouds and began its slow descent to the ground ten thousand feet below, like spent grapeshot falling through the trees. The wind shifted constantly, blowing clouds of white powder back and forth across our path. The air was so cold it seared my throat when I inhaled.

Bear's height, together with the size of the horse he was riding, made me feel like a dwarf astride the chestnut as we picked our way single-file down the side of the mountain, me in front. My escort rode with his Spencer across the pommel of his saddle, his buckskin-gloved hands crossed over it and holding the reins. In front of him, a gunny sack hung on either side of the dun from the saddle horn in the middle. One of them held his scalps. I hadn't seen inside the second sack, but I had a pretty good idea of what it contained. I filed this hunch away in my memory for future reference.

We approached the Crack from the northern end, where it leveled out after a steep climb of nearly two hundred feet from its lowest depth. For us, the climb would be twice as dangerous; we were going down, not up.

Halfway down, the mare lost its footing, and I had to haul hard on the reins, pulling it back onto its haunches to keep both of us from tumbling all the way to the bottom. Behind me, Bear halted his mount and waited until I was in control again before continuing. I glanced at him once over my shoulder. Both his and the dun's heads were enveloped in vapor, like gargoyles snorting steam out their nostrils.

The snow at the bottom of the crevice was piled up to the horses' breasts. It struck me that finding Rocking Wolf's body beneath that muck was not going to be an easy task. Not that it mattered, of course; we had all the time in the world.

Noon found us nearly a mile into Devil's Crack, with the snow still falling softly around us. The horses were lathered and wheezing from struggling through the snow; I was about to suggest that we stop and rest when Bear grunted suddenly and thrust a finger the size of an ear of corn out ahead of him. I looked to see where he was pointing. A couple of yards ahead, a horse's foreleg protruded stiffly straight up from the bank of white. Another few seconds and we'd have stumbled over it.

We dismounted, and together we worked feverishly to claw the snow off our find. It was slow going, as the stuff was wet and heavy and we had no shovels to work with. After about twenty minutes we had cleared away enough of it to see that the leg belonged to Rocking Wolf's stallion. It lay twisted half onto its back, its eyes still wide in its final spasm of terror and a froth of blood frozen on its lips. Its back was broken. Now there remained only one corpse to find.

An hour later, we had cleared out a ragged circle ten feet in diameter around the dead horse down to the bare ground, and still there was no sign of Rocking Wolf's body. Bear and I stared at each other over the dead animal. His expression, bewildered at first, slowly grew thoughtful. He looked as if he was about to speak when a voice floated down to us from somewhere far above our heads.

"One for you, white skin!" Carried on the wind, the voice had an unnatural quality, rendering it almost unrecognizable. "Now it becomes my turn."

Rocking Wolf's words echoed along the walls of the crevice until they became part of the wind itself, and then it was impossible to tell where they left off and the gale began.

# CHAPTER 8

"What now?" I asked Bear, after the initial shock had worn off. I had to shout to make myself heard over the mounting wind.

"Why ask me? It's you he was talking to!"

Even as he said it, I realized he was right. If Rocking Wolf had suspected I was leading him into a trap before, he was sure of it now.

"Look for his rifle," I said. "It must be here somewhere. If he still had it, we'd both be dead." I began kicking holes in the banks of snow beyond the clearing.

"No time." The scalp-hunter's tone was clipped. "If we're going to be out of here by nightfall, we'd best be heading south, and that's one climb I'm not going to risk after dark."

"Then what?"

"You leave that to me." He mounted the dun.

I had to crane my neck to look up at him, he was that tall and the horse was that big. "I hope you're not planning on heading east around the mountain. Church and his bunch are waiting to bushwack you on the other side. You and anyone riding with you."

"Figured that. Mount up."

The sun was a bloody gash between the overcast and the horizon when we vaulted out of the Crack at its southern end. No sooner had we emerged than Bear turned his horse's head east.

"Why don't you just shoot yourself in the head and save time?" I exclaimed.

"There ain't nothing west of here but more mountain and blizzards." His beard bristled over his set jaw. "I'd heaps rather take my chances with men."

"You don't know Church."

Travel at night was impossible with the moon obscured by clouds. We made camp at sundown on a shelf of wind-swept rock on what was now the lee side of the mountain, where firewood was nonexistent and we were forced to share a stiff piece of salt pork from my saddlebags, more of the rations I had bought in Staghorn. Staghorn. Right then, it seemed as far away as San Francisco.

"Give me your hands," said Bear, after we'd finished eating.

"Why?"

"Just give them here." He spoke gruffly.

I extended my hands. Something hard and cold snapped shut around each of my wrists. In that instant I realized that my handcuffs were no longer hanging on my belt. Before I could protest, he smacked me in the chest so hard with the flat of his hand that I lost my balance and toppled over onto my back. A leather thong was wound around both my ankles and pulled taut with a jerk that sent pain shoot-ing straight up my legs. It was all over in the space of a few seconds.

"It must be my honest face," I said acidly.

"I ain't survived fifteen years in the high rocks by taking unnecessary chances," he told me. "Keep that buckhide dry or it'll tighten up on you and bust your feet. You got to relieve yourself, roll over to the edge of the shelf and do it. Try not to fall off." He tossed me my blanket.

"What are you going to do?"

"Sleep." He sat down with his back against the mountain and gathered his bearskin around him, his rifle lying across his lap.

"Good," I said. "See if you can get some for me, too."

I did sleep, though fitfully. Several times I opened my eyes to see Bear's bulk against the scarcely lighter background of the mountain, still awake and tossing an occasional rock at the wolves slinking back and forth beneath the shelf. When he struck one, it would yelp and leap to one side, then snarl up at us, its teeth forming a ghastly white semicircle against the black of its body. "Not tonight, you lop-eared son of a bitch," the scalp-hunter muttered once. But all he got in reply was a rippling growl.

That long night bled almost imperceptibly into a bleak and snowy dawn. It had been snowing steadily for twenty-four hours, and now the entire range was a clean chalk sketch on a background of dirty linen. First light found us entering a narrow pass between the base of Spirit Peak and a rocky knoll to the south.

"If I were planning to ambush anyone, this is where I'd do it," I told my companion, rubbing my wrists where the handcuffs, now removed, had chafed them during the night.

That had about as much effect on him as dropping a stone down a bottomless well and waiting for the splash, so I let it slide. Being unarmed in the midst of danger creates a strange feeling of detachment anyway; knowing that you can't do anything to defend yourself no matter what the circumstances, you don't care what happens. But the feeling wasn't enough to prevent me from keeping an eye on the promontories that flanked our path. That detached I wasn't.

I saw the glint while we were riding abreast through a relatively flat section of pass, and was out of my saddle in the same instant. I struck Bear shoulder-first. I had the fleeting impression, as the pain of impact spread through me, that he wasn't going to budge, but then, like a huge tree whose roots have rotted away, he toppled. We hit the ground in a heap.

He made a growling noise and crooked a huge arm around my neck, catching my adam's apple inside his elbow and crushing it. "A gun!" I managed to croak, before my voice was choked off. I pointed to the top of the cliff.

It sank in on him belatedly. Slowly he released his grip. I inhaled in desperation.

Far above us, feeble sunlight painted a pale strip along something long and metallic sticking out from the top of a line of rocks on the north side of the pass. Beyond that, the blur of what was unmistakably a human face showed light against the bare granite.

"I thought you said he didn't have no rifle," said Bear quietly.

"It could be Church."

"That's dandy. Now all's we got to do is figure out which one of them is going to kill us."

"I might be able to get up there if you'll keep him busy down here," I suggested.

"Why don't you keep him busy whilst I go on up?" His tone was suspicious.

"What am I supposed to do, jump up and down and holler? You've got the only gun."

He repeated the growling noise. Twisting to look down at him, I thought I saw his eyes wander toward the gunny sacks tied to the dun's saddle. For a moment it looked as if he might relent. Then he shook his head, as if he had just won a battle with himself. "Go on up," he said. "Stick to the shadow."

"Give me your knife."

He glowered at me for a moment, then passed over the big bowie. "I expect that back afterwards."

"Stick around. Maybe you can take it off my body."

Using the horses for cover, I crept along the base of the knoll until I was in shadow, then took a deep breath and sprinted across to the opposite side of the pass. There, I flattened out against the mountain and waited for the shots. There were none. I looked up. From this angle, the rifle barrel was invisible, if indeed it was still there. I hoped it was. If there was any moving around to be done up there, I wanted to be the one who did it. I shuffled sideways until I came to a spot where some ancient avalanche had piled a makeshift staircase of stones at the base of the mountain and began to climb. After a while I took off my gloves and put them in my pocket to make the job easier.

It grew steeper as I ascended, until I was crawling straight up a vertical wall with only a shallow foothold here and there and an occasional crag over which I could curl my numb fingers. Once my foot slipped and I had to smack the wall hard with the palm of my right hand to keep from plummeting fifty feet to the jagged pile of rocks at the bottom. The hand tingled as I felt around with my foot for support, but not until I came to a ledge deep enough for me to support myself on my elbows did I notice that I had scraped most of the skin off the palm. I decided that if I ever got out of this alive, Judge Blackthorne was going to be slapped with a lot of medical bills.

At length my head drew level with the line of rocks from which the rifle had thrust itself earlier. I cast wary glances to right and left and, finding no one in sight, pulled myself up and over the edge. Then I drew the knife from my boot—the leather-bound handle stung the raw surface of my hand—and crept forward with the remainder of the mountain at my right shoulder.

I came upon him lying on his stomach with a boulder on either side of him and his cheek resting against the stock of a Remington rifle, the barrel protruding out past the rocks. Before he could move, I flung myself full-length on top of him, crooked my left arm around his throat the way Bear had done with me earlier, and placed the point of the bowie against the tender flesh beneath his chin.

"Let go of the rifle!" I commanded.

There was no response, not even a gasp. After a beat I twisted his head so that I could get a look at his face. It was Homer Strakey, Jr., and he was as dead as the stone ledge upon which he was lying.

He was gun-barrel stiff and his flesh was like ice. I got up off him and turned him over with the toe of my boot; it was like rolling a log. His hands were locked tight around the Remington's action. His eyes were wide open. The wound that had killed him—the one Bear had inflicted—was a gaping black hole in his abdomen just above the belt. There was no sign of bleeding on the ledge. He had been dead a long time and he hadn't been alive when he was put there.

I stepped to the edge of the shelf and waved my arm to get Bear's attention. It worked, because a shot rang out the instant I showed myself and a bullet whanged off the rock just below my left boot. I leaped back away from the edge.

"Are you crazy?" I shouted, once my heart had resumed beating. "It's me!"

"Sorry!"

I called to him to come on up. When his enormous face

appeared above the rocks some thirty minutes later, I placed the muzzle of the Remington between his eyes.

"Sorry isn't enough," I said.

The hopelessness of his situation was borne in on him slowly. He had his Spencer slung over his left shoulder by its leather strap and both his hands were engaged in maintaining his grip on the slippery rocks. Even a skull as thick as his would have been blasted apart by a bullet from the Remington at that range.

"You told me to keep him busy," he grumbled at length. "How was I to know you'd be damn fool enough to show yourself like that?"

"Why don't you look before you shoot?" I demanded. "I'd be just as dead whether you meant it for me or not."

"If I was out to kill you, you'd be dead. I don't miss no shot like that."

"Then you knew it was me, damn you!"

"You planning to shoot that, or are you going to talk me to death?"

"I can't." I lowered the rifle, reluctantly. "Firing pin's broken."

"Figured that." He swept the barrel with a huge hand and heaved himself up onto the shelf. Standing, he towered over me by nearly a head.

"How?"

"If it wasn't, you'd of shot me the minute I showed. That's the easiest way out of the mess you're in, and if I remember right, you never was one to take the high road when you didn't have to." He spotted young Strakey's body lying a few feet away beneath a film of freshly fallen snow. "You do that?"

"Not me. You. He was dead when I got here."

He nodded. "That explains the busted firing pin. If this Church is the heller you told me about, he wouldn't go off and leave no working gun with a dead man for anybody to pick up."

"He didn't die here," I said. "There's no blood, and he wasn't strong enough to climb up here without help. Question is, why'd they go to all this trouble?"

"Trying to slow us down, most likely."

"Why, when they could just as well shoot us from ambush?"

He shook his leonine head. "I don't know. I was him, I'd try to hedge my bet, set some sort of trap that can't go wrong. Can't think why he'd pass up a set-up like this." His brow furrowed, and stayed that way for a long moment. Then something dawned over his features. "Unless he thought of a better one." He swung around and took a step toward the edge over which he had just climbed. "Let's ride."

"What's your hurry?"

He didn't reply. He began backing down the way he had come.

"What about him?" I jabbed the barrel of the Remington toward Strakey's body.

He looked at it hard, as if seeing it for the first time. "Pitch him over. Maybe he'll keep Old Lop Ear off our backs for a night."

We put in a lot of saddle time during the next two days. That day we rode until long after dark, camped for six hours, and were moving again before sunup. This time he didn't bother handcuffing me, which I supposed meant something, but I was too exhausted to puzzle it out. Maybe it had something to do with me telling him about the broken firing pin when I might have tried to use the Remington to bluff him

out of his own firearm. Whatever his reasons, I had somewhere along the line gained a measure of his trust, which
wasn't an easy thing to do.

I had not, however, gained all of it. He wouldn't explain
why we were in such a hurry, for instance; when I pressed
him, he would give his horse a kick and surge ahead of me
until my words were drowned out in the drumming of the
dun's hoofs. He spoke rarely, and then only in monosylla-
bles when silence became inconvenient. Snow came in
spurts, now light, now so heavy it was impossible to see past
the flurry of dollar-sized flakes. By noon of the second day
it had let up enough for us to see the cabin huddled against
the south face of a lopsided mountain on the western fringe
of the Bitterroot.

Even then, it would have been invisible but for a pale gray
ribbon of smoke drifting up from the rough stone chimney;
wedged into a triangular chink in the mountain itself, the
log structure appeared at first glance to be nothing more
than a pile of wind-toppled trees. Only upon closer inspec-
tion did the semi-symmetrical nature of its construction become apparent. In the spring and summer, it was probably
masked by foliage. Now, it was little more than a black strip
showing above the banks of snow which were piled up to
its single tiny window.

We were perched midway down a slope that graded gently downward before us for another two hundred yards before leveling out in front of the cabin. Bear swung his great
head in a slow arc from left to right, noting each detail in
the landscape like a minister studying his scripture. Then
he hooked the thumb and little finger of his right hand inside his mouth and whistled shrilly. The sound pierced the
brittle air and echoed from the mountaintops; from a distance, it might have been a bird calling to its mate.

When perhaps a minute had crawled past without an answer, he whistled again. Again it was met with silence. The horses fidgeted and snorted steam out their nostrils.

"What I was afeared of," said Bear.

No sooner had he said it than the door of the cabin swung open with a bang that reverberated like a pistol shot around the circle of mountains and Church stepped out into the open.

His right arm was locked around the throat of an Indian woman with a shape like a sack of feed. At that distance, her features were a blur, but her complexion, braided hair, and drab costume of skins left no question about her race. In his left hand, the bounty hunter gripped his Navy Colt with the barrel buried in the folds of her stout neck.

"You got yourself a brave squaw, Anderson!" He shouted twice as loud as he had to, to make himself heard. The mountains rang with his nasal tenor. "She'd of let me bust her arm before she whistled back. I'm kind of glad she didn't, though. I like this way better."

"Your squaw?" I queried, out of the corner of my mouth.

Bear nodded. "Bought her off a Blackfoot sub-chief from the plains, along with a hunnert pounds of cracked corn for Pike, here. He wouldn't make the deal unless she went with it."

"What's it going to be, Anderson?" shouted Church. "Do you come in guns down, or do I make a mess right here in front of your cabin?"

"You're too late, Church!" I called out. "This man's in my custody."

Bear glanced at me suspiciously. I ignored it.

"That you, Murdock?" called the bounty hunter.

I told him it was.

"I can't see your badge from here. You might be an

accomplice pulling my leg. Not knowing any better, I might accidentally blow your head off."

"How bad do you want her back?" I asked Bear.

"She's an awful good cook."

"I was afraid you'd say something like that. Stall him."

The scalp-hunter raised his voice. "How much time I got to think about it?"

"Don't care for her much, do you?" It was a threat.

"I'm tired, damn it! Give me time!"

Church squinted toward the pale glimmering of light beyond the clouds. "One hour," he said. "You better come up with the right answer, though. One more dead injun won't mean much in this part of the country." His arm still around the woman, he backed into the cabin and slammed the door.

We retreated up the slope into the cover of a stand of skeletal maple trees and dismounted.

"Is that your cabin?" I asked my companion.

"Built it two years ago. Ain't four people in the whole range know about it besides me and Little Tree, there, and all of them's Blackfoot."

"How'd Church find out about it?"

He shrugged his massive shoulders. "Nothing's secret if more than one knows about it. Old White Mane hunts these parts all year long; he'd sell out his tribe for a bottle of good whiskey. Anyhow, it don't matter how they found out. I expected something like this when I seen that dead man they left behind to slow us down. I said before that Church was the kind that likes to make sure nothing goes wrong." He rubbed a thumb thoughtfully along the scarred portion of his jaw. "How soon can you get around behind that cabin?"

"What behind? There isn't any behind. You built the damn thing right into the mountain!"

"You climb good. You proved that back at the pass."

I searched his face for some sign of deceit. I found none. "You're getting awfully trusting suddenly," I said. "Back at the pass you didn't want me out of your sight."

He grunted. "You can move without being seen. They'd spot me a mile away."

"Church is no fool. It'll be guarded."

"I didn't say it'd be easy."

"What do I do once I get there?"

He untied one of the gunny sacks from the horn of his saddle—the one without the scalps—and set it on the ground. Reaching inside, he drew out a kerosene lantern of rusted metal and glass. "As soon as you get up on top of the roof, I want you to chuck this down the chimney." He held it out for me to take. Liquid sloshed around inside the base.

"Are you serious? That'll go off like dynamite! What about your squaw?"

"She'll be outside when you do it. Just wait for my signal." He jiggled the lantern impatiently. I took it.

"How about giving me the rest of what's in that sack?" I asked him.

He started as if struck in the face. "What you talking about?"

I nodded toward the sack, which he had been in the act of tying back onto his saddle. "There's a .45 caliber Deane-Adams five-shot revolver in that bundle. Leslie Brainard took it off me and you took it off the Indians who got it from him. There was a rifle too, a Winchester, but you don't have that. Likely he threw it away after emptying it at the Indians. What I'm interested in right now is the revolver. How about it? You're going to be in need of another gun hand when the shooting starts."

"Why should I trust you with a gun when I didn't trust you with my knife? You never gave that back, come to think on it."

"I didn't stick it into your ribs either. That should prove something."

He dipped into the sack without another word and handed me the holster and gun. I strapped it on, drew the revolver, and spun the cylinder to make sure it was loaded. It wasn't. Grinning at him, I loaded it from the supply of shells on the belt. "You don't miss a trick, do you?"

"Just don't get no ideas about using it on me," he warned. "That's been tried before."

I gave him a mock salute and moved off in a crouch through the trees.

"One thing." Bear's low murmur crackled in the crisp air.

I stopped and looked back at him. In his shaggy bearskin he resembled a hoary old oak standing among the anemic maples.

"Underneath all that snow there's an inch of dried acorns on the roof. I put them there last summer to let me know if some injun was trying what you're about to."

"Is that all?" I snapped. "What about a moat and crocodiles?"

"Nope. Just acorns."

It took me the better part of our allotted hour to circle around to where the cabin was socked away in the mountain's broad base; brush being scarce, I had to take advantage of intermittent fierce squalls of snow in order to dash from one scrub patch to another, a clear enough target for anyone watching closely through the window. I hoped that whoever was manning that station was too busy rubbing the frost off the glass to spot me during those brief periods. Fortunately, that seemed to be the case, because by the end of the hour I was scaling the craggy surface of the rock toward the snow-covered cabin roof, and there were no holes in me.

My relief was short-lived. I was six feet off the ground when a gun was cocked loudly behind me and Ira Longbow offered me the choice of either coming back down or taking a bullet in the back of the head. I chose the former.

# CHAPTER 9

I glanced back over my shoulder. He was standing a couple of yards back from the rock wall, Dance in hand. His tracks in the snow indicated that he'd just come around from the other side of the cabin, where he had undoubtedly been watching my approach.

"Who says lawmen are dumb?" he said approvingly as I began my descent. "You know, I'd of killed you right where you was if Church wasn't so soft on that badge. I think he'd like to wear one hisself. Drop the gun."

I was still hanging on with both hands. Balancing myself precariously, I reached back with two fingers and flipped the revolver out of its holster. It landed in the snow with a muffled thump.

"That's real good. Down, boy."

The snow was slippery where I'd trampled it while searching for my first foothold on the way up. I tested it carefully with one foot before I let all my weight down on the ground. Then I slipped.

Longbow reacted as I'd hoped he would. Faced with a similar situation, a professional would have stepped back out of the danger zone; not the half-breed. He lunged forward, thrusting the barrel of the six-shooter at me. I tucked his outstretched arm beneath my right armpit and twisted left, grasping his wrist in my free hand as I did so. This accomplished two things: First, it jarred the bone of his wrist against my left hipbone, making him release the gun; second it allowed me to throw all my weight onto my right leg and fling him, head first, into the stone wall down which I'd just climbed. He folded into a heap at the base of the wall.

Time was running out. In another minute Church would emerge from the cabin to learn Bear's answer to his ultimatum; I was fairly sure he hadn't heard the commotion over the whistling of the wind about the structure's thick walls, but I couldn't afford to have him find me there, not when he had the Indian woman for a shield and another man with a gun inside. If Old Man Strakey hadn't been armed before, he certainly was now that his son had no further use for the percussion cap pistol he'd been carrying. I located my gun and, after knocking snow out of the barrel, put it in its holster. Then I dragged Longbow's unconscious form around the curve of the mountain, threw snow over it, and did what I could to smooth over the tracks on my way back. I was counting on the bounty hunter being too busy watching the top of the slope to notice the footprints that remained. Deciding not to try and find the Dance in the snowbank where it had fallen, I began climbing the wall once again.

I had just cleared the corner of the roof and was still moving when Church came out dragging Little Tree. I held my breath. Hanging by both hands, I was unable to get to my gun. If he looked up I was dead.

But he didn't look up. His attention was centered on the stand of maples at the top of the slope. I continued my upward progress.

"Time's up, Anderson!" he shouted. "What's your answer?"

Seconds ticked by, during which I placed my feet carefully in each foothold lest he hear the noise in the overpowering silence that followed his call. Even the wind had died. He cocked the Colt with a dry click. The woman gasped. Anderson had appeared atop the slope.

I stepped down onto the roof, first one foot, then the other. Beneath twelve inches of snow there was a muffled crunch as I released my hold on the mountain. I froze. Church didn't turn. Slowly I removed the lantern from my right shoulder, over which I had slung it by its metal bail.

"Don't shoot!" Bear's strident voice, so high-pitched for a man his size, echoed throughout the clearing. "I'm coming in."

Church made a sound of satisfaction deep in his throat. "Now you're getting smart! Remember, I got two men inside the cabin with guns."

That was a bluff. He was keeping Ira Longbow as his ace in the hole.

Bear hurled the Spencer out ahead of him. It executed three complete spins and landed butt-first in the snow, its barrel pointing skyward. He gave his horse a gentle kick and the two of them moved forward down the slope.

The chimney was a column of soot-blackened stones sticking two feet up out of the snow on the opposite corner of the roof. I made my way over to it, stepping carefully on the layer of acorns beneath the snow. My pants legs were soaked above the tops of my boots.

"Hold it!" roared the bounty hunter. I stopped, reaching toward my gun. "Where's Murdock?"

There was a tense moment while the question repeated itself again and again among the high rocks. Slowly, Church's head began to turn.

"Ira?" For the first time since I had met him, the arrogance was missing from his tone. Half-formed fear played about the edges.

A hundred yards beyond the cabin, Bear raised his right arm above his head and brought it down with a savage slicing motion. It was the signal.

I lifted the lantern high over the smoking chimney and heaved it down through the opening. It struck bottom with a crash. I leaped back in the same instant, but not in time to avoid singeing my eyebrows in the jet of flames that erupted up out of the chimney.

Someone screamed inside the cabin. By that time Church had already swung about, his arm still around the woman, gun barrel rotating in search of a target. I launched myself from the roof and came down on top of both of them. The squaw squirmed free.

The bounty hunter and I grappled in the snow, rolling over and over as he tried to maneuver his Colt into firing position. Both my hands were locked around his wrist, but it didn't budge. He had the wiry strength of a mountain lion. His other hand closed around my throat in a death-grip. The blood pounded in my broken head. Finally I let go of his wrist with my right hand and clouted him on the chin, once, twice. The gun dropped from his hand.

The cabin door banged open and a human pillar of flame ran bellowing out into the open. It was Homer Strakey, Sr., ablaze from head to foot. He fell headlong into the snow and began rolling, shrieking incoherently and slapping at the flames that engulfed him.

I was getting up off the stunned Church when something hard and cold was pressed against the base of my skull and I heard a deep, fury-wracked voice at my ear. "This is where you finish up, Murdock!"

I didn't stop to think. Dropping to one knee, I swept my left arm around, catching the arm holding the gun with my elbow and knocking it to one side. Ira Longbow, his hair matted on one side and his face streaked with blood from the cut I'd opened on his head earlier, stumbled backward, reeling to catch his balance. He succeeded, and brought the Dance around to fire. At the same time, I reached for my own gun. A crawling sensation took hold of my insides. My holster was empty.

The Deane-Adams lay in the snow between us where it had fallen when I'd left the roof. There was a pause while the half-breed came to realize the superiority of his position. Behind him, the window and open door of the cabin blazed brightly; against that background, the leer that came over his lean features was diabolic. His finger tightened on the trigger.

The air throbbed with a sudden explosion. The whole right side of Longbow's face burst open and his head spun halfway around on his neck. His gun flipped from his hand, he pirouetted on his left foot, and crumpled into the cinder-blackened snow. After a few kicks he lay there without moving, eyes and mouth wide open, the good side of his face turned as though looking back at me over his shoulder. The sound of the fire greedily devouring the log cabin dominated the scene.

I turned. Fifty yards up the slope, Bear Anderson lay on his stomach in the snow where he had dived when the action started, his Spencer braced against his right shoulder and supported on his elbows. The echo of his shot could still be heard receding into the distance.

He couldn't have thrown the rifle into a more convenient spot if he'd been practicing for a week. It had been no accident; he hadn't survived a decade and a half of Flathead enmity by leaving things to chance. It was no wonder that the Indian women regarded him as the embodiment of the evil spirit.

Church was beginning to stir. I picked up my gun and got hold of his Navy Colt before he could retrieve it. He cursed, spat out what looked like a piece of a tooth, and climbed unsteadily to his feet. "Goddamn you, Murdock."

"It wouldn't surprise me if He did." I returned my gun to its holster and stuck the Colt inside my belt. Then I stood back. "Get going."

The bounty hunter remained motionless, eyeing me suspiciously.

"What in *hell* do you think you're doing?" Bear approached on foot, leading his horse and carrying the Spencer.

Near the burning cabin, Little Tree had gotten up out of the snow and was watching the scene with glittering black eyes. Her face, although round, was smooth and unwrinkled and somewhat pleasant. Her ordeal hadn't seemed to upset her as much as might be expected, but then she was living with the most dangerous man in the Northwest and was probably used to such conditions.

"Now we're even," I told Church. "Pick up your friend and go."

"What about my gun?" he asked.

"I'm fair," I said. "I'm not stupid. You need something to shoot game, you've got Strakey's pistol."

He stood his ground a moment longer, watching me, or so I thought, in his cockeyed fashion. Then he nodded. "We left our horses on the other side of the mountain." He turned to see to his partner.

Old man Strakey's hands and face had gotten the worst of the burning; blisters the size of Michigan cherries were beginning to swell on the skin. But he got up with Church's help and staggered off supported by the bounty hunter, his tattered clothes still smoking. When their backs were turned, Bear raised his rifle and sighted down the barrel. I grabbed it and pushed it away. The scalp-hunter glared and made as if to strike me with the butt, only to check the motion when he found himself staring down the bore of my revolver.

"I've got this jackass sense of honor that will probably get me killed someday," I explained. "But he handed me my life once, and now I'm returning the favor."

"I'm obliged, Murdock." Church had stopped just past the corner of the cabin, now a flaming shell, to look back. Despite his lack of size, he appeared to have no difficulty supporting his companion's bulk. "It won't get you no prizes, though," he added. "Now I only got to split that five thousand two ways."

Bear was forced to watch them leave while I kept him covered. When they were out of sight and my gun had been put away, he turned to the woman and barked at her in rapid Blackfoot. She replied softly in the same tongue. He nodded once, curtly.

"Let's ride," he said.

"Where to?" I asked.

"There's a Blackfoot village a day's ride west of here, in the plains. I'm going to leave Little Tree with her own people until this is over. Which it would of been but for you."

He had his foot in the stirrup and was about to mount the dun when he arched his back suddenly and toppled backward seven feet to the ground, where he lay as lifelessly as Ira Longbow's mutilated corpse.

# CHAPTER 10

The heat of the fire was terrific on the back of my neck as I loosened the rough woolen scarf that enveloped Bear's throat beneath the collar of the bearskin. His great chest swelled with his first unfettered breath, then relaxed as he exhaled mightily. His face was flushed and slick with perspiration. He blinked and looked at me.

"What happened?"

"That's my question," I said.

"Don't know. Everything went gray and I felt myself going over." He gritted his teeth and grunted as if undertaking some superhuman effort, but succeeded only in lifting his head a fraction of an inch up out of the snow. Gasping, he let it drop back. "I can't move."

I prodded his slablike ribcage with my fist. "Feel that?"

"No."

"How about this?" I smacked his left thigh with the flat of my hand.

He shook his head.

"Try lifting your hands."

His right hand came up readily. Its mate remained still at his side. Something glimmered in his clear blue eyes. Fear?

I looked at Little Tree, who had knelt in the snow on the other side of him. "Do you speak English?"

"Some little." Her voice was soft, almost inaudible.

"Help me get him into the shelter of that rock." I jerked my head in the direction of the mountain, where internal stresses had long ago thrust a broken shard of rock several yards square away from the mountain so that it formed an awning four feet above the ground.

We were half an hour pulling and shoving Bear's three hundred and fifty pounds through the snow to where the sloping shelf formed a bulwark against the elements. That done, I directed the squaw to fetch my horse from among the maples at the top of the slope where I had tethered it. "We'll stay here for tonight," I told Bear, once I'd caught my breath. "Tomorrow we start for Staghorn."

"We will like hell!" Again he tried to get up, with the same results. He fell back panting.

"That bullet you picked up is a lot deeper than you let on," I said. "The same thing happened to the captain of my out-fit at Gettysburg. He had a ball from a Confederate rifle pressing against his spine, paralyzing him. Your lead must have just shifted. If it shifts back in the right direction, you might be able to move again."

"And if it don't?"

"It will probably kill you."

"Can't you get it out?"

"I'm not even going to try. If I made a mistake, I'd either kill you or paralyze you for life. I've got to get you to a doctor."

He snorted. "Why bother? Me dying is the only way you're going to get back to town with your scalp."

"That wouldn't say much for me, would it? You've saved my hide twice."

"I reckon you was right," he said, after a pause.

"About what?"

"About that honor of yours getting you killed."

"Staghorn's only a couple of days' ride from here," I said, ignoring the remark. "What they've got for a doctor is worse than no doctor at all, but if I can get you to town I may be able to send for one that can do some good."

"No go Staghorn," said Little Tree.

I looked up. She had finished tethering my mare to a stripling that grew flush with the wall of the mountain and was standing just beyond the shelf with her fists clenched at her sides. Her expression was wooden.

"Why not?" I asked.

"Bear hang."

"How did you find out about that?"

She shrugged. "White man's way. Kill men, white man hang. No go Staghorn."

"We don't know that he'll hang," I said, and looked at Bear. "It's your decision. You can either go to town and take your chances with the law or stay here and wait for Church."

"Some choice," he growled.

"Sorry, but I don't have anything better to offer."

"Go Blackfoot village," said Little Tree. "Medicine man there."

I shook my head. "I have nothing against your beliefs, but no amount of wailing and shaking of rattles is going to get that bullet out of his back. It's Staghorn or nowhere."

"How you going to get me over the mountains?" challenged the scalp-hunter. "I don't roll easy."

"We can fix up a litter."

"What you mean 'we'?"

"Little Tree and I. Don't say she's not going; there's a blizzard coming, and it's been too long since I rode the Bitterroot regularly for me to attack it in weather like that without a guide. You'd be no help at all in your condition. If you decide to go, she's coming along."

He didn't like it, but there was no fighting my logic. "Ain't you afeared all that moving might shove the bullet the wrong way?" he said, after a moment.

"It's a chance we have to take. But I wouldn't worry too much about it. If it were going to shift that easily, it probably would have while we were moving you just now."

His brow darkened. "They why in hell did you do it?"

At that moment, the entire front of the blazing cabin collapsed with a resounding *frump*, sending fiery logs rolling and skidding across the snow. Now the structure was nothing more than a pile of burning timber with a stone chimney rising naked from one corner.

"Would you rather we left you there to fry?" I asked him.

He appeared to think things over. Finally he said, "You might as well go ahead and build the litter. We won't live to see morning anyway."

"What's that supposed to mean?"

His eyes slid past my shoulder. I turned to follow his gaze. At the top of the slope, dozens of sleek gray forms milled about among the bare maples, sniffing the ground from time to time and exposing lolling red tongues to the frigid air. There were more than a hundred of them. One, a big monster with a shaggy mane and a dangling ear, stood partway down the grade with its legs straddling our trail, staring at the smoldering wreckage of the cabin as if mesmerized by the flames.

"Didn't take them as long to finish off that dead bounty hunter as I figured," Bear said.

I gave Little Tree the bowie knife and instructed her to cut some brush for a windbreak while I disposed of Ira Longbow's body in a snowbank as far away from the shelter as possible. On her way to the scrub, the squaw picked up the Spencer from the ground where Bear had dropped it when he fell and took it along for protection from the wolves. I swept up Longbow's revolver and stuck it into my belt beside Church's Colt. All told, and assuming that Bear had enough ammunition on him for another full load, I estimated we had approximately forty rounds among us. If the woman and I were lucky enough to down an animal with each shot, that left us with only about sixty wolves to deal with. What was I worrying about?

That afternoon we built a fire using sticks of unburned wood from the ruins of the cabin and left an opening a foot wide in the windbreak for the smoke to escape. Over it Little Tree cooked a neck of venison that she had rescued from a small storage cellar beneath the wreckage—we had no time for Bear's special method of roasting—and afterward we ate in silence while snow piled up outside the shelter. I thought that if this weather continued, most of the mountain passes would soon be blocked, and wondered if perhaps the Flatheads weren't already on their way to the plains to winter and make plans for the spring uprising, new moon or no. I didn't dwell on it. I had enough to occupy my mind without wasting time on something over which I had no control.

I used what brush I could rustle up to construct a litter, bound together with the last of the fringe from Bear's buckskin shirt. When it was finished it didn't look as if it would support his tremendous weight, but it was the best I could manage without access to the maples atop the ridge, where the wolves had bedded down to wait out the remaining daylight. We'd find out for sure tomorrow—if any of us lived that long.

Night settled like lampblack over the mountains. Bear

slept quietly beneath his blanket, Little Tree beside him wrapped in mine, while I took the first watch at the opening. I had the scalp-hunter's Spencer across my lap.

The warmth inside the shelter with the fire going made me drowsy. More than once I caught myself just before my chin hit my chest and was forced to scrub my face with handfuls of snow taken from outside the opening to wake up. After a while, though, even that became useless, and I dozed off around ten.

I awoke to find the fire guttering among chunks of glowing charcoal and the snow in front of the shelter alive with wolves. Then I realized that it had been the horses' frantic neighing that had awakened me. I started involuntarily. The movement startled a big male that had been sniffing curiously at the windbreak into going for my right hand. I jerked it back. The wolf's jaws closed over empty air with a snap. Before it could react, I swung the Spencer around and caught it on the end of the snout with the butt. It yelped in rage and pain and lunged forward through the opening, jaws working like a sewing machine.

Its breath was hot and rank on my face when I swung the rifle back the other way, thrust the muzzle into the thick fur at the animal's throat, and pulled the trigger. The air exploded inside the shelter. Blood and meat and tufts of fur flew all over. The wolf slumped over me heavily, its jaws still agape, eyes wide open and glassy.

Bear and the woman were awake—what else could they be?—but if they were talking I couldn't hear them, because my ears were still ringing from the blast. My clothes were slimy with blood from my collar to the tops of my boots. Bits of fur floated down all around me. The air stank of cordite and something else just as strong. Burning hair. I looked down and saw that the animal's coat was smoldering where its hindquarters had come to rest in the middle of the dying fire. Using both hands, I rolled the limp body off my legs and with some effort succeeded in pushing it out through the opening with my feet. Immediately it was fallen upon by its fellows, who tore at it and dragged it away, fighting over it among themselves. In the center of the melee, the rangy male with one limp ear lunged this way and that, drawing blood from flanks and shoulders until order was restored. Then, holding the pack at bay with threatening snarls, it stepped forward and helped itself to the bounty. At length some of the others joined in cautiously, but the majority was left to pace restlessly back and forth and watch the proceedings with twitching tails and murder in their eyes. In no time at all there was nothing left of the corpse but bones and hair.

Little Tree insisted upon helping me off with my coat and pants, and while I huddled next to the rebuilt fire wrapped in the blanket she had just relinquished, scrubbed them in the snow outside the opening to remove the worst of the blood. The wolves, their appetites sated temporarily, eyed her from a safe distance beyond reach of the flames. Their eyes glittered greenly from time to time in the reflected firelight. When she was finished she hung the garments from the windbreak to dry.

"Now we got one less cartridge than we had before," Bear said. He was staring up at the stone ceiling, snug beneath his coarse-woven Indian blanket. His voice came faintly, as if from a long way off; the whining noise in my ears had only just begun to fade.

"What should I have done? Strangle him?"

"You got my knife, ain't you?"

I reached down to feel the hilt of the bowie in the top of my right boot, where I had stuck it after Little Tree had returned it to me. "I never thought about it," I admitted. "Much as I'd have liked to try my hand at killing a full-grown timber wolf with a knife while it was gnawing happily away at my throat. Especially after that same knife had been used to cut brush."

He had no answer for that. Or, if he had, he kept it to himself. In any case he did not pursue the point.

"I see to horses," said Little Tree. She picked up the Spencer and stepped out through the opening.

There was silence inside the shelter after that, while Bear and I listened to the wind whistle past the opening. It gusted at intervals, hooting gleefully as it buckled the fragile walls of the enclosure and blew smoke into our faces. Razor-edged blasts spat bits of snow through chinks in the windbreak.

"I fell asleep," I said.

"Figured that," Bear replied.

"I figured you did. That's why I admitted it."

The squaw returned. "Horses all right. I watch now. You sleep."

I was in no mood to argue. My head was throbbing and I was tired of propping my eyelids open with my thumbs. I drew the blanket up to my chin and stretched out beside the fire. I was asleep before my head hit the floor of the shelter, which was merciful, because it was frozen hard as rock.

The blizzard was upon us in full force when we broke camp the next morning. Wind roared past our ears, whipped stinging grains of ice like bits of ground glass into our faces, whited out the landscape until it was impossible to sort out earth from sky. Under such conditions, I was glad I'd held firm on the subject of Little Tree going along to act as guide. She would ride the mare while I hauled her mate behind the big dun.

Although the litter creaked beneath Bear's weight when

we lifted one end of it, it proved strong enough to support him, and once I had flattened the ends of the wooden supports with the blade of the bowie to form runners, the entire burden slid across the surface of the snow as easily as any sled. I secured the litter with a thong to the scalp-hunter's saddle so that it dragged behind the dun, and mounted gingerly, the way any experienced rider does when stepping into a strange pair of stirrups. The big horse fidgeted beneath the rig and the unfamiliar weight on its back, but at a word from its prostrate master it adjusted itself grudgingly to the situation. I stroked its sleek mahogany neck to show it who was in command.

"Everything all right back there?" I shouted to Bear, over the howling gale.

"Let's just ride."

We started with a jolt. Leather creaked, limb groaned against green limb, makeshift runners scraped over fresh powder. In our wake rode Little Tree to keep an eye on our progress. I cast a glance back in her direction. Beyond her, vague gray shapes bounded through the flying snow toward the bank in which I had buried Ira Longbow. They swarmed over it, digging with all four paws. Soon, however, even that scene was lost amid the swirling particles of white.

# CHAPTER 11

**W**e were crossing over old ground in the beginning, but if we hadn't known what direction we were going, none of us would have realized it. What had been hills of snow were now sinkholes, hollowed out by the wind, while level spots through which Bear and I had passed without hindrance a few days earlier were heaped as high as ten feet. Whole stands of pine and maple had been all but obliterated; in other places they had been swept clean where before only their pointed tops had shown. What landmarks remained were blurred behind drifting clouds of white powder so that they resembled features in a grainy tintype.

The wind was tearing out of the east at between forty and fifty miles per hour. I had my kerchief tied over the lower part of my face as feeble protection against frostbite, while Little Tree rode with her chin huddled in the collar of her fur-faced cowhide jacket, one of a handful of items she had been able to salvage from the unburned cellar of the cabin. Bear, the most likely candidate for death by freezing due to his immobile state, was wrapped from head to foot in every available blanket. But for the snow, we might have been veiled mourners transporting the mummified remains of our king to a tomb on the banks of the Nile.

What was two days' ride for a man alone on horseback was considerably more for a man and a woman hauling a litter through one of the worst blizzards on record. Missing Devil's Crack cost us a full thirty-six hours. Most of the passes being closed to us, we were forced to rely on mountain trails and narrow clefts in the high rocks, some of them so cramped we had to dismount and walk our horses single file, Little Tree leading the mare by its bridle, me driving the big dun from behind as if it were an ox plowing a field. At these times we stopped often to disengage the broad litter where it had wedged itself between the rocks. In three days we made barely twenty miles.

I had been wrong when I'd told Bear not to worry about the bullet in his back shifting while he was being moved. At intervals his paralysis gave way to agony as the lead wobbled about next to his spinal column, relieving his numbness just long enough for the pain to set in. Although he bore it without complaint, his suffering was evident in his features. That's the essential difference between man and beast. I'd have shot a dog before letting it go through the hell he accepted as a matter of course.

We were emerging from one of these clefts on a downhill grade toward the close of the third day when I stopped short and signaled the squaw, who was walking behind me, to draw back from the opening. A hundred yards beyond, the entire Flathead nation was pouring onto the circular plateau below us from a forest to the east. At its head rode Chief Two Sisters.

He wore a white woven coat decorated with broad bands of green—the labor, most likely, of the squaw of some ambitious brave. His tarnished-silver hair was braided in front, loose in back, and bound with ornaments bearing the Salish symbols of strength and virility. In the waning light, his face was old and drawn but hard, the eyes sunken beneath his square, jutting brow, mouth turned downward into a permanent scowl. He shifted uncomfortably from time to time on his horse's back, but I gathered that this was not so much from pain as from discomfort caused by the strip of deerhide that was wound tightly around his injured ribcage, part of which peeped above the V of his coat as he leaned over to dig a lump of ice out of the top of his moccasin boot. Like his braves, he rode with a rifle slung over his left shoulder. The difference was that while most of the others carried single-shot Springfields—the kind the army had given them several years earlier as a token of good faith— his was the Henry repeater that had been taken from me by Rocking Wolf. Apparently he didn't share his nephew's contempt for the weapon.

At his side rode a muscular-looking individual in a buffalo robe, the only visible part of his face a narrow strip of flesh showing between a scarf wrapped around his lower features and a headdress crowned by a pair of curving buffalo horns. This had to be the medicine man whose antipathy toward me I had sensed in the chief's lodge something over a lifetime ago. His eyes were hard and shifty, like those of medicine men everywhere.

I watched from the cover of a vertical pillar of rock while the mass of warriors, with an occasional feminine face sprinkled among their numbers, slowed to a halt behind the chief's raised right hand. Silence prevailed while Two Sisters scanned his surroundings. His eyes swung in my direction and I froze, my hand gripping the butt of the Deane-Adams. But they moved on without pausing, and when it was apparent that he had satisfied himself that they were alone on the plateau, the chief turned and said something to the man mounted at his side. The wind drowned out his words. Which was all right, because I wouldn't have understood them anyway. The medicine man heard him out, then pulled down his scarf to reply. That's when I received my second shock of the day.

The face beneath the headdress was dusky, the nose broad and flat, the lips thick. Against this background, the whites of his eyes were startling. It was the kind of face you expected to see beneath the cap of a Pullman porter, or bent over your boots and grinning at its reflection in the fresh shine. The last place you would have looked for it was beside the chief of the most powerful Indian tribe in the Bitterroot. I'd known that some tribes took in Negroes out of spite for the white man, but I could think of no other instance in which one of these foundlings had risen to such influential rank. The entire party could have charged us at that moment and I would have been unable to react, I was that stunned.

For a while it seemed that there was some disagreement between the two about whether they should camp there for the night or proceed into the cleft in which the three of us were crouched. At length, however, the order was given to dismount, and as darkness crept over them, the Flatheads began setting up their lodges.

"We'll camp here for tonight," I whispered to Little Tree, after withdrawing from the opening. "Pull out before dawn, the way we came in. If they find us here we'll be wolf-meat by tomorrow night."

"Lose one day," the squaw pointed out.

"Better a day than our scalps."

"Ain't no need to pull out," said Bear.

I looked at him. Bundled up as he was aboard the litter, only his blue eyes showed, staring up at the sky.

"Suicide must look pretty good from where you sit," I said dryly.

"How many injuns we got?" he asked me.

"Four or five hundred. The whole shebang. Why?"

"You know how long it takes to shove four or five hunnert riders single file through this crack?"

"What are you getting at?"

"Them Flatheads is anxious to clear these mountains before every pass gets blocked twixt here and the plains. Many as there are, they'll save at least a day by going around the long way. Besides, Two Sisters ain't exactly the kind to favor placing his whole tribe in a situation where they could get bushwacked as easy as in here. Just sit tight. They'll be on their way by sunup tomorrow."

"And if they aren't?"

He met my gaze. "You reckon we can survive an extra day in this blizzard?"

"No."

"Then I don't see as we got much choice."

That ended the discussion. Above us, the wind squealed between broken pinnacles of ice and rock, casting bushels of dry white granules over us at ragged intervals. "How's the back?" I asked Bear.

"It ain't good," he said. "Every now and then, I get so's I can move my legs a little; sometimes I almost figure I can get up. But it don't last long."

I nodded. Then, "What do you know of a black man who rides with the Flatheads?"

The scalp-hunter stiffened. "He with them now?"

"You know him?"

"That's Black Kettle, or so he calls himself." His voice was taut. "Blackfeet talk about him all the time. According to them, he worked as a slave on a plantation down in Georgia until he got caught up in an uprising and was wounded when the overseer's men moved in with shotguns. They cut down about a dozen of them. Slaves ain't cheap, so they patched him up, give him a whipping, and told him to get back to work. Sometime later he knifed the overseer and lit a shuck for the Northwest. That's the story he give the Flatheads, anyhow. I reckon he was heading for Canada when he got took prisoner by Two Sisters."

"He dresses like a medicine man," I said.

"That's what he is. Injuns and niggers take to each other like hot corn and butter, and crazy men are powerful medicine. He had to make it sooner or later."

"Black Kettle's crazy?"

"If he was a dog, he'd of been shot a long time ago."

"I take it he doesn't care for white men."

Bear laughed, but without humor. "Next to him, Rocking Wolf is a Presbyterian minister."

"That explains it," I said.

"Explains what?"

"Why your parents were killed. I'd always wondered what prompted Two Sisters to go on the warpath that year. I'm surprised you didn't see it."

"I saw it."

"Then how come his scalp isn't in that bag?" I nodded toward the gunny sack hanging from the horn of the dun's saddle.

"Don't think I ain't tried," he said. "He's crafty. He never leaves camp, and I ain't got to the point where I'm ready to take on more than one or two hunnert Flatheads at a shot."

"Meaning that someday you will?"

"Meaning that someday I'm going to take Black Kettle's kinky scalp."

We fell silent for a moment, listening to the wind and the faint noises drifting up from the camp below us. Finally, Bear said, "Any sign of Rocking Wolf?"

"No. Maybe he'd dead. I don't see how he could make it out there with neither horse nor rifle."

"We don't know for sure that he don't have a rifle. Besides, survival is an injun's business; it's the first thing he learns before he gets his feather. Likely they missed him somewhere."

"That's one feat I hope we can duplicate," I muttered.

Little Tree and I unhitched the litter and did what we could to make ourselves comfortable, which proved to be a wasted effort. The cleft acted like a bellows in reverse, sucking in cold air and cascades of snow that rattled in gusts against our heavy clothing and burned our skin like hot ashes wherever it found a chink. We didn't dare light a fire; for warmth we wrapped ourselves in our blankets and huddled together around Bear with our backs to the wind like cattle. Now and then a scent of wood smoke wafted over us from the direction of the plateau, which did nothing to improve our spirits. Further, there was no escaping the conviction that behind us, the shadows swarmed with wolves. It was going to be a long night for the three of us.

Sunup—if it could be called that, hidden as it was behind the pewter-colored overcast—found me struggling to get to my feet, working the rust out of joints I hadn't known I possessed until that morning. After relieving Little Tree of the Spencer, I crept forward to the granite promontory I had manned the previous afternoon. The plateau was a beehive of activity; Indians milled around leading horses, striking huts, extinguishing fires—in general, getting ready to depart. In the center of everything sat Two Sisters astride his painted horse, barking orders and directing the operation with sweeping gestures. While he was thus engaged, Black Kettle rode up to him. Immediately the two appeared to resume the argument they had carried out the day before, the medicine man gesticulating like a madman while his chief shook his head stubbornly. Watching, I got the impression that this was a common scene between them. Eventually Black Kettle threw up his hands, wheeled his horse, and cantered out of sight beyond the rock behind which I was crouching.

That Two Sisters had won the argument was evident. The only question that remained was what stand he had taken. Had he opted to go around the mountain the long way, or was it his intention to defy what Bear had said about him and lead the tribe straight through the cleft? If it was the latter, we were as good as dead. There was no way we were going to hitch up Bear's litter, turn around, and get out of there before the first Indian entered. I cursed myself for having taken the advice of an invalid who was more than likely suffering from delirium.

"What our plans?"

I started and swung the Spencer around, narrowly missing Little Tree's head with the side of the barrel as I did so. She had come up behind me so silently that I hadn't known she was there until she'd spoken. She was holding Ira Longbow's Dance, which I'd given her previously, in her right hand. I relaxed my hold on the rifle.

"You're doing fine," I told her. "Just keep that gun handy. If they come this way, we're going to sell our lives as dearly as possible. It worked for Custer."

Either the speech sounded better then than it does now, or Little Tree's training kept her from commenting. At any rate, it seemed to satisfy her, because she stopped asking questions I couldn't answer.

You had to hand it to the Flatheads for efficiency. Within ten minutes they had the plateau stripped of any evidence that their camp had ever existed, and were mounted and lined up along the northern edge waiting for the order to move. Beyond them, Black Kettle rode restlessly back and forth, a gray presence behind the driving sheets of snow.

For a moment Two Sisters appeared to hesitate, which was understandable. If Bear's assumption was correct, the chief had not heard from Rocking Wolf for days, and like any other uncle he was loath to depart without knowing his nephew's fate. Finally, however, he made his decision; without a word he kneed his mount forward and led the way north—around the mountain.

We watched in silence as the column of Flatheads paraded past the opening. Last to leave was the medicine man, who spent some time trotting about the deserted camp as if to blow off steam, casting frustrated glances in the direction of the cleft. The squaw and I flattened ourselves against the ice-covered rock wall and listened to the beating of our own hearts, louder at this point than the shrieking wind. Minutes crept by, or maybe they were just seconds; it was impossible to judge. At last Black Kettle spun the horse about and, with an angry whoop, galloped off in the others' wake.

I let out my breath and lowered the rifle, the sights of which I'd had lined up on the black man's broad chest. Beside me, Little Tree replaced the Dance's hammer with a sigh of sliding metal. For a stretch neither of us spoke.

"Hitch up the litter," I said at last. I was surprised at the steadiness of my own voice.

We took our time crossing the plateau, to avoid being spotted by stragglers as much as to ensure the scalp-hunter a comfortable ride, and reached the cover of the woods after an hour. From there we descended to the edge of a river some forty feet wide at its broadest point, where we stopped. It was one of those countless tributaries that take so many twists and turns on their way through the mountains that they wind up with either a dozen names or none at all. The wind had swept this one clean of snow, leaving the silvery surface of the ice bare but for serpentine ribbons of powder writhing across it in the wind. Its banks were lined with pine and cattails, the latter bowed beneath the weight of cling-ing frost and so deceptively fragile in appearance that they seemed ready to fall apart at the touch of a finger. Ice-laden hulks of fallen trees formed natural bridges across the wa-ter where they had been torn out of the ground in past storms.

"We cross?" asked Little Tree.

"I don't know," I replied. "It took a lot of punishment when the Flatheads crossed. Let me have the mare." I dis-mounted.

"What you do?" She got down off the chestnut and handed me the reins.

"I'll have a better idea of how much this ice can hold once I cross over." I swung into the mare's saddle. "Wait for the high sign before you start across with Bear. Lead, don't ride. If you hear it start to crack, get the hell off fast."

Out in the open, the wind was ruthless. It plucked at the brim of my hat and found its way inside my coat, billowing it out behind me. My breath froze in my nostrils and clung in crystals to the stubble on my cheeks and chin. Updrafts snatched my pants legs out of my boots, exposing bare skin to blasts of peppery snow.

Suddenly, something hard struck the ice at the mare's feet, sending up a geyser of splinters and shooting cracks out in all directions. Coming upon its heels, the sound of the shot was an anticlimax.

# CHAPTER 12

I left the saddle just as the mare reared, striking the ice hard on my right shoulder and rolling. The horse fled slipping and sliding in the direction from which we had come. I clawed my gun out of its holster and lay on my stomach gripping the weapon in both hands, my elbows propped up on the ice.

There was nothing to shoot at. An unbroken line of brush and pine formed a barrier along the opposite bank, behind which an army could have hidden. Even the cloud of metallic gray gunsmoke drifting across the scene had been snatched away by the wind so fast that it was impossible to tell where it had originated. In a game of snipers, I was the only visible target for miles.

"Get up, white skin!"

Nearly drowned out as it was by the wailing gale, there was still no mistaking that voice. I remained prone.

Another bullet spanged off the ice near my left elbow, spitting bits of crystal into my face. The shot echoed growlingly into the distance. I got up.

"I would have bet money you'd lost your rifle back at Devil's Crack," I told Rocking Wolf. I held the gun against my right hip.

"You would have lost."

I tried to place where the voice was coming from, but the wind roaring in my ears made that impossible.

"You did well, white skin," it continued. "I have the use of only one leg. When last we spoke the pain was too great for me to take aim. Since then I have grown used to it. Had I not, I would never have been able to come this far, where I knew you would one day pass." He snapped off another shot, which whizzed past my ear and struck the ice ten feet behind me. Hairline cracks leaped out across the surface.

"Where is Mountain That Walks?"

I hesitated a beat before answering. It had just dawned on me that from where Rocking Wolf was—wherever he was—Bear and his squaw were invisible. "He's dead," I said.

"You lie." A fourth bullet pierced the ice directly in front of me. Water splattered over my boots. I leaped backward.

"It's the truth." I spread my legs to distribute my weight; the surface was growing spongy. "He had a bullet in his back, put there by the bounty hunters we met west of the Crack. The bullet finally moved. I buried him twenty miles back."

There was no reply. I began to feel cold where my body had come into contact with the clammy surface of the ice. Finally the voice called out again.

"Surrender your gun, white skin. Slide it across the ice. The one in your belt as well."

I obeyed. The revolver skidded ten feet and came to a stop just past the halfway point. The Colt followed, sliding beyond that and losing itself in the cattails on the other side. At that moment Rocking Wolf stepped out from behind a tangle of brambles and began hobbling toward me.

Purple bruises had swollen his face into a caricature; his left eye was a crescent glittering between folds of puffy flesh

and his lips were thick and torn. His bearskin hung in tat-
ters from his thickset frame. He held the Winchester cra-
dled in his left arm, the right supporting his weight upon a
forked limb thrust beneath the armpit. The leg on that
side—shattered, most likely, in his fall—dragged uselessly
behind him. Any pretense he had made previously of mask-
ing his emotions had been abandoned, for the face that
confronted me was twisted with hatred beyond even its
physical mutilation.

He stopped with his feet planted on either side of the
abandoned Deane-Adams and raised the rifle to the level of
my chest. "Do not turn away," he barked. His swollen lips
got in the way of his consonants, slurring them. "You should
be prepared to face your handiwork."

"I don't suppose it would do any good to deny I had anything to do with it," I said.

"Do not waste my time. I am through listening." He
shifted the makeshift crutch a little so that he could steady
the rifle with his other hand. Not that he really had to, at
that range, but he wanted to prolong the moment.

I decided that if Little Tree were going to make a
move from the cover of the brush behind me, she would have
done so by now. Stooping suddenly, I scooped the bowie
knife out of my right boot and followed through in an under-
hand fling, sending the blade whistling in the general direction of the Indian's squat torso.

It didn't land point first, of course; that was too much to
hope for under the circumstances. What mattered was that
Rocking Wolf thought it would. He moved to dodge it even
as the leather-bound handle swung around and bounced
harmlessly off his chest; in so doing, he threw too much
weight onto the crutch and it slipped out from under him.
By that time I was in motion, charging head down like a

maddened bull. He fired. Something hot seared my right cheek, too late. I struck him head first in the midsection, and we went down together. The rifle spun from his grip and clattered away out of reach.

A town-bred white man is no match for a wild Indian at the best of times, but I'd counted on Rocking Wolf's injury giving me an edge. What I hadn't counted on was my own injury. Mountain air goes no further toward healing a fractured skull than that at sea level, and in any case it isn't advisable to use the damaged instrument as a weapon. My vision blurred, doubled. I saw two Deane-Adams revolvers lying side by side on the ice and grabbed for the wrong one, coming up with a handful of empty air. By that time the Indian had found his wind; cocking his good leg, he planted his foot against my chest and pushed hard. I reeled backward and was forced to execute a fancy roll to avoid splitting my head open all over again when I struck the ice.

The Indian reached out blindly and closed his fingers over the bowie knife. Rolling over onto his stomach, he pulled himself toward me frantically, dragging his useless right leg behind him, one hand clutching the knife like an ice pick. When he was close enough, he raised the weapon high over his head and stabbed downward. I rolled again, just as the blade shattered the ice where my head had been, and before he could react, I straddled his back, locking my arms around his throat from behind.

It was no good; though my vision had corrected itself, my head was pounding and I was weak as a baby. He stabbed back and up with the knife, forcing me to break my grip to keep the blade from slashing open my ribcage. At the same time he hooked my ankle with his good left leg and arched his back, flipping me off. The impact of my fall blinded me for an instant. The first thing I saw when my senses returned

was Rocking Wolf on his knees before me, the hand holding the knife poised over his head in striking position.

He had started the downward swing when a shot rang out
and his forehead exploded. Blood and bits of bone spattered
my face. The knife dropped from his hand and clattered to
the ice. Slowly, as if he had changed his mind, he sank back
onto his heels and just as slowly toppled over sideways. His
body jerked spasmodically for a moment, then lay still.

I didn't waste any time after that. When you hear a shot
you weren't expecting, the first rule is that you look around
for a weapon. I wasn't about to throw away my cards without knowing for sure whether it was Little Tree who had
fired. I flopped over onto my stomach and began crawling
toward my gun.

I was within reach of it when there was another explosion and the revolver spun away from me, arcing across the
now-wet surface of the ice. Immediately I rolled in the opposite direction and came to rest on my stomach behind
Rocking Wolf's still form. Once there I risked a quick glance
toward the bank where I had left my companions, for it was
there that the shots had originated.

Church was standing on the edge of the ice holding Bear's
Spencer in both hands. His undersize frame was impossible to mistake even in that driving snow. The butt of what I
took to be Ira Longbow's Dance protruded above his holster. Behind him, Homer Strakey's equally recognizable
bulk stood in a position where he could keep an eye on both
Bear and Little Tree. His stance told me he was armed. Although I couldn't see it, I knew he had his dead son's old-
fashioned percussion cap pistol in one hand. What with the
blizzard and the drama that had been taking place on the
ice, it had been no feat for the two to sneak up on my companions and relieve them of their weapons. Now I knew why

Little Tree hadn't fired at the Indian when it seemed she'd had the chance.

"Looks like you owe me again, Murdock!" cried Church. His scarf was tied loosely around his scrawny neck, the ends flapping in the wind. "I can't abide watching no injun kill no white man."

"So you'll do it instead," I finished.

"Got to. You got so's I can't go around you no more, and I'm tired of dogging you. Now, get up from behind that dead injun."

"I'd rather not."

His sloping shoulders heaved in a mighty sigh. "We got to go through this all over again? Homer!"

On cue, Strakey stepped forward and stretched out his right arm, placing the muzzle of the pistol against the squaw's right temple. She stood still as the tree for which she was named.

"Why don't you just move on?" I demanded, stalling for time. "You've got Anderson."

"I do for a fact—all wrapped up like Christmas morning. How'd he get that way?"

I told him.

"Well, well." He sounded pleased. "So one of us did hit him, after all. The offer's tempting, Murdock, but it ain't enough."

"Why not?"

"There's a good day's ride between here and Staghorn; I think me and the old man would enjoy it more if we didn't have to spend all our time looking over our shoulders. I'll take my chances on the squaw, but you're another brand of bacon. Now, are you going to get up from behind that stiff or am I going to have to ask Homer to put a ball through the squaw's head? He's been itching to use that thing ever since you turned him into a candle back at Anderson's cabin."

"What makes you think that'll work with me?" I asked. "Maybe I don't care what happens to her."

"All right, Homer, blow her brains out."

"Hold it! I'll get up."

Still I hesitated, but not just because I didn't want to get killed, which of course I didn't. In stepping forward to put the pistol against Little Tree's head, Strakey had turned his back on Bear's litter. That was evidently the opportunity for which the scalp-hunter had been waiting. Awkwardly and with great effort—he was, after all, shaking off the paralysis of days—he swung his legs out from under the covers and rose like a gigantic specter behind the old man's tensed form.

"Come on!" To show he meant business, Church slapped a bullet from the Spencer into Rocking Wolf's body. The corpse jerked like a kicked sandbag. Another cartridge was racked into place. I climbed to my feet.

"Step clear of the stiff," ordered the bounty hunter.

I took my time obeying. He grew impatient.

"Homer!"

But Homer wasn't listening. At that moment, the scalp-hunter threw his massive arms around the big old man and squeezed, lifting him up in the air as he did so to throw the pistol off target. The ball was released with a snap, missing Little Tree by a least a foot. Simultaneously I heard the crackling noise of ribs giving away beneath the pressure. Strakey screamed through his teeth, a high, chuckling wail that put me in mind of his dead son's nervous giggle.

Church's reaction was not immediate; he had called to his partner and had heard the expected shot. But at the sound of the scream he took a step backward and turned his head. It was just what I needed.

He realized his mistake almost in the next instant, but by then it was too late. I had already dived and come up on my knees with the Deane-Adams gripped in both hands, and when he snapped his head back in my direction I pumped all five bullets into his chest.

For a space I regretted that it wasn't a six-shooter, as the bounty hunter hovered there seemingly unaffected by his wounds, the rifle firmly in his grip. But then his knees buckled and he folded to the ground. The Spencer flopped free.

Homer Strakey's spine snapped with a report like a pistol shot. Bear, who had lifted the old man's body high over his head to deliver the final blow, flung it, rag-doll fashion, to the earth. Clad in skins as he was, his features blurred by the swirling snow, the mountaineer might have been one of those legendary manlike beasts the Indians of the North call the Sasquatch. Then his knees began to shake and the image was dispelled.

I made my way over to the bank, but not before reloading my revolver from the dwindling supply of cartridges on my belt, on the off chance that one of the bounty hunters might still be alive. I needn't have bothered; neither of them was about to get up this side of Judgment Day. I picked up the Spencer and freed Church's body of his gun belt and the Dance he had taken from Little Tree. Strakey's cap-and-ball I left to the elements like the useless toy it was once its load had been fired.

"Anybody hurt?" I inquired.

Little Tree shook her head. She had gone to her mate's side and had an arm around him; he cast it off and stood there swaying. "Let's ride," he said. "Likely them Flatheads heard all that shooting and are on their way here already."

"When did the bullet shift?" I asked him.

"Just before we stopped." He had turned and, walking on

unsteady legs, crossed over to his horse to unhitch the litter. "I didn't say nothing at the time because I wasn't sure. It was just a tingle. What difference does it make? It shifted. Find that nag of yours and let's ride."

"Ease up. If that bullet's as mobile as that, you're running a risk every time you take a step."

"Save that stuff for when you hang out your shingle," he retorted, tossing the litter aside with a powerful thrust of the left arm. He winced and placed what he thought was a surreptitious hand against his injury. I pretended not to notice.

The mare hadn't wandered far. I found it munching at a blackberry bush on the edge of the forest and led it back to the riverbank, where it became so troublesome at the scent of gunpowder and death that I had to tether it to the trunk of a storm-shattered pine while I sought out the bounty hunters' horses. These were hobbled a hundred yards upstream behind a steep snowbank. I chose one—a black with a yellow blaze and stockings to match—for Little Tree, and after removing the other's saddle and bridle, cut it loose and shooed it away. There was no sense in making things easy for Lop Ear and company. Only as I stood watching it canter away toward the comparative openness of the forest did I realize that I had just released a mount far better than the one I was riding. Well, I had gotten used to the aging chestnut anyway. I threw the extra saddle and bridle into the snowbank and rejoined Bear and Little Tree with the black.

Crossing was tricky. I went first, leading the mare, and when I had reached the opposite bank, Little Tree struck out with her new mount, followed by Bear leading the big dun. When he was halfway across, the ice hammocked, squirting water up through its cracks and groaning ominously. He stopped, but as the noise continued it became apparent that standing still was no safer than moving and he resumed with caution. There were two inches of water on top of the ice by the time he and the horse stepped up onto dry land, but the surface remained intact. From a distance it might have been two feet thick.

"We'll stop here," Bear said.

"We've eight hours of daylight left," I pointed out. "What about the Indians?"

"This is where we make our stand."

"Nice last words. Too bad there won't be anybody left to carve them on your tombstone." I spoke bitterly.

"We ain't about to outrun them, that's for sure. And a river's good a place as any to face off. Better than most." He held out his hand for the Spencer. I gave it to him reluctantly.

"Tether the horses clear of the firing line," he told Little Tree, handing her his reins. When she moved off, leading all three animals, he inclined his head toward the gun in my holster. "You're going to have to use a little more economy when it comes to shooting Flatheads. You used four too many on Church."

"Do I tell you how to scalp Indians?" I snapped.

"Just a suggestion."

The Indians came at noon. By that time, entrenched amid the cattails between Bear and the squaw—who was armed once again with the Dance—my gun in hand and the rest of the captured iron within reach, I had given up on them entirely. I was about to say so when the sound of galloping hoofs reached me faintly over the incessant whine of the wind. A soft rumble at first, in seconds it swelled to a roar. The scalp-hunter settled his Spencer into a groove he had hollowed out previously atop an old muskrat den and sighted in on the spot across the river where he had left the bodies for bait.

"Don't nobody fire until I give the word," he said.

They came streaming out of the forest on the other side, a loose wedge of warriors with Two Sisters and Black Kettle mounted at the point. From there the momentum slowed until, drawing near the corpses, they halted. A brave sprang down from his horse and stooped to examine each of the bodies. Rising, he cast a glance across the river, spotted Rocking Wolf sprawled face down in the middle, and pointed.

The chief had already noticed. He nodded reflectively, after which he and the medicine man fell into animated conversation. At one point the latter paused to gaze along the opposite bank, then suddenly raised his right arm and thrust a finger straight at us. I buried my face in my arms. When no bullets followed the gesture, however, I returned my attention to the Indians. It appeared that Two Sisters and Black Kettle were arguing once again, this time over whether they should charge across and begin pursuit immediately or follow the bank and cross farther upstream to avoid a possible ambush, with the medicine man in favor of the former. This time he won. Under instructions from the chief, punctuated once again by numerous gestures, the Flatheads lined up along the riverbank in what my old cavalry sergeant would call charge formation.

"Remember," Bear muttered, "not until I give the word."

They started across in a tight line, unslinging their bows and rifles as they went. The ice bowed dangerously beneath their collective weight. I stretched out full length on my stomach and held the Deane-Adams with my arms resting on a knot of tangled cattails, awaiting the order to fire. It didn't come when I expected it, with the result that I almost gave the game away with a premature shot. Even then Bear remained silent. Out of the corner of my eye I caught a glimpse of his bearded profile; his teeth were showing and the skin over his brow was taut. By that time the Indians were so close I imagined I could smell the mingled stenches of horse and rancid bear grease.

"Fire!" His voice was shrill.

Our first shots crackled like burning wood. Two braves fell, shrieking as they spun from their horses. The third bullet—I think it came from the Spencer—struck Black Kettle's horse and it crashed over onto its side, spilling the medicine man off its back and smashing through the ice where it fell. That sparked off a chain reaction, and as we continued firing the river became a confused tangle of tumbling warriors and horses screaming and thrashing in the black water. Bodies, both of horses and men, were so thick that there was no longer any need to take aim; we just kept pumping lead into the fray like hunters heading off a herd of stampeding buffalo. In seconds the holes in the ice were rounded up with bobbing corpses.

I had emptied both the five-shot and Church's Navy Colt and was reaching for Rocking Wolf's Winchester when Two Sisters gave the order to retreat. Ducking lead, the braves gathered up what dead they could get their hands on and thrashed their way back toward the opposite bank, twisting around now and then to snap off a shot in our direction. Bear and I kept hammering away at their backs until they vanished among the trees.

"They'll try again," said the scalp-hunter. "Next time they'll be more savvy."

He took in his breath suddenly, and I paused in my reloading to look at him. He was staring in the direction of the river. I followed his gaze. Something was bobbing in the water.

At first I thought it was a corpse the Indians had overlooked, but as I watched I saw that it wasn't a corpse at all, but a live warrior swimming frantically toward the broken edge of the ice. I squinted through the flying snow; it was Black Kettle. Unseated from his horse, he had plunged into the river and was straining every muscle to reach the safety of the ice before he was either dragged down by the weight of his furs or picked off by our guns. Tight, glistening wet curls spilled over his shoulders and down his back, his buffalo horn headgear having been discarded.

"Let me have the knife." Bear's tone was strained. When I hesitated, he reached back and snatched the bowie out of my boot. In another moment he was on his feet and striding out over what was left of the ice.

"Bear!" I shouted. It was no good. He had eyes and ears only for the man in the water.

He reached the jagged edge just as Black Kettle lunged forward and grabbed hold of it with both hands. The medicine man's gasp of relief was choked off as he saw the fur boots planted in front of him and looked up at Anderson's towering figure. I saw the whites of his eyes bulge in horror, and then Bear bent down, snatched a handful of his kinky hair, and with the other hand swept the blade of the bowie from left to right across Black Kettle's throat. Arterial blood spurted out three feet in a bright red stream; his gurgling cry was torn to shreds by the wind. The water turned pink around him. Now only Bear's grip on his hair kept the medicine man from sliding beneath the surface, and in another moment, as the scalp-hunter gathered a bigger fistful and made use of the knife once again, the river snatched away the final traces and swept them—body, blood and all—downstream.

I had seen too much in one day. When Bear straightened, holding aloft his bloody trophy for all to see, I turned my head and was sick.

# CHAPTER 13

Lying beside me, Little Tree was strangely silent. I over-
came my nausea long enough to ask if she was all right.
She wasn't.

"Bear!"

I had to call a second time before he heard me. Finally
he turned and, still holding the dripping scalp, made his way
shakily across the ice; the sluggishness in his right leg told
me that some of the paralysis was still with him. "What is
it?" he demanded, his chest heaving.

"Your squaw's dead."

I had been in no mood to break it to him gently. Now I
regretted my bluntness. He dropped the scalp and fell to his
knees at Little Tree's side, gathered her in his arms and tried
to get her to raise herself. It was no use; the blood was already beginning to congeal where a bullet from a Flathead
rifle had made jelly out of the back of her head on its way
out of her brain.

"I hope the scalp was worth it," I said.

I regretted that too, but for a more personal reason, as
without warning he let go of the corpse and swept his knife
around in a broad arc with the intent of decapitating me. I
ducked just as the blade swished past, knocking off my
hat. Before he could come back the other way I fisted my
revolver and, taking advantage of his hunched-over position,

threw all my weight into a punch straight at his bearded jaw. I felt the jar all the way to my shoulder as I connected. That was more than I could say for Bear, who shook his head as if to rid himself of a moth trapped in his whiskers, gathered the front of my collar in one tremendous fist, and without so much as a grunt of exertion lifted me off my feet and held me dangling twenty-four inches above the ground. His eyes were bloodshot, his face purple.

"Now," he said, balancing the knife in his other hand, "let's see what you et for breakfast."

"You'll have to take my word for it." I stretched out my right arm, which was only now beginning to ache, and planted the muzzle of the Deane-Adams between his bushy brows. "This time there's no broken firing pin."

I could tell it wasn't working. He was going to use the knife, and it didn't matter whether I pulled the trigger or not, because with his last reflex he was going to let open my belly. We were both dead. All that remained was the burying. Judge Blackthorne was going to be confused as hell when he learned what had happened to me. I began to squeeze the trigger.

The cylinder was already turning when the scalp-hunter's face twisted into a mask of pain and he lost his grip on the knife. It hit the snow only an instant before he did. I pulled loose from his weakened hold on my collar, landed on my feet, and prepared to finish the job I had started, for the gun was still in my hand.

He was stretched before me, unable to move. All my experience told me to fire and get it over with. Even if he wasn't bluffing, and the bullet in his back had in fact shifted, we would both be better off if I put him out his misery and rode on. There was no doubt in my mind that that was the only thing to do, so of course I didn't do it. I let the hammer down gently and put the gun away.

"How bad is it this time?" I asked him.

"Don't know." His feet shifted slightly in the snow. "I'm starting to feel something. A tingle."

"You're lucky. It probably moved again when you hit the ground. It could just as easily have cut a cord and killed you. Can you ride?"

"Go to hell."

"I'm sorry about Little Tree," I said. "But she's dead and those Indians are due back any time. If you can't ride, I'll have to rig another litter. From now on we keep moving until we get to town."

"Do what you want. I'm staying."

"Like hell you are. Little Tree and I didn't bring you this far just to let you commit suicide. She's dead because of you. Are you saying that doesn't mean anything?"

He didn't reply. I gaped at him.

"That's what you're saying, isn't it?" I arranged my face into a sneer. "You're pathetic. It wasn't enough that you threw away your life on vengeance; you had to toss hers out too. Now that it's come down to a choice, you've chosen to go out in a blaze of glory. Glory, hell! You're giving up."

Roaring in rage, he threw himself over onto his stomach and wriggled through the snow toward where he had left his Spencer. He had his hand on it when I took two steps and pinned it, hand and all, beneath my boot.

" 'Mountain That Walks!' " I taunted, sneering down at him. "You can't even crawl."

He let his face fall forward into the snow.

I reached down, snatched the rifle out of his grip, and jacked out all the shells. "Better pick them up," I advised, tossing the weapon down beside him. "You haven't got that many to spare."

He was still lying there when I mounted the mare and rode off. I can't say now whether I intended to leave him to his fate or if I thought my leaving might shake him out of it and get him to follow me. I was sure he could ride. How I really felt is a moot point, though, because I hadn't made half a mile through the steep drifts that blanketed the foot-hills when I spotted the blue uniforms riding toward me from the direction of Staghorn. I reined in and threw a leg over the horn of my saddle to wait.

They seemed to be taking an inordinately long time about approaching until I realized that they were doing so by de-sign. They had heard shooting and had come running. As far as they were concerned, I was the enemy. My suspicions were confirmed when drawing within rifle range, they spread out, dismounted, and knelt in the snow beside their horses with their rifles braced in firing position. There were fifteen of them, wearing army blue oilskin slickers over their woolen winter uniforms.

"You there!" This from a rail-thin horse soldier near the center of the line, a sunburned youthful type with a hollow, drillmaster's voice, matter-of-fact and without inflection. "Throw down your weapons and dismount!"

I didn't argue. I unholstered the Deane-Adams for the ten thousandth time and flung it away out of temptation's reach. Next came Church's Colt, and then the rifle I had captured from Rocking Wolf. I got out of the saddle as slowly as I could without losing my balance and falling, which would undoubtedly have provoked the order to fire; he had that kind of voice.

"Now the hat. Remove it with two fingers and scale it away."

He was no fool. I did as directed. None of the men left his ready crouch even then.

"Identify yourself."

"Page Murdock, deputy U.S. marshal, Helena." I was careful to keep my hands within sight. "I have a badge, if you'd care to see it."

Apparently he didn't. He gave the order to mount, and after much floundering and soldierly cursing I was surrounded by men on horseback.

"Sergeant, his weapons." Up close, the officer wasn't quite the young man I'd thought him to be; he had a blond moustache and creases beneath his vague gray eyes. His face was gaunt beneath the brim of his campaign hat, his complexion nearly as dark as an Indian's. Little lumps of determination stood out on either side of his jaw.

The sergeant, whose square, black-moustached features looked as if they had come up against more than one bony fist in their time—once quite recently—dismounted and fished the revolvers and rifle out of the snow where I'd thrown them, then handed them to his superior, who examined them in an offhanded fashion.

"Captain Amos Trainer, Fort Benton," he said in his clipped monotone. He made Two Sisters sound emotional by comparison.

"You're a long way from home, Captain."

He ignored that, pretending to be interested in the engraving on the side of the rifle. "We were told by the sheriff in Staghorn to look out for a mean-looking bastard riding a no-good chestnut mare. His description, not mine."

"You didn't seem to have any trouble identifying me by it," I said. "How is Henry?" I bent to retrieve my hat.

"He's dead."

I paused in mid-stoop, then snatched hold of the hat and

shook it free of snow, as if that were the most important job in the world. I put it on and carefully creased the brim. "Who?"

"Nobody you'd know. About a week ago, a punk shell from Wyoming got drunk and called him out."

"Faster?"

He shook his head. "Fast as. They fired at the same time. The punk was dead when he hit the floor. Goodnight died the next morning. He never regained consciousness."

"Two years ago the punk would never have cleared leather. Who's the new sheriff?"

"You're looking at him. When there was no word from the man we sent here, General Clifton sent out his patrol to hunt down and arrest Bear Anderson, the Indian murderer. Goodnight was shot the evening we arrived. I wired the general, who wired the governor, who placed me in charge until the local citizenry can hold an election."

"Bet that pleased the general."

Something bordering on a smile passed across the officer's gaunt features. He swung open the rifle's lever, found the chamber empty, frowned, replaced it. "I was told you'd gone into the mountains after an escaped prisoner. Where is he?"

"You don't want to stand out here in this blizzard while I tell you that one," I assured him.

"We heard some shooting a while ago. You can start with that."

"I had a run-in with Two Sisters about a half-mile back."

"Alone? How many guns can you fire at one time, Deputy?"

I sighed. "I'm tired of arguing, Captain. Bear Anderson's back there, and he needs medical help."

He glared at me. "I think you'd better start explaining."

I took a deep breath and told him what I could, including the fate of the bounty hunters his commanding officer had hired. He listened in silence.

"Mount up, Sergeant," he said when I had finished.

The sergeant had been standing behind me. Now he stepped into leather, oilskin rustling, and accepted the revolvers and rifles from his superior.

"I'm going along," I said.

"That's what you think. Sergeant!"

"Yes, sir." The sergeant saluted. He spoke with a Georgia drawl; I found myself wondering what rank he had held in the Confederate Army, and if we might have met somewhere before, across a smoke-enshrouded battlefield. He was too old not to have served.

"Detail two men to stay here and keep an eye on Mr. Murdock. Orders are to shoot if he tries anything." He gathered up his reins and reached back to flick open the flap securing his side arm in its holster. It was an Army Colt; what else was there, here in Colt country?

"I'm going along for your protection," I explained. "If you go in there half-cocked, you're going to lose most of your men."

He smiled twistedly. "Against one man, Deputy? One *wounded* man?"

I said, "The Flatheads number over five hundred, and they haven't been able to take him in fifteen years. And wounded or not, he just killed two men, one of them with his bare hands. If he sees me with you—armed—he might go with you peacefully."

"You're not sure?"

"He tried to kill me a little while ago."

"You don't inspire confidence, Deputy."

"That's your job, Captain. I'm just a public servant."

"Very well. Sergeant!" He nodded at the non-com, who handed me my weapons. I accepted them and returned each to its proper holder.

"But, remember," added the officer, "my orders stand to shoot to kill in the event you cross us."

"I expected no less from the U.S. Army," I replied, and mounted the mare.

Heading back toward the river, I asked Captain Trainer what he was doing out there.

"We were on our way back from our first patrol when he heard the shots," he said.

"Isn't that neglecting your responsibilities as sheriff?" I asked.

"Not at all. There's no reason I can't fulfill my duties to the U.S. government as well as to the voters."

"Funny, I thought they were one and the same."

"Column of twos, Sergeant," he said, ignoring my comment.

We came upon him just as he was preparing to straddle the dun. Little Tree's body was nowhere to be seen; a mound of snow, marked at one end by a pine bough standing upright, explained his delay in leaving. He saw us approaching, but made no move toward the Spencer in his saddle scabbard. He mounted carefully and sat watching us.

"You said he was wounded," snapped Trainer, drawing his Colt. He signaled halt.

"I said wounded. Not dead."

"Look at the size of him." This from the sergeant. "I wish I'd brought my buffalo gun."

"Just keep him covered." Trainer raised his voice. "Bear Anderson! This is the U.S. Army! Throw down your weapons and surrender!"

The wind whistled.

"Prepare to dismount, Sergeant."

"Prepare to dismount!" bawled the sergeant. Leather creaked.

"You with them, Page?" The scalp-hunter spoke quietly.

I said I was. He nodded. "Just as well. I was getting too slow anyway." He slid the Spencer from its scabbard—the captain cocked the hammer of his Colt—and, swinging the rifle by its barrel, hurled it out into the middle of the river. It struck with a crash, bobbed once, and slid beneath the surface.

The unexpected action distracted us. While we were watching it, Bear unsheathed his bowie knife and plunged it into his breast.

# CHAPTER 14

I had started forward before he hit the ground. Trainer grabbed my arm.

"Stay back! It might be a trick."

I pulled my arm free and kicked the mare forward. Bear was lying in a hunched position at his horse's feet, breathing heavily. The big dun, anxious, shifted its weight from one front hoof to the other and snorted steam. I dismounted and turned the scalp-hunter over onto his back. The bowie was jammed up to its hilt just below the curve of his chest; blood was spreading slowly.

"Who's got a clean kerchief?" I demanded of the troopers who had come forward to look down at the legend of the Bitterroot.

"Ain't nobody got a clean kerchief after three days on patrol," the sergeant said, dismounting. "But here." He untied the yellow cloth from around his neck and handed it to me.

Pulling the knife from Bear's breast was only a little easier than loosening an axe sunk in a maple stump, but by grabbing hold of the hilt and bracing my other hand against his shoulder I succeeded in drawing it out. Then the bleeding began in earnest. I tore open his bearskin and shirt and poked the end of the kerchief into the wound. He shuddered.

"Some scalp-hunter you are," I told him. "You can't even kill yourself. That bearskin saved your life."

"I always did hate it," he said, grunting through his teeth.

I undid my belt, pulled it free, and strapped it around his chest inside his shirt to secure the makeshift bandage. It barely reached. I had to use the bloody knife to make a new hole in the leather before I could fasten it.

"How long do you think that will hold?" Trainer asked.

"Long enough to get him into Staghorn, I hope," I said. "If he lives that long."

"He won't."

"Ordinarily, I'd agree with you. But people like Bear Anderson don't just die."

"I can't understand it. If he wanted to commit suicide, why didn't he just let us shoot him?"

"I like to do some things for myself," Bear grunted. Then he lost consciousness.

"Will you look at that!" the sergeant exclaimed suddenly.

I looked up. He was pointing across the river.

A pack of wolves thronged the opposite bank, snarling and slashing at one another over the bounty hunters' now-frozen bodies. On the outer edge of the pack, Lop Ear himself, head down and teeth bared, eyed the soldiers warily. His hackles bristled. The sergeant hooked his rifle out of its scabbard, nestled the butt against his shoulders, and fired.

The pack scattered, all except Lop Ear, who stood his ground. The sergeant fired again. This time the big leader howled and tried to rear, but the bullet had smashed a hind leg. The rifle crashed a third time. The wolf fell over onto its right shoulder, kicked, and lay still. Steam rose from its body.

"Wolves," spat the sergeant, lowering the rifle. "I hate 'em."

Expecting Bear to ride with a bullet in his back and a knife wound in his chest was out of the question, so the soldiers and I set about constructing a new litter while the captain paced the riverbank, twisting a gloved fist in a gloved palm and firing anxious glances from time to time across the water, where the Indians remained an unseen presence. On that side, gangs of wolves heaved and tore at the carcasses of the bounty hunters and their dead leader, bolting great bloody chunks of meat and hair in their eagerness to fill their bellies before they were shouldered aside by the others. Pleading low ammunition, Trainer had put a stop to any more shooting of the animals, and so we were forced to work to the accompaniment of their greedy slurps and snarls. At last we had the scalp-hunter secured to the rig and hitched once again behind the dun; with me in charge of it and troopers leading my mare and the black behind their mounts, we pulled out.

The blizzard had begun to wind down by the time we reached the foothills. That night the cloud cover broke, allowing a ragged splinter of moon to glimmer down and set aglow the rolling whiteness that surrounded us. We made no camp, having fed and watered our horses at the river. As it turned out, though, we needn't have been concerned about pursuit, as by sunrise—a brilliant, sparkling sunrise, the first such in many days—we had yet to be overtaken. Already it seemed that Black Kettle's loss had begun to change the character of the Flathead nation. We stopped for a short rest at noon, and by the close of the second day we were on the outskirts of Staghorn, where the smell of wood smoke quickened the pace of even the most exhausted of our mounts.

The main street was deserted, which came as no surprise since it was piled with snow up to the tops of the hitching rails on either side. We came to a halt in front of the darkened barbershop.

"Sergeant, see if you can wake Staghorn's excuse for a doctor," ordered Captain Trainer.

"Not him," I said.

"Open your eyes, Deputy. Right now, Ezra Wilson is the only thing available. Every road to town is blocked."

"I'd rather do the job myself."

The sergeant banged on the door with the butt of his revolver and kept banging until a light came on inside the shop. The door flew inward and Ezra Wilson, in nightshirt and cap, started out onto the threshold.

"What the hell—oh, good evening, Captain." He had spotted the mounted troopers.

"We've a wounded man here, Wilson," said the captain. "How are you at surgery?"

"At this hour?"

"At any hour. Never mind. Get moving, Sergeant. I want two strong men on each end of that litter. Get him inside."

It was the work of two minutes for the delegated men to unhitch the litter, hoist it, and staggering beneath their burden, shuttle it past Wilson into the shop. The troopers transferred the patient from the litter to the bed in the back room.

"Who in perdition is *that*?" Wilson stared popeyed at the giant that was revealed when the blankets covering him were peeled back. Bear was conscious and breathing with great effort.

"That there's the man who might just make you famous if you pull him through, Doc," volunteered the sergeant. "That there's Bear Anderson."

The eyes started farther. "Anderson? The scalp-hunter?"

"Is there any other?" I retorted. "Look, he's got a bullet in his back, and I think it's leaning up against his spine. Can you take it out?"

"I don't know. I never tried anything like that. And I'm not about to try now. I don't treat murderers."

"You'll treat this one." I drew my gun.

Wilson stared at it for a moment. Then he smiled. "You wouldn't shoot."

I shattered the glass chimney of the lamp he was holding with one shot. He lost his grip on the base and had to stoop to catch it before it hit the floor. The flame flickered violently.

"Are you crazy?" Trainer exclaimed. "You could have burned us up!"

I removed the empty shell from the cylinder and replaced it with a fresh cartridge. "I have faith in Wilson. He's good with his hands. That's why he's a barber." I spun the cylinder. "What about it, Ezra? Are you going to operate?"

He was standing there holding the still-burning lamp in both hands. He opened his mouth, closed it. "I'll wash up." He set down the lamp and stepped out through the side door.

"You're something new in lawmen," said the captain, studying me curiously.

I holstered the gun, looked around, found another lamp, and transferred its chimney to the one the barber had just relinquished. "You and my boss would get along famously," I told him. "He says the same thing."

Ezra Wilson returned a few minutes later wearing the same clothes he'd had on when I left his shop the last time. "Turn him over," he mumbled, opening his medical bag and setting out the contents on the table beside the bed.

"See to his chest first," I said. "He's been stabbed."

"Anything else?" His tone was ironic.

"What would you like?"

"Room. I need room to work."

Captain Trainer dismissed everyone except the sergeant.

Then the non-com and I helped Wilson strip off Bear's shirt and bearskin. His chest was a battlefield of scars old and new, but the barber was interested in only one. He undid the belt I had fastened around the huge torso and slowly drew out the kerchief.

"Christ," he said, looking at the bloody relic. "Why didn't you stuff your hat in while you were at it?"

He opened a bottle of alcohol and poured it into the wound. The scalp-hunter arched his back, sucking air in through his teeth.

"Laudanum!" Wilson barked. "Cabinet, top shelf. Hurry!"

The captain reached down the square bottle and handed it to him. He pulled out the stopper with his teeth, measured a portion of its contents into a shot glass on the table, put it to Bear's lips. The big man gulped it down greedily, his head supported by the barber's other hand. Almost immediately he relaxed and his breathing returned to normal. Wilson looked at me sideways.

"It does have its uses, you see," he said.

He finished cleaning the wound and applied a patch, securing it with sticking-plaster, then nodded to us. The sergeant and I helped him turn the patient over onto his chest. "Turn up the lamp," said Wilson. I obeyed. A warm yellow glow spread over the bed. Fresh shadows crawled up the wall on the other side.

"It's healed over," the barber observed. "I'll have to re-open." He reached for the laudanum bottle and glass. I took hold of his arm.

"He's had enough," I said.

He looked at me. "It's not for him."

I hesitated. He held his hands up in front of my face. They were shaking. I released my grip.

I watched the expressions on the two soldiers' faces as the barber poured himself a measure of the narcotic—nearly twice what he'd given Bear—and tossed it down as if it were a shot of watered-down whiskey. To say that they were thunderstruck would be an understatement. But they kept their mouths shut.

There was a clock somewhere in the building; the ticks reverberated like explosions in that overheated room as Wilson cut with his scalpel and probed inside the wound with alcohol-soaked fingers. At length he straightened and wiped the blood off on a towel.

"It's deep," he said. "Maybe too deep. I'm just a barber. I don't know anything about backs."

"Can you get it out?" I asked.

"No question about that. The question is, what'll happen when I do it? It's fifty-fifty I might kill or cripple him." He looked at the captain. "Will you take the responsibility?"

That was a tough one. I could see Trainer weighing the odds. It was a decision that could affect his career, and not for the better. Finally he nodded. "Go ahead," he said. "Whatever happens, I'll back you up."

Under Wilson's direction, I poured more alcohol over his hands while he held them over a basin on the table. He shook them dry. Then he seized a pair of metal tongs and had me repeat the procedure with them.

"Hold up the lamp," he told me. As I did so, allowing the light to flood into the gaping hole, he spread the flesh around it with his fingers. A drop of sweat rolled down his nose. He wiped it off on his rolled-up sleeve.

"There it is," he said. "See it?"

I leaned over for a closer look. Framed between his fingers, a dark and shadowy something showed deep in the wound. "So that's what they look like after they hit," I said.

"Of course. What did you expect?"

"I don't know. I put them in. I don't take them out."

"You've got the easy job."

He inserted the tongs. As he worked, a fresh bud of perspiration started out on the bridge of his nose and began the long crawl downward. I removed my kerchief—this time clean didn't matter—and mopped his face gently. His breath came sibilantly through his nostrils. After what seemed an eternity he drew out the tongs, straightened, and with an exhausted sweep of his right arm hurled the offending substance clanging into the basin.

"What's the verdict?" I asked him.

He picked up the discarded scalpel from the basin and extended it to me. "Care to do the honors?"

I stared at him uncomprehendingly. Finally he shrugged and used the pointed end of the instrument to prick Bear's right leg. It jumped.

"He's a lucky man," he said, tossing back the scalpel. "He'll be able to walk to the gallows."

The sergeant's breath came out in a whoosh. "Good work, Doc! Remind me to talk to you about sending a case of that loudium stuff to Doc Hollander back at Fort Benton."

Wilson ceased bandaging to glare at him. "That's not funny, Sergeant," he said. "Not funny at all."

"How long before he can be moved?" asked Trainer.

"Couple of days. This is twice you've booted me out of my bed, Murdock. This time I hope I get paid."

"I'll settle my bill before I leave town," I assured him. "For the rest, you'll have to talk to the captain. He's his prisoner, not mine."

The captain adjusted his slicker. "If you're not too tired, Deputy, I'd like to see you in the sheriff's office in a few minutes."

"I'm not paying the bill."

"Your sense of humor wears thin after a while." He strode toward the front of the shop and the exit. "Sergeant, I want a guard posted in front of this building at all times. I'll send someone to spell you in an hour."

The sergeant grumbled something unintelligible, which may or may not have contained the words, "Yes, sir."

I remained behind a few minutes to make sure Bear was resting comfortably, then left to join the captain at the jail. At the door, I almost bumped into a big trooper who was on his way out. I had never seen this one before. He had a coarse face overhung by massive black brows and shoulders like a workhorse; by most standards I suppose he was huge, but I had just spent ten days with the biggest, so I was less than impressed. He brushed past me without a word.

Inside, Henry's coffee pot was sizzling away atop the stove, filling the room with its familiar acrid odor. Henry's rifles and shotgun were locked in the rack where he'd left them. Captain Trainer, still wearing the slicker, was sitting behind Henry's desk smoking one of Henry's cigars and reading one of the wanted circulars Henry had stacked there. A puddle was spreading beneath Trainer's hat where he had dropped it atop the desk.

"Who's the buffalo?" I asked.

"That's Corporal Patterson. He's been filling in as sheriff in my absence. He'll be back after supper. Sit down."

"He looks capable." I dropped into the chair before the desk and tilted my hat forward over my eyes. Moisture seeped from the brim down into my collar; I let it.

"He should be," he said. "He was a sergeant-major before I broke him for striking an officer."

"Anyone I know?"

He let that one slide. I heard the water dripping from his oilskin to the floor.

"We're both exhausted," he began, "so I'll make this short and sweet. Will you agree to testify against Bear Anderson at his trial?"

That sank in slowly. "What do you care one way or the other?" I asked finally. "You won't have anything to do with it once you turn him over to the civil authorities."

"I'm not turning him over to the civil authorities. As soon as he's well enough, he'll be tried in military court-martial."

I straightened my hat and sat up. "Anderson's a civilian. The military has no jurisdiction over him."

He sent a jet of blue smoke toward the darkened ceiling. "It's perfectly legal. Federal law states that the military may intervene in cases where the civil courts have ceased to function. Staghorn has no permanent judge, and the circuit judge can't get in until the passes are cleared. Technically, due process of law has been suspended."

"Nothing in the law says you can't wait until spring."

"Nothing in the law says I have to."

"Whoever heard of a captain presiding over a military court-martial?"

"The circumstances are unique. There will be no peace between the Indians and the settlers while Anderson goes unpunished. Delay on our part will be construed by Two Sisters as official sanction for his actions. And it's not just him. The Blackfeet are getting restless and so are the Crows. The fact that they're no friends of the Flatheads means little as long as a renegade white is allowed to go around killing Indians. If we don't act now, next year's thaw will bring a full-scale war like this territory hasn't seen since the Little

Big Horn. A wire to General Clifton should remove most of the legal obstacles that remain."

"You've got it all figured out, haven't you? All that's left is to measure the rope."

"Fifteen feet, I should think, allowing for the knots and Anderson's height and weight."

I showed him my gun. His expression didn't change.

"That's not your style, Murdock. Even if it were, you'd have no place to go afterwards."

"Murder is relative," I told him. But I put the gun away. Instead, I gripped the edges of the desk and leaned forward until our faces were only inches apart. "I'll tell you what is my style. I'm no lawyer, but I've seen my share of them in action in Judge Blackthorne's court. When that court-martial convenes, I'm representing Bear Anderson."

The twisted smile returned. "Suit yourself. The outcome will be the same regardless of what you do or say."

I straightened. "You're the enemy," I said. "Not Bear. Not the Indians. You."

His cigar had gone out. He relit it, lifting the chimney of the lamp on the desk and leaning forward to engage the flame. "That's all for now, Deputy," he said, between puffs. "I suppose we'll meet again in court."

# CHAPTER 15

He was scheduled to hang shortly after dawn on a bleak day in December.

As expected, the trial had been a joke. Chief witness for the prosecution was old White Mane, whose whiskey-roughened voice shook as he described the aftermath of what was already being whispered about abroad as the Spring Thaw Massacre, and repeated the dying words of its sole survivor. It mattered little that this was pure hearsay, or that a significant number of the details had changed since the first time he had recounted the story to Bart Goddard, or even that every time he opened his mouth the air reeked of the profitable side of Goddard's mercantile. It didn't matter at all that I raised objections remarking upon each of these points. Trainer turned such arguments aside with the grace of a boxer feeling out his opponent—never actually landing a punch, but rendering mine ineffective through simple footwork. The emotion-swaying tricks I'd learned observing the transplanted eastern attorneys in Helena were useless in the stylized atmosphere of a military court-martial. Bear was twisting in the wind before the first bang of the gavel.

Before the trial, I had made several attempts to wire Judge Blackthorne to inform him of Trainer's unorthodox proceedings, only to be turned away each time by armed guards stationed at the door of the telegraph office. The captain, they told me, had declared martial law in view of the "Flathead danger," and put a stop to all messages traveling into and out of town. The restriction was eventually lifted, but by that time high winds had taken down the telegraph lines, thus severing Staghorn's last link with civilization. Trainer couldn't have planned it any better.

But weather is a fickle thing that recognizes no ally.

For two weeks following the passage of sentence, blizzards kept the troopers from carrying it out. Even then, two of the men assigned to construct a gallows behind the jail were killed when a sudden blast of wind from the North tore the supports from beneath them, hurled them to the ground, and brought half a ton of fresh lumber crashing down on top of them. Not counting the Indians we'd slaughtered back at the crossing, that made it nine dead just since I'd renewed my acquaintance with Bear Anderson. Bringing him to task was proving an expensive proposition for whoever tried it.

At length, however, the gallows were built, and beneath a pale sun the citizens of Staghorn gathered in the old firebreak behind the jail, stamping their feet and pounding their shoulders with gloved and mittened fists to keep the circulation moving while they waited for the back door to open. It was an impressive gathering; merchants had closed their shops, and farmers, trappers, and cattlemen had braved the arduous journey to town in order to see history in the making. It wasn't every day you got to see a legend die.

And they were not the only spectators.

Since dawn they had begun to accumulate along the rocky ridge overlooking town, and by the time the jail door opened, the skyline was filled with mounted Indians decked in all their ceremonial finery. For the first time in memory, the Flatheads had not made their regular migration to the plains west of the Bitterroot to await the spring thaw. Two Sisters had chosen to winter in the mountains rather than miss the hanging.

On the gallows itself, backs to the wind, stood Captain Trainer and Corporal Patterson. Patterson was a last-minute substitution for the sergeant, who, upon learning that he was to be the hangman, had gotten drunk and started a brawl that wrecked Goddard's saloon just after the old bastard had finished repairing the damage wrought by Ira Longbow. Trainer had locked him up in the cell adjacent to the scalp-hunter's pending possible court-martial. I saw the sergeant come to the window of his cell from time to time to glance down at the proceedings; from the expression on his face I wondered if he had been as drunk as he'd seemed, or if his one-man riot had been staged to keep him from being the one who sprang the trap.

The local minister—pudgy, bespectacled, and mumbling from a Bible held open in his mittened hands—was the first to descend the long flight of wooden steps that led from the back door of the jail to ground level. Behind him walked Bear, bareheaded and in chains, his hands manacled behind his back. A chorus of mingled gasps and murmurs greeted him as he ducked his head and swiveled sideways to get through the doorway; most of those present had never seen him, and to a generation that considered a man over six feet tall to be gigantic, the sight of Anderson's nearly seven feet of gristle was beyond belief. Trailing him were the remaining eleven troopers. The captain wasn't taking any chances here, as the odd man followed at a safe distance with his side arm in hand, while behind him the others marched in a column of twos with their rifles in parade position at their shoulders. There was no drum; the condemned man was a civilian, after all, and some of the conventions had to be honored. So silence reigned.

Fourteen steps led to the scaffold. The extra had been added as an afterthought to compensate for Bear's great height, even as the strongest rope in town had been sought to support his tremendous weight. He mounted them with ease in spite of the chains that linked his ankles and wrists. His expression was impossible to read.

The first trooper followed him to the top while the others took up a position of attention on the ground in front of the gallows. There, a buckboard with an empty coffin on the back and a teamster with a bad cold waited to transport the body to the cemetery south of town. At intervals the teamster helped himself to a healthy swig from a bottle he had on the seat beside him to relieve his sniffles; the gurgling noise it made as he tipped it up sounded ridiculously loud in the charged atmosphere of the firebreak.

I was standing in the alley between the jail and the deserted dress shop next door, a vantage point the crowd had overlooked, probably because of the icy gusts that whistled unhampered through the narrow gap. From there I had a good view of the scaffold and the Indians on the ridge. I spotted Two Sisters mounted at the northern end of the line, wearing ceremonial feathers and a coat pieced together from the kind of pelts the Flatheads considered too fine to waste in trade with the other nations. His feelings concerning the scene unfolding below him must have been mixed; no doubt he was pleased to see his people's killer punished, but at the same time he was losing the one excuse he needed to unite the northwestern tribes in a war against the whites.

"Any last words?" Trainer asked Bear, as the noose was slipped over his head.

"I come here to die, not make a speech," he said. "Let's ride."

The reply was a disappointment to some of the spectators, who had evidently been hoping to hear something of historical or biblical origin. I saw Jack Dodsworth of the Staghorn *Republican* flip shut his notepad with a disgusted gesture. They couldn't know that those last two words were a summary of Bear's whole life.

There was nothing else to do, but do it. A glance passed between Trainer and the corporal, and at a nod from the captain the noose was drawn tight and a black cloth hood was tugged down over the magnificent leonine head. Patterson stepped away from the trap and stood with his hand on the wooden lever, waiting. Trainer's arm came up, stopped. For a space they might have been puppets on a miniature stage, Goliath and his armorers in a biblical reenactment, awaiting David's entrance. Then the arm came down. The lever was released with a squeak.

The trap fell, banging at the end of the leather straps that held it. Bear plunged through the opening. The rope jerked taut, stretched—and broke.

The shattered end sprang upward, wrapping itself around the gallows' wooden arm. Bear, still wearing the noose, hit the ground hard and lay kicking in the mud and slush. He was strangling.

I was halfway down to the firebreak when Trainer recovered from his initial shock and ran down the steps, taking them two at a time. By the time he got there, Ezra Wilson, who had been standing by waiting to sign the death certificate, was kneeling beside the body and struggling to loosen the noose with his hands. The officer reached past him and sawed at the rope with his knife. It parted and fell. Wilson tore away the black hood.

"Pierce!" shouted the captain. "Another rope! On the double!"

A trooper left formation and took off at a sprint up the slope. The others dropped their rifles to hip level and moved forward to drive back the pressing crowd. I slipped past them.

"You tried once," I panted, reaching Trainer. "Isn't that enough?"

He turned his vague gray eyes in my direction, but said nothing.

"Somebody'd better do something, and fast." Wilson was straining every muscle to hold down Bear's heaving shoulders. "His neck is broken."

"Hurry up with that rope!" the captain roared.

The trooper returned a moment later bearing a coil of rope, and he and Patterson secured one end and slung the other over the gallows arm. While a noose was being fashioned, Trainer, another trooper, and I lifted Bear to his feet and hustled him up the steps. If I couldn't help him any other way, I could at least help him die.

This time Patterson didn't bother with the hood and he didn't wait for the order to drop the trap. As soon as the noose was in place he tripped the lever.

This time the rope held. The gallows creaked, the scaffold swayed; for a moment it seemed as if the entire structure might collapse. Bear kicked twice and dangled.

A gust of wind caught the gallows arm and twisted it around, straining still further the nails and pegs that held the structure together. Then it died. The great body swung in silence.

The minister remembered his job suddenly and began reading from the Book of Genesis.

I think it was that first failure on the part of the hangman that led to the rumor, which persists, that Bear Anderson survived that day, and that someone else was hanged in his stead. It doesn't seem to matter that any attempt to sneak him out would have had to have taken place in front of more than a hundred witnesses, not counting the Indians, and that nobody but a perfect double could have taken his place the second time, as that time he was hanged without the hood over his head. Legends don't perish that easily. As late as last year he was seen in St. Louis driving a trolley, and there's no indication that these sightings will cease until time makes his further survival impossible.

I do nothing to discourage such talk. Although I stopped carrying a badge six years ago, when Judge Blackthorne died and they brought in an assistant district attorney from New Hampshire to replace him, people still seek me out on occasion to ask about Bear and the time we rode together up in the Bitterroot. When the conversation approaches the hanging, I change the subject. They'd resent me if I tried to force the truth down their throats, and in any case they wouldn't believe me. It's easier among the Indians, where there is no written history and the storytellers can leave out the last part in order to keep the myth going. Now that Two Sisters and most of the braves who were there that day are gone, and the Flatheads themselves are socked away on reservations, it's an easy thing for them to believe that Mountain That Walks still prowls those rocks on the back of his big dun horse, his belt a tangle of bloody scalps, looking for fresh victims. He's become part of their heritage, and when the bad feelings are done between red and white, and scholars begin collecting these stories and putting them down on paper, you can bet that Bear will be there in some form. That's when he'll prove to be as indestructible as the legends say.

On that day, however, there was no doubt. When it was certain that the rope had done its job, Captain Trainer undid the knot that anchored it and allowed the body to fall of its own weight to the ground. Wilson bent over it, pried open each eyelid, and straightened.

"He's dead."

The statement carried up to the ridge, and after a few minutes Chief Two Sisters wheeled his horse and led his braves back into the shelter of the high rocks.

# STAMPING GROUND

*For Louise Baraksadic Stamenoff,*
*my grandmother—the last pioneer*

## From an Old Commander

As near as I can estimate, there were in 1865 about nine and a half million of buffaloes on the plains between the Missouri River and the Rocky Mountains; all are now gone—killed for their meat, their skins and bones.

This seems like desecration, cruelty, and murder, yet they have been replaced by twice as many *neat* cattle. At that date there were about 165,000 Pawnees, Sioux, Cheyennes, Kiowas, and Arapahoes, who depended on these buffaloes for their yearly food. They, too, are gone, and have been replaced by twice or thrice as many white men and women, who have made the earth to blossom as the rose, and who can be counted, taxed and governed by the laws of nature and civilization. This change has been salutary and will go on to the end.

—GENERAL WILLIAM TECUMSEH SHERMAN
to William F. Cody, June 29, 1887, as quoted
in the latter's autobiography, *Life and Adventures
of Buffalo Bill*

# CHAPTER 1

"**S**immer down, Page. Northern Dakota isn't the end of the world."

As he spoke, Judge Blackthorne ran the fingers of his gavel hand through his raven chin-whiskers. I suppose he thought that made him appear wise and fatherly, but the effect was more satanic than usual. His gaunt, Lincolnesque features were set off by steady gray eyes with soaring brows and a high, shiny forehead peaked with a great mane of black hair of which he was more than a little vain, there being not a breath of silver in it. His dress when he was not on the bench was dudish: Prince Albert coats and Vanderbilt ascots tucked inside the collars of ruffled shirts and secured with a tiny golden horseshoe studded with diamond chips. His resemblance to Lucifer was heightened by a constant, tight-lipped smile. Something had gone wrong with his teeth when he was down in Mexico helping the U.S. Army show the natives their error in refusing to cede several hundred million acres of land now known as California, Nevada, Utah, New Mexico, Arizona, Colorado, and Wyoming to their neighbors to the north. He had a nice new set of white porcelains, but found them uncomfortable and never wore them except when eating or in the courtroom; they made a most authoritative clack when he set his jaw. The result when he smiled without them was straight out of

*Paradise Lost.* The last time he had presented me with this particular expression was during the Panic of '73, just before he cut my salary. And now he was telling me that northern Dakota was not the end of the world.

"That's easy for you to say," I retorted. "You aren't going there."

I'd almost said, "You've never been there," but changed my mind. I was fairly certain he hadn't, but he was forever surprising me, bringing forth reminiscences I hadn't known he possessed to support his argument, and I wasn't about to blunder into *that* trap. If he had visited our neighboring territory, however, he knew why I objected to going there. I'd passed through Dakota on a cattle drive to Montana six years before and had seen enough of sudden blizzards, spring floods, and Mormon crickets to last a lifetime. When I'd learned at the end of the drive in Helena that the trail boss was planning to return to the ranch along the same route, I'd turned in my rope and taken the first job that was offered me, namely that of deputy U.S. marshal for the court of Judge Harlan Blackthorne in the territory of Montana, the place of my birth. Neither his nor the usurped power of President Rutherford Birchard Hayes was going to make me go back without a damned good reason.

He busied himself with the case records on his broad oaken desk. The one on top dealt with a French Canadian fur trapper who had been apprehended in Deer Lodge trying to sell a load of beaver skins bearing the mark of a small band of Blackfeet found murdered the month before near the Canadian border. But Blackthorne had sentenced the Canuck to hang earlier that week, so I knew he was stalling.

I sighed and sat down in the straight-backed wooden chair that faced his desk, hanging my hat on my knee. Daylight shone through a ragged rent in the crown where a renegade Crow had come within an inch of separating my scalp from my skull with a tomahawk before I altered his plans with three grouped shots from my English revolver in the center of his face. "All right, spill it. What's the real reason you're sending me?"

He pretended to interest himself in the case of the executed trapper a moment longer, then abandoned the pose. He had a keen sense of the absurd, which was one of the reasons I tolerated him as an employer. Our gazes locked.

"I owe a friend a favor," he said at length. "Abel Flood, the federal judge in Dakota, is an old classmate. If not for his intervention on my behalf, I would have lost the appointment in Helena back in sixty-four to a young pup from North Carolina." He drawled the name of the state exaggeratedly. His contempt for the South was equaled only by his distrust of youth in general. "He's short on marshals at the moment—they've all been gobbled up by the army for scouts, the Indian situation being what it is—and he's called in my marker. I promised him my best man. You're going to Bismarck."

"Is that supposed to be an argument on your side? I'm supposed to drop everything and go to that privy-pit because you owe somebody a good turn? I thought you knew me better than that."

"You wanted the truth. Besides, it can't be as bad there as you paint it. I understand the territory's going through the biggest land boom in its history."

"The railroads can sell manure to hog farmers."

That isn't exactly the way I said it, but a thing like that sounds better in person than it looks on the printed page. He rose. When he did that he lost a good deal of his authority.

In a pair of high-heeled Texas boots he would still have had to stretch to see over a five-and-a-half-foot fence. It was his turn to sigh.

"I wish you'd be a little more co-operative about this, Page. You know how much I hate to pull rank."

"About as much as a whore hates to charge."

"You leave me no choice." He donned his courtroom scowl. "Page Murdock, I'm placing you under arrest for the murder last year of Lucas Church, the bounty hunter."

That one took me by surprise. "It won't wash," I said, after the shock had worn off. "You know as well as I do that that was a case of self-defense. He was trying to take Bear Anderson away from me for the bounty when I was bringing him in on the scalp-hunting charge. I turned in a detailed report at the time."

"It will be introduced as evidence."

"A case like that will take a week to unravel!"

"More like six. The wheels of justice grind slowly and exceedingly small."

"What will I live on in the meantime?"

"Bread and water, most likely. That's up to the jailer. Of course, I could take another look at your report and reconsider the case."

"While I'm in Dakota?" No answer. I glared at him. "Did you ever find out who your father was?"

"Be sure and pack your waterproof," he said, plainly fighting off the return of the diabolic smile. "I'm told it's wet on the Missouri Plateau this time of year."

Here I had the choice of complying or handing in my badge and being done with it. He had no case and he knew it. But I'd found my niche and, in what the papers back East referred to as the "emerging West," jobs were scarce for thirty-five-year-old ex-rawhiders who knew nothing but how to handle a rope and where to place a bullet so it will do the most good. I could always cheat on my expenses. Anyway, six years was a long time. Maybe Dakota had changed. And maybe elves lived in General Grant's beard.

It was mostly steamboat travel from Helena down the Missouri to the railhead of Bismarck. It would have been rail all the way had not the Panic ground construction and just about everything else to a halt five years before, but wishing didn't straighten out the bends in the river. My fellow passengers, aside from a group of close-mouthed prospectors on their way to the gold strikes in the Black Hills, included an aged Scandinavian with a two-word English vocabulary and a battered brass trumpet screwed constantly into his left ear, and a woman who was on her way to visit her husband, the adjutant at Fort Abraham Lincoln. Neither had much to say in any language, both were ugly, and the only thing we appeared to have in common was an all-consuming dread of our destination.

I didn't recognize the place when I got there. The tent town I had passed through riding drag for Ford Harper, then known as Carleton City, had given way since the coming of the trains and the gold rush of 1874 to a city of neat wooden and log buildings, every other one a saloon, complete with courthouse and the requisite number of churches. In my time the settlement had been a mile or so farther downriver, but when the railroad came through in 1873 it was decided to move the tracks north of the ford to beat the land-grabbers out of their profit. When it came to stealing, the Northern Pacific brooked no competition. The new location was dubbed Point Pleasant, but troopers from nearby Fort McKeen called it Whiskey Point for obvious reasons. Gold mines opening around Deadwood two hundred miles south brought in the rough element, and the city's bloodstained history dates from that time. Now, construction was going on everywhere and the streets were jammed with traffic, evidence enough that the much-vaunted Dakota land boom was more than a figment of some railroad magnate's imagination.

I picked out a likely looking hotel from the dozen or so that confronted me upon leaving my torture cell of the past several days and struck off in that direction carrying my valise. It was a hot day for June—in northern Dakota it was unprecedented. Stepping into the narrow coolness of the shallow lobby was like plunging fully clothed into a lake. The room was deserted except for a sallow youth who sat behind the desk flipping through the latest dime novel from Fargo. He didn't look up as I approached.

The thud of my valise hitting the floor from two feet up brought him lazily to his feet. He marked his place in the novel with a forefinger. "Yes?" He was younger than I'd thought. He had long, slicked-back dishwater-brown hair and a thin face mottled with clusters of pimples. His eyelids drooped insolently behind steel-rimmed spectacles. The gray suit he was almost wearing had to have looked better in the catalogue or the fellow who had worn it before him would never have ordered it.

I asked for a room. His upper lip curled.

"We're full up. Happens every spring, when the prospectors come in from Deadwood to pick up equipment. Try us in September." He opened his book and started to sit back down.

"Tell me something." I leaned my elbows on the desk. This put my grimy, unshaven face inches from his relatively clean one. He paused, knees bent. "What would you do if an important visitor from another country showed up without warning and asked for a room?"

The lip curled farther. I decided that was his smile. "Well, in a case like that, I suppose we could always scrape up something."

I eased my gun from its holster and laid it atop the desk. "This was made in London. We room together."

His eyes dropped to the gun, then roamed the lobby, looking for law. That made him fresh from the East. After a few months on the frontier you get out of the habit. I grunted, reached inside my breast pocket, and plunked the tin star down beside the gun. One glance was enough. He swung the big register around, dipped a pen into his inkwell, and handed it to me.

I scribbled my name and flung down the pen, squirting watered-down ink over the page. "Where's the nearest tub?"

"The Chinese Baths are just around the corner." He frowned at the spots on the yellowed cream paper. Then the lip curled again. "Of course, there's Amity Morgan's place on Third Street. If you're not too tired—"

"I'm too tired." I put away the gun and badge, lifted my valise, and headed toward the stairs, leaving him there with his mouth open. Apparently there were some things you didn't admit to in Bismarck, and being too tired for a roll between perfumed sheets was one of them. I was too tired to care.

The End of Track Saloon, located at the north end of Mandan Street, was as new as its name. Construction was still going on inside and the smells of fresh lumber and turpentine held their own against the more insidious odors of beer and sweat and brimming spittoons. It was dark inside, oil being sold at gold-rush prices out here where it was hard to get. I welcomed its cool interior even more than the hotel's, since the Chinese Baths had opened my pores and I was sweating freely beneath my clean clothes. Even at that

early hour the place was packed. Gritty miners up from
Deadwood literally rubbed elbows with fat land speculators
just off the train and dusty troopers on leave from the adjacent Fort Lincoln. I shouldered my way up to the bar and
shouted for whiskey over the clatter of the carpenters' hammers. A bartender with furry forearms and heavy Prussian
features splashed amber liquid into an un-chipped glass,
shoved it at me, and scooped up the coin I dropped without
a wasted movement. I wondered if he was one of the im-
migrants a destitute Northern Pacific had lured there by
naming the settlement after Germany's Iron Chancellor. If
he was, it didn't look as if he thought he'd gotten the best of
the deal.

Liquor in a new glass was too rare a thing to waste at a
crowded bar. I had beaten two unsuccessful-looking prospectors to a freshly vacated table in the far corner and
was toasting my good fortune when a pair of hand-tooled
Mexican boots with a man standing in them stopped beside my chair. I ignored him and went on drinking. There
was a good deal of Missouri River in with the Minnesota
whiskey.

"Deputy Murdock."

It was a declaration rather than a question. Something
about the tone in which it was delivered lifted the hairs on
the back of my neck. I raised my eyes from the glass as
slowly as possible. That trick had saved my hide more than
once, for the tension it created could usually be counted
upon to force the hand of a would-be gunslinger before he
was ready. If it didn't, then I was up against someone with
experience, which was good to know. This time it didn't. I
raised them past pinstriped brown pants and a well-fed belly
over which was buttoned a vest and a hip-length coat, to a
huge black handlebar moustache and a vulture's beak of a

nose the color of raw iron. A pair of bright blue eyes glittered beneath the shade of a black hat so new it gleamed in the pale light filtering through the open front door. There being no holster visible, I looked to the next most likely place and noticed a familiar bulge beneath the man's left armpit. I noticed something else as well: two points of a star poking out from under the lapel of his coat.

"I'm Murdock. Who are you?"

"A. C. Hudspeth, federal marshal, Dakota Territory. I got a complaint you threatened a hotel clerk a little while ago with a gun."

"It got heavy in my holster. I put it on top of the desk to rest. Like this." I lifted the five-shot .45 from my lap and deposited it, still cocked, atop the table. His buzzard's beak turned crimson.

"Where's your badge?"

I flashed metal.

"Why don't you wear it?"

"For the same reason I don't paint a big red bull's-eye on the back of my coat."

"You need a lesson in good manners," he said. "Judge Flood's expecting you over to the courthouse. He's been waiting ever since we got word an hour ago you were in town. He don't like to be left hanging."

"Neither do most of the defendants in his court. But that doesn't keep them off the scaffold."

That was a shot to the groin. Abel Flood's record of hangings was no worse than that of any other judge in the territories, where prisons were a long way apart and lumber for building gallows came cheaper than armed escorts. But when they leave openings like that, I leap through.

All of Hudspeth's emotions showed in his nose, which was beginning to resemble a railroader's lantern. It was a knotted lump of flesh trussed like a rodeo calf with hundreds of tiny burst blood vessels. You saw a lot of noses like it in canteens throughout the West, not uncommonly on men who wore badges, but seldom on federal marshals, who, like cavalry officers, were usually selected for their heroic good looks and little else. I decided he was probably a pretty good lawman, because he certainly had nothing else going for him. I might even have admired him if he weren't such a pain. I let him stew while I tossed down the rest of my drink the way they do in the dime novels, in one confident jerk. You could do that when most of it was water.

His voice was choked, as if he'd emptied the glass himself. "If you're through, the judge wants to see you. Now."

I took just enough time leathering the five-shot and getting up to let him know what I thought of his implied ultimatum without seeming self-conscious about it. I found when I stood that he had a couple of inches on me and that I'd been all wrong in thinking him soft. Although he was thick in the middle, his weight was pretty evenly distributed upon a heavy frame, and solid. His eyes were as clear and bright as bullets fresh from the mold.

"Strictly speaking," Judge Blackthorne had explained before I'd left Helena, "Bismarck shouldn't even have a federal judge, Yankton being the territorial capital. But there's talk in Congress of dividing Dakota in two once it becomes a state, and it's a sure bet it'll *be* the capital of the northern half soon now that the railroad's in. That's why Flood keeps his chambers in the county courthouse."

This structure was a squat log affair within smelling distance of the river, identified by a sign that swung from a rusted iron rod with crude letters burned into the wood. Hudspeth entered without knocking and tracked mud across a big room with a judge's bench, three rows of seats, and

empty echoes in the rafters. An American flag, spanking
new (nothing in Bismarck was old), hung on the wall behind
the bench at a discreet distance from a much-missed spit-
toon near the witness-box. Beyond that was a door before
which the marshal stopped and rapped upon with a ponderous fist. A voice like two blasts on a steam whistle bade
us enter.

Fat law books crowded the shelves of the corner cubicle
in which Flood shared chambers with the county magis-
trate. He got them in sets straight from New York City and
never read them, or so I divined from the lack of wear on
the expensive leather bindings. Unlike Blackthorne, who
had scrimped and worked nights to buy a book at a time
while putting himself through college, and had studied each
until he knew it by heart, Flood had come from a family of
rich eastern politicians who had been only too happy to
grease the skids. "Don't let him fool you, though," the
judge—my judge—had warned. "The old bastard knows
more about human nature than you'll find in any legal record, and that's all it takes to dispense the brand of justice
our founding fathers talked about."

A quarter ton of flesh wrapped in twenty yards of black
broadcloth was seated in a stuffed leather armchair near the
window as we entered, that day's edition of the Bismarck
*Tribune* spread open across his fat knees. His bald head
shone like a wet egg in a nest of cobwebby fringe, and black-
rimmed pince-nez wobbled astride his round pink nose. He
was clean-shaven except for fluffy side-whiskers. The knot
of a narrow black necktie was obscured beneath the folds
of his chin. He looked as if he had never been out of that
chair. The room had been built around him while he sat
there reading his newspaper. Looking at him, I wondered
how I had ever thought of A. C. Hudspeth as fat. A gold

watch was attached by a chain to his swollen vest, and this he was consulting in the palm of a pudgy flipper.

"One hour and six minutes," he bellowed, snapping shut the face of the watch. "I'll have the accountant deduct that from your salary at the end of the month."

I was to learn presently that this was his normal speaking voice, and that he was almost deaf. The trials over which he presided, I was told later, with both sides shouting to be heard by the man who wielded the gavel, could be followed from halfway across town. The *Tribune*'s court reporter had only to sit next to an open window in the newspaper office and take notes.

I didn't say anything, but scooped out a handful of crumpled scraps of paper from my left hip pocket and dumped them over the newspaper in his lap.

"What's all this?"

"Receipts," I said, and repeated it in a louder voice when he cocked his ear. "Food. Boat fare. A bath. Whiskey. Judge Blackthorne said you'd reimburse me."

"For the necessities! The taxpayers of the United States will not subsidize your self-indulgence!"

"All right, forget the bath."

The top of his head grew pink. His scalp and Hudspeth's nose made good barometers. I took pity on him and stopped being smart.

"I'm kidding. The whiskey's on me."

To my surprise, the fat judge broke into a guffaw that set the window behind him to rattling in its frame. He handed the receipts to the marshal.

"See that Deputy Murdock is compensated for his expenses. All of them, including whiskey." He returned his attention to me. "I'm a man of temperance myself, but I can appreciate the importance of that first drink after the journey downriver. Henceforth, however, the spirits will indeed be on you. Well, what do you think of our little community?"

"The prices are too high and it's full of bastards. Aside from that it's a nice little trap."

That didn't amuse him at all. I was having difficulty getting his range.

"Well, no matter," he said finally. "You won't be here long. Tomorrow I'm sending you to Fargo."

"Why Fargo?"

"You're picking someone up."

"A prisoner?"

"No." He smiled secretly—the kind of expression you get by practicing for hours in front of a mirror—and removed his pince-nez to polish them with an acre of white silk handkerchief taken from his breast pocket. His eyes, in contrast to the marshal's, were vague and lifeless. "Not yet, anyway. It'll be your job to make him one. The gentleman's name is Ghost Shirt, but as far as the Dakota Cheyenne are concerned he's the Second Coming of Jesus Christ. The families of one hundred and forty-nine men, women and children massacred by his band in the Black Hills last year might not agree. I hope you find the rest of the territory more to your taste than Bismarck, Deputy. You're likely to see a lot of it before you finish this assignment."

# CHAPTER 2

The Indian they called Ghost Shirt might have died a minor sub-chief of the Cheyenne nation had not George Custer's 7th Cavalry discovered gold in the Black Hills of southern Dakota in 1874.

The following year, frustrated by its consistent failure to reach a treaty with the resident Casts No Shadow and his Cheyenne followers, the federal government opened the hills to gold-seekers in an attempt to force the Indians out. Casts No Shadow, a provincial brave who had never ventured east of the Red River of the North, struck back by attacking and slaughtering the first wagon trainload of prospectors that rolled into his stamping ground. Then the army came, and after the chief's two sons were killed in a skirmish with the cavalry, he lost heart, surrendered himself, and was hanged six weeks later for his part in the massacre. His brother, Kills Bear, who had departed with half the tribe for Montana at the time of the surrender, threw in his lot with Sitting Bull at the Little Big Horn and, in the charged aftermath of Custer's slaughter, fled to Canada in '77 to escape the vengeance of the new administration in Washington City.

With him was Ghost Shirt, a young nephew filled with an all-consuming hatred for the white man nurtured throughout the three years he had spent in the East learn-

ing the ways of the enemy. During the trek north he grew
restless and peeled forty braves off the main shaft for his
own foray into the Black Hills. The immediate result was
the Dry Hole Massacre.

Dry Hole was a tent city erected near the gold strikes fifteen miles from Deadwood, where some seventy miners
had settled with their families while they eked out a bare
living chipping away at an anemic vein above a tributary of
the Belle Fourche River. Ghost Shirt and his warriors came
upon the settlement one morning soon after the men had left
to work their claims. Without warning the Indians swept
down on the women and children who remained behind.
The few miners who heard the commotion in time to go
back and do something about it ran straight into an ambush.
By the time the others returned in force, they found their
tents and wagons in flames and the camp a litter of corpses.
The Indians had salvaged everything of value and fled.

That was the first. Others were to follow. Names like
Teamstrike and Crooked Creek and Blind Man's Hollow
conjured up images of smoldering bodies and babies dashed
against trees and women in the final stages of pregnancy
writhing at the ends of lances skewering them to the ground.
The newspapers back East were crammed with wild-eyed
descriptions of how the renegades ate the hearts and livers
of their victims and wore leggings made of human flesh.
These last were fabrications, but the troopers sent out to
investigate the disturbances knew that the reality was far
worse.

The near eradication of a large cavalry patrol from Fort
Abraham Lincoln by the diminutive band of braves at Elk
Creek in December of '77 opened the floodgates. With Sit-
ting Bull and Kills Bear in Canada, Ghost Shirt became the
Red Man's Great Hope. From all over the Northwest they

flocked to his standard—Cheyenne, Sioux, Arapaho, and even a disgruntled few of the despised Crow, all united for the first time in living memory. Rumor had it that the battle-wise Cheyenne who had accompanied the old chief into exile were trickling south to join the "loinclothed Messiah," as General of the Army Sherman referred to him bitterly during an unguarded moment at a press conference. The War Department made hurried preparations for a stepped-up Indian war. New forts were planned, while existing ones as far away from the seat of trouble as Fort Buford near the border of northern Montana were reinforced to capacity, and a massive recruitment campaign was launched throughout the eastern states in an effort to bring the peacetime army up to its Civil War strength. Within two months of Ghost Shirt's return, all of Dakota had become an armed camp.

On New Year's Day, 1878, four hundred troopers under the command of General Baldur Scott descended on a Cheyenne camp south of Castle Rock and slaughtered everything that moved. When the carnage was over, it developed that Ghost Shirt was not present and that most of those killed were old men, women, and children. Never one to let slip an opportunity, Scott ordered everything burned so that the warriors would have nothing to come back to and then took off in pursuit.

Ghost Shirt now was on the run for the second time in his young life. At the head of his band of homeless braves, he struck out across the Badlands toward Canada, but was forced to turn east when two cavalry regiments from Fort Yates opened fire on them at Thunder Creek, and crossed the Missouri River below Mobridge. A forced march followed, with pursuers and pursued covering a hundred miles in two days. The Indians were nearly overtaken at Napoleon and again at Jamestown, only to escape with bullets singing about their ears. Outnumbered two to one, they made a stand, aptly enough, at the Sheyenne River and were all but annihilated at the cost of one hundred and twenty-six troopers. Ghost Shirt was wounded in the leg and taken prisoner along with three warriors. The rest fell in battle. The survivors were incarcerated at Fort Ransom and tried within the week for the Black Hills massacres. The verdict was guilty. At the age of twenty-two, the nephew of the last chief of the Cheyenne nation was sentenced to hang.

He and his trio of condemned followers were kept in the guardhouse under close watch while work progressed on a special gallows designed to accommodate four men at once. Shortly after the changing of the guard on a starless night in March, an argument broke out among the prisoners, blows were exchanged, and Ghost Shirt collapsed. The guards thrust bayoneted rifles between the bars and held the others at bay while the door was unlocked and a delegation entered to examine the stricken man. Suddenly a strangled cry rang out. A sergeant who had been stooping over Ghost Shirt reeled back, clawing at a bloody shard of wood protruding from the socket where his right eye had been. In the confusion that followed, one of the Indians snatched the rifle out of the hands of a guard and placed the bayonet point against a paralyzed trooper's throat. Then Ghost Shirt, who had sprung to his feet after attacking the sergeant, relieved the private of his side arm and got the drop on the remaining trooper in the guardhouse. It was all over within seconds.

With one of their comrades in his death agonies and two more in the hands of the prisoners, the troopers outside the cell were forced to stand and watch while Ghost Shirt and his companions prodded their hostages before them through the opening and backed across the compound into

the shadows along the east wall with them in tow. Not until
they were out of sight did the soldiers act. They ran for the
wall, raising the alarm as they went, and snapped off shots
at gray figures spotted scaling the ladder to the battlements.
One brave, Standing Calf, fell at the foot of the ladder when
a bullet crashed through his brain. Another, identified later
as Ghost Shirt's cousin Bad Antelope, was struck twice in
the back as he teetered atop the wall, and toppled into the
Sheyenne River on the other side. A third, a Crow called
Silent Dog because his tongue had been cut out when as a
youth he had been captured by the Iroquois, was taken prisoner before he could reach the ladder but was killed later
under mysterious circumstances which the army was still
investigating. Ghost Shirt was nowhere in sight.

The bodies of the two troopers who had been taken hos-
tage were found lying in pools of blood at the bottom of the
ladder, their throats slashed by the captured bayonet.

The next day, a search party discovered Bad Antelope's
corpse bobbing against a rock at a bend in the river a mile
south of the fort. When a week of searching failed to turn up
either Ghost Shirt or his tracks, it was decided that he had
perished while trying to swim the rapid waters of the Sheyenne at spring thaw, and that his body was already halfway
to Minnesota, if it hadn't snaggled on a fallen limb in some
uninhabited part of the territory. The search was called off
after ten days, and Washington began processing new orders
for the now unnecessary reinforcement troops in Dakota.

Then, two weeks after the escape, a Swedish farmer was
found murdered in his cabin two miles east of Fort Ransom.
A neighbor who called on him from time to time became
alarmed when the immigrant, an aged widower, failed to
answer his knock, and entered through the unlocked front

door. The house was a shambles. Someone had gone through the cupboards, scattered their contents over the floor, overturned flour barrels, dumped out the woodbox, torn out drawers, and pawed through the linens and clothing inside. Amid this confusion lay the elderly Swede, naked except for a nightshirt, the latter stained where he had been disemboweled with some sharp instrument the moment he stepped out of his bedroom.

Further investigation revealed that there was not a scrap of food left in the house. Missing also was the dead man's only weapon, a pre–Civil War Colt pistol which he was known to have kept next to his bed. That he had been carrying it when he went out to investigate the strange noises in the other room seemed a reasonable assumption. His buggy horse was gone as well. The hasp on the barn door had been forced with great difficulty and the animal removed by a man wearing moccasins—as shown by the tracks left in the soft earth inside. The considerable effort that had gone into breaking the hasp was borne out by the shattered half of a bayonet blade found in the grass beside the door.

The discovery sparked panic among settlers throughout the territory. The commanding officer at Fort Ransom issued a hasty statement to the press declaring the evidence inconclusive, but as no other explanation was forthcoming his words went unheeded. Washington was bombarded with telegrams demanding protection from the Antichrist in the settlers' midst. Congress, still involved with its investigation into the more interesting legacies of the Grant Administration, sent a terse directive to the General of the Army: Either deal with Ghost Shirt once and for all or learn to get along without allocations from next year's budget. Sherman's immediate reaction to this ultimatum went unrecorded, as this

time no reporters were present. Nevertheless the laborious
process of reassigning men who were already enroute to
their new posts was begun.

The turnaround was too slow. In mid-April, while the
troop strength at Fort Ransom was still at low ebb, Ghost
Shirt, accompanied by twenty renegades believed to have
been recruited from among the disgruntled Sioux south of
the Red River Valley, raided the post armory and made off
with a wagonload of rifles and ammunition, enough to equip
a force five times as large. They struck while the troopers
were busy fighting a fire the braves had set at the north wall,
and, in a bloodless battle—the first such since the trouble
had begun—shot their way out through the gate, wagon,
horses, and all. The weapons stolen were part of a new ship-
ment of unissued .56-caliber Spencer repeating rifles, which
made the outlaw braves among the best-armed Indians in
the West. The average cavalryman was still carrying the
single-shot Springfield that had helped lose the Civil
War for the Confederates. A pursuit patrol dispatched within
minutes of the raid came upon the wagon half a mile west
of the fort, its bed a jumble of empty crates. After that the
fates appeared to be on Ghost Shirt's side, as at that moment one of those sudden downpours for which the region
surrounding the Red River of the North was notorious
opened up and washed out all traces of the Indians' escape
route.

Nothing more was heard of the renegades or their activi-
ties after that. Repeated forays by the U.S. Cavalry between
the Black Hills and the Minnesota border failed to turn
up the slightest hint as to their whereabouts. This time, however, no one was optimistic enough to advance any theories
regarding the death of Ghost Shirt. It was believed that he
was busy raising a brand new army with which he would

launch a series of massacres that would make those in the hills pale by comparison. If the current land boom was any indication, Easterners were confident of the Indians' imminent capture or destruction, but as far as those already in residence were concerned, the entire territory was a powder charge primed and ready to blow as soon as Ghost Shirt lit the fuse.

I was aware of all this, but as it gave me time to study the angles, I let Judge Flood prattle on until his thunderous voice grew raspy at the edges. Then I broke in.

"What's Fargo got to do with it?"

The fat judge cleared his throat, a sound that reminded me of coal sliding down a chute. "A people who call themselves the métis keep a small camp a couple of miles south of there," he said. "They're part Algonquin, part French, and they know more about the territory than any other friendly Indians you're likely to find. You'll want to engage one or two of them as guides. Also, Fort Ransom is only three days' ride to the southwest. The commanding officer, Colonel Broderick, is an acquaintance of mine. I'll give you a letter of introduction and he'll fill you in on the latest details. Any other questions?"

"Several hundred. To begin with, what am I supposed to do that the army can't?"

"The reason that bunch has been so hard to find up until now is that the cavalry can't move without being heard for miles. Too many men, too much equipment. But one man or a small band, provided they know what they're doing, can penetrate that region unobserved. Since half the problem is locating them, you'll have a head start."

"What do I do once I've located them? Surround them?"

"You won't be alone. I'm sending Marshal Hudspeth with you."

"Dandy. That makes the odds only ten to one."

"That's why time is of the essence. Army intelligence has reported a general exodus from Sioux and Cheyenne reservations throughout Montana and Dakota over the last few weeks. It's no mystery why they're leaving. Your job will be to capture Ghost Shirt and bring him here for hanging before they can join up with him. Otherwise there'll be hell to pay."

"I thought he was scheduled to hang at Fort Ransom."

"He was." All this time Flood had been polishing his spectacles. Now he stopped and held them up to the light. Apparently satisfied with their sparkle, he placed them in a hinged leather case, snapped it shut, and slid it into his breast pocket along with the handkerchief, neatly folded. "I've rescheduled it for Bismarck because I feel it's imperative that the citizens of Dakota witness the execution. The present situation hasn't affected the land rush so far, but if Ghost Shirt is captured and hanged in some remote place like Fort Ransom there's going to be talk that he wasn't apprehended at all, that the army's covering up, and accusations like that have a habit of sticking. Right now our sole advantage is that Bismarck is the end of the line. By this time next year that will no longer be true. The Northern Pacific plans to resume operations next spring. Let one suspicious rumor get started and the settlers will keep going as far as the rails will take them. The only way to prevent such a situation is to make this a civil matter and invite the public to the hanging."

"And you expect this Colonel Broderick to co-operate?"

"He has no choice. If Ghost Shirt is not brought to justice soon he faces court-martial for criminal negligence. You will find him most eager to help."

"What's your interest in this?"

A fresh guffaw exploded from him. "Harlan was right, by thunder! You're nobody's fool. Very well, I'll be honest." He folded his hands upon the swell of his stomach, which for him was quite a reach. "I have interests in several hundred acres of land situated along the railroad right-of-way. If the land boom fizzles, so do my interests. But that's only a small part of it. I'm genuinely concerned with the welfare of the territory, and I'll make use of all the power I possess to insure its future. It will never be anything more than a rest stop between stations if everyone who passes through thinks he has to hold onto his scalp with both hands for fear of losing it. It's in your power to change that. Will you accept the assignment?"

"I didn't realize I had a choice."

"Of course you do. I can't order a man to go on a mission from which the odds are he won't return. Hudspeth has volunteered. If you wish, you can be on the next boat back to Helena and no one will think less of you because of it."

"What makes you think I can do the job at all?"

He smiled, I think. At least, something stirred his mammoth jowls. "I've done my homework. Anyone who takes on the entire Flathead nation as you did last year and lives to tell about it is capable."

"You're doing your damnedest to make it impossible for me to refuse."

He shrugged.

"What the hell?" I said. "I couldn't face another boat ride so soon anyway." That kind of breezy nonchalance fit me like a tent, but something was going on here that he wasn't telling, and since I had gone to all the trouble of coming to my least favorite spot on earth I decided I might as well find out the reason. I figured he'd buy my vanity act, that being the West's most available commodity. "When do we leave?"

"Tomorrow morning, on the six-fifteen to Fargo. As I said, time is of the essence."

I put on my hat. "In that case I'll be seeing you. I've got just enough time to grab a meal and a bath and get some sleep."

"I thought you had a bath." This from the marshal, in a suspicious tone. He was still holding my receipts.

"Don't worry. I won't charge this one to the taxpayers."

Hudspeth leered. "Amity Morgan," he said knowingly. "Just be sure and keep an eye on your poke. Her girls would steal the pennies off a dead man's eyes."

"I'm not dead yet."

I looked to the judge to see if that was worth another belly laugh, but he didn't appear to be paying attention, frowning as he was at his enormous paunch and pushing his lips in and out. He was preoccupied with something, and I had a pretty good idea what it was. I'd been overconfident in assuming he hadn't seen through my act. I should have known better. A liar is quick to recognize a peer.

# CHAPTER 3

**H**udspeth didn't like trains. That much was obvious once we had taken seats in the coach and, precisely on the stroke of six-fifteen, jolted into motion. He gripped the arms of his seat as if clutching the brasswork of a storm-tossed clipper and held on, eyes staring straight ahead and the veins in his nose standing out, until we had left the station and topped off at a steady twenty-five miles per hour. Then he relaxed by degrees until his teeth stopped grinding and the color returned to his knuckles.

The seat opposite us, like most of the others in the car, was empty. But the crowded runs west more than made up for the deadheads away from the land of opportunity. I settled back into the plush upholstery and stretched out my legs in the half acre that separated the seats. Space was George Pullman's long suit.

"You don't look like the kind that volunteers," I ventured after five or six miles. I watched the telegraph poles flitting past the window. They were more interesting than the flat scenery beyond, scrawny and misshapen as they were. Trees were scarce in northern Dakota, and the linemen made use of what they could get.

"Neither do you." His voice sounded almost normal. "So how come we're here?"

"I asked you first."

He grumbled some and shifted around on the cushions. But he could see that didn't satisfy me, so he sighed and stared at the floor. That bought him some more time. "I won't lie," he said at length. "I've petered down to considerable less of a lawman than I was when I started out. My eyes ain't half what they was, and you can cook and eat a fair-size meal in the time it takes me to get a gun out of a holster. That's why I hide it under my arm."

"I noticed. It's obvious as hell."

He scowled, as at the unwanted logic of an impertinent child, and went on. "I got two years before my thirty's in, then I can retire and collect my pension. That's if I can stick it out without getting fired. The judge has been handing out some heavy hints lately, mostly about my drinking. He's a damn dyed-in-the-wool teetotaler, and in his thinking every man who takes a sip now and then is a drunk. Anyhow, he doubts my ability to carry out my duties, he says, and with the territory filling with settlers like it is he's wondering if some young jackanapes from out East might be more suitable. Then he brings up this Ghost Shirt business. It's blackmail, pure and simple, but what've I got to put up against it? I'm too old to drive teams any more, and that's all I know how to do besides enforcing the law."

"I guess all judges are alike," I said, and related how I came to be in Dakota. He snorted.

"Them law schools ought to be made illegal. They turn out more crooks than the prisons."

I agreed. "Flood, for instance. Assuming we can pull off the impossible and beat the army to Ghost Shirt, what's he to gain? I don't for one minute buy his story about land interests, and that's easier to swallow than the one about saving this glorious territory." I waved a hand toward the window just as we happened to be passing a group of ragged bone-pickers reaping the rotting harvest of last winter's buffalo slaughter along the railroad right-of-way.

"The White House. That's what he's got to gain." The marshal slid a metal flask from the inside breast pocket of his coat and uncorked it. As he did so, the coat buckled and I caught a glimpse of the gun reposing in a special pocket of his vest beneath his left armpit. Small wonder it bulged. It was an army-size Smith & Wesson .44 caliber, christened the American, big and heavy enough to drive nails with the butt. The Deane-Adams English .45 I carried in my hip holster looked insignificant by comparison. This one was about as suited to be carried beneath a man's arm as a grand piano was to be played in a third-floor cathouse. He took a long pull at the flask's acrid contents—the odor of bad traveling whiskey assaulted my nostrils—replaced the cork, although without conviction, and returned the container to his pocket. His bright little eyes clouded for an instant, then cleared brighter than ever.

"The White House?" I prompted.

He nodded. "Flood ain't been satisfied just being judge since he first clumb onto the bench. He made two tries for governor of the territory and damn near got the appointment the second time. He would of, too, if some nosy reporter on the *Tribune* hadn't wrote that he took money from the Northern Pacific back in seventy-one to clear a track foreman of a charge of murdering a Chinaman on government property."

"Did he?"

"Kill the Chinaman? I reckon so."

"Not that. Did Flood take the money?"

"Oh, that. Who knows. I'd be mighty damn surprised if he didn't. Everybody takes money from the railroads. The only reason the choice went against him is he got caught.

That didn't cool him off any, though. He just aimed higher."
Hudspeth went for the flask again, then changed directions
and, instead, loosened his gun in its leather-lined sheath as
if that had been his intention all along. I recognized the
standard drunk's way of cutting down: Take plenty of liquor
along just in case, but only hit it half as hard. Flood's threats
worried him more than he would admit. "Ever since Custer
got it," he went on, "being an injun fighter brings in more
votes than promising to cut taxes. The judge figures if he
can get to Ghost Shirt ahead of the army and hang him in
Bismarck, he'll collect enough publicity between now and
eighteen eighty to step into Hayes's shoes."

"In that case, why send just us? Why not a posse?"

"That's easy. If the posse gets wiped out, he has to explain to Washington City what they was doing butting in on
the army's business, and probably get himself impeached, or
whatever it is they call firing a judge. This way, if we don't
make it back—which strikes me as more than likely—he
can say we was acting on our own or at most just offering
our services to the authorities already involved. Two more
scalps on Ghost Shirt's belt don't make a hell of a lot of
difference in them drawing rooms back East. Besides, the
judge can spare me, and since you ain't his man anyway he
can afford to toss you down the same hole. It's like betting
someone else's money on a fair hand. He's got nothing to
lose and the whole pot to gain."

"He's told you this?"

"A skunk don't have to announce himself for you to know
he's there. My nose is as good as any lard-bucket newspaper reporter's."

"Greedy, isn't he?"

"Your judge ain't?"

I returned my attention to the landscape beyond the window. We were shuddering now through the buttes—huge, flat-topped stumps of weathered granite whose red sandstone caps glistened with the remnants of a recent rain. Beyond them to the northeast, gunmetal-colored clouds were gathering for a fresh offensive upon the newly planted, still vulnerable crops in the Red River Valley. If it wasn't torrential rains, it was drought. If it wasn't drought, it was grasshoppers, "Mormon crickets," that swarmed in by the hundreds of millions to blight everything in their path. Fate and the elements stood in line for a lick at the unsuspecting settlers who dared take a plow to God's country. For the rest of us He saved the Indians and the politicians.

"I hate Dakota," I said.

The canvas-to-clapboard story in Bismarck found its echo in Fargo but intensified a hundredfold. Here, where the busy, backward-flowing Red River of the North transected the railroad jumping-off point for merchants and developers laden with hard-to-get goods and peddled dreams from Minnesota and points east, Chinamen, Scots, Germans, French and Scandinavians teemed the muddy streets and temporary shacks in greater variety than anywhere else west of the Old World. Hudspeth and I hoisted the bedrolls, slickers, saddles and rifles (his a single-shot Springfield, mine a Winchester so new it squeaked) that were our only luggage down from the rack and stepped into the sea of humanity on the platform in search of a livery.

"It used to be over there," said the marshal, pointing out a building two blocks down the street, which now, if the sign was to be believed, sheltered the Golden West Emporium and Tonsorial Parlor.

"It's come up in the world," I observed.

On our third try we found someone who spoke English well enough to direct us to a livery on a street with the optimistic name of Broadway. There, we haggled with the stony-faced old Scot who ran the place over some serviceable-looking horseflesh, including a pack animal, and at length agreed upon a mutually unreasonable price, for the payment of which we asked for and were given receipts made out in flowing European script that neither Flood nor even a skinflint like Blackthorne could doubt. One hour, a meal, and four exorbitantly priced drinks later we were astride our new mounts and on our way to a métis camp which the bartender at the Old Fargo Saloon assured us was two miles south of the city limits. We were still riding five miles beyond that point.

"I thought you said you knew where the camp was," I growled at Hudspeth. Light was fading fast and the weeks between me and my last hard ride were beginning to tell in various places.

"I did once. I can't help it if they moved."

"They must move a lot. The bartender said they were camped an hour's ride back just last night."

"You can't believe everything a bartender says."

"You should know."

Half a mile farther on we spotted scattered fires in the distance, and another twenty minutes found us on the outskirts of a village of primitive lodges and skin tents. The usual menagerie of yapping mongrels heralded our arrival. Despite the racket, the dogs were all that crowded around us, snapping at the horses' heels as we made our way through the camp. I was unprepared for this reception, or lack of it. Where I came from, a visit by whites to an Indian camp was an event worthy of note, if it was anything less than suicide. A brave who let a stranger, any stranger, within a mile of his lodge without raising the alarm wasn't worth his feathers. We had gone a hundred yards before we came across the first sign that the place was inhabited at all. This was a boy with long black hair cropped straight across the back of his neck at the nape, wearing a bright calico shirt and new Levi's cut down and stuffed into the tops of calf-high moccasins (the only part of his attire that could have come from inside the village), who was busy sewing up a rip in the side of a lodge covered with scraped buffalo hides. He paid us no attention as we rode up to where he sat cross-legged on the ground bent over his labors. Although he couldn't have been older than ten or eleven, he manipulated the bone needle and gut thong with the assurance of an old squaw stitching a new ornament onto her warrior's tunic.

"We're looking for Pere Jac," Hudspeth announced.

The boy looked up uncomprehendingly. The light of the torch that blazed before the lodge fell across a set of features finer than I'd expected, set off by flashing black eyes and lashes that swept his dark cheeks. The marshal repeated the query, or one like it, in bastard French. After a moment the boy nodded and pointed with the needle toward the rusty glow of a large fire east of camp. Hudspeth thanked him and we moved off in that direction. The boy resumed working.

"Do they all get that excited over white men?" I asked the marshal.

"What did you expect? They're more than half white themselves."

The métis, I was to learn, were no less mongrel than their pets. Also called *bois brûlés*, or "burnt wood," because of their swarthy complexions, most were descended from Huron or Algonquin women and foreign trappers who had come west in the middle of the last century and married into the tribes. Since then interbreeding had become a way of life, until now there was precious little to separate them from the equally dark French Canadians who were prevalent in the area. Nevertheless they retained their essentially Indian ways. They were nomadic and depended for their existence almost entirely upon the buffalo of which they were undisciplined butchers. They also knew every rock and bush in Dakota territory by its first name, which was the reason we were here.

Whatever was going on inside the circle of firelight, it was receiving the full-throated approval of the colorfully clad mob that surrounded it. Their shouted encouragement was a stew of English, French, and one or two other languages I couldn't identify. It was so loud it almost drowned out the sound of blows.

The free-for-all was well in progress by the time we got there. In the center of the circle, cheered on by the howling spectators, half-naked men shining with the sweat of their exertions wrestled and fought in a tangled throng, grunting, snarling and muttering oaths in a variety of tongues as colorful as their audience's garb. Kicking seemed to be in, as was biting and eye-gouging. It was an elimination contest. Every now and then a man battered and torn beyond his limits staggered or was carried from the action over the outstretched forms of his predecessors, while in the middle the melee raged on without flagging. Those left sported shiners and smeared lips like I hadn't seen since the bank runs in the early days of the Panic. All about their feet bloody teeth twinkled in the firelight.

One brawler in particular, a squat breed whose powerful build belied the iron-gray hair falling about his shoulders, looked to be giving more than he got, as he answered his opponents' blows with Helena Haymakers that sent them reeling back into the crowd of spectators. Little by little, as

Hudspeth and I watched from the backs of our horses, the heaving mass dwindled until only a handful remained to slug it out among themselves, with the old man in the heart of it. The air was heavy with the rank smell of turned earth and sweat.

All in all, I reflected, this spectacle was playing hell with what I'd been told about the gentle ways of the métis. But then there are exceptions to every rule.

Down to the bare boards, the rules of combat underwent a subtle change. The younger men, apparently recognizing the threat to their reputations should they fall to someone thirty years their senior, stopped fighting each other and teamed up, at odds of six to one, to take out the old man. They whooped and hollered and charged headlong into a beehive.

He was a magnificent specimen, this old breed who could have been anywhere from fifty to seventy-five but fought like a Blackfoot brave in his twenties. Muscles writhed beneath his naked torso like snakes beneath a sheet, and scars thick as cables crisscrossed his great chest and shoulders. He reminded me of a king buffalo I had once seen defending its throne. Old and grizzled though he was, he was still more than a match for the youngsters who challenged his authority. Besieged from all sides, he met them in silence, snaggled teeth bared in a determined grin as he felled this one with a blow and hooked that one viciously in the groin with the toe of a moccasin. Those lucky enough to connect found their best shots glancing off him like a blacksmith's hammer bounding from an anvil. Then a clout from an axe-like fist would bring their participation to an end. In this manner he disposed of four assailants in as many minutes.

He had both arms wrapped around a fifth and was bear-hugging him into unconsciousness when the sixth, a lean young breed with features more Indian than white, snatched up a chunk of wood from the fire and charged him from behind, swinging the glowing end above his head. I have no special love for rules, but this seemed to be going astray from the spirit of healthy competition. I drew my revolver and was debating whether I should drop him and risk the hostility of the tribe or gamble on a dime-novel try at shooting the club out of his hand, when a shot like the Fourth of July in Chinatown crashed within a foot of my left ear. The young breed shrieked, dropped his weapon, and clapped a hand to the side of his head. It came back bloody.

Every eye in the vicinity, including mine, swung to the big man astride the horse next to my own. A plume of metallic gray smoke wandered from the snout of the Smith & Wesson in Hudspeth's right hand while with the other he struggled to keep his startled mount under control. He had drawn the clumsy thing from its unlikely position beneath his left arm and fired while I was still figuring the angles. And he said he was slowing down.

The old man wasn't one to let the grass grow. While his would-be attacker was still hopping around and lamenting the loss of his right ear, he whirled and slung the limp breed he was holding six feet into the other's arms. One hundred and sixty pounds of métis struck him full in the chest, tore the wind from his lungs in a loud *woof*, and bore him, a tangle of arms and legs, to the ground on the other side of the fire.

For a long moment there was silence. Then the air erupted and the crowd surged forward, closing in on the old breed, the women babbling excitedly, the men pumping his hands and slapping him on the back. Our presence was forgotten. A half-full whiskey bottle was produced from some hoarder's lodge and, after it had been admired for a while, was presented to the victor with a flourish. He seized it in a bloodied right hand and tipped it up, letting the contents gurgle down his throat without seeming to swallow. Two more tilts and he slung the empty vessel away over his shoulder. It bounced once in the grass and rolled after the retreating form of the vanquished breed as if pursuing him. Everyone seemed to find that amusing. Everyone, that is, except the old man, who caught the eye of a dark-skinned young woman standing on the edge of the crowd and jerked his head toward the injured man. She nodded and moved off to follow him. The old man's will, it appeared, was law— rare among Indians, where a leader usually led by example only and would not presume to issue anything so harsh as an order.

"Hey, Pere Jac!" called Hudspeth, dismounting.

"A.C.!" The aged métis squinted through the gathering gloom. "A.C., is that you?"

"Who the hell else would waste a bullet on your worthless hide?" He started leading his buckskin in that direction. I stepped down to follow.

Pere Jac barked something in French to the man nearest him, who took the reins from Hudspeth and those of my bay and led them toward camp.

"They will be fed and rubbed down well," the old man explained.

He had a French accent you couldn't suck through a straw. "How are you, A.C.? That was respectable shooting." He seized the marshal's outstretched hand and shook it every bit as energetically as his own had been shaken moments before.

"Not as good as it looked," said the other, wincing as he disengaged his hand from the other's grasp. "I was trying to put one between his eyes."

"I am glad that you did not. He is my sister's only son."
He looked at me curiously. He was almost a foot shorter
than I, but built like a warhorse. He had well-shaped features despite the numerous bruises and swellings, and eyes
of washed-out blue in contrast to the mahogany hue of his
skin. His jaw was fine, almost delicate, his face shot through
with tiny creases and wrinkles, as if it had been crumpled
into a tight ball and then smoothed out again. His gray hair,
dark with sweat, hung in lank strands to his shoulders. Perspiration glistened on his skin in the firelight and trickled
down the cleft that divided his chest into twin slabs of lean
meat. Yet he was not the least bit winded.

Hudspeth introduced us and we shook hands. His grip
wasn't much, if you were used to sticking your hand inside
a corn-sheller and turning the handle.

"Page Murdock," he said, with unfeigned interest. "You
are the man who brought Bear Anderson out of the Bitterroot Mountains last winter, one step ahead of the Flatheads."

I said that I was. I could see that those were the words
someone was going to carve on my tombstone.

"And yet you do not look like a foolish man," he observed.

I grinned. "Pere Jac," I said, "you and I are going to get
along."

"My name is Jacques St. Jean. Marshal Hudspeth and
these others insist upon calling me Pere Jac because for a
brief period in my foolish youth I sought the clergy. The
clergy, alas, did not share my enthusiasm. Now I content myself with reciting the Scriptures and instructing my people
in the ways of the Lord."

"That was some Bible-reading we caught just now," said
Hudspeth dryly.

"Man is an imperfect animal, full of hostility and sin. He

must be given the opportunity to cleanse himself of both from time to time if he is ever to pass through Purgatory."

"You do this often?"

"Every other Wednesday, without fail."

"How about sin?"

"Sin is for Tuesday. But you have not come all this way to speak of religion, A.C."

"We need an experienced tracker, Jac, and unless there's someone around here who reads sign as good as you I guess you're it."

"That is what I thought. Come with me to the river." He signaled for a torch to be brought. When one was handed him, he motioned the others to remain where they were and strode away, carrying the flaming instrument. As we hastened to catch up: "How much are you offering this time, A.C.?"

"I was thinking four cases."

"A man's thoughts are his own, *mon ami*. But that one is beneath notice."

"That's the price we agreed on last time!"

"The last time was four years ago. It costs much more to subsist in these days of revolution and expansion."

"We're talking about whiskey, not money. And you got no more bellies to fill now than you had four years back. All right, six cases. But that's as high as I go. We're talking about taxpayers' money."

"I do not think that ten cases would upset the economy."

"Ten cases!" Hudspeth stopped walking. At the base of the grassy slope, the Red River hissed and gurgled at high water. But the métis kept walking, so he had to sprint to catch up.

"Seven cases," he said.

Pere Jac made no reply.

"Eight, damn it! But you'd better guarantee results."

We were at the river now. The old man handed me the torch and stepped off the bank, Levi's, moccasins and all. He dipped his swollen and bleeding hands into the water and splashed it over his face and chest.

"Eight it shall be," he said at last. "But I guarantee nothing." He dug a finger into his mouth, withdrew a loosened tooth, saw it was gold, and thrust it into a hip pocket. "Who are we going after, A.C.?"

"A Cheyenne by the name of Ghost Shirt."

The dusky-skinned woman Jac had sent earlier to look after the wounded breed appeared bearing a bundle of clothing. She held out a calico shirt while he stepped out of the water, and helped him on with it. I figured her for his granddaughter; she turned out later to be his squaw. He shook his head at her offer of a dry pair of leather leggings, accepted a military-style red sash instead, and knotted it about his waist. "I think, A.C.," he said finally, "that you had better give us the whiskey in advance."

# CHAPTER 4

**W**e were Pere Jac's guests for the night, which meant that despite our protests, he, his woman and his three children slept outside and the lodge was ours. This was the same structure we had seen being repaired earlier by the boy who turned out to be Jac's son Lucien. Sleeping on buffalo robes didn't come easy after an extended period of city life, but I'd got along on worse and so had Hudspeth. We drifted off in short order—me from exhaustion after the unsettling activity of the past few days, the marshal after reacquainting himself with the flask in his pocket.

It rained sometime during the night without our knowing it. There were puddles on the ground the next morning and the air had that damp metallic smell, but the sultry and unseasonal heat that had dogged me since leaving Montana had not been washed away. If anything, the atmosphere was more oppressive than ever. It hung from last night's burned-out torches, beaded on the outside of the lodges in droplets of moisture, clung like moldy rags to our throats and the insides of our nostrils when we tried to breathe. The very act of taking in oxygen was exhausting. Two steps outside the shelter I felt as if I hadn't slept at all.

Our host and his family were wet but cheerful—the métis' natural state—and greeted us warmly in order of rank. We muttered something in response and sat down on the

ground to a breakfast of dried buffalo meat and herbs fresh
from the soil. That finished, Hudspeth mounted his buckskin and took off to fetch supplies and the pack horse we
had left in Fargo, and to make arrangements for the deliv-
ery of Pere Jac's eight cases of whiskey, while I stayed behind to get to know our guide. This was more important
than it sounds. Armed men forced to travel in each other's
company for an indefinite period are well advised to get ac-
quainted before they set out, or the first argument on the
trail could well be the last.

I had nothing to worry about in Jac. He packed no side
arm but carried a Sharps carbine and rode an unprepossess-
ing paint pony, and the confident but careful way he handled both as he made ready for the trip reflected a familiarity
with the rugged life that earned my approval. One of his few
concessions to the white man's way was a weatherbeaten
McClellan saddle complete with a pair of army issue bags.
Into these he packed a leatherbound copy of the Scriptures
and enough pemmican to last three weeks on the trail—
roughly an ounce and a half of dried buffalo, berries and
sugar pounded into a hard cake the size of a cowboy's brass
buckle. These were his only provisions.

His woman's name was Arabella. Save for the dusky
brown of her features and a thoroughly Algonquin mode of
dress, from the polished snail shells strung around her neck
to her elkskin moccasins, there was very little about her that
said she was part Indian. Her hair was chestnut and hung
in braids to her breasts. Her eyes, more oriental than native,
rode at a slight tilt atop high cheekbones. Her mouth was
wide but handsomely sculpted, the line of her jaw strong but
not stubborn. She seldom spoke in Jac's presence. In that
respect at least she was all squaw.

The children took after their father in looks, with Lucien, the oldest at ten, already beginning to show in the girth of his chest the beginnings of Jac's warrior build, and Jerome, six, and little, black-haired Paulette, three, watching every step of the preparations for departure with identical pairs of the old man's pale blue eyes staring out of their chocolate faces.

This, I had been told over breakfast, was Pere Jac's second family. His first wife had been killed fifteen years before when a herd of buffalo spooked prematurely during a hunt near Pembina and trampled the camp. His first son, now grown, left shortly before Jac's second mating along with his own squaw to start a new métis settlement below the Nebraska line. The old chief had taken Arabella as his bride after her first husband, his brother, succumbed to smallpox in the epidemic of '67. Jac remarked with pride that two of his five grandchildren were older than Lucien, and that Arabella was expecting another child in November.

Once the paint and my bay were saddled and ready to go, we sat down in the shade of the only tree for miles, a cottonwood beginning to die out at the top, and swapped a lie or two about past manhunts while he charged a stubby clay pipe from a pouch he carried on his belt and lit it with a sulphur match. Then we sat and listened to a faint breeze too high to reach us stir the branches twenty feet above our heads.

"Ghost Shirt," I said then. "What do you know about him?"

"Only what I have heard." He was having trouble keeping the tobacco burning. He struck a fresh match, puffed at the anemic glow in the bowl, got it going, shook out the match. Bluish smoke curled before his bruised and weathered features. "There is nothing haughtier than a full-blooded Cheyenne in his prime. Tell him that he is Christ reborn, as they have done with Ghost Shirt since he was old enough to understand, and he becomes impossible. Ten days before his birth, it is said, Ghost Shirt's father, Paints His Lodge, dreamed that he saw the sun rising from his squaw's loins. When the story was repeated to him, the tribal shaman prophesied that a son would be born who would lead his people to greater glories than had ever been known, a son who was destined to be a god, yet who would remain on earth to guide the Cheyenne to their rightful place as conquerors of the land.

"It did not help matters that the boy proved himself a superior athlete long before the time came for his test of manhood, nor that when that time came he fulfilled all of the requirements with ease. Sent east to study the white man's world, he returned after three years seething with hatred for the entire race. He commanded the right flank of his uncle Kills Bear's warrior band in the Custer fight and proved himself an adept tactician as well as a born leader of men. Had the Little Big Horn never happened, Ghost Shirt might have enjoyed limited authority for a number of years and attained the rank of chief sometime in middle life. As it is, he has risen too fast too soon. He is a rash young man with more power than he knows what to do with. Unfortunately, of late he has been finding uses for it."

"Is he as crafty as they say he is, or just lucky?"

"Craft and luck are difficult things to separate. A man must have a little of both if he is ever to be successful. Ghost Shirt is fortunate. Moreover, he is brilliant. It is a dangerous combination if you are not on his side."

"You're describing a young Sitting Bull."

"Or a young Napoleon," said Jac.

He thought about it, then shook his head. "No. Not like Sitting Bull. He at least has learned to temper his distaste for the white man with wisdom. There is no wisdom in Ghost Shirt's brilliance. Only hate. He cares not for the future of his people, only for revenge. He will be the ruin of the Cheyenne nation. You have a saying for it: He burns down the barn in order to destroy the rats."

Pere Jac was silent for a time. A dead seed came rattling down between us from the cottonwood's upper branches. A crow had come to light upon a high twig and began to scold us raucously. A newcomer, screaming for those already there to leave. Thus harangued, I understood for a moment the feelings of Ghost Shirt and his followers. But only for a moment.

"You are to kill him?" asked Pere Jac.

I hesitated, thinking at first that he was talking about the crow. "No," I said, catching his drift. "We've strict orders to bring him back alive for execution in Bismarck."

"That is a foolish thing. Dead, he is a threat ended. Alive, he remains an open sore. There is always the hope among his people that he will return to lead them. If we are able to capture him, our troubles will just be beginning."

"Look at the bright side. We won't live long enough to take him prisoner."

He laughed and brushed at the sparks that had showered from his pipe down onto his leather leggings. "You are right, Page Murdock," he said. "We are going to get along."

We basked in the warmth of that for a while. Then the sound of galloping hoofs shattered the late morning stillness and Hudspeth, the loaded pack horse tethered behind his own mount, reined to a dusty halt in front of us and heaved himself out of the saddle, nearly going down on one knee as he landed on his feet with a jarring thud. His nose was flame-red and his eyes held an urgent glitter. He barely gave us time to scramble out from under the tree before he thrust a crumple of paper into my face.

"This was waiting at the telegraph office," he announced. "It's from Judge Flood. A force of twenty injuns ambushed a patrol out of Fort Ransom last night and killed Colonel Broderick and twelve others. Ghost Shirt was leading them."

# CHAPTER 5

"**W**hy?" I looked up from the scrap, torn and wilted from being jammed into a pocket and carried across eight miles of Dakota territory.

"How in hell should I know why?" Hudspeth demanded. "He's crazy mad. He'll do anything."

"I don't think so. If he were that crazy he'd have been dead long ago. Ghost Shirt must have had a reason to attack that patrol."

"It don't much matter if he did or didn't. What matters is he went ahead and attacked it. I wired Flood to tell him we got the message, and Fort Ransom to let them know we're coming."

"Any answer from the fort?"

He shook his head. "Likely they're on alert. Operator's too busy hunting up reinforcements to acknowledge." He grunted and flicked a drop of sweat from his beacon of a nose with the tip of a blunt forefinger. "The only good thing about this whole business is now we know he ain't met up yet with the Sioux and Cheyenne from around the territories."

"Maybe. Or maybe it's a trap."

"We'll know soon enough." He swung back into the saddle. "Mount up. We're heading out."

I straddled the bay. "What'll we do once we get there?"

"We'll think of something on the way." He wheeled west.

Pere Jac didn't move. "Where is my whiskey, A.C.?"

The marshal reached into a saddle bag, hoisted out a quart bottle full of tobacco-colored liquid, and tossed it to the breed, who caught it in one hand. "There's ninety-five more coming day after tomorrow," Hudspeth told him. "You want to see the receipt?"

Jac drew the cork and helped himself to a swig. "I trust you, A.C.," he said, wiping his mouth with the back of his hand.

The métis slid the bottle in with his other belongings, said his good-byes all around, and stepped into the paint's leather with the ease of a man forty years his junior. Five minutes later we were clear of camp and heading southwest, fifty miles of which separated us from our destination.

We reached the Sheyenne at dusk. There, a shallow ford stretched between us and the fort, which was a purple blemish on the muted red glare of the setting sun. No sooner had Hudspeth set a hoof in the water than a shot rang out. Riding behind him, I heard a *thup* and saw his broad-brimmed black hat tilt over his left ear. He hauled back on the reins to keep his horse from spooking, but it was too late. The buckskin kicked up its heels and arched its back, whinnying and trying to turn so it could bolt. The marshal spun it around three times before dizziness took over and the animal stopped to regain its bearings.

"Halt! Who goes there?"

A lanky trooper stood up to his knees in water in the middle of the river, a rifle braced against his shoulder, smoke draining from its barrel. The challenge lost a great deal of its force, however, when the young voice issuing it cracked in the middle.

Hudspeth let out a roar and sprang to the ground. He hit

the water running, tore the rifle from the trooper's hands before he could react, and sent it spinning far out into the river. Then he swept the trooper off his feet and prepared to send him after it.

"Do it, and you'll be dead before he hits the water." A harsh croak, dry and empty as a spent cartridge. It crackled in the charged air.

The marshal froze, legs spread apart, the trooper squirming in his arms. He turned his head slowly in the direction of the voice.

Three soldiers were mounted on horseback on the opposite bank, each with a rifle snuggled against his cheek. The broad brims of their dusty campaign hats left their faces in shadow. Two of them, anyway. The man on the left, although obviously cavalry, wore the cocked forage cap of an infantryman, a style of headgear made famous by both sides during the late unpleasantness out East. A rain cape hung to his waist, performing double duty as a duster. His features were invisible against the sun. Softer now, the wallowing light glinted off gold epaulets on the square shoulders of the man in the middle. A hammer was thumbed back with a brittle crunch. Late, but persuasive as hell. Hudspeth returned the trooper, a callow youth with blond hair and freckles, to his feet. He put several yards between himself and the marshal as quickly as possible.

"Hands up, all of you."

We did as directed, raising our open palms above our shoulders. Hudspeth was last to comply.

"Now suppose you tell me who you are and what you're doing here."

"We're federal officers," growled Hudspeth, after a pause. "I'm Hudspeth. The mean-looking one is Murdock. Here from Bismarck on the injun problem. I got a letter from Abel

Flood, federal judge for the territory of Dakota, for Colonel Broderick." He started to reach inside his coat but
stopped when all three rifles rattled.

"Keep your hands up!" The command was metallic.
"Colonel Broderick is dead."

"I know. I wired you this morning to tell you we was
coming."

The officer turned his head a fraction of an inch toward
the soldier Hudspeth had just released. "Go to the telegraph
shack. See if there's a wire from someone named Hudspeth."
When the youth had gone: "The Indian. I suppose he's a federal officer too."

"He's our guide, and I bet he's got more white in him than
you."

The pause that followed put an extra twist in the tension.

"You make a bad first impression, friend." The words
were bitten off.

After about a year of silence, the trooper returned bearing a telegraph blank with a spike-hole in the center of it.
The officer glanced at it, then handed it back. He lowered
his rifle. At a signal from him the others followed suit a moment later. Then he spurred his big black forward into the
water. He stopped in front of Hudspeth and ran his eyes over
the three of us. They were brown eyes, with flecks of silver
in them. His heavy brows were startlingly black in comparison, downward-drawn and prevented from running into
each other only by a thin pucker line that went up until it
disappeared beneath the forward tilt of his campaign hat.
His beard too was black and cropped close to the skin so
that it resembled General Grant's. That came as no surprise.
In spite of his dismal presidency, in spite of the endless
congressional investigations that had hounded him during his last days in office and after, Grant was still the

hero of Appomattox, the hard man on the white horse whose preference for whiskers had inspired men from New York to California to lay aside their razors. Among army officers there were two distinct types, the Grants and the Custers, and you didn't venture into many posts without finding yourself virtually surrounded by either long-hairs in buckskin jackets or silent men who fingered their beards meaningfully when they could think of nothing significant to say.

This officer—a major, now that I could make out his insignia away from the sun's glare—had a long, one might say Roman, nose and the beginnings of jowls beneath his whiskers, which had undoubtedly contributed to his decision to grow them. The sun had burned his flesh to match the red Dakota dust on his saddle. His eyes were not the steely type one expected in men accustomed to command, but large and luminous and cowlike, strangely unintelligent—like Grant's. His physique beneath the coarse blue tunic (buttoned to the neck, even in that heat) was powerful but beginning to loosen around the thighs and belly. I placed his age at about forty.

His side arm was an Army Colt with a smooth wooden grip, the rifle he held across his lap, a Spencer. Like his uniform, both were covered with a skin of fine dust. Beneath him his horse was lathered and blowing.

He took in my face, clothes, horse, the Deane-Adams in my holster, the Winchester in its scabbard, then went on for a similar inventory of Pere Jac. Then he returned to Hudspeth.

"You owe the U.S. Government the price of a new Springfield rifle, Marshal."

"Tell them to take it out of my taxes."

I stifled a grin. Either the lawman had qualities I hadn't

suspected or a little of me was beginning to rub off on him. I was starting to enjoy my subordinate role in this thing.

He wasn't finished. "I told you who we are. It's polite to introduce yourself back, ain't it, Lieutenant?"

"It's Major," snapped the other. "Major Quincy Harms, acting commanding officer at Fort Ransom until Washington City appoints a permanent replacement for Colonel Broderick. I'm sorry, Marshal, for all the inconvenience, but you must understand that the situation here is tense. We can trust no one." There was no apology in his tone.

"So you shoot everyone on sight?"

"Trooper Gordon will be reprimanded for his lapse in judgment. I believe you mentioned a letter from Judge Flood." He held out a hand.

The marshal drew out the paper Flood had given him the morning of our departure and handed it over. Harms unfolded it and read. The muscles in his jaw twitched. Then he thrust the letter inside his tunic.

"Sergeant Burdett, relieve Trooper Gordon of his duties and place him under house arrest until further orders."

An infantryman, the private had no side arm to be taken from him. The man in the forage cap merely leaned down, screwed the muzzle of his rifle into the other's collar, and began walking his horse forward. Rather than be trampled, the trooper let himself be prodded along like a stray calf. Somehow I got the impression that he was going to be punished not so much for firing a premature shot as for allowing himself to be overpowered by a civilian.

"Come with me, please, all of you. Bring your horses." The major reined his black around and splashed through the water toward the fort entrance. The third rider, a middle-aged corporal with a plug of tobacco bulging beneath his lower lip, followed him.

"Damn tin soldiers," muttered Hudspeth as he mounted the subdued buckskin.

One half of the huge double slat gate swung inward to allow us entrance, then was pushed shut by two troopers and secured with a timber bar that must have been shipped, like the logs of which the fort's framework was constructed, downriver from Montana or by rail from Minnesota. From there we rode past crowds of hard-eyed men in uniform who watched us with hands clasped tightly around their Springfields and Spencers. They had the desperate look of animals left too long at the ends of their tethers. Before the post livery a company of troopers was dismounting wearily, their horses, faces and uniforms covered with a mud of sweat and dust. Among them was a pair of empty mounts bearing the army's brand.

From the porch overhang of a long adobe building swung a sign that identified it as the garrison commander's office. The major and corporal left their saddles in exhausted unison, their square-topped boots double-crunching on the carted-in gravel. Jac and Hudspeth and I dismounted more earthily and hitched up at the watering trough, where the horses wet their noses eagerly. Harms handed his reins to the corporal.

"The right front needs reshoeing. And see to it that our guests' mounts are rubbed down and fed. They're dead on their feet."

The corporal saluted and led off his and the major's mounts.

The office smelled of coffee and stale tobacco. The walls were bare adobe reinforced by wooden timbers, and the floor was made of pine planks eight inches wide and scrubbed white as bears' teeth by some miserable trooper on punishment detail with a scouring pad and a toothbrush for the cracks. The desk was battered, scarred in numerous places where matches had been struck against its scaly surface, and covered by a large-scale map of eastern Dakota. Holes in the corners and a pale spot on the wall behind the desk indicated that the map had been taken down recently for close study. A curled corner was held in place beneath a white china mug with damp brown grains clustered in the bottom. Behind the desk stood a high-backed swivel chair, its dark wood covered to within an inch of the age-polished edges by hard, dry leather secured with large brass tacks. From fort to fort, the decor never varied.

Major Harms peeled off his hat and pegged it beside the door. His hair, like his beard, was jet black, short at the temples and neck and full on top. A bald spot the size of a ten-dollar goldpiece showed defiantly at the back of his head. He made no attempt to conceal it. He stepped around behind the desk and dropped into the swivel chair in a cloud of powdery dust. His forehead just beneath the hairline was ringed unevenly with several different shades of tan where he'd settled and resettled his hat under the scorching sun.

Hudspeth sat down on the edge of the sturdy captain's chair that faced the desk as if easing himself into a scalding tub of water. Evidently it had been some time since he'd sat a saddle as long as he had during the past few days. I chose a bench that ran along the right wall and wished it were the back of my horse, it was that hard. Pere Jac remained standing. In his dusty half-Indian, half-white man's attire, his pewter-colored hair loose about his shoulders, eyes impassive as the heads of newly driven nails, he might have been posing for the stamp on a penny. The mingled scents of leather and dust and sour sweat and, faintly, old bear grease wafted from him. Aside from the grease, I was at a loss to determine how much of it was his and how much mine.

"Frankly, gentlemen, I don't see how I can help you, nor why I should try." Harms folded aside the map on his desk, revealing mottled traces of green blotter paper beneath a pattern of dead black ink.

"The letter calls for your co-operation," Hudspeth rapped.

"Not mine, Broderick's. And it calls for something which was not his to give. He had no authority to bring in an outside party. Hostile Indians fall within the jurisdiction of the U.S. Army and no other. Their crimes are not a matter for the civil courts."

"Judge Flood thinks different."

"Judge Flood can go to bloody hell." The words came lashing out. He fell silent, rolled the map back farther, found a hand-worked wooden humidor standing on the corner of the desk, and removed the cover. He drew out a cigar the length of his wrist, struck a match—placing a fresh groove on a previously unmarred section of desk—and ignited it. Blue smoke came billowing out in true Grant style. I don't smoke, but it would have been nice if he'd offered us one. He used the same match to light a lamp with a milky white glass shade on the opposite corner and sat back as the soft glow gulped up the shadows.

"Forgive me, gentlemen," he said. This time he sounded sincere. "I've been in the saddle eighteen hours straight. We're short-handed, but it's important we show the enemy a stern face. I'm tired and my patience is on a short halter."

"Any luck?"

He looked at me quickly. "Luck? Doing what?"

I didn't answer. Finally he shook his head.

"We hit every arroyo and dry wash between here and Jamestown. No trace of Ghost Shirt or his warriors. Two of my Indian scouts deserted. They're afraid the Great Spirit is on the other side. Superstitious heathens!" He puffed furiously. His features swam behind an azure haze.

"You're lying, Major."

He stared. Something akin to rage glimmered in his dull brown eyes. I went on before he could blow.

"Your horse was heaving and covered with froth. They don't get that way unless they're ridden fast and hard. Two riderless horses came in with the patrol, and I know enough about Indians to know they don't desert on foot in this country. My guess is you buried what was left of those scouts after Ghost Shirt got through with them, then took off in pursuit. Where's he holed up?"

Harms made a thing out of picking all the lint off his cigar.

"We sent them on ahead to scout out the territory." He spoke slowly. "When they stopped leaving sign we tracked them to the James River. We found them hanging upside down from a cottonwood over a smoldering fire. Their skulls had exploded from the heat."

"Ghost Shirt. Where is he?"

For a moment it looked as if he might answer. Then his dazed expression cleared and the stubborn glint returned to his eyes. "That's army business. So far all the casualties in this quadrant have been sustained by the military. I won't take the responsibility for any civilian deaths here."

"Colonel Broderick—" Hudspeth began.

"Colonel Broderick was a good soldier, but he was weak. He worried more about holding onto his command than keeping the peace in his sector. As a result he lost his own life and those of a dozen of his men while on routine patrol. There will be no such blunders beneath my command. As long as you three are here you are welcome, within limits, to the facilities of the post, but you will not be allowed to leave until the situation is in hand." He started to rise.

"What was a full colonel doing leading a routine patrol?" I pressed. "That's a job for a captain or a lieutenant."

He looked at me again. A faint smile played over his lips but fell short of his eyes. "You served?"

"I was with Schoepf at Mill Springs and with Rosecrans at Murfreesboro. A ball smashed my leg there and I sat out the rest of my enlistment in splints."

"I thought I'd noticed a slight limp. You must have been very young."

"I was nineteen when I signed up."

"Why did you leave?"

"I don't like officers."

That ended the friendly coversation. He stalked toward the door and clapped on his hat. "Sergeant Burdett will be in to show you to your quarters."

"You didn't answer my question, Major," I said.

He ignored me and tugged open the door. I went on. "Colonel Broderick was tracking Ghost Shirt, wasn't he? He got too close and the Indians attacked. Which means you have a fair idea where their stronghold is."

He turned back. Beyond his shoulder, purple twilight had settled over the compound, silhouetting the sentries on the wall in liquid black. "What makes you think it's a stronghold?"

"You took thirty men and came back with twenty-eight. If you'd met Ghost Shirt in the open you'd have killed at least a few of his braves and lost more than two scouts. The only explanation is they're holed up someplace where you can't dig them out. All I'm asking is where."

"Suppose I told you. What can you do that we can't, one underarmed deputy and two old has-beens?"

The marshal sprang from his chair and lunged toward the major, who clawed at his holster. I stuck out a leg, tripping Hudspeth. He threw out his arms and struck the floor hard on his face. The china mug fell from the desk, clunked against the planks, and rolled around in a lazy circle, coming to rest against the lawman's left boot.

Pere Jac remained rooted in the middle of the floor. He hadn't moved. I had already pegged him as a born survivor.

"You're forgetting that one of these old has-beens almost turned one of your men into fishbait a little while ago," I reminded the major.

He put away the Colt and secured the strap that held it in place. "It's a moot point, Deputy," he said. "You're confined to the post for the duration."

"We can make it as hot in here as it is out there." I slid out the Deane-Adams and pointed it in the general direction of his groin. He kept his calm.

"I don't think you will. You're sworn to uphold the law."

I grinned and pulled back the hammer. As I did so I heard another weapon being cocked behind me. It could have been an echo. I knew it wasn't.

Harms smiled, this time all the way. "It might be a good idea to give me the gun." He came forward with his hand outstretched. "Sergeant Burdett has a Spencer rifle pointed at the back of your head."

"He speaks the truth, Page." Jac's tone was noncommittal.

I shifted my head just far enough to take in the outline of the man leaning through the open window behind my right shoulder, a rifle in his hands. I held onto the revolver. Something in my expression halted the officer in mid-step. His smile drained from his features.

"You know," I said, "everyone thinks the gun at a man's back is deadlier than the one in his hand, but that's not true. They both kill just the same."

Drops of moisture sparkled on Harms's tanned forehead. This wasn't his game, I could tell. He was used to shooting it out with rifles and howitzers across several hundred yards of open ground until one side or the other gave up or ran out of ammunition. Here there was no room for his brand of bravery. Face to face with .45-caliber death in that narrow room, he felt fear for what was probably the first time in his career.

In that instant I threw myself from the bench, hit the floor, and rolled. There was an explosion and a cloud of splinters near my head and something hot seared my right cheek, but I kept moving. I came up flat against the wall with my gun still in my grip.

As the sergeant maneuvered to get something worthwhile in his sights, I grabbed the Spencer's barrel with my free hand and jerked it downward. It throbbed in my hand, belched flame. One of the broad white planks in the floor splintered and split down the middle from one end of the room to the other. The simultaneous roar set my ears to jangling and brought dust and loose dirt showering down from the rafters. I twisted the gun from Burdett's desperate grasp and pulled it through the window.

Harms went for his Colt. He was pretty fast. He had the strap almost undone by the time Hudspeth, back on his feet, hauled out his Smith & Wesson and clapped the muzzle to the major's temple.

"Go for it," he said. "Please go for it."

Harms left the Colt where it was.

I had Burdett covered with the Deane-Adams. Short and thickset, he had sunken eyes overhung with black, bushy brows and a cleft chin bunched up like a fist. Tiny blue specks peppered the left side of his face just beneath the leathery skin. Some time or other he had come within a hair's breadth of having his head blown off by a shotgun blast. His left eye glittered unnaturally in the lamplight, and I knew it was glass. His nose was an incongruous pug, but he had filled the gap between it and his wide mouth with a thick black moustache. I counted to ten, then extended the Spencer to him. He stared at it as if he'd never seen it before, then, gingerly, as if he thought it might blow up, took hold of it and hauled it back through the opening. Hudspeth watched, thunderstruck.

"What the hell—"

"Three men don't stand a lot of chance against a garrison full of soldiers." I handed Harms my revolver. He took it hesitantly. "Give him yours before somebody gets hurt," I told the marshal. I was having trouble talking. I relaxed my face muscles and realized I'd been grinning all this time.

It took a few seconds, but finally Hudspeth sighed and turned his weapon over to the major.

"One underarmed deputy and two old has-beens, Major." My resistance to temptation never was much to speak of.

Harms rattled the revolvers together, stared from one face to the other. Then:

"They're all yours, Sergeant. Put them up in Colonel Broderick's quarters and post a guard at the door. And try to resist the urge to give Murdock your rifle again." He turned and strode out stiffly. The troopers who had crowded around the door at the sound of gunfire stood aside to let him through.

"Some fight, A.C.," said Pere Jac on our way out.

"Sure you was close enough to see it?" snarled Hudspeth.

"It is the meek who shall inherit the earth. I fight only for what is mine."

"At least you didn't try to break my neck." Bright eyes slid murderously in my direction.

"Better a broken neck than a bullet in the belly," I said.

Burdett told us to be quiet.

Broderick's late home, one of a row of officers' quarters housed in a single building near the north wall of the fort, was equipped with a sitting room and a bedchamber with two narrow beds. We were told he had shared it with his wife before the Indian troubles had forced her to return to their permanent home in Ohio. The furnishings were spartan and, except for the hand-sewn lace curtains beginning to yellow on the windows of the bedroom, masculine. The rooms smelled strongly of bootblack.

Hudspeth and I wrestled for a while with a supper of stringy long-horn beef and vegetables taken from what was left of the colonel's wife's garden, which was brought in to us by a seasoned-looking horse soldier, then we gave up and pushed our plates aside. Only Jac, his teeth and gums toughened by years of gnawing at leather-tough pemmican, went on eating. His chewing and the ticking of the clock on the mantel were the loudest sounds for some time. Outside, the boards on the porch creaked beneath the shifting weight of our restless guard.

"This is your stamping ground, Jac," Hudspeth said finally. The sound of a human voice after all that silence made me jump. "Where's the best place around here for a bunch of injuns to hole up?"

"The possibilities are endless." The old métis dipped a spoon in the gravy on his plate and began drawing lines on the bare surface of the table. "There are many buttes and sheltered washes, any one of which would serve Ghost Shirt's purpose. The best is here, just west of the James River." He made a wet X on the other side of the line that represented the body of water. "An abandoned mission, once used by Mormons and built to withstand fierce attack. Twenty well-armed braves could stand off an army from its battlements for months."

"You think that's it?"

He shrugged. "Who is to say? If he is the brilliant chief the stories claim he is, that is where he will be. But I have never met him, and so I have nothing else on which to base my judgment."

"I've heard them same stories, so there must be something to 'em. I'll gamble on it. Murdock?"

"I'm in the pot." I had gotten up from the table to listen for the guard. I laid my hand upon one of the rock-solid timbers that held up the wall of our prison. "Now all we have to do is figure out a way to get past the guard, fight our way through a hundred or so armed troopers, and scale a sixteen-foot wall. I hope one of you has something in mind, because I'm fresh out of suggestions."

" 'The foolish despise wisdom and instruction,' " quoted Pere Jac approvingly. Something in the way he said it made Hudspeth and me look at him. Smiling, he was tracing pagan symbols absent-mindedly on the table with the edge of his spoon.

# CHAPTER 6

They made quite a pile, the lighter items such as Mrs. Broderick's lace curtains and the sheets and ticking from the beds on the bottom with the colonel's heavy uniforms and whatever else we could find that would burn heaped on top. Hudspeth and I had done most of the work, gathering the stuff and throwing it into the middle of the sitting room floor while Jac supervised. All of this was done with a minimum of noise and with one ear cocked toward the door, where the squeaking and groaning of the porch boards beneath our guard's feet told us whether he was listening at the keyhole or just pacing back and forth. When the pile was four feet high Jac signaled us to stop, picked up the coal-oil lamp from the table where we had eaten, extinguished it, and saturated the linens and woolens on the floor with its contents. Then he struck a match on the edge of the table.

"You sure this will work?" whispered the marshal. "I always wanted a funeral with an open coffin."

"I offer no guarantees." The métis watched the sulphur flare and waited for it to burn down to the wood. "This is not the sort of thing one can practice. Since there is no other way out of this fort, however, we must convince Major Harms that it is in his own best interests to release us."

"Ghost Shirt made it out without all this."

"Ghost Shirt lost three men doing it and killed that many soldiers. I assume that you wish to spill as little of your own countrymen's blood as possible."

"Meanwhile," I pointed out impatiently, "the smell of that coal oil is drifting toward our friend outside."

"Quite right." Pere Jac squatted and touched the match to the hem of a lace curtain.

The flame caught, burned slowly at first, then spread to engulf the pile with a hollow, sucking sound. A pillar of oily black smoke rose to the ceiling and sent greasy curls unwinding into all the corners of the room. The choking stench of burning rags followed. We got down on the floor where the air was sweeter and waited for results.

We didn't wait long. There was shouting outside the door and pounding, and then a key rattled in the lock and the trooper on guard, a grizzled old campaigner with leathern features and a great swelling belly solid as a sack of lead shot, burst into the room, coughing and digging his fists into his eyes as a wall of smoke hit him square in the face. He stumbled about, clawing at the air and calling for assistance between fits of hacking. In another moment the room was full of troopers in varying states of undress, but all of them armed. Finally buckets of water were produced and emptied in the general direction of the flames, which hissed and spat and sent up thicker and more fragrant columns of smoke than before. The firefighters' curses were colorful and, as a rule, had to do with someone's ancestry. A muck of water and soot darkened the muted colors in the Brodericks' carpet, which was the kind you bought out East and had shipped back here.

Quincy Harms came striding in just as the troopers were slapping out the last of the flames with coats and army blankets. He was in his shirtsleeves, and the scrubbed cleanliness of his face and hands in contrast to the grimy cross-hatching on his neck and wrists indicated that he had been shaving, or more likely trimming his beard, when the alarm had sounded. His suspenders were twisted from having been hastily drawn up over his shoulders. He circled the room, taking in the smoking, charred debris on the floor, the soot on the walls and ceiling, the objects overturned and smashed in the commotion that had followed the troopers' arrival. Our guard, his face streaked black and glistening with sweat, saluted and began to tell his side of the story, but the major cut him off with a slashing motion.

By this time the air had cleared and the three of us were sitting around the table with innocent expressions pasted on our faces. Harms kicked aside a smoldering scrap of tunic and stalked up to us, fists clenched at his sides. He was livid.

"Something wrong, Major?" I was seated nearest him.

His left fist caught me on the corner of the jaw. I went over backwards, chair and all, and hit the floor hard. I bounced up quicker than he expected and cocked my own left.

"Page."

Jac spoke warningly. I shifted my gaze, followed his, and got a spectacular view of the inside of the old trooper's Army Colt pointed at my breast. I lowered my arm.

At a nod from Harms the gun was returned to leather. Cutting loose had calmed him somewhat. His color was closer to normal, but the silver flecks in his eyes swam and glittered in the light of the one lamp left burning.

"What did you gain by that?" He addressed himself to Hudspeth.

"We're expensive pets to keep," I replied, making him face me. "We just wanted to show you how expensive we can be."

"Is that a threat? Because if it is I can throw you in the guardhouse and be done with it."

"You did that with Ghost Shirt."

"We've learned a bit since then."

"Like what?" Hudspeth put in. "Doubling the guard? You can't spare that many men with things like they are. You said yourself you're short-handed."

"The fact of it is, Major," I went on, "we're more trouble than we're worth. You can take away our guns and our matches, tie us up and throw us in a deep hole, and we'll still make it hot for you and your men. You can weather it, but why should you have to? You've enough to worry about with all hell breaking loose outside."

While I had been speaking, patches of color had appeared on his cheeks, glowing as if from fever, and I braced myself to meet another blow. But he held himself in check. When he spoke, the strain showed in his voice, raising it from its normal moderate level to a quivering tenor.

"Just whose side are you on, Murdock?"

"That's easy. Mine."

This time I was sure he was going to make a move, but he fooled me again. For an hour, or maybe it was just ten seconds, he stood there staring at me without seeing me. Then, without turning, he spoke to the old trooper.

"See that their mounts are saddled and their pack horse loaded and ready to go. They're leaving tonight."

"Tomorrow morning's soon enough," I said magnanimously. "We promise not to burn down any buildings before then."

"I wasn't offering you a choice. It's tonight or never." The glint in his cow eyes was as steely as it got. "I'll read Scripture over your grave, Murdock."

Half the stars in the sky were blotted out behind a black

overcast as we saddled up (never trust that job to anyone else, least of all a trooper who hates your guts), and by the time we were ready to move out they were all gone and thunder was belching faintly in the distance.

Our guns were returned to us in the livery by the old trooper who had been our guard. I slid my Winchester into its scabbard, inspected the Deane-Adams to make sure it was still loaded, and caught the horse soldier's eye over the cylinder. He avoided my gaze.

He was old enough to be a general, but his faded blue sleeves bore a single stripe. Most likely he'd risen in rank and been busted back down more than once, probably for brawling. The scar tissue over his eyes and fistlike, many-times-broken nose gave me that much. Those eyes were deep in their sockets and shadowed beneath shaggy white brows. They wouldn't blacken noticeably no matter how many times they were hit, nor how hard. He wore his handlebar a third longer than Hudspeth's. Also white, it was stained yellow at the fringe—chewing tobacco—and at the moment its ends were being gnawed by a set of mail-order teeth that buzzed when he spoke, which he hadn't done for some time. Unlike Blackthorne, he appeared not to mind wearing them. His complexion was breadcrust-brown and cracked all over like a riverbed gone dry. The sagging flesh beneath his chin was gathered together at the buttoned collar of his field-stained tunic. Crisp white stubble showed where his razor had missed that morning, a circle of sticking-plaster where it hadn't. We played tag with the eye contact for a while and then I lost my patience.

"All right, disgorge." I holstered the five-shot. "You look like you swallowed a powder keg."

"I can't do it," he said. His voice fell somewhere between a whisper and the sound you get when you try to rack a shell into the chamber of a repeater with sand in the action. "I don't care if they bust me again, I can't watch you three go out there without telling you what's waiting."

Hudspeth gave his cinch a yank and then all was silence. The ticking of the blacksmith's forge as it cooled grew loud. Somewhere a horse snored.

"Well?" The word exploded from the marshal.

The trooper lurched ahead without further preamble. His eyes were black hollows beneath the heavy brows. "I'm Hoxie, Jed Hoxie. Twenty years in the service, not counting the two I spent with Stonewall Jackson. I was with that patrol that got hit last night. Cap'n Francis—he was one of them got kilt—he headed it up till one of the injun scouts found the trail of a couple dozen unshod ponies this side of the James. It could of been friendlies, maybe even métis, but nobody believed that for a minute. None of them has budged a inch from their camps and reservations since this whole thing started, except to hunt, and there ain't no hunting along the Jim this time of year. No, we knowed who it was all right. When you been out here as long as some of us you get so you can smell 'em. Francis ordered halt and sent a messenger back to the fort for orders from Colonel Broderick. But instead of sending 'em, the old man rode back hisself and took charge of the patrol. He said it was time the job got done right, and he wasn't going to trust it to no one else. There was forty of us—more than enough, I guess he figured, to deal with Ghost Shirt.

"Their trail crossed the river a couple of miles south of Jamestown. It was so fresh there was puddles of water in the tracks on the other side. We caught sight of dust clouds a hour or so later. There wasn't much, what with all the grass, but you can always count on twenty horses kicking up a little when they're rid hard. This was the hilly country in the Drift Prairie, and the dust was all we seen of 'em. Broderick called column of twos and we give chase at a canter. We was still following the dust cloud when they hit us.

"They come at us from two sides, one half hitting us in the flank from the left, the other taking us at a angle near the front from the right, just like a pair of scissors. Neatest split cavalry charge I ever did see. They come out of nowhere, whooping it up to beat the band and pounding away with them Spencer repeaters they took from our armory. Broderick went first. Bullet tore clean through his left eye and knocked off the back of his head on its way out. Captain Francis took two in the chest and one in the thigh and bled to death before we could get him back to the fort. We lost our bugler whilst he was blowing recall. He went down with one in his back, wailing on that horn like a sick calf. Bullets was flying all over the place. Once I felt someone tugging at my sleeve, but when I turned to see who it was, there was nobody there. What was there was a hole in the elbow where a hunk of lead kissed it. The injuns made one pass, then turned around and done it again, only backwards, and all the time they was pouring lead into us like grease through a tin horn. We'd of lost a hell of a lot more than twelve men if injuns was any kind of shots."

"Did you hit any of them?" I asked.

He shook his head, working his store-bought teeth like a mouthful of chew. "Can't say for sure. There was a lot of metal buzzing back and forth, and the way them injuns shriek you don't know if they're hit or just mad. But if we didn't at least nick one or two of 'em it'd be a miracle."

"Was Ghost Shirt with them?"

"Oh, he was with 'em all right. I seen too much of him when he was here in the stockade not to recognize him when I seen him again, and he wasn't wearing no war paint like the others. He rode point on the bunch that hit us from the front."

"Why wasn't he wearing paint?"

"How the hell should I know? Them injuns don't think the same as people. All I know is that paint's supposed to turn away bullets. Maybe he figures he don't need it."

"Whose dust were you following when they attacked?" Hudspeth asked. He peered into the buckskin sack of cartridges he carried in his saddle bag to see if they were all there.

"Likely that belonged to the womenfolk, dragging buffalo robes and bushes behind their horses to make it look like the whole party. It's the oldest trick in the book, but it works most every time. Hell, what can you do to fight it?"

"You can go back to the fort." This from Pere Jac, without intonation. The comment drew a hostile glance from the horse soldier.

"I'd expect that from a breed," he snarled. "We're the army. We're trained to fight."

"And die," said the other. "In the end, what have you gained?"

Hoxie's complexion turned a high copper. I stepped between him and the métis.

"Steady, soldier. We're all on the same side."

"I don't take to nobody with injun blood in his veins calling me a fool," he said. But his violent mood had subsided.

"Nobody called anybody anything. Where was this fight?"

He grew furtive. "I said enough. If the major finds out I told you what I done already he'll bust me out of the service. I just didn't want nobody running off and getting kilt without knowing the score. What you do now is your business." He tugged his hat down and took a step toward the stable door. I laid a hand on his shoulder. It felt like a chunk of the scrawny meat we'd had for supper. He stopped and glared up at me from his inferior height, eyes glittering beneath the shelf of his brows.

"If you tell us where Ghost Shirt is hiding, the major will never know you told us anything."

He started as if slapped in the face. For a moment disbelief and consternation chased each other across his features in the greasy glow of the coal-oil lantern that hung on a rusty nail beside the door. His eyes searched mine for some sign that I was bluffing. He didn't find anything. I sit a good game of poker.

"That stinks," he said.

"To high heaven," I agreed.

"They give him a lot of slack out here. He could call it high treason in time of war and have me shot."

"That's up to you."

"Even if I get away, he'll send Sergeant Burdett after me. Broderick used to sic him on deserters like a trained hunting dog. He never brought any of them back alive."

I said nothing. The forge had grown silent, and now there was only the liquid hiss of the lantern behind me to underscore the stillness. At last the trooper fixed me with an expression that made me feel the way I'd felt when I looked down the barrel of his gun in Broderick's quarters. I rested a thumb on the butt of the Deane-Adams, just in case.

"There's a old stone building six, eight miles west of the river, a fort of some kind. Sergeant Burdett told me that Harms's patrol got within a couple of hundred yards of it this morning when a bunch of bucks on the wall opened fire and the major called retreat. It'd take a force three times what we got a month to blast its way in there. A twelve-pounder wouldn't knock the mortar out from between the rocks in the wall."

"The Mormon mission," said Jac.

I nodded. "Thanks, Private. You're clear with us."

He muttered something indelicate and stamped out.

The first drop banged my hat while I was mounting up outside the door. It was the last individual drop I heard. The rest came down in a roar so sudden Hudspeth and I were thoroughly soaked by the time we got our black slickers out and on. Pere Jac merely removed his nice calico shirt and stored it safely in a saddle bag, facing the elements half naked.

"Couldn't wait till tomorrow to get kicked out, could you?" grumbled the marshal.

Jac smiled and quoted something from Mark, or maybe it was Matthew.

The water was streaming from the brims of our hats—those of us who had hats—as we rode out through the open gate. It glistened on the old breed's broad back, magnifying the scars of battles old and new. There was a light in the window of Major Harms's office, and I knew he was bidding us good riddance. I considered tipping my hat, thought better of it, and kicked the bay into a canter just in time to splatter mud over the uniforms of the troopers waiting to close the gates behind us. Whatever they called me was drowned out by the downpour.

# CHAPTER 7

The wind rose and lightning stabbed at the ground, throwing the landscape into dazzling negative, as we stopped to camp on the high ground west of Fort Ransom. But the hard rain was over, and that which hissed down around us now was the kind that could go on for days, flooding the lowlands and washing away farmers' crops as it fed rivers still swollen from the spring thaw. Hudspeth and I used our rifles to make tents of our oilcloth slickers and crawled under them while Pere Jac wrapped himself up from head to foot in his saddle blanket and began snoring almost immediately. If I slept at all I never realized it, shivering in my wet clothes and listening to the drops drumming the surface of my temporary shelter as I thought about how nice it would be to hear them tapping the roof of the officers' quarters back at the fort from the depths of a warm featherbed.

It was still raining when I arose at sunup to find the marshal already at work over a small fire, frying bacon in the cast-iron skillet he carried in one of his saddle bags. The smell of sweet grease clawed at my stomach, reminding me that I hadn't eaten anything to speak of since breakfast the day before. The longhorn beef at Fort Ransom didn't count. I swigged water from my canteen, sloshed it around

and spat it out to clear away some of the fuzz, and stepped
closer just to smell.

"Where in hell did you find dry wood?" I asked him.

"Not wood, buffalo chips." His voice was hoarse and
thick with phlegm, the way it was every morning. After several days with him I knew that it didn't begin to clear until
he'd been up half an hour. "Best damn fuel there is, and it
never gets so soaked you can't start it burning with a little
work."

"I'm surprised the métis have left buffalo in Dakota to
make enough to get a fire started." I glowered at Pere Jac,
who sat on his wet blanket gnawing at his pemmican. I re-
sented the ease with which he had fallen asleep the night
before. He went on chewing as if he hadn't heard.

The bacon was a little too crisp for my taste, but after
nearly starving to death I wasn't complaining. Jac preferred
the saddle leather he was eating, but he did accept a tin cup
of coffee when it was offered. I did too, but only to wash
the grease from the roof of my mouth. The stuff tasted like
burnt grain. We crouched around the fire sipping in moody
silence.

"What are we doing out here?" growled Hudspeth.
"Bouncing around all over the territory, getting saddle sores
and wet asses, and for what? A hunk of lead between the
eyes and six feet of Dakota on our faces."

"Flood's your boss, not mine. You tell me." I swallowed
the dregs in the cup carefully, having already scalded my
tongue and throat with the first gulp. I hooked the pot out
of the fire with my kerchief wrapped around my hand and
poured a second cupful. Glutton for punishment, that's me.

"Me I can answer for." He produced his flask and poured
a ration of whiskey into his coffee. "I'm out of a job if I
don't. Jac's got whiskey coming, if the rest of his tribe don't

drink it all up before he gets back. You're the one I can't figure. What's in this for you?"

"The thrill of the hunt, the glory of the kill."

"No, really."

I warmed my hands around the tin cup. "I've never walked away from anything once it's started. I suppose this was as good a place to start as any, and I probably would have if I hadn't risked my scalp fighting the Flatheads in the Bitterroots last year. If I didn't turn my back on that, why should I do it now? Besides, I'd kind of like to see if we can get away with it. So do you, but you won't admit it."

"Maybe so, but it's a damn poor reason to get killed."

"I've yet to hear a good one."

He threw the dregs of his coffee into the fire and got up. That was another of his quirks. He never drank the last of anything, not even whiskey. "Well, if we got to die, it might as well be sooner as later. Saddle up." He kicked mud and clumps of wet grass into the fire. It went out grudgingly.

Pere Jac drained his cup and rose with none of the complaints you expect from an old man climbing to his feet after a long interval. He shook out his blanket, wrung it out thoroughly, used it to rub down his shivering paint, wrung it out again, tossed it over the pony's back, and saddled it. I did the same, using the bay's blanket for rubdown, then wringing out my bedroll and strapping it behind the cantle of my saddle. We fed the horses two handfuls of grain apiece and were on our way by the time sunlight turned the sky from black to charcoal gray.

It was twenty-five miles from where we'd camped to the James River, with mud the color of rust squirting up around the horses' hoofs at every step. There's nothing exciting about a trek across the flat country east of the Drift Prairie, especially with rain bleeding down and turning everything

a mildewy gray. Suffice it to say that one Dakota river basin looks pretty much like all the others.

By the same token, there was nothing spectacular about
the James, even at high water. Sodden, grassy banks dotted
sparsely with scrawny cottonwoods and box elders sunk to
their lower branches in muddy, liver-colored water do not
inspire great poetry. The current was swift but hardly torrential, so the damned thing didn't even have danger going
for it. It was just another river in a territory chock full of
just anothers. Nevertheless we had made pretty good time
in reaching it, as there was still an hour of daylight sitting
somewhere beyond the overcast when we got off to water
the horses and fill our canteens.

"We'll camp here tonight," I said. "Cross in the morning."

"What for? It's early yet." Hudspeth wiped his running
nose on the sleeve of his coat and removed a clot of floating
grass from the mouth of his canteen between thumb and
forefinger.

"I don't know about you, but I'll sleep better with a river
between me and Ghost Shirt."

"Afraid?"

"Yes."

There were no fires that night, nor the next morning. Even
if there had been buffalo chips available, the chance of an
Indian spotting the smoke was too great. We ate some of
the salt pork Hudspeth and I had bought in Fargo—Jac stuck
to his pemmican—and washed it down with water from our
canteens. That night we took turns standing watch, me first.
I kept awake slapping at the mosquitoes that descended over
me in swarms.

The rain had stopped by the time we were ready to pull
out, not that it made much difference with the sun still hidden by clouds and the wet grass cloying around our knees

and a strip of water thirty feet wide waiting to be crossed. I dreaded that. Horses hate to cross the stuff at the best of times, but when it's over chest-high they forget who their masters are and make for the nearest dry land regardless of what happens to the weight on their backs. I felt the bay gasp when the bottom fell out from under it. Before it could spook, I grabbed a double armload of its neck and raked its flanks with my spurs. It screamed and swam for dear life. I closed my eyes and held on until there was solid ground beneath me once again. Hudspeth was there waiting for me, the pack horse in tow. Pere Jac crossed over a moment later.

"How far?" I asked the latter.

"Seven miles." He pointed toward the southwest. "It is the only building around still standing."

"What's the best way to approach it?" asked Hudspeth.

"With the cavalry."

We decided to risk a frontal approach rather than lose another day by circling around, and headed southwest. Half an hour later the sun broke through the overcast. Droplets of moisture sparkled on the blades of tall grass like broken glass after a barroom fight. Gradually the flat plain gave way to rolling prairie. The landscape was deceptive. From a distance it looked as if you could see everything for miles, but you could miss half the Cheyenne nation hiding in the hollows between the hills. We slowed our pace accordingly.

After four miles we came to a broad swath running from north to south where what grass that had not been trampled beneath many hoofs was grazed almost to the ground. The horses nickered when we stopped, and shifted their weight nervously from hoof to hoof. The métis dismounted, crouched, and spent some moments studying the turned earth. Then he rose with a grim expression on his weathered countenance.

"Unshod ponies," he said. "Heading south. One, perhaps two hours ago."

"Ghost Shirt?" I suggested.

He shook his head. "Not unless he has picked up many new braves."

"How many?"

"More than I can count."

He climbed back into the saddle and we continued for another hour. Jac reined in at the crown of a hill and thrust a long, wrinkled finger at arm's length before him. "There!"

I followed his gesture. At first I couldn't see anything. Then I spotted it, an irregularity on the horizon, hardly more than a blur, but obvious enough against a skyline nearly devoid of trees.

"The mission?"

Jac nodded.

"I can't see a damn thing." The marshal drew a battered army-issue telescope from his saddle bag, extended it to its full length, and screwed it into his left eye socket. He spent some time twisting it. "Yeah, I see it," he said then. "It's—" He stiffened.

"What is it?" I demanded, after a couple of seconds had slithered past in silence.

"I think we're too late." He handed me the glass.

I trained it toward the object atop the distant rise. It was a stone fortress, thirty years old if it was a day, with broken battlements along the top of the front wall and a ravaged bell tower rising from the middle, the bell intact and naked to the elements. I panned away from the structure, saw something belatedly, went back. I twisted the scope for sharper focus.

A mounted phalanx of perhaps three hundred Indians loaded down with full war regalia was on its way toward the mission's yawning entrance from the north. Even as they approached, a small group of similarly attired warriors galloped out to meet them. When they were a hundred yards apart they stopped, and the leader of each band peeled off for a private parley in the center of the clearing. The glass wasn't powerful enough for me to make out their features, but it didn't really matter. Never having seen Ghost Shirt, I wouldn't have recognized him anyway.

# CHAPTER 8

"You're the injun expert," Hudspeth informed me sourly. "What do we do now?"

I played for time, studying the doll-size figures on horseback in the center of the magnified circle. Short of a Great Southwestern desert after a brief rain, when everything is in blossom and the sagebrush looks like it's on fire, there's nothing more colorful than a large group of Plains Indians girded for war. Many of them half naked, the rest wearing fringed and beaded vests or jackets or the remnants of blue cavalry tunics with the sleeves cut off, the warriors had painted their skin red and black and yellow and white and decorated themselves with shells and beads and the claws and teeth of various predators. The braves from the mission were all armed with rifles, the others with only an occasional firearm among the lances, clubs, and bows and arrows, all of which were lowered as a gesture of peace and good faith.

They wore buckskin leggings and wolf pelts and summer moccasins with fringes that dangled below the bellies of their mounts. Coup sticks trailing eagle feathers and the traditional Cheyenne and Sioux symbols of strength and virility, fashioned of leather and polished wood and rattling at the ends of buckhide thongs knotted to the buffalo bone cross-pieces, stuck up at crazy angles above the heads of the warriors holding them. Here and there the white bulb of a bleached human skull decorated the top of a pike.

One Indian—he who had ridden out alone to greet the leader of the newcomers—wore neither paint nor decoration. Naked to the waist, he was attired only in leggings, moccasins, and a breechclout of what looked like faded red burlap, dyed by a squaw's patient hand. It was the only splash of color on his person. He rode bareback astride a muscular roan with a white blaze and stockings, whose full sides suggested grain and not grass feeding—hardly an Indian pony. A couple of hundred yards closer and I might have been able to make out the army brand on its sleek rump. The rider was built thick about the chest and upper arms, and his nut-brown flesh glistened with grease or sweat or both. He wore his black hair long. That was as much as I could tell about him from my vantage point. He didn't look much like a god, but then I'm no authority.

The other chief was decked out in fine buckskins and a feathered headdress whose tail descended below his waist and rested on the back of one of those hide-stripping wooden saddles with which some savages insisted upon torturing their mounts. Strips of ermine dangled in front of his ears, and when he turned once to gesture with a long, fringed arm over the Indians at his back the sunlight shone on a row of polished stones in the headband. It was a sight that kings and Russian grand dukes came halfway around the world to see, only to return home in disappointment when they didn't. Somehow, though, in the presence of the other's unadorned simplicity, the visitor's splendor came off as pompous and a shade ludicrous. I passed the telescope to Pere Jac.

"The one in the headdress. Recognize him?"

The métis was unfamiliar with the instrument. Carefully

he placed it against his right eye, waved it back and forth a little, settled down finally, and sat motionless for about a minute. Then he returned the glass to me.

"His name is Many Ponies," he said. "He used to trade with the métis before the wars. Some of the Miniconjou Sioux elected to follow him at the time of the breakup following Custer's death. The last I heard of him he was in Canada."

"He's back."

Jac went on. "Tall Dog, also a Miniconjou, is there as well. I was told he had retired to the Standing Rock reservation. Also Broken Jaw, a Cheyenne warrior, and Blood on His Lance, who was a sub-chief under the great Oglala Crazy Horse. The others I do not know."

"That's all right. That's enough."

"So what do we do?" repeated the marshal.

"Why ask me?" I swung the glass back to him. The movement startled him. He jumped, then grabbed the instrument with both hands. "You're the ramrod in this outfit."

"You've fought injuns. I never been closer to one than a cigar store."

"I shot at a few. That's not the same as fighting them."

"It's close enough for me."

"While we are arguing," Pere Jac put in, "I suggest that we get down behind this hill before they see us against the horizon."

"Congratulations," I told him. "You just became our new Indian expert."

We wheeled our horses and withdrew below the crest of the rise. There we dismounted and squatted to confer, holding onto the animals' reins in the absence of a place to tether them. We kept our voices low, which was ridiculous, considering the distance that separated us from the Indians at the mission. Fear does strange things to people.

"It is obvious that one of us must go back for the soldiers while the rest remain here to keep an eye on the Indians." Jac took out his stubby pipe and sucked air through it noisily. "The question is, which of us shall it be?"

We exchanged glances for a while, but no one seemed inclined to volunteer. There was no telling what kind of reception awaited the one who returned to the fort alone. Ghost Shirt, however, was something on which we could count. At length the métis shrugged and plucked a handful of stiff new grass from the ground at his feet. He spent some time sorting through the blades, decided on three, discarded the others, then made a show of clearing his throat, like the foreman of a jury milking his moment in the sun before delivering the verdict.

"We will draw straws. The holder of the short straw will go."

I shook my head. "I don't like it."

"Why not?" Hudspeth demanded. "It seems fair enough."

"That's why I don't like it."

Jac shuffled the bits of stubble in such a way that we couldn't see what he was doing, and held out a fist from the top of which the ends barely protruded.

Hudspeth selected the first one and held it up. It was about two inches long. His breath came out in a sigh.

I stared at the two remaining until the breed began to show signs of impatience—which, taking into account his natural stoic disposition, should give some idea of how long I stalled. I took a deep breath and plucked out the one on the right. It fell just short of an inch.

We looked at Jac. He was enjoying his role. He kept us

in suspense for as long as was prudent, and when Hudspeth's nose began to flush he opened his fist. A straw an inch and a half long lay in the hollow of his palm.

"I told you I didn't like it." I threw down the evidence and got up to remount. "I'll be back when I can." The bay grunted in protest when I swung a leg over its back, as if it knew where we were going.

"Just a minute." Hudspeth took hold of the bit chain. "If you bring the army and they help us catch Ghost Shirt, how are we going to get him away from them to hang in Bismarck?"

I leaned forward and, taking his wrist between thumb and forefinger, removed his hand from the bit. "You worry too much," I said. "We'll never live to see Bismarck again anyway."

"Good luck, Page." Pere Jac's expression was blank.

I could see he really meant it, so I choked back the response I had all set, nodded curtly, and laid down tracks east.

The rain in Dakota, I learned, doesn't stop during the wet season. It just moves on, leaving the places where it's been to dry and cake and the crops to wither while it washes away what's left of the green that's already given up waiting for it elsewhere. The storm that had hit us after leaving Fort Ransom was in the north now, a black crescent on the skyline looking like the charred fringe of a towel left too close to the fire, dumping water over the higher country up around Fargo. The prehistoric lake bed that stretched from the Drift Prairie to the Red River took the runoff and channeled it into the James River. At that point the lazy stream we had crossed a couple of hours earlier became a snarling torrent forty feet wide at its narrowest point and swift enough to sweep downriver a horse and rider faster than a man can curse. I no longer recognized it.

I wasted half a day riding up and down in search of a place to cross. A mile north of the spot where we'd come over, the river broadened into a lake, which was no good at all, and the farther south I rode the swifter grew the current. It was late afternoon when I gave up and turned back toward the mission, and damned near sundown before I galloped up the rise where I'd left my companions.

At least I thought it was where I'd left them. Those swells all looked alike when there was no one there. I called their names a couple of times, being careful to keep my voice from carrying as far as the mission. When after two or three minutes there was no answer, I rode to the top of the hill and looked around. There was the mission on the sky-line, looking to be about the same distance away as it had been that morning. There was no sign of life on any of the other hills in the area. I turned and cantered back below the crest for a second look.

It was the spot, all right. Dismounting, I saw that the ground was chewed up where our horses had stood fidgeting and pawing the earth while we squatted talking, and in a bare spot I saw the pointed toe of a footprint that could only have been made by one of Hudspeth's fancy Mexican boots. As I bent over to study it, something cold and slimy slithered up my spine. I mounted again and spurred the bay back to the crest. What I saw there made me reach back automatically to grip the butt of my revolver.

On the ridge about three hundred yards away, a solitary rider sat facing me astride a roan horse with no saddle. The figure's hair hung down in plaits on either side of its naked chest. It was holding a rifle upright with the butt resting upon one thigh; a cloth of some sort drooping from its barrel and stirring ever so slightly in the minimal breeze. I was only dimly aware that this was Pere Jac's beloved calico shirt. The Indian looked as if he had been there for hours, which was impossible, since I'd just looked in that direction a few minutes before and seen nothing. The slimy thing crawled back down my backbone.

"Page Murdock." Warped and distorted by distance, the unfamiliar voice was felt rather than heard, stroking my eardrums in such a way that it set my teeth on edge. "You have the choice of dying in the mission with your friends or dying out here alone. I await your answer."

# CHAPTER 9

I waited until the words died away before, slowly, as if a sudden movement might spook my game, I squeaked my Winchester from its scabbard and raised it to my shoulder. Ghost Shirt didn't stir. I wondered if he thought his flag of truce might save him, or if he really believed he was indestructible. If so, his brilliance was overrated. Allowing for distance and the updraft from the hills that rolled between us, I drew a bead on a point just above his left shoulder and took a deep breath, half of which I planned to let out before I squeezed the trigger. Still he didn't move.

But something did.

Thirty feet in front of my nose, the ground heaved and spewed up a dozen black-faced braves on horseback. They exploded over the crest of the next ridge, teeth bared white—or as close to white as Indians' teeth got—against the ebony goo they had smeared over themselves from hairline to breechclout, Spencer repeaters braced one-armed against their biceps in that impossible-to-hit-anything way they had. At that range, however, they couldn't *all* miss. They were all over me in two blinks, stabbing the bay's bit before it could rear, snatching the carbine out of my hands, jerking my Deane-Adams from its holster. I was overpowered by the stench of hot sweat and bad grease, of lathered horseflesh and paint. No hands reached for me. They didn't have to. I was ringed in.

They were Cheyenne. One, a brave with a nose like a razor and a lightning-streak of yellow slashing diagonally across his blackened features, wore one of those human-finger necklaces for which the tribe was notorious, its macabre pendants brown and wrinkled and shrunken so that the nails stood out like claws. They didn't look as if they had ever strung a bow or braided beads into a horse's mane or, to put an even grimmer face on it, drawn a needle through an embroidery hoop or followed a passage in a family Bible. Interspersed among these were tiny medicine bags that looked to have been fashioned from human flesh. The ornament carried strong medicine, too strong for an ordinary warrior. But there was only one chief in Ghost Shirt's crowd, so he must have been no more than a sub-chief or a brave who had proved himself in many battles. Possibly a medicine man. In any case, he seemed to be the leader of this band, as my Winchester was turned over to him without hesitation by the Indian who had seized it. He eyed it lovingly, passed a hand over the engraving on the action, then, decisively, thrust his own dusty Spencer into the hands of the brave nearest him and tucked the carbine under his arm. He grunted a terse order. The point of a broad-bladed knife was thrust inside my left nostril and hands rooted around inside my saddle bags. At length my cartridge boxes were produced and tossed to the ranking warrior. The sharp scent of steel tickled the hairs inside my nose. I controlled myself with an effort. A sneeze now could have cost me a substantial amount of blood, to say nothing of what a startled Indian might do. Not that I was going to live long enough to see the last of the sun, wallowing now in a blood-red pool behind the fortress on the distant ridge.

Another order was given in guttural Cheyenne and my horse began moving with no encouragement from me. In a mass we struck out toward the mission. I glanced in that direction, but Ghost Shirt was no longer there. Having served his purpose as bait, he had left the situation in the hands of his subordinates and returned to his stronghold. Such confidence in the obedience of his warriors bordered on arrogance.

Up close, the wall of the mission turned out to be constructed of weathered stone, tightly mortared and forming a barrier nearly twenty feet high around the buildings inside. Three decades or more ago it had served as a place of refuge for the settlers who had dwelled nearby in farmhouses long since reduced to their foundations by fire and the elements. A few pulls on the great bell that swung in the central tower and the Mormons would come streaming in for protection from Indians, blizzards, or religious persecution, three of the many dangers they had learned to live with in order to uphold their creed. I wondered which of the three had brought an end to it all in this lonely quarter, or if they had simply thrown everything over to join Brigham Young's exodus to Utah. Whatever the reason, only this fire-blackened, bullet-chipped fortress remained as a monument to the brotherly existence they preached.

The gate was made of logs bound and pegged together vertically, all but petrified with age. It swung open in one piece to admit us, then was secured by a handful of Indians who lowered another log into steel cleats on either side of the opening, much as at Fort Ransom. The ground inside the enclosure had been pounded over the years into a dust fine as face powder and loosened by the activity of the present occupants to form a layer two inches deep. It puffed up around the horses' fetlocks in reddish clouds that drifted across the compound like gunsmoke across a busy battle-field. Fresh rope ladders hung from the catwalks on all four walls, atop which Sioux and Cheyenne sentries stood watching me, their eyes hostile slits in faces dried and cracked beyond their years by constant exposure to sun, wind, and grit.

There were women and children in the compound, which surprised me, although there was no reason it should have. Sex and age were of little consequence among a people for whom hardship and danger were a way of life. It didn't matter to the children running naked, their ribs showing beneath their brown hides, that there was a war on, nor to the stout squaws who hardly glanced at me as they sat cross-legged in the hot sun chewing on large squares of buckskin to make soft leggings for their braves or lugged clay pots of water and baskets of dried buffalo chips to their cooking fires. They were doing the work their mothers and grand-mothers had done before them, all the way back to when the Earth-Shaker fashioned the first woman out of clay to mate with and free the first brave for hunting and making weapons.

Except for the stone bell tower, now in the early stages of decay, the structures inside the compound were made of less sturdy stuff than the wall. Soddies mostly, with here and there a long, low adobe building scattered among them, its thatched roof sagging in the middle like a Conestoga wagon, they were ramshackle affairs slapped together more for shelter during the hours of sleep than for actual living purposes, and had begun falling apart twenty years before. Cones of buffalo hide strewn about the grounds offered mute testimony to some Indians' contempt for the white man's idea of quarters.

The foundation of the tower—which, if the weatherbeaten

wooden cross pegged into the mortar on the front of it was
any indication, had once been the mission chapel—was
square, sunk below the ground, and entered by means of a
shallow flight of earthen steps leading down to a low plank
door. Rough hands yanked me from my horse and half-
carried, half-dragged me to the top of the steps. Teetering
on the edge, I was patted all over for hidden weapons, relieved of the knife I carried in my right boot, and shoved
head first down the stairwell. I sailed through the air just
long enough to experience that eerie weightless sensation
you get when falling in a dream, then, suddenly, slammed
into a great blank wall of nothing.

Someday, when they build a home for retired lawmen,
they'll have to provide a row of chairs in which those fortunate few who survive the profession may sit while they
stare at the wall. I had scarcely gotten rid of the headache
I'd acquired last winter when a wife-murderer I'd been escorting back to Helena had parted my hair with a rock
during an unguarded moment, and now, as I swam to consciousness through a pool of thick, multicolored glue, I
wondered why Grant and Lee were fighting the Battle of the
Wilderness, complete with thundering twelve-pounders and
rattling musketry, all over again inside my skull.

I was flat on my back on what had to be the hardest stone
floor this side of Yuma prison. My first act, after the necessary vomiting, was to raise a gentle hand to the top of my
head to see if anything was leaking out. A white-hot bolt
of pure pain shot straight down to my toes when the tip of
my index finger stroked a lump the size of a cobblestone in
a nest of matted, sticky hair. After that I quit. At least this
time my skull was in one piece. That was a relief, even if
whatever was locked up inside it was pounding to get out.

Nobody ever told me if we're allowed more than one cracked head to a lifetime.

I decided that I was inside the chapel. If so, I now saw where the work that had not gone into the other buildings on the mission grounds went. I ran a palm over the surface of the floor. It was made of flat rocks, polished to as high a finish as sandstone ever achieved, and bunted up against one another so snugly that in places I couldn't squeeze my fingertips between them. Above me, the crudely vaulted ceiling opened into a shaft that shot straight up to the sky, where the rusted bell stood out in sharp relief against the jagged, moon-washed square beyond. The thing must have weighed half a ton. One good tug on the frayed old rope that dangled down between the rotted rafters, I thought detachedly, and the great hunk of iron would come singing down and squash me like a roach. With my head in its present condition I didn't much care.

Now and then a solitary bat flapped its pendulous course to and fro inside the rim, the framework of its membrane-covered wings etched starkly against the pale sky. The sight of it jarred me into reality. How long had I been out?

"Two hours."

My head jerked around in the direction of the unexpected voice, the pain following close behind. When the popping lights and purple spots faded, I saw moonlight playing over the angular bones of Pere Jac's face in the darkened corner where he was sitting. The orange glow of his pipe brightened as he sucked on the other end, then faded as he took it from between invisible lips. He was shirtless, which came as no surprise since I'd seen the garment hanging from Ghost Shirt's rifle earlier.

"It is the third question a man asks when he comes to after a blow," he went on without salutation. "First he asks himself where he is, then what happened. When he has answered those he is left with the passage of time, to which only another can reply."

"Sounds like the voice of experience." My tongue moved sluggishly. My face began to burn and I realized that my forehead and the bridge of my nose were skinned where I had come into contact with whatever I had come into contact with.

"A man who has reached my age without being knocked senseless at least once has not lived. They carried you in here after it became apparent that they could not open the door simply by throwing you against it. Not that they did not come close. Two of the boards you sprang will never be the same."

"Neither will my head." I rolled over onto my side so that I could see him without straining my eyeballs, which creaked in their sockets. It was then that I discovered that every muscle in my body was in the same condition as my skull. "Where's Hudspeth?"

"Beside me, sleeping. Can you not hear his snores?"

I'd thought it was the foundation settling. Now I became aware of the rhythm in the rumbling noise coming from the blackness at the base of the wall. I had to hand it to the marshal. He could sleep on the gallows.

"Care to tell me the story?"

"It is very exciting." The red glow arced upward, flared, faded again. Black against the milky-water color of the moonlight, threads of smoke unraveled up the shaft. "An hour after you left we decided to bed down the horses so that they would be fresh for whatever would be expected of them when you returned. I heard a noise on the other side of the hill as I was unsaddling. I was reaching for my Sharps when a Cheyenne lance pierced my right shoulder. A.C. shot the brave in the throat with his revolver while he was turning to draw his knife at the top of the hill. The bullet nearly took his head off. Before he hit the ground fourteen or fifteen Indians came whooping and shrieking over the crest, waving rifles and those hatchets my French ancestors traded their great-grandfathers for furs and blankets. A.C. killed two and wounded a third, but there were too many of them and they were too fast, even on foot. They fell on him and would have torn him to pieces then and there had not Ghost Shirt stepped in to prevent it."

"That doesn't fit in with what I've heard about him."

"I think that he has something special in mind for A.C."

And yet he slept. I shook my head in wonder. Judge Flood didn't know the quality of the iron he was getting set to toss on the scrap heap.

"How'd they know you were there?" I asked Jac.

"Perhaps they spotted us when we were watching them earlier. It is more likely that someone noticed the sunlight glancing off the lens of the spyglass."

"Seems to me I should have heard the gunshots. I wasn't that far away."

"You wouldn't. These hills soak up noise."

"That's not all they've soaked up. How's the shoulder?"

He shrugged, then right away regretted it. I heard a sharp intake of breath in the darkness. He let it out carefully, through his nostrils. "They have applied a bandage, of sorts. The medicine man—Lame Horse, I think he is called, my Cheyenne is rusty—said some words over it. I shall live in spite of them."

"Decent of them to have left you your pipe, matches and tobacco."

"We are the only things here that will burn. Am I to assume that the army is not coming?"

I told him about the river. He sighed.

"'For it is better,'" he quoted, "'if the will of God be so, that ye suffer for well doing, than for evil doing.'"

There isn't much you can say to a thing like that, so I let it stand. Hudspeth's snoring dominated everything for a time. Then, from outside, a high, thin wail was borne in on the night air. An unearthly sound, brazen and eerie. It raised the hairs on the back of my neck.

"What in hell was *that*?"

"A bugle." He knocked out his pipe against the wall at his back. A shower of sparks fell to the floor, glowed there for a while, then blinked out, one by one. "Captured, I suppose, when they attacked Colonel Broderick's patrol. They have been taking turns blowing it for the past hour. Probably they hope to use it to confuse the soldiers next time they fight."

"It won't work unless they know the calls. The way they're blowing it sounds chilling as hell."

"That is the next best thing."

We listened to it for a while.

"How come we're still alive?" I asked then.

He hesitated. "I have been wondering the same thing. It worries me."

"Hostages?"

"I think not. What would they have to bargain for? They have their freedom. No, I fear that they have some other use for us. The reason I fear is that I have no idea what it is."

Outside, the bugle fell silent. We listened to that for a while.

I said, "Ghost Shirt knew my name."

"Of course he did. I told him."

That took a minute to sink in. I'd suspected it, of course,

but I hadn't expected him to admit it so readily. "What do you plan to do with the thirty pieces of silver?" I asked then.

He chuckled, without humor. "Page, you have an exaggerated sense of your own importance. He asked me who was with us. I might have said no one. He would have read the ground and seen that there were three sets of tracks, not counting those made by the pack horse. Hudspeth and I would have been strung up by our heels over a fire until we either talked or our skulls burst. I thought it best that we were all spared the trouble. Can you honestly say that you would have acted differently?"

"I might have made him work for it a little."

"That is where our characters differ. I fight only for what is mine. It is enough that I lost a fine shirt. Besides, once he had us dangling over that fire he would not have bothered to have us cut down whether we talked or not. This way it was more of a burden for him to do it than to undo it."

There was no arguing with logic like that, but I was in that kind of mood, so we hashed it out for another five minutes or so. We were so busy neither of us noticed when Hudspeth ceased snoring.

"Can't you bastards shut the hell up and let a man sleep?" He sat up, lifting his head and shoulders into the pale light. His face was a map of cuts, swellings and bruises. One half of his handlebar was cocked upward where his upper lip was puffed and crusted over with dark blood.

"Jesus, you're hard to look at," I said.

"That's your problem." Absent-mindedly he reached for his flask, grumbled when he came up with a handful of air. "One of them black-faced sons of bitches took the time to lift my whiskey whilst the others was kicking me around." He hawked and spat out a jet of what looked to be blood that had collected in his mouth. It splattered loudly on the stone floor.

"It is fortunate that they did not lift your scalp as well." Jac blew the sludge out of his pipe with a sound that put me in mind of a boy blasting on a broken whistle.

"Wouldn't much matter if they had, since they're going to anyway. This ain't no weekend in St. Louis we been invited on."

"They don't usually take the scalp of an enemy not killed in battle," I said. "They might, however, hollow out your skull and use it for a bowl to grind meal in. That is, if it isn't solid bone."

"You should talk. You took a look at that door you knocked on with your forehead?"

I had a snappy retort all ready, but I didn't get to use it. Pere Jac made a noise like steam escaping from a boiler and clutched our wrists in a vise grip, listening.

A short scraping sound, such as might have been made by a human foot wrapped in dead animal flesh scuffing hard earth, reached us from just outside the door. A heavy bolt was shot back and moonlight fanned out across the flagstones. Two Indians stood outside the doorway, one a little behind the other because there was not enough room for them to stand side by side in the narrow passage. Cold light painted silver stripes along the barrels of their rifles. The one in front signaled for us to stand up. When we obeyed, he covered us with his rifle while his companion slid in past him, carrying coils of what looked like buckskin thong. He stepped behind us.

I knew what was coming. I put my hands behind me so he'd have no excuse to yank, and in a few seconds he had the first cord wound tightly around my wrists. Tight as it was, though, he gave it an extra tug that almost pitched me forward onto my face, then secured it and spat on the knot. He did the same with Jac, but when he got to Hudspeth he surpassed himself, forcing the marshal to curse through his teeth when the knot was set. That finished, the other Indian came in and joined his partner. Steel dug into my back and we started forward.

"I feel like a bride on her wedding night," I whispered to Pere Jac as we approached the steps. "What do you say when you meet a god?" Then the gun punched me behind the ribs and I shut up.

# CHAPTER 10

Dakota nights being cool the year around, there was a snap in the air as we made our way across camp, our Indian escorts close behind. I shivered in my thin canvas coat and wondered how Pere Jac, naked to the waist, managed to keep from turning blue. But he was a native and accustomed to extremes of temperature. The fact that his breath, like mine and Hudspeth's, was visible in gray jets of vapor seemed to bother him not at all. He seemed equally unconcerned with the boiled strip of buffalo hide that swathed his injured right shoulder, which, now dry, must have chafed his skin at the edges like rusty barbed wire. The blood had dried into a yellow-brown stain on the hide. Around us, firelight glimmered cozily behind panes of oiled paper in the windows of the soddies and huts and behind the skin walls of the tipis. The smell of wood smoke teased my nostrils and caused my stomach to grind when I detected in it the sweet aroma of roasting meat. I hadn't eaten since I'd shared a piece of salt pork with the marshal that morning, a hundred years ago.

We were conducted to a large adobe building near the south wall, which had, I supposed, served as a place for the Mormons to meet and be preached at and marry their legions of wives. The door had long since been blown off or taken down and chopped up for firewood or used for lumber in a country where wood fetched higher prices than whiskey, and now a buffalo robe hung in its place over the opening. The barrel of a Spencer blocked my way as I was about to step inside. Its owner, one of our guards, held us at bay with the business end while his companion went in. Half a minute later he returned and pulled the robe aside for us to enter. The other brave resumed his position behind us as I stepped across a threshold worn hollow by foot traffic, followed closely by Jac and Hudspeth.

The room was long and narrow, the mud-and-timber walls unpaneled, the floor earthen. At the far end a fire of wood scraps and buffalo chips burned bluish and smokeless in the grate of a large stone fireplace, casting its buttery light over the floor and walls, where giant shadows licked and flickered against a dingy yellow background. The owner of one of them sat in a rickety wooden chair with his back to the fire, a colorful blanket draped shawl-like over his bare shoulders and my gun belt buckled around his waist, the Deane-Adams resting in its holster. That came as no surprise. The five-shot was a rare piece this side of the Atlantic. Any Indian, even a Messiah who had been educated at the hands of the white man, would find it enough of a novelty to prefer it over Hudspeth's Smith & Wesson or any of the other more common firearms seized over the past several weeks. There was no sign of my Winchester, but then it was dark in the room and I doubted that he'd let a weapon so obviously superior to the Spencers his tribe was using get very far out of his sight, even if it had already been claimed by someone else.

Seen up close, his features, which had once been described as "satanic" by a newspaper writer who had never been west of Manhattan, were rather ordinary, although even enough to be considered handsome by some mooneyed schoolgirl with visions of being abducted by a virile savage to a tipi in some far-off prairie. His nose was strong but hooked only slightly, his lips full for an Indian and sculpted, his chin square. Somewhere along the line someone had told him his eyes were hypnotic, and he played them for all they were worth, glaring at each of us in turn from beneath drawn brows, like Napoleon in his portraits. He did his best to make the rough-hewn old chair look like a throne by sitting as erect as possible, and I have to admit that the effort wasn't altogether unsuccessful. He might even have pulled it off if he weren't suffering from a bad summer cold.

His eyelids were puffy and he wiped his nose from time to time with the edge of the blanket, but that only made his sniffles worse. The idea that he was prey to the same ills that plagued the rest of us plainly bothered him more than the cold. It showed in his expression. His face was more easily readable than the average Indian's, which irritated him no less. He would be that kind, I thought, growing more disgusted with himself each day for his inability to live up to his reputation. It was a weakness he shared with many another legend I had known. I filed the knowledge away in my memory for future reference.

All the same, he made me feel old. At the age of twenty-two I had been a penniless veteran with a game leg and no prospects. Thirteen years had healed my leg and improved my outlook, but that was about all. At twenty-two, Ghost Shirt was the undisputed chief of all the renegade tribes in the Northwest, with more braves flocking to his standard every day. Is it a white man's trait always to be comparing his lot with others? In any case, we did have one thing in common, and that was that in our respective occupations

we both stood a better than even chance of being dead tomorrow. At the moment, however, the odds of it happening
to me were much the stronger.

But there must have been something to the god theory,
because it wasn't until I had exhausted myself on Ghost
Shirt that I noticed the room's other three occupants. One,
a scruffy, grime-yellow dog of uncertain forebears, lay
stretched across the hearth with its chin on its front paws,
bright eyes resting on Ghost Shirt, whom I took to be its
master. Its tail had been bobbed, from the look of the ragged
stub, by a jack knife or some other instrument just as inad-
equate. It twitched whenever the chief's eyes flickered in
that direction. The others in attendance were not seated—
partly, I assumed, out of respect for the chief and partly because most Indians were uncomfortable sitting on chairs,
and the floor was too hard and cold even for them. For some
reason I knew that the Sioux standing near the farthest of
the four windows was the Miniconjou whom Jac had identified earlier as Many Ponies, even though I had seen him
before only at a distance and he had since doffed his paint
and feathers. But he carried himself like a chief, and the
strong, beak-nosed face, partially in shadow, was too old
and seamed to belong to a warrior one would choose to take
along on such an arduous campaign as this. He appeared to
be more interested in the moonlight-drenched scenery beyond the window than anything inside the room. The third
was a nervous sort with a sharp face and lean brown body
set off by sun-bleached buckskins, who hadn't stopped pacing since we'd entered. He too had scraped off his paint,
but I recognized him instantly as the streak-faced warrior
who had commanded the party that had taken me prisoner.
He had exchanged his necklace of human fingers for a more
conventional one of copper and semiprecious stones. Ap-

parently he felt no need for strong medicine in the presence of his chief. I hadn't noticed it before, but now that he was on foot I couldn't miss his withered left leg, which looked as if it had been shattered in his childhood and stunted, so that his foot dragged sibilantly across the floor as he paced up and down the length of the room.

On the long, low table that stood before Ghost Shirt, chunks of lean red meat, the remains of a meal, floated in a pool of bloody juice in a pottery bowl. My stomach began to work all over again at the sight of it. I tried to devour it with my eyes, but that was less than satisfying. But since it was the next best thing to eating I kept my eyes on it from then on. I even imagined that I could smell it, although there was no steam rising from it and it was probably cold as ice. As far as I was concerned it was tender sirloin hot off the griddle.

The warrior with the game leg was holding forth in a harsh guttural I took to be Cheyenne. His voice was a nasty bleat and he spoke with a pronounced, buzzing lisp. He was angry as hell about something and his tone reflected it as he continued to pace rapidly in spite of the dead limb, gesturing agitatedly with his long, bony arms. Although he pointedly avoided looking in our direction, it was plain enough who were the subjects of his tirade. Ghost Shirt waited until he had finished, then blew his nose on the edge of the blanket and said something over his shoulder to Many Ponies. His voice was moderate but high strung. It's unfair to pass judgment on a man's tones when he's speaking in a foreign tongue, and more so when his adenoids are swollen, but I blamed the tension on the pressure of command. You'll hear the same quality in the calmest of voices at an officers' cotillion if you've an ear for it.

He didn't say much, but whatever it was it had a question

mark on the end of it. Reluctantly, as if afraid he'd miss something outside, Many Ponies turned his face from the window long enough to flick his eyes over us, then returned them to the landscape beyond the empty pane. His lids were bald where he plucked his lashes, and deep crow's feet pulled them down at the corners, giving his elderly face—he might have been forty-eight, far past prime for an Indian—a sad expression. His reply, in Sioux, was brief and without inflection.

Gimpy launched a fresh tantrum—or maybe it was the same one—as if he'd been holding it back during the others' exchange only with great effort. But he pulled up short when Ghost Shirt held up a callused palm. Annoyance glittered in the lame brave's eye. He'd had more to say.

Unlike his fellow tribesman, the Cheyenne chief kept his attention fixed on one or the other of us all the while he spoke, and he spoke at length. He was calm for the most part, but certain words brought out his emotions from time to time, twisting his face into a mask of hatred and rasping harshly off his tongue like the buzz from a snake's rattle. Once I caught the Sioux word for the Arapaho nation—uttered, no doubt, for the Miniconjou's benefit—when it came lashing out in this manner. I wondered about that, since the Cheyenne and the Arapaho were supposed to be like brothers, but perhaps this was a matter of personal preference. From there he dovetailed deliberately into more placid speech. Broken occasionally by interruptions from the gimp, which were themselves cut off when Ghost Shirt resumed as if unchecked, the monologue went on for about five minutes, at the end of which stretched a silence complete enough to reveal that the warriors in the compound had returned for a fresh go at the bugle. I could have sworn once that I heard the opening bars of "The Campbells Are Coming," but it was probably just coincidence.

We had not been addressed, nor had we heard a word of English since we'd been ushered into the room. It wasn't ignorance, because Ghost Shirt had spent enough time in the East to have picked up at least the rudiments of the language. I saw his strategy. As long as he refused to acknowledge our intelligence by speaking to us, we were less than human. He had nothing to gain by it other than revenge, but then that must have been one of the things that ate at him when he was locked up at Fort Ransom. It meant something else as well, although I dared not put it into anything so dangerous as a hope: As long as he preferred to play this kind of game with us, we were going to live.

Evidently this was lost on Hudspeth, who had also seen Ghost Shirt's motives, as his flush had spread beyond his nose over his forehead and down into his collar. His buckskins creaked as he worked his wrists. Before he could blow I ground my heel surreptitiously into the toe of his Mexican boot. Rage gurgled in his throat and he glared murder at me out of the corner of his eye, but he held himself back. I had succeeded in splitting his anger into two channels and preventing him from saying or doing something that would cost us our hides.

The lame Cheyenne plainly didn't like what was going on. He stamped around a few seconds longer, flapping his arms and dragging his useless foot and not looking at us, slid an eye toward the door as if longing for the nerve to stalk out, gave up finally, and turned his back on the room to see what was outside the window that Many Ponies found so diverting. At that point the Sioux apparently decided that anything the other might find worth looking at wasn't, and turned his attention to the rafters atop the opposite wall. I got the impression the two were less than eager comrades.

A pair of sharp notes delivered on the bugle seemed to bring the young chief out of the funk into which he'd fallen. He said something to the guards, waving a hand toward the door. One of the Spencers nudged Jac and we turned to leave, but not before Ghost Shirt spoke his first two words in English.

"Here, Custer," he said, and leaned down to set the bowl of meat scraps on the floor for the dog.

Back in the chapel, Hudspeth waited until the door was slammed shut and barred, then sat down on the floor and tugged off his left boot. "You damn near busted my foot!" He massaged the injured area.

"Better that than some buck wearing our fingers on a cord around his neck." I rubbed my wrists to get back the circulation cut off by the thong, which had been removed.

"The hell with that! First you trip me, then you try to screw my foot to the floor. You're more dangerous than the injuns!"

I ignored him, looking at Pere Jac. "What was that all about, anyway?"

The activity had started the métis' wound bleeding again. He leaned back in the semidarkness and staunched it by pressing the heel of his hand against the bandage and holding it there.

"They argued over us. Lame Horse—the one who limps, he is the medicine man who dressed my wound—wanted us dead. It seems he has dreamt that white men in their midst will bring them ill fortune. He was quite vehement about it. Colorful, too. You should have heard what he wanted to do with your head, A.C."

The marshal muttered something unintelligible and wiggled his toes to see if they still worked.

"What about Many Ponies?" I asked.

"He had no opinion about it one way or the other. He has brought a new squaw with him and he was anxious to get back to her. When Ghost Shirt asked him how he voted, he said that he would go along with whatever the others decided."

"And Ghost Shirt?"

Jac's brow furrowed. "He is not so simple. He hates us worst of all, and I think that if he had his choice he would agree with Lame Horse. But he has other things on his mind. Many Ponies has not been able to deliver as many braves as promised. The Sioux sub-chief, Blood on His Lance, has a child down with fever and could not come to tonight's meeting as he is the medicine man of his band. The Cheyenne lost three of his best braves in the fight with A.C. this morning. The fourth is not expected to survive the night. I think he was strongly tempted to see us roasted to a turn."

"So why aren't we roasting?"

"I am getting to that. Now that the army knows where he is, he has decided to leave the mission before more soldiers come. Spotted Cat, the Arapaho chief, is camped with eight hundred warriors just this side of the Black Hills. Ghost Shirt plans to meet up with him there and, with his help, fight the blue coats on his own ground. He knows now that final victory is impossible, but he wishes to teach the whites a great lesson before he goes to join Kills Bear and Sitting Bull in the land of the white grandmother. He wishes, he said, to make the whites speak his name henceforth in whispers, like old women around a campfire."

"He's a fool. Eleven hundred Indians don't stand a chance against the U.S. Army."

"Against the entire army, no. But they can do great damage to a single garrison that is not expecting them, to say nothing of what will happen when they descend upon the unprotected gold camps in the Black Hills. Further, there are as many as two thousand Indians unaccounted for on reservations throughout the Northwest. Once the news of what Ghost Shirt is up to spreads, there is little doubt around whom they will rally, and then many lives will be lost."

Here the métis smiled sardonically. The tight-lipped expression reminded me of Judge Blackthorne and made me homesick all over again. "Spotted Cat," he said, "is no friend of Ghost Shirt's. But he needs Spotted Cat's warriors, and he is confident that a generous gift will seal the rift that separates them, at least for the time being."

"Let me guess," I said. "We're the gift."

He nodded, still smiling. The mirth fell short of his eyes. In front of the door, Hudspeth stopped playing with his foot and gaped at him.

"Torture is Spotted Cat's specialty." His bleeding under control now, the breed got out his pipe and blew lint from the bowl. Then he began poking tobacco into it. "Moreover, he shares Ghost Shirt's sympathies concerning white men and half-breeds. The Cheyenne feels that the gift of two white federal lawmen and a métis will ensure his alliance in the forthcoming struggle." His face was bathed briefly in the flare of the match as he puffed life into the pipe. Then he shook out the flame and retreated into shadow once more.

"So when are we leaving?" Hudspeth demanded.

"First light."

Later I wished the marshal hadn't asked that question. I was the rest of the night trying to get to sleep.

# CHAPTER 11

**T**hree hundred warriors, their women, dogs, three prisoners, and assorted children don't set out on a long journey at the drop of a hat, but the dust had hardly settled on the crown when we began moving through the heavy mist of dawn of what was shaping up to be another humid day. War ponies and their riders were first out the gate, followed by the relief string herded along by the women, with travois of all sizes bringing up the rear behind plugs too old and worn out for any other duty. These last contraptions were simply lodge poles roped together to carry weapons and ammunition and folded tipis and jerked buffalo meat and infants, which had to be dragged slowly to keep down the dust and friction, standard hazards among a people who had never developed the wheel. Once outside, the warrior band split into thirds, with Ghost Shirt riding point at the head of his Cheyenne and Many Ponies and Blood on His Lance, a Miniconjou who looked to be in his late twenties and wore his hair in plaits braided with otter skin, protecting the flanks with their Sioux. None of them wore paint, but then they weren't anticipating any fights just yet or they would have been stripped down to keep the wounds clean. Jac, Hudspeth, and I ate dust astride our own mounts behind the leading band of Cheyenne.

At least we weren't traveling on empty stomachs. Even

Ghost Shirt had been forced to admit that dead men made
poor torture victims, and so we had each been treated to a
heaping bowlful of half-raw horse, or maybe it was dog. If
the latter, it wasn't the one Ghost Shirt called Custer, as I
saw him darting in and out among the horses' shanks later
as we'd been getting ready to leave. Whatever it was, it
stayed down, and that's all I'd been asking of my meals for
some time. Nobody had bothered to tie us up, which was
a compliment to our common sense. You don't outrun an
Indian on horseback, not astride anything that eats grain or
grass.

I'd thought riding with two partners was dusty but I hadn't
seen clouds like this since the army. Tying my kerchief over
my nose and mouth wasn't much help. The stuff was so fine
it came right through the cloth into my nostrils and down
my throat. By midday I'd eaten that peck of dirt we're allotted during our lifetime. Reddish mud caked my clothes, skin
and horse. My armpits were chafed raw from the grit, my
eyelids gummed so tight I had to pry them open with
my fingers to see. I could only imagine what it was like at
the rear of the column.

We traveled slowly, climbing the Missouri Plateau twenty
miles west of the James River shortly before sunset and
camping on the edge of a watering hole just beyond effective rifle range of the buttes that lined the eastern ridge. For
supper we were issued buffalo jerky and warned, in the halt-
ing English of the glowering Cheyenne who gave it to us,
to make it last because that was all we were going to get
between now and trail's end. I gnawed at my portion in silence and, after the same brave had bound my hands and
feet, turned in without a word to my companions. After all
the time we had spent together we had very little to say to
each other.

The blue-coated Indian was standing atop the central ridge of the nearest butte when I awoke the next morning. Not for long, though; one moment he was there, the next he had vanished. I kept still about it until our guard had cut us free of our bonds and walked away to attend to other matters.

"See him?" I asked of my fellow prisoners as we crouched together, grinding away at our jerky.

Jac nodded. "Crow, most likely. Or Arikara. Some of them still scout for the army. He has been with us since before dawn."

"What do you think they'll do?"

"Follow us until their messenger brings back reinforcements from Fort Abraham Lincoln, or Fort Yates, or both. Then they will attack, probably while we are preparing to move out."

I glanced around. We were not the only ones who had noticed our observer. Here and there a brave was smearing black paint over himself from a hollow horn, while others tested their bowstrings or loaded their rifles, stopping at one or two shells because ammunition was limited and some Indians believed that a fully loaded rifle led to extravagance. A Sioux crouching a few yards away used the point of his knife to scrape a cake of excess powder from the action of his Spencer. I winced. Give an Indian a brand new firearm and inside of a month he'll turn it into junk.

"What makes you so sure they won't hit us now, while we're sitting?" asked the marshal.

"For the same reason that cavalry does not storm an artillery emplacement without infantry support," Jac said, chewing. "They would be cut to pieces. Besides, there is a little matter of their being outnumbered nearly two to one."

"In that case, why don't the injuns force a fight right now?"

"They are unaware of their advantage. Only we know Harms's strength. And even if they did, the soldiers will not fight with the odds so strong against them. We would be here forever. In the meantime Spotted Cat may move beyond Ghost Shirt's reach. Here he will not gamble. So all the paint you see being applied will go to waste."

"How long before the reinforcements come?" I asked.

Pere Jac shrugged his good shoulder and thrust his jerky away inside his left moccasin. "If the messenger heads north and waylays the train from Fargo to Bismarck, three days. Otherwise, a week. Give or take a day. Two riders left this camp an hour ago, heading west. I suspect their mission is to try to catch and kill the messenger. If that fails, it will be a forced march all the way to the Black Hills."

I followed his example and put away my own strip of jerked meat. "Why don't they wire the other forts?"

"If Ghost Shirt has not had the telegraph line cut by now, he is unworthy of his reputation."

"All the same it's stupid," said Hudspeth, still gnawing. "That's what alerted Fort Ransom."

"He had no choice. It was either that or take the chance of finding himself knee-deep in soldiers before he reached the Missouri River."

"Hell of a note, us being scared of our own army."

Jac said, "Now you know how the Indians feel."

Lame Horse approached, shuffling his dead foot and carrying a buckskin sack. He was painted and wore his grisly necklace and something new, a headdress made from a wolf's head with the fangs of the upper jaw encircling his brow and a fur mantle hanging down the back of his head like a cowl to the shoulders. His deformity was concealed

beneath a buffalo robe that swept from his neck to his heels.
The flame-yellow streak knifing diagonally across the middle of his blackened face was starting to run at the edges
where he had already begun to sweat. Without a word he
squatted beside Jac, tossed the robe back from his shoulders,
and undid the dressing that covered the métis' wound. He
then smeared the ugly, jagged gash with a piece of buckskin
soaked in some greenish, evil-smelling salve carried in a
hollow horn taken from the sack and bound it afresh with
cured hide. The way he shoved his patient around as he
treated him said little for his bedside manner, but then you
don't expect a lot of courtesy from someone who was calling for your death a little over twenty-four hours ago. Finally he drew out a rattle with a bone handle and a head
made from the painted skull of some small animal, possibly a prairie dog, tilted back his head so that the dead wolf's
glass-bead eyes glittered in the light of the rising sun, shook
the rattle perfunctorily three times in each of the four
directions, chanted something in an emotionless drone,
packed up, and left, dragging his half-developed leg behind
him beneath the trailing robe. No pipe smoking, no ritual
of purification, no change of song. Either he had disposed
of all that the first time around or he didn't think his patient was worth the bother.

"Tender, is he not?" commented Jac.

"Wait till you get his bill," I told him. Then our guard
jostled me from behind and we saddled up.

There are people who spend their lives studying the mi-
grating habits of western nomadic tribes, for whom these
next few pages might make fascinating reading, but I was
too preoccupied to take notes even if I'd had the necessary
material. Back-breaking hours in the saddle, sleeping on
damp, hard ground with one eye open for rattlesnakes,

wrists chafed bloody and hands swollen by rawhide thongs drawn too tightly during the hours of darkness when an escape attempt might be made, mosquitoes the size of horseflies that whined in our ears when we tried to sleep and drew blood, leaving crusts of it all around the hole, days so hot the sweat seemed to sizzle when it hit the air, nights so cold our perspiration-soaked garments grew stiff and crackled when we moved, the salty leather taste of jerky morning and night, the ache in our jaws from trying to chew it, wading through fresh horse manure and old buffalo chips, horse froth drying white and stinking on our pants legs, warm water drunk from earthen jugs, blisters on our palms, boils on our backsides, dogs barking, babies crying, horses snorting, men sweating, dust, dust, dust. Dust in our eyes, noses and throats. Dust in our boots and pockets. Dust that rose and rose in great, strangling clouds that obscured the sun and stained sky and grass the color of old blood. Dust so fine we couldn't feel it between our fingers but which stirred and shifted in our lungs when we coughed, and we coughed often, hacking so hard it seemed our throats would turn inside out with the pain of it. Dust that never settled but continued to drift aimlessly hours after we had camped, etching swirling black shadows against the pale night sky. Dust so thick a finger drawn down a cheek left a furrow a blind man could feel. Each day was like the one before, only it was worse because we were older and less able to take it.

Meanwhile, to the east of us, a cloud only slightly smaller than the one we were trailing held parallel to our route along the horizon. When one of us finally made mention of it, Jac merely nodded and said, "He missed the train."

It was on the fifth night that Happy—thus we had nicknamed the anonymous dour brave who looked after us—

made his mistake. It wasn't that he was stupid or careless, nor that we were especially smart, but that circumstances made it impossible for any of us to be anything else. We were within listening distance of the Missouri River fifteen miles south of Fort Yates, camped in a grassy hollow just off the east bank, where patrols from the fort would have to cross over to engage us and the animals could graze without being outlined against the horizon and the sentries could lie concealed in the tall grass around the rim. Rounded stones, deposited when the prehistoric lake that had occupied the spot receded, studded the ground. Before this, Happy had always made sure that there were no such tools around before he settled his prisoners, but since there were too many of them here and most were anchored down more or less permanently, he compromised by choosing a spot where the stones were relatively smooth and devoid of those jagged edges that came in handy for sawing through bonds, flung away the undesirables, tethered us carefully, and wrapped himself up in his buffalo robe to take up his nightly vigil. As usual, he was asleep within minutes.

I waited until I was sure he was under good and deep, then struggled into a sitting position and shifted around from rock to rock until I found one that felt like it might do. Hudspeth and Jac did the same. Mine was edgeless, but the surface was like sandpaper and might conceivably be expected to wear its way through the stiff, dry leather thong that bound my hands behind my back between now and sunup. I made myself as comfortable as possible and started rubbing.

The next couple of hours were the hardest. Every muscle in my body cried out for rest, and the tedious rhythm of my wrists scraping up and down the surface of the rock acted like the swinging motion of a baby's cradle, heaping a couple of hundred pounds onto my eyelids. I dozed off twice, the second time so deeply that when I jolted awake I had no idea how long I'd been out, and redoubled my efforts to make up for lost time. But by then the crisis had passed and staying alert was no longer a problem, because the pain made sleep impossible. It started as a dull ache between my shoulder blades and ended up a sharp, stinging sensation like something left by an angry hornet. Worse, I had begun sweating in spite of the cold, and salty rivulets came trickling down my wrists, burning against the raw flesh and drawing the thong even tighter. My hands grew slippery with blood from the chafing. With all this to occupy my mind I hardly noticed the numbness of my rump where I sat on the iron-hard ground.

I heard snoring and looked up to see that Hudspeth, seated a few yards away, had fallen asleep in the middle of his labors, his chin on his chest and the ends of his moustache fluttering as he inhaled and exhaled mightily through his big red nose. I whistled softly through my teeth at Jac, who was working away at a rock not far from the marshal, and inclined my head toward his dozing bulk. Jac nodded and kicked at the marshal's feet until he came awake with a start. He looked around in bewilderment for a moment, then caught on to where he was and what he was supposed to be doing and resumed scraping.

The damp chill of approaching dawn had seeped into my clothes when my thong came apart with a resounding pop. Pere Jac's parted at almost the same instant. We stared at each other for a second like a couple of kids who had risen ahead of the rest of the family on Christmas morning. Then we tore away the scraps and bent forward to undo the thongs on our feet. The marshal, who hated being last in anything, set his jaw and worked his hands until I could have sworn I saw smoke rising behind him.

I finished ahead of the métis and, once I had mastered the fine art of achieving one's balance after the circulation has been cut off for hours, crept over to see what I could do for Hudspeth. But he was less than two-thirds of the way through his bonds, so I left him there and went off in search of a knife.

The nearest one was on Happy's belt. Since he couldn't very well be expected to give it up without protest, I selected a likely looking rock from among the dozens imbedded in the ground around me and tested it for heft. Rocks are vastly underrated as weapons, as I'd learned at the receiving end last winter. Deciding that this one would suit my purposes, I pulled off my boots and tiptoed over to where the guard was lying enveloped in his hide cocoon.

Right away I regretted having named him Happy. You don't do that, any more than you make a pet of the hog you're planning to butcher for Easter dinner. It didn't matter to me how many white scalps he may have taken, nor how many half-grown girls he may have raped before slashing them open from belly to breast, nor if he preferred using both hands or just one when swinging a baby by its heels and dashing its brains out against a tree. Being shallow, I was concerned only with the fact that he had never done any of us any actual harm, other than causing us a little discomfort, and that only on orders from the top. It had me all torn up for maybe a second and a half. Then I brought the rock crashing down squarely onto his exposed right temple.

Even so, I was just in time, as at the last instant his eyes sprang open and he went for his knife. But there was no way he was going to fumble his way out of his covers before the rock struck. He arched his back, but by then it was just nerves because he was already dead.

I looked around quickly. The sounds I'd heard before were the same sounds I was hearing now, nothing missing, nothing new. Apparently the slight noises the Cheyenne had made in dying had not been enough to alert his confederates. I let out my breath, only then realizing that I'd been holding it all this time, and returned to my task. Freeing the knife took some prying, clenched as it was in his fist. At length, however, I had my hand around the smooth bone handle.

I felt a presence behind me and spun around, swinging the knife in a wide arc from left to right. Pere Jac leaped backward but not far enough to keep the flat of the blade from scraping the top of his breechclout.

"Sorry," I said, in the overwhelming silence that followed.

"My widow would have been gratified to hear that," he replied dryly. But the closeness of the call was discernible on his face.

"Next time maybe you'll remember to keep your distance."

"You will forgive me if in my prayers I request that there be no next time."

"There sure as hell won't be if you two don't quit jawing and cut me loose!" Hudspeth's whisper was as good as another man's shout.

I slashed both his trusses—hands and feet—and told him to stay put. Before he could protest I turned away and returned to the dead guard. Somehow I kept my jerky from coming back up long enough to roll the body clear of its wrap and slide the robe on over my shoulders. I considered discarding my hat, thought better of it when I remembered the merciless Dakota sun, and crumpled and jammed it into my belt instead. My chances of passing as an Indian were about as good as they were of surviving the next half hour, but it was all I had.

"Stay where you are!" I hissed at the marshal, who had been struggling to get up. "Maybe I don't look much like a Sioux or a Cheyenne, but I come a hell of a lot closer than you. Wait until I get you a weapon."

He didn't like it, but he was no fool. He kept his position.

I handed the knife to Pere Jac. "You they'll believe," I said. "Cut out three good horses from the relief string. Hit the sentry before he can cry out or we'll be skinned and dressed by sunup. I'll get us some firepower."

"With what? I have the knife."

"Weren't you watching the first time? When you get the horses, give us three owl hoots, then count to twenty. If we're not there by then, ride like hell."

He nodded and slid away into the shadows to the west, where the horses were hobbled.

It was pathetically easy. They say a leaf dropping will bring an Indian out of a sound sleep, but that doesn't hold true when the Indian is surrounded by hundreds of his own kind and he's played out from five days of hard riding. I thumped the first one just in front of the ear while he lay sprawled beneath on ornate blanket. It wasn't as thorough a job as with Happy. At the last moment he stirred in his sleep and I missed the vital spot, fracturing his skull but not killing him. That was all right, because I hadn't intended to do away with anyone in the first place. You just can't be as accurate with a hunk of stone as with a gun or a knife. In any case he was out of action, although still breathing. A search of his body yielded up another knife and a Spencer rifle tucked beneath the blanket. I checked the breech and had all I could do to keep from cursing at the top of my lungs.

What had he planned to do if the cavalry attacked while he was armed with an unloaded piece?

I went over him again, more carefully this time, and came up empty. I took a deep breath and let it out slowly, to think. Then I grinned and pulled open his buckskin shirt. There they were, seventeen .56-caliber cartridges, pierced through their lead noses and strung on a leather thong around his neck. I yanked it loose and loaded the rifle up tight, swinging the lever forward and back slowly and quietly to rack one into the chamber, then added another cartridge. I thrust the string containing the remaining ten in my pocket.

Having served its purpose, the rock was cast aside and the knife took its place. This one was store-bought, with a cowhide-wrapped haft and a blade of tempered steel, probably the former property of some long-dead soldier or scout. I laid the Spencer aside for the time being and, holding the knife underhanded, crept up to the next sleeping form.

I withdrew the blade and wiped it thoroughly on the dead brave's blanket. Then I began my search. This time I hit paydirt. Not only had he a fully loaded Spencer, but a revolver stuck in his belt as well. I looked at it in the light, and damned if it wasn't Hudspeth's Smith & Wesson. The odds against that happening weren't as great as you might think, since we were camped in the middle of the Cheyenne and they had been the ones who had captured Jac and the marshal. Twenty to one. No, make it eighteen, since I'd just disposed of two of his comrades. I'd have bet half a month's pay on odds like those. I thrust the revolver into my own belt, collected the rifle and the one I had taken from the other Indian, picked up that one's blanket, and gave everything but one rifle and the knife to Hudspeth. His bright little eyes lit up as he curled his hand around the Smith's heavy grip.

"Where in hell—"

I hissed. "Wrap that blanket around yourself and keep your chin tucked in so the handlebar doesn't show. And ditch that hat."

Three owl hoots sounded faintly to the west. I put my boots on and helped him to his feet.

"Wait a minute!" He stood his ground. "What about Ghost Shirt?"

"For Christ's sake, shut up!" I would have throttled him if the circumstances were different and he weren't so big. We crept off.

Within a hundred yards of the horses I halted and threw out an arm to stop Hudspeth. Someone was speaking in harsh Cheyenne.

As my eyes grew accustomed to the shadows on this side of the hollow, I made out Pere Jac standing motionless among the horses' milling forms. At his feet, just as motionless, sprawled a figure which I took to be that of the Indian assigned to watch over the horses. Something about his position told me that his responsibility was ended. Jac was gazing up at the rim. I followed his line of sight and spotted an Indian sentry silhouetted against the lightening sky.

He must have risen from the grass when he heard noises. He had a rifle braced against his shoulder and was scanning the scene below in search of a target. He repeated his challenge.

I raised my own Spencer and drew a bead on his chest. I was set to fire when a shot rang out from an unexpected quarter. The sentry's rifle tumbled from his hands and he crumpled into the tall grass. Then a bugle sounded and the world fell apart in tiny, glittering pieces.

## CHAPTER 12

The first wave came thundering over the western rim spread out in charge formation, bugle wailing, Springfields popping, scattering the riderless horses left and right in spite of their hobbles. Officers' sabers flashed in the first pink rays of dawn. Sabers, by God. I gave Hudspeth a shove between the shoulder blades with the flat of my hand so that he lost his balance and pitched forward onto his face, and joined him an instant later. Hoofs shook the ground on either side of us. The wind of them bounding overhead stirred the hairs on the back of my neck. I heard the dust sifting down all around me, my senses were that acute. Not that it did me any good. It seemed we lay there for hours while rider after rider pounded past, although it couldn't have been more than a couple of minutes. Even so, at the rate they were traveling that added up to a hell of a lot of cavalry.

I waited until I was sure the last straggler had passed, then leaped to my feet, still clutching the Spencer. Hudspeth got up more slowly, but I could see he wasn't hurt, unless you count being mad as hell as a handicap. Pere Jac, who had himself flattened out when the sentry fell, was already up, clutching the mane of his own paint—dumb luck—and shouting something at me that I couldn't hear because hoofbeats were still echoing in my head. But I caught his drift and snatched at the mane of the horse nearest me, an ex-

cited army gray that was trying to gallop and gnaw at the
thong that bound its forelegs at the same time. Hudspeth had
the misfortune to grab onto a mustang that fit him about as
well as a size 5 corset fit the Statue of Liberty, now arriv-
ing piecemeal from France. But we all had mounts and, as
far as I could tell in the haze of settling dust, were still
armed.

The Indians had been taken completely by surprise. They
were running all over the place, whooping up their courage and firing their rifles at flitting shadows, grabbing for the
manes and tails of panicky horses, while the soldiers rode
through with their reins wrapped about their forearms and
picked them off with rifles and side arms first from this side,
then that. Gunsmoke glazed the battleground. Sabers slashed
randomly at tipis and running figures. It was a killing frenzy.
A brave armed only with a flint tomahawk leaped onto the
back of a horse behind the soldier who was riding it, but
before he could swing his weapon a bullet from a nearby
Springfield splintered his head and he tumbled off. Another
soldier leaned down from his saddle, revolver in one hand,
and tore aside the flap of a squat tipi. The young squaw
inside thrust the muzzle of a Spencer up his nose and
pulled the trigger. His horse screamed and reared. He somersaulted backward over its rump and landed on his face,
which didn't matter because he no longer had one. A fat
squaw waddling as fast as she could go with a child in her
arms ran straight into the downswing of a young lieutenant's
saber. Her head came off slick as a kicked cabbage and
her body ran for several more steps before it stumbled
and fell, spilling the infant out onto the ground. A soldier's
horse came clattering toward the yowling, naked baby where
it lay sprawled in the grass. I turned my head away just as
the first hoof struck.

Major Harms, or whoever was calling the shots if not him, was a student of General Nelson Miles. The second wave, which came in from the northeast, was backed up by squares of infantry, the kind of troops the armchair generals back in Washington City swore were hopelessly ineffective against Plains Indians, but which Miles had been using to great advantage since the beginning of the wars. By this time Sioux and Cheyenne snipers had taken up positions along the eastern rim, and as they took aim the horse soldiers hit them at breechclout level with their 45-70 single-shots. The cavalry just kept coming. I had no idea how many there were, but it was obvious that both Fort Lincoln and Fort Yates had been all but emptied out for reinforcements and that the Indians' superior weaponry wasn't worth a leaf in a torrent against numbers like these.

Now that the focus of battle had shifted to the other side of the hollow, a handful of troopers from the first attack took advantage of the lull in this quarter to grab a few scalps. I wasn't shocked. The first one taken was worth a bonus or a furlough depending upon who was in command, and anyway they weren't worth much to the corpses from which they were lifted. What bothered me was the officers back East who acquired the trophies without any risk except to their pocketbooks and either sold them at a profit or hung them in their parlors to add weight to their tales of personal prowess told to entice fashionable young ladies into bed. Barbarians come in all types and colors.

Jac and I cut away the hobbles on our captured mounts, including Hudspeth's, and were about to make a run for it when the marshal cried out and pointed behind me. I swung around, hugging the rifle to my hip.

Ghost Shirt, astride his roan, had broken through along with half a dozen warriors and was making for the high ground west of camp. At his side rode Lame Horse, minus paint. The soldiers who had been cutting dead hair fired in unison. Two Indians fell. Ghost Shirt clapped a hand to his head and reeled. His horse whinnied in terror, wheeled right, and blundered into the milling relief herd. The remaining braves, one of them the medicine man, returned fire. The troopers dived for cover as they galloped through, then sprang up and snapped shots at their backs. Another Indian tumbled from his horse, I couldn't tell which.

While the soldiers' backs were turned, the chief, his mount trapped among its fellows, lost his grip on the mane and slid like a rag doll to the ground.

"Get him!" I snapped at Jac, who was closest to the herd. "Before he's trampled."

He left his paint, calmer now that it had recognized its master, and sidled his way in between the horses. Hudspeth held my gray while I went in to help.

Ghost Shirt was lying on his face next to the roan. Together we turned him over. He had a crease on the left side of his head where a bullet had grazed it—I couldn't tell how badly, there was too much blood—but he was still breathing. So much for the god theory. Being the only one of us with a shirt, I tore a long strip from the tail of mine, used it to clean away what blood I could, and bound it tightly around his head. My Winchester was slung over his shoulder by a makeshift strap, a welcome sight but hardly a surprise. It was too good a weapon to leave in the hands of a subordinate. I transferred it to my person, unbuckled the gun belt containing my Deane-Adams, and strapped it on around my waist. That made me feel fifty per cent human again. I inspected both guns to see if they were loaded and found that they were, which completed the cure. Then Jac and I heaved the unconscious Cheyenne up and over the back of his horse. The métis held the animal while I braided two more strips into an approximation of a rope and tied Ghost Shirt's hands and feet together beneath its belly. If he survived that, I decided, I might reconsider my opinion of his so-called immortality.

I picked up the confiscated Spencer from the ground where I'd left it, and then I said something that wasn't clever. I said, "Happy birthday," and handed it to Pere Jac. To show how much strain we were under, we both laughed like idiots.

Hudspeth had our saddles, bags, and blankets laid out on the ground when we emerged, leading the roan by its army bridle, and was cinching his rig onto the mustang's back. He could move fast when he had to. We'd left them where I'd killed the guard because it's hard to look like an Indian when you're carrying fifty pounds of leather over your shoulder, and Hudspeth had run there, loaded them up, and gotten back before his mount could stray out of reach, with bullets flying all over hell. He flicked his eyes over our burden and yanked tight the cinch.

"You got him," he grunted. "Good."

I could have clubbed him with the butt of the Winchester. Jac had his eight cases of whiskey and I still had my job whether we brought back the Indian or not. We had risked our hides to help him keep his badge, and all the thanks we got was something my father said when his hunting dog fetched its first duck. Even the dog got a pat on the head. But I supposed that was as high as he gushed, so I let it slide.

"Why don't you give me the mustang and take the gray?" I asked him. "You'll scuff your fancy boots dragging them on the ground."

"I grabbed it, I'll keep it. You'll find fresh jerky in your

saddle bags, both of you, and them buckskin bags hanging
on your horns is half full of water. I got 'em from a bot-
tomed-up tipi."

"That's not all you got," I said, one hand in my saddle
bag. I drew out a box of Deane-Adams cartridges.

"I found that on the ground. The injun must of dropped
it when he got shot."

I dropped it back into the bag. "Where's that Spencer I
gave you?" I had just noticed he was no longer carrying it.

He snorted. "It wasn't worth the extra weight. The action
was jammed full of powder. I wouldn't trust no gun of mine
with no redskin if it meant my life. I heard once—"

A bullet nicked the top of his saddle. He ducked behind
the horse, drawing his revolver. Jac and I shouldered our
rifles.

"Come out of there, you onion-skinned sons of bitches!"
A master sergeant's voice if I ever heard one, Ohio twang
roughened by weather and grit and years of bawling orders
at green recruits.

The herd had begun crowding around us, blocking our
view of the cavalry stragglers. Now, gray light perforated
the shadows and the horses shied away before the harsh bellow, and in the clearing beyond stood a heavy-chested
trooper in a dusty uniform with a knife in one hand and an
Army Colt in the other. There were others with him armed
similarly, but he was the one who had shouted. A .45-caliber
bullet had pierced the right cheek of the Sioux lying at his
feet and carried away the left half of his skull on its way
out. I had to admit that the trooper was dedicated. He had
given up the chance at a furlough—or a bonus—in order to
take a few prisoners.

I said, calmly as possible, "You need spectacles."

This being friendly country, more or less, we had doffed

our disguises and put on our hats, not counting Jac, who wore none. The sergeant (his stripes were visible now) had expected Indians, and at worst he might have been prepared for other soldiers, but two white civilians and an elderly half-breed were too much for him to sort out at one time. But they're conditioned to hold onto their guns when in doubt, and this one held true to his training.

"Just who the hell are you, and what you doing with that there dead injun?" His features were Scandinavian, deeply tanned and dusted across chin and cheeks with blond stubble. He had pale blue eyes, which contrasted vividly with the burnished copper of his complexion, and yellow side-whiskers that came to the corners of a jaw so square a carpenter could have used it for a miter. The hand holding the gun had an equally square black thumbnail and knuckles banded with white scar tissue. He had burst them on his share of out-thrust chins.

"In the first place," I said, "he's not dead. As for the rest, we're civilian peace officers on special assignment with Major Quincy Harms and this is our prisoner." That was a gamble. If the sergeant and his companions were from Fort Ransom we were sunk.

He scraped his chin with the back of the hand holding the knife, ostensibly on the theory that it helped him think. Still he didn't lower the revolver.

"I don't know. You got a badge?"

That request was beginning to wear thin on me. I was standing behind the gray; resting the carbine across its rump, I fished out the star with my left hand and held it up. There's no doubt that pinning it to your shirt simplifies things, but anywhere you wear it, it's too close to your heart. Hudspeth pulled open his coat to show his. The sergeant squinted from one to the other in thoughtful silence.

"All right, so you got tin. That comes cheap. Anything else?"

"For Christ's sake, can't you see we're white?" One of these days, I thought, the marshal's nose was going to explode in a big red cloud.

The sergeant glared at him. He was going to say, "Shut up, fat boy," or something as inflammatory. It was on his lips. When he did, Hudspeth was going to throw lead and we would all die right there, smack in the middle of the earth's left armpit. I wondered how St. Peter would take it when he asked me what I was doing at the gates so early and I told him I had acted in defense of my partner's waistline, and the marshal was standing behind me in line broad as a chuck wagon across the beam. My grip tightened on the Winchester.

But I was disappointed, although I doubt that's the proper word for what I felt. Instead of saying it, the sergeant nodded curtly, as if he had just come to the decision that we were, indeed, white. He wasn't finished yet, however.

"What about Grandpa?" he challenged, jerking his chin toward Jac. "Don't tell me R. B. Hayes is deputizing half-breeds now."

I explained who he was and what he was doing there. The sergeant's eyes left me and took in our gear lying on the ground a couple of yards away. I answered his next question before he could ask it.

"Our horses were shot out from under us. Pere Jac, there, took a lance in his shoulder as he went down. We're in the midst of changing mounts."

I must have been pretty convincing, because the top kick glanced down impatiently at the Sioux he'd been preparing to scalp. He was losing interest. But for duty's sake he got in one more lick, a good one.

"What's so all-fired important about that particular in-jun?" he demanded. "There'll be hundreds to choose from in a few minutes."

"This ain't no ordinary—" Hudspeth began. But before he could finish he had something else to occupy him, namely the pain in his ankle where I had struck it with the side of my boot.

"It's one of Ghost Shirt's inner circle," I broke in quickly, to draw attention from Hudspeth's cry. "Tall Dog, a Chey-enne warrior. He may be able to shed some light on his boss's plans."

The sergeant snorted. "Hell, that's no secret. He was on his way to link up with Spotted Cat and his Arapahoes down south. What he didn't know was they surrendered to Gen-eral Crook last week."

"Surrendered?" It flew out. Right after it did I knew it was a mistake.

He nodded. It hadn't dawned on him yet. "Every last one of 'em, right outside Deadwood. Not a shot fired. Christ, ev-eryone's talking—" He broke off. Realization flushed over his face. He'd been about to holster his weapon, but now he raised it again. "Say, where you been? If you was with Major Harms all this time like you say, you would of knowed all about the surrender. It's all over the army. Speak up!"

I could have given myself a swift kick. Not because I had opened my trap without thinking, which was reason enough, but because of what happened next and what it meant. If I hadn't been all aglow inside over how glib I was and how I was going to talk us out of this, I might have seen it com-ing, as Jac had, and taken steps to counteract it—as Jac had. All the time the sergeant was questioning me, the métis had taken advantage of the fact that all eyes were on me and had sidled around the horses until he was standing within lunging distance of a quaking trooper who looked too young for the uniform he was wearing and who was having trouble holding onto his revolver with both hands. When the sergeant raised his Colt again, Jac dropped his Spencer noiselessly in the grass, curled one of his trunklike arms around the trooper's windpipe, pinioned one of his ankles in the crook of a knee so that he was balanced precariously on one leg, and thrust the point of his knife against the tender flesh beneath the young man's chin. At the same time, the half-breed bumped him from behind with his pelvis and the revolver sprang from his hands like a slippery frog. All without a sound, until the trooper went and spoiled it by crying out.

I was sure the sergeant was an old-line campaigner who knew better than to let his attention be distracted from his primary objective no matter what. I still think that, even though he did what he did. A man on the shady side of forty doesn't give up the reactions of a lifetime just because a little brown book tells him they're no good. He turned his head just far enough to see what the noise was about, realized his mistake, and turned back, but by then it was too late. The muzzle of my Winchester came swinging around, cracked against the back of the hand holding the Colt, and was staring at the third button down from the collar of his tunic by the time the revolver hit the ground. My nerves were strung so tight I nearly blew him into the next world when he doubled over, hugging his shattered hand between his knees.

"This carbine fires a forty-four caliber round," I told him, "and so does the revolver the marshal has trained on the man behind you. One of them is enough to make a corpse your loved ones won't want to kiss before they lower it into the ground, but they don't kill any deader than the knife Pere Jac is holding at Tom Sawyer's throat there. That leaves two soldiers uncovered. Are you a gambling man, Sergeant?"

He took enough time to swallow twice, but I can't say if he used it for that purpose. I was looking at his eyes. I saw in them that although he was still doubled over, the pain in his hand was no longer a priority. He was figuring the odds. So he was a gambling man. A smart one too, if what I read there next was on target.

It was. "Drop your guns," he told his men. When there was no response he repeated it, bellowing this time. Two Colts and a Springfield thumped the grassy ground.

"The belt gun too," I said to the man who had discarded the rifle. He hesitated, then unbuckled the belt one-handed and let it fall. Hudspeth stared at it.

"Hey," he said. "Is that a Smith American?" The trooper said it was. "I'll be damned!" He stepped forward, hugging his own Smith against his rib cage, and picked up the belt, which was loaded with cartridges.

"Get all of them while you're at it," I told him.

"You won't make a mile." The drillmaster's bawl had shrunk to a croak. Now that the decision had been made, the throbbing in the sergeant's hand must have been terrific. I risked a downward glance and felt a twinge of remorse. I hadn't meant to finish his army career. As far as a lifer like this was concerned, I supposed, I might just as well have killed him. I decided to let him have the last word. I was out of smart answers anyway.

The marshal came back carrying the discarded iron. I told him to unload the pieces and leave them there in a pile. We were carrying too much weight as it was, and I didn't want to leave the troopers unarmed in the middle of a fight.

We were still on the same side, no matter how it looked. Hudspeth obeyed but retained the belt full of .44's.

I kept them covered while he and Jac, who had released the callow soldier, saddled up and stepped into leather. Behind us, the whooping and shooting continued, farther away now as the Indians were bottled up against the high southern rim of the lake bed. Bright yellow flames blossomed in scattered places as the tipis were set afire. Another ten or fifteen minutes and it would all be over for everyone but the buzzards. I leathered the five-shot, mounted, and together we broke into gallop and topped the western rise in the direction of the Missouri River. The troopers dived for their weapons, but by the time they had them loaded we were well out of range. Their popping was drowned out by the drumming of our mounts' hoofs.

We stopped at the river to water the horses and fill the buckskin bags Hudspeth had liberated from camp, then wheeled right and headed north. Ghost Shirt was still alive, no thanks to us. I had bunched my bedroll under his chin to keep his head up; the gash above his ear was bleeding again, but slower now. He was still out. I wondered if he would ever come to, and if he didn't, if Flood would still insist upon hanging him. I decided that he would. In the judge's case, the quality of mercy was strained through a sheet.

After a couple of hours of hard riding—tempered, of course, by the condition of our prisoner—we got off and led the horses to give them a rest. No one had spoken since leaving camp.

"Where to now?" asked the marshal. He seemed more out of sorts than usual, which was understandable after several miles on the back of a horse three sizes too small.

"The scenic route," I replied. "In another few miles we'll swing east for three days or so and then north again. We can't take the chance of being spotted by whatever troopers might be left in Fort Yates, and if Dakota's like anywhere else there's too much civilization strung out along the river. It'll take us a hundred miles out of our way, but with any luck we'll be able to catch the train to Bismarck and be there by the end of next week. Whenever that is."

"That's one hell of a long ways to travel with a red-hot injun, even if he does live. Some of them Cheyenne got through back there, you know. And don't forget the army."

"The Cheyenne will be too busy licking their wounds for some time, and the army's got its hands full. Worry about them later."

"I got as much confidence in that as I do in Jac. He's the one said they wouldn't attack unless we was moving."

Jac shrugged, both shoulders this time. His wound was coming along. "I did not expect infantry support."

"Stop grousing," I said. "You didn't think we'd capture Ghost Shirt in the first place."

"Now the hard part begins." Pere Jac's face was wooden.

# CHAPTER 13

The first words Ghost Shirt uttered upon coming to were English, and they weren't very nice.

We had set up camp in the shadow of the buttes along the edge of the plateau twenty-five miles northeast of the hollow where the battle had taken place. Jac and Hudspeth were breaking out the jerky and I had a hand under the Indian's head and a buckskin bag full of water in the other when his eyes opened without any fluttering and he spoke the words, which needn't be quoted here. I clucked my tongue.

"Shame on you. Is that any way to talk to someone who helped save your life?"

He said something else just as colorful. Apparently he had picked up quite a few of our quainter expressions during the time he had spent among us in his youth. But he didn't resist when I forced the neck of the water bag between his lips. He drank greedily. Then he closed his eyes again. I lowered his head gently onto the extra horse blanket I had folded beneath it. The even rise and fall of his chest told me he was asleep, or doing a good imitation of it.

"He ought to eat," grumbled the marshal. His jaw worked as he ground away at a piece of jerked meat. I shook my head.

"He needs rest more. When he's ready to eat, he'll eat. Besides, with his head in the condition it's in, he'd be lucky if he didn't break open the wound just chewing on this saddle leather." I produced my own strip, looked at it, sighed, took a bite, sighed again, and put it away. I was hungry, but my teeth were still sore from the last meal. "I hate Dakota," I said.

Pere Jac had finished his meal and was looking over his pony, grazing with the others at the end of their tethers on the other side of camp. He muttered an oath, the first I had ever heard from his lips.

"What's wrong?" I asked.

"Split hoof." He was inspecting the pony's right front. "He has not yet begun to limp, but he will. If I get another day's ride out of him it will be a holy miracle."

"That's what you get for not shoeing him," said Hudspeth.

"Are there any settlements nearby?" I asked Jac.

He released the hoof and straightened. "A ranch, three miles the other side of the buttes. It belongs to an old Scot named Tyrone, or it did. It has been many years since I saw him. Perhaps he is dead."

"Any horses?"

"He raises them, or used to. But he will charge an arm and a leg."

"So long as he don't charge money," put in the marshal. "We ain't got none of that to spare."

"Get it up, both of you." I got out my wallet and spread the bills on the ground. "Thirty-three dollars. See if you can sweeten it."

Hudspeth carried a dilapidated billfold with a picture of Lola Montez on the back of an advertisement for chewing tobacco. Reluctantly he drew out a pair of ten-spots and six ones and placed them next to mine. Neither of us was carrying pocket change because you don't go Indian-hunting with anything on you that jingles. I looked up at Pere Jac.

"No bills," he said. "How about this?" He reached into the leather poke he carried and handed me a lump of yellow something the size of a tooth, which was exactly what it was. I recognized it as the loosened gold molar he had extracted from his mouth the night we had met in the métis camp. I hefted it in the palm of my hand.

"Quarter of an ounce, maybe a little more," I judged. "Let's say nine dollars."

"It cost me twelve."

"Someone saw you coming. All right, that gives us sixty-eight dollars, enough to buy two good horses in Helena."

"It won't buy us one from Tyrone." He drew up the poke and returned it to his saddle bag.

"We'll worry about that tomorrow."

Tomorrow was bleeding into the purple overhead like cheap red dye when I awoke to find Jac standing over me, moccasined feet spread apart and the muzzle of his Spencer dangling in front of my face. I thought, *You can't trust anyone*, pushed it away before it could blow off one of my best features, and drew the Deane-Adams, pointing it at his groin.

The movement startled him. He stepped back quickly and glanced down at me as if he'd forgotten I was there. He hadn't been watching me at all, but something far beyond me. The muzzle of the five-shot brought him back in a hurry. Without a word he raised his arm and pointed in the direction he'd been looking. That trick being as old as the rock that had been digging into the small of my back all night long, I didn't look right away but climbed out of my bedroll and took two steps backward, keeping him covered. Then I looked.

My first thought when I saw the curl of black smoke drifting up against the distant haze was that I had made a horse's
ass of myself again. Then the significance of it hit me and
that didn't seem so important any more. A spot of bright
yellow flickered at the base of the curl. The group of dark
lumps clustered around it might have been rocks, but they
weren't.

"How long?"

"I cannot say. I noticed it at first light."

"Get Hudspeth up."

"Too late. I'm up."

I turned to my left. The marshal was standing next to his
bedroll facing west, where the campfire was. No doubt about
it, I'd been living too soft of late, sleeping too soundly. It
didn't comfort me that I'd come off watch only three hours
before. "Got your glass?"

He thrust it at me. "I reckon the injuns found the ammo
in my saddle bags more interesting. But you won't see anything."

"My eyes are ten years younger than yours." I pointed the
glass in the direction of the fire and twisted it. Behind me
the sun had begun to top the buttes, casting their shadows
just short of the other camp. When I had the flames in good
and clear I shifted a little to the right. As I did so, one of
the lumps stirred, cast something into the fire, and stood up.
It was dressed in black. No, blue. It turned to look up at the
buttes and sunlight glittered off the tiny, polished surface
of what had to be a glass eye. I lowered the telescope.

"Shades of the U.S. Army," I said.

"Harms?" suggested Hudspeth.

"Worse, if what Jed Hoxie told us is worth anything. Sergeant Burdett."

"How many with him?" He took back the glass and

trained it in that direction, as if the fresh knowledge might improve his vision.

"Eight or ten. Either they don't know we've got Ghost Shirt or Burdett talked the major out of loading him down with more men than he needed. I'm betting on the second."

"How good you figure this guy is?"

"If he's good enough to have followed us this far, he's good enough for us not to worry about trying to cover up our tracks from here on in. We'd just be wasting our time. He wants us to know he's there, or he wouldn't have lit that fire. He hopes we'll panic and make mistakes."

While we had been talking, Pere Jac had begun to saddle the horses. "Speaking of wasting time," he said pointedly. We took the hint and turned to break camp.

I walked over to where Ghost Shirt was lying with a blanket drawn up to his chin and watched his face for a second or two. His eyes were closed and his breathing was even. "Get up," I said. "I know you're with us." I nudged him gently in the ribs with the toe of my boot.

Something the size of a newborn calf came roaring up from beneath the blankets and struck me full in the chest, knocking me down hard on my back. I found myself looking up into a savage face with hatred in its eyes and a double row of sharp, curving teeth in a gaping mouth. The jaws closed on my right arm when I went for my gun. I tried to extract it and felt the flesh tearing away from the bone. Hot breath seared my face. My ears rang with the thing's frenzied snarling, which grew shriller as I fought to keep it from my throat. It shook my wrist like a dead snake. I had about given up the battle when something blurred across my vision, there was a loud thump followed by an earsplitting yelp of rage and pain, a name was called sharply, and suddenly the weight was gone from my chest.

"Are you all right, Page?" Pere Jac was standing over me, gripping his Spencer by the barrel like a club—which was an appropriate comparison, since that's what he had just used it for. Behind him, Hudspeth had his Smith & Wesson out to cover Ghost Shirt, who was on his feet now, and Custer, the yellow mongrel I'd seen him with back at the mission, who was at the Indian's side. The dog was scrubbing its head against the grass to clean the blood from the cut Jac had opened over its right eye. It was still snarling.

I got up, holding my torn wrist together with the other hand. Almost reluctantly, I peeled back the ragged sleeve to inspect the damage. It wasn't as bad as I'd feared, although it was bad enough. A good deal of meat had been exposed and rearranged, but as far as I could tell the muscle was intact. I tore a fresh strip from what was left of my shirttail and began to bind it up. Jac finished the job.

"All right," I said, once the blood was out of sight. "Where'd the animal come from and how'd he get into camp? It wasn't during my watch."

"Nor mine," said Jac. "I never left this spot."

We looked at Hudspeth. He fidgeted.

"It must of been after I stepped into them bushes." He jerked his head toward a prairie rose bramble fifty yards away. There was no apology in his tone. "It was only a couple of minutes. Hell, a man's got to—"

"Damn smart dog, picking just that moment to sneak into camp."

"He is smart."

It was Ghost Shirt who had spoken. He was down on one knee beside the dog with his hand on its bleeding head. Not stroking it or patting it, just holding it there, the way he might handle anything else that belonged to him.

"He is trained to follow me at a distance and to join me

at night in silence." The commanding strain had not left his speech in spite of his captive state. Although he spoke without accent, the fact that he gave each syllable its proper value made it clear that for him English was a foreign tongue. "I did not train him to attack in my defense. That he does naturally."

He sneezed, winced at the shock to his own injured head, and climbed unsteadily to his feet. I was surprised. It was the first time we had stood face to face, and even then we weren't, not exactly. I knew that most Indians only ran to about five and a half feet, but from his reputation I had expected this one to top off a lot taller. The crown of his head came to my nose. It didn't make me feel superior, though. Some of the hardest fights I've had have been with runts.

He was a fine specimen, at that. The shirt he wore sashed about his waist, once red, now faded to a desert tan, barely contained his chest and shoulders, and his solid, heavy-muscled thighs strained the seams of his buckskin leggings. From there they swelled into powerful calves, then tapered to trim ankles and a pair of feet small and delicate-looking enough in their fringeless moccasins to arouse the envy of a beautiful woman. His reddish brown breechclout nearly swept the earth.

"Why'd you call him off?" I asked.

I got the hypnotic stare. "For his own safety. One more blow like the first would have killed him."

"Is he going to behave himself now?"

"He always has. I said that he is trained."

"Let me put it another way. Are you going to behave yourself?"

He smiled then, which took me aback. I hadn't seen him do that before. It didn't suit him. "I have not been unconscious all the time," he said. "I have overheard your conversation.

With what will you threaten me? I am worth nothing to you dead."

Daring me. Just like a twenty-two-year-old boy. Aloud I said, "We'd rather keep you alive, sure, but we'd heaps rather stay alive ourselves. If you're the genius they say you are you'll try to fix it so we won't have to choose. Besides, there's a group of men in blue coats back there who don't care whether they bring you back sitting a saddle or draped over it. If you decide to pitch pennies you'd better be sure where they'll land."

I'd expected that last statement to go over his head, but he understood. He hadn't spent all his time while out East inside the classroom. Anyway, the smile was gone.

Hudspeth mounted the mustang. In spite of the situation and the pain in my wrist I suppressed a grin. He looked like a fat padre on a scrawny burro. He scowled at the dog.

"If that mutt goes with us he eats grass," he said. "We ain't got enough jerky we can afford to waste it on no mangy cur."

"He is Cheyenne. He will hunt for his food," said Ghost Shirt.

We straddled our horses, Jac favoring his wounded shoulder, me my wrist, the Indian his head. Only Hudspeth remained unimpaired, unless you counted the fact that he was deprived of his whiskey and that he was riding a horse that didn't fit him. Followed by a dog with a burst scalp, we must have looked like a hospital train returning from a battlefield as we steered single file down the narrow trail that led to the flatlands. I turned in my saddle for one final glance at our pursuers before we passed below the ridge. There was now no sign of a fire.

The haze burned off around five o'clock, when the air turned hot and dry as the inside of a brick chimney. The grass had gone from green to brittle brown. The harsh smell of baked earth stung our nostrils. Suddenly I missed the sultriness of the past several days. The back of my neck grew skillet-hot and water splashed into my mouth from the buckskin bag I carried seemed to evaporate before it reached my tongue. The landscape swam behind shimmering waves of heat.

Tyrone, it turned out, owned several sections on the western edge of the Drift Prairie, smack in the middle of which stood a tiny sod hut with a privy behind it and a corral roughly the size of Montana. Here and there horses grazed in groups or galloped off alone to kick up their heels in the open acreage. A windmill towered over the hut, its blades stock still. It was either tied down or the air was just as stagnant up there as it was at ground level.

To the northwest, beyond the fenced-in section, several hundred acres had been turned over quite recently. As a matter of fact, it was being turned as we approached it, by a pair of huge workhorses pulling a large plow with a scrawny old man at the handles. As he pushed, he kept up a steady rhythm of curses in a rich, bellowing cant that carried for miles. Since there was no one else around to receive them, it was evident that they were directed at the two grays straining at the traces. The horses didn't appear to be paying any attention to the abuses he was hurling at them as they worked. They were probably used to it by now and couldn't function without it.

We had reached the west end of the plowed field when the farmer rounded the opposite corner. Maybe I was getting old, but I was sure he hadn't noticed us yet. The bullet that struck the ground in front of my gray's hoofs and kicked dirt up over its fetlocks told me different.

# CHAPTER 14

**"I** spent too much time plowing these furrows to mess them up with a bunch of graves. But I'll make the sacrifice if I don't start hearing some names I trust damn soon."

However many years it had taken Tyrone to pick up the American way of speech west of the Mississippi, they hadn't been enough to eradicate his Scottish burr, which showed itself most prominently in the acrobatics his *r*'s went through before they left his tongue. His voice was deep and rich, the way it had been when he was cursing at the horses earlier. He was standing behind the giant grays holding a Remington rolling-block he had hooked from a special scabbard on the plow handle as he was coming around the end of his last furrow, so smoothly that I hadn't realized what he was doing until the shot rang out.

The breed spoke up. "Tyrone, do you not remember me?"

"Jacques!" It was strange hearing Jac called by his right name. I found myself resenting it without knowing why. For all his obvious delight, however, the Scot maintained his grip on the rifle. "Where have you been these twenty years? I thought you were dead."

Several items of gossip were exchanged, none of which is crucial to this narrative. We did learn that the rancher was breaking ground for late oats after an argument with his feed supplier had resulted in their terminating their working agreement. Then Jac introduced us—all except Ghost Shirt, to whom he referred simply as our prisoner. Only then did Tyrone step out from behind the horses and approach us, still holding the rifle. His figure beneath the shapeless work clothes was small and wiry and he walked with a definite bounce. A worn tweed hat with a slouched, finger-marked brim was crushed on top of his head. The lower half of his face was completely hidden behind a reddish beard, streaked with white and cut square at the bottom. Over this swooped a moustache that must have dressed out at a pound and a half, the waxed ends of which dipped down to the corners of his jaw before jutting back up to tickle his ears. A pair of wire-rimmed spectacles glittered astride a bulb of flesh in the middle of his face. I placed his age at about sixty, but it could have fallen ten years either side of that. He got to within a few yards of us when he stopped short, his face reddened, and he raised the Remington to his stringy shoulder.

"Ghost Shirt!" He made it sound like one of the names he had been calling the horses. The dog, which had just caught up with us, hunkered down and growled threateningly at him through bared teeth.

"You know him?" I asked.

"I saw him in the stockade at Fort Ransom last March when I went there to raise hell about the Crows stealing my horses. What are you doing with him?"

"Judge Flood plans to decorate a pole with him in Bismarck if we can keep ahead of the army." I made a quick decision based on what Jac had told me of the Scot's character on the way there and gave him a rundown. He listened in silence.

"How far are they behind you?" he asked, when I had finished.

"Not more than a couple of hours."

"So why are you stopping?"

For an answer, Pere Jac stepped down and held up his pony's damaged hoof for him to see. Tyrone nodded.

"I can give you a good price on a three-year-old I broke last fall. What've you got to spend?"

"*You* broke him?" Hudspeth cut in. He had all the discretion of a heckler at a church service.

"Somebody had to." Tyrone glared up at him defiantly. "Every last hand I had lit out when Ghost Shirt broke jail. I was busting broncos before you were born."

"Did they have horses then?"

I decided to steer the conversation back onto the main track before bullets flew. "What can you give us for sixty-five dollars?"

The Scot discovered he had a mouthful of worms. There is no other way to describe that expression.

"You've guts, I'll give you that. Not that they'll do you any good now or in the long run. In your situation I could soak you a thousand dollars."

"Not when sixty-five is all we have." I sighed. All right, so maybe that was overdoing it a little. I was tired. "I guess you've got us figured out. I was saving some for emergencies. Sixty-eight dollars."

Worms again. "Get off my land."

"Seems to me it would be worth the difference to keep three of your fellow citizens from becoming criminals and robbing you." I didn't draw my gun. That would have been too obvious, and fatal under the circumstances. But I shifted my weight in the saddle to bring the butt of the Deane-Adams within easy reach.

"Is that how it is?"

"You certainly have a way with words," I said.

I'll give him credit for one thing: He didn't say, "You're sworn to uphold the law" or anything like that, although I could see that he was considering it. I had a whole speech made out for that one. But what he did say was just as predictable.

"This Remington is trained on your belly. Are you betting that your hand is quicker than my finger on this trigger?"

Another gambler. The West was full of them. I said nothing. There's a time to raise and a time to stand pat.

"Maybe you didn't hear his name before." Hudspeth was backing my play. "This here's Page Murdock. He's the one brought in that scalp hunter Bear Anderson last year in Montana, right under the noses of Chief Two Sisters and the *en*-tire Flathead nation."

I thought he was laying it on a little thick, but it appeared that Tyrone was not a man to be subtle with. His murky green eyes did things behind the spectacles. He was a strong man, and a brave one, but sustained tension is a hard thing for anyone to take. I knew, because I was on the other end of the same taut string. Five or six seconds shuffled by. My shoulder began to ache from holding my arm in the same position. I supposed the rifle was growing heavy in the old Scot's hands, although you wouldn't have guessed it by the way he held it. Finally he lowered the piece about the width of a butterfly's eyelash.

"You throwing in the pinto?"

Jac said he was.

"You're getting a good pony damned cheap."

I had handed the treasury over to Pere Jac on the trail. He reached into his poke, withdrew the crumpled bills and the gold tooth, and turned them over to Tyrone, who took them in one hand while he balanced the Remington in the other. I could have taken him then had I wanted to, but there

was no longer any reason and anyway I liked him. Maybe I
was looking at myself in thirty years.

He held up the tooth. "What's this?"

"What's it look like?"

"How do I know it's real?"

"Bite it."

"I'm not going to bite anything that was in somebody
else's mouth."

"Then you'll have to trust us. Where's the animal?"

"In the corral next to the house." He pointed. "That's it,
the piebald grazing at the fence. Watch him. He's spirited."

Jac mounted and said, "We will leave the paint as agreed.
That and sixty-eight dollars should buy us the best horse
in the West."

"That's the only kind I raise."

"Burdett and his men will be around before noon," I told
the Scot. "When they come—"

"I know. Tell them you went the other way."

I shook my head. "They know better. Tell them the truth,
but lie first. They won't expect you to level with them the first
time around. Wait until they press you, then give it to them
straight. It will save you a lot of pain. Real pain. These aren't
your run-of-the-mill horse soldiers. They play for keeps."

"Who doesn't, out here?"

The piebald was a good pony, broke to saddle but not in
spirit, as Pere Jac discovered when he went to mount after
cinching up, and found himself swinging a leg over empty
air. The pony was on the other side of the corral, tossing its
triangular head and champing at the bit, by the time its
would-be rider hit the ground amid a swirl of yellow dust.

"Maybe he doesn't like Indians," I suggested, helping the
métis to his feet. "Next time try mounting from the left."

Getting near it was a problem this time, but at length Jac

got a foot planted in the left stirrup and his hindquarters in the saddle. His unfamiliar weight threw the animal into a panic, but after a couple of wild gallops around the corral the two were inseparable. The old man may have been half and half, but when it came to riding he was all Indian. I could tell he was satisfied, because when it came time to leave he ignored the gate standing open and bounded over the fence. It was a four-railer, and the stallion cleared it with room to spare.

By noon we had come upon the trail the war party had left coming out. Small wonder the army had found no difficulty in locating us. A grass fire left a harder path to follow. All those hoofs and moccasins and travois had churned the grass into a band of red dust a quarter-mile wide and eight inches deep, meandering drunkenly to the horizon. At that point we veered straight north. None of us felt any need to eat more earth, and there was no sense in making things easy for Sergeant Burden.

A wind had come up from the northeast. It rippled across the tall grass so that the writhing blades resembled not so much the waves of the ocean (a favorite comparison among visiting Easterners) as the bristling hackles of a great angry beast. The first gust came out of nowhere as we topped a rise, lifting my hat from my sweat-greased brow with a sucking sound that reminded me uncomfortably of the noise made when a scalp is pulled away from the skull. I caught it just in time—the hat, not my scalp—and jammed it down to my ears. The air hitting my face was hot and stale, like an expelled breath. Then it died, but before the ground swell retreated over the last hill in the southwest it came up again, and from then on the intervals between gusts grew shorter and shorter until we were bucking a constant gale.

A jackrabbit exploded out from beneath the gray's hoof as we were cantering down one of the hillocks and thumped through the grass toward a burrow some twenty yards away. Ghost Shirt's dog was after it an instant later. There aren't many dogs that can catch a jack on the run, but Custer was no ordinary mongrel. A rabbit has only one trick, when you come down to it, and that's that it can stop and turn on a dime. Nine times out of ten nothing else is needed. It'll run so far, then halt suddenly. Almost invariably its pursuer, unable to duplicate the feat, will run right past, and before it can turn the rabbit has already reversed directions and gotten a head start that nothing short of a horse at full gallop can touch. Fifteen feet short of the hole this jack chose to rely on the odds and stopped abruptly. In the next instant Custer was upon it. There was a savage snarl, a squeal of pain and terror, and then the dog tore away its throat and settled down to devour the warm flesh. It was all over in less than a second.

"He won't eat grass today," I told Hudspeth. He made no answer. For another four or five miles, in fact, he said nothing. Then, as we were nearing the crest of yet another of the endless swells:

"We got company."

The marshal was riding at my left and a little to the rear. When I turned to look at him he jerked his head backward. As he did the wind caught the brim of his hat and folded it back against the crown, Indian scout style. Weeks on the trail had beaten all the newness out of it. I looked beyond his shoulder.

He had sharp eyes, despite what I had said that morning when he was unable to spot the soldiers through the spyglass. Far to the southwest, a flying wedge made up of dark, irregular shapes had just come into view atop one of the undulating hills and was traveling with great speed down its face.

"Making up for lost time," I said. "They've gained an hour on us."

Jac said, "They cannot keep up that pace. Even so they will be upon us by nightfall. Something should be done."

"That's what I like, a man who makes decisions." That burning wind in my face had dried up my patience. It wasn't as bad as the "hot southerlies" that blew up from Mexico from time to time, baking the beds of rivers and turning grassland into desert, but it would do until one came along. "How about making one that's worth something?"

Hudspeth reined in next to a burned-up wild rose bramble and leaped down from the saddle. My common sense was deadened by the heat. For a moment I thought he had decided to make a stand against eight or ten seasoned troopers and get it all over with, but when he stooped and twisted off the bramble at its stem I couldn't see how that fit and abandoned the theory. Sun and lack of rain had cooked its branches brittle and many of its tiny, shriveled leaves shook loose and rattled to the ground with a sound like shot falling through the trees as he worried it from its moorings. Then he straightened, holding the trophy as if it were a priceless artifact.

"Matches." He held out a hand to Pere Jac.

The métis caught on at the same time I did. After only a beat he reached into his belt and produced the square of oilcloth in which he kept his matches and tobacco. Hudspeth struck one on the heel of his boot and, shielding the flame from the wind with his body, touched off the bramble. The dry leaves caught like pitch and went up in a bright orange blaze. After returning the package to Jac, he mounted up, holding the makeshift torch at arm's length to avoid frightening the mustang, then leaned down from the saddle and set fire to the brown grass where he had been standing.

"Start riding," he shouted over the wind and the fierce crackling, controlling with his free hand the horse, which had begun dancing backward nervously from the spreading flames. "If this wind shifts we'll all be fried where we sit." He galloped west, touched off fires in two more places, then hurled the burning bush in the direction of the distant riders and wheeled to join us in our northern flight.

I heard a raucous noise just behind me and twisted in my saddle, drawing my gun. A yellow blur dashed past me. I realized then that it was Custer just catching up with us after finishing a fresh meal. The dog had darted straight through the flames without a qualm. It had its master's grit.

"Where did you get an idea like that?" I asked Hudspeth as he drew alongside me.

"From my parents, though they never knowed it." His face was flushed from the heat of the flames. "Once when I was ten years old I come home from school and found a smoking black hole where our cabin used to be. Land charred for a square mile. Turned out a spark from the ungreased hub of our neighbor's Red River cart sparked off a fire on our south forty. My ma and pa was inside eating when it hit the cabin. It come so fast there was nothing they could do. I buried what was left of them in one hole."

I never know what to say in a situation like that, so I kept my mouth shut. That's usually the best course anyway. Behind us, the grass went up like tinder as the high winds whipped the flames westward at unbelievable speed and sent a great cloak of black smoke spreading over the prairie. Over my shoulder I caught a glimpse of the dark-clad riders as they reined in a mile or so shy of the blaze, but then the smoke from three separate sources came together and blotted them out.

"And there came out a fire from the Lord, and consumed them," said Pere Jac, but he was speaking so low that I doubt anyone heard him but myself and his God.

# CHAPTER 15

**N**othing breeds co-operation like a common enemy. Once the threat of Sergeant Burdett and his pack of two-legged hounds was ended, however, it came time to think about restraining Ghost Shirt. For this purpose I produced from my saddle bags the special pair of handcuffs a blacksmith had struck to my order in Montana some years back and used them to secure his hands behind him as we were preparing to bed down. I hadn't brought them out before because they were shiny and sent out a flash in the bright sunlight that a half-blind drummer couldn't miss, but with the hostiles, red and white, out of the running for at least the present it seemed safe to put them to work now. That the Indians had left them in the bag said something about the way things had changed over the past couple of decades. When the wagon trains began rolling west they would have sold their souls for such an attractive bauble, but now they shoved it aside in their search for ammunition. If they'd known what use I'd be putting it to the story would have been different.

A tiny spring inside the mechanism—an addition of my own—locked them automatically with a metallic snick when I closed the manacles about his wiry wrists. Since Indians are as dangerous with their feet as with their hands I used a length of rawhide left over from our captivity to bind his ankles where he lay on his blanket. He made no protest, but then I hadn't expected him to. His kind didn't do much talking when not among its own, and never when words were useless. The dog slunk toward him as I was tucking him in, but he snapped something at it in Cheyenne and it returned to its place beside the fire. That was wise. He knew that it wouldn't be able to resist attacking me next morning when I came near its master, and had no wish to spend the rest of a brief life in those irons. Hudspeth, Jac, and I took turns standing watch as always.

The procedure was repeated the next night. Mornings I released him from the cuffs to eat and undid the thong around his ankles, then after breakfast manacled him again, this time with his hands in front so he could ride, and kept him ahead of us on the trail to remove temptation. It was late in the morning of the second day since the fire that we came upon the rails of the Northern Pacific some five or six miles west of the James. We crossed them and set up camp just out of sight but not out of earshot of the next train.

Nearby was an ancient buffalo wallow, low on water but high on wallow, with a stand of half a dozen spindly cottonwoods growing on its north shore. That was an unexpected stroke of luck. More than half certain that we wouldn't survive to see the railroad, I hadn't given much thought to how we were going to stop the train once we got there. You don't just stand in the middle of the tracks and wave one down in the midst of hostile Indian territory, not and expect to spend the rest of eternity as anything but a grease slick along the cinder bed. The sight of those trees in the middle of a barren land was enough to make me a believer in manna from heaven if I hadn't known that a water-loving cottonwood sprang up wherever a man spat. Fortunately, Hudspeth had seized a hatchet along with the other provisions he took from the Indian camp, and by the time I had Ghost Shirt trussed up to make sure he behaved, the marshal was three quarters of the way through the first trunk. When that was on the ground I spelled him on the hatchet while he and Jac lugged the tree down to the rails. When they were all lying beside the tracks we went to work cutting them into six-foot lengths. Within a couple of hours of our arrival we had a respectable pile stacked four feet high across the irons.

I was depositing the last spindly chunks atop the heap when something buzzed past my right ear and struck the end of one of the logs, splintering the bark. Then I heard the shot. I tossed away my burden and dived behind the woodpile as more firearms opened up from the same general direction, their bullets pelting the ground and spanging off the rails. One of them struck the heel of my left boot while I was in flight. I came down hard on the ties, rolled, and ended up in a crouch next to Hudspeth, who had been standing behind the pile when the commotion began and now was down on one knee in the same spot, his Smith & Wesson in hand. His moustache was bristling. A lot of things annoyed him, but none so much as being shot at. I drew my Deane-Adams.

Jac, who had been on his way back from checking on our prisoner, charging his pipe as he went, lay motionless on his stomach in the tall grass twenty feet away. At first I thought he'd been hit, but then I saw his ear twitch and I realized he was just lying low. His Spencer was leaning against the woodpile on the other side where he'd left it, the end of its barrel taunting me over the top of the barrier. My Winchester was still in its scabbard with the horses in camp. Two bad mistakes when you come to think of it, the métis going unarmed to inspect a dangerous captive and me leaving a firearm near that same captive, who was trussed up but still had a brain. Worse, we both knew better. Reaching the railroad against all those odds had made us all cockier than we had any right to be under the circumstances.

Beyond the stack of wood, where the shots had originated, yawned open prairie, unbroken except for an occasional brown bush, too low and spindly to conceal a man, let alone several. For several there were, unless that was a Gatling gun out there, which still meant more than one because you don't exactly carry that kind of firepower on the back of a horse. To look out there, though, you would have sworn we were all alone. Which meant only one thing.

"Burdett?" whispered Hudspeth at that point, as if he'd been reading my mind. I shook my head.

"Indians. Only they can hide like that in the middle of open grassland. And only they can use up that much ammunition without hitting anything worthwhile."

"You mean Lame Horse?"

"Who else? He probably saw us leave camp with Ghost Shirt at the Missouri and guessed where we were heading. He's been paralleling the tracks ever since or he would have been caught in the same fire that pushed back Burdett. How much lead have you got on you?"

"Just what's in my gun. The belt's back in my saddle bags. How about you?"

"Five in the cylinder and another ten in my belt. The rest is in my bags. If you carried a forty-five Peacemaker like almost everyone else I might risk giving you some. At least it wouldn't blow up in your face."

"Look who's talking, you and that little toy you pack."

I stoked up my courage and raised myself just enough to snatch hold of the barrel of Jac's rifle and hook it back over the woodpile. Three guns opened up as I did so. One bullet actually struck the wood four feet to the left of my exposed hand, their marksmanship had improved that much. A log thicker than most was dislodged from the top and landed with a crash across the rails. That let daylight in. I removed my hat to reduce the target and crawled on my knees to the end of the stack to take aim at a likely-looking movement in the grass thirty yards south of the tracks and squeezed off a shot. A jackrabbit barreled out heading east.

Hudspeth had better luck. Crouched peering through a chink where the uneven surfaces of two logs failed to meet, he spotted the white plume of a single eagle feather protruding above a patch of brush too far away for a revolver to reach with any accuracy at the same time I did, aimed high, and sent a lean, black-painted brave reeling over backward with a scarlet smear where his collarbone met his throat. That's why I said luck. It had to have been an incredibly bad shot to hit anything at that distance.

That lessened the odds somewhat, although I couldn't say by how much since there was no way of knowing how many Indians had slipped past the army besides those few we had seen with Lame Horse back on the plateau. But I was heartened by the evidence that the enemy was flesh and blood after all. No sooner had this one hit the ground than a comrade lost his head and snapped off a shot that whizzed two yards over Hudspeth's hat. I fired at the puff of gunsmoke. Nothing spectacular happened as a result, but there was no answering shot from that quarter, which may have meant something or nothing.

For a long spell nothing happened, unless you count being eaten alive by mosquitoes as the afternoon wore on and we were enveloped in shadow. Drought killed off everything but them, which figured. Nevertheless we were better off than Jac, who was forced to lie out there baking in the sun with the shade of the woodpile only a scamper away. The temptation must have been staggering. There wasn't enough Indian in him to keep his naked back from turning as red as Hudspeth's nose, but he was old-man stubborn enough not to move a hair. As for the full-bloods, they burned too, but more slowly, and since they were used to such hardship we couldn't claim much advantage.

The apparent impasse did prove one thing. If Lame Horse was in charge as I suspected, he came nowhere near Ghost Shirt as a strategist. He had pinned everything on wiping us out in the first volley, and when that failed he was at a loss over what to do next. Whether or not it had yet become evident to him, though, his course now was obvious. I said as much to the marshal.

"Wait for nightfall?" he repeated, in his stage whisper. "I thought injuns never attacked at night."

"That's true of some, but only because they believe that if they're killed their souls won't be able to find their way to the Happy Hunting Ground in the dark. Lame Horse is pretty sure of himself, and if he loses a brave or two it doesn't concern him as long as he isn't one of them. He isn't a company man like most of the others in his tribe. His performance back at the mission convinced me of that. And if he's as powerful a medicine man as I think he is the others'll do as he says because they're afraid of him. Which leaves us with a choice."

"What's that?"

"We can either die fighting or turn Ghost Shirt over to them. He's what they're after anyway."

"Think they'll let us go if we do?"

"I doubt it. That crippled bastard's wanted our scalps ever since that first night."

"So why did you even bring it up?"

"It was bound to come up sooner or later. Just thought I'd get it out of the way."

"Well, you know what my answer is."

There being hours to go before sundown, we settled in for a long wait. As I crouched there, taking an occasional potshot at nothing in particular to let them know we were still in the running but mostly just crouching, I realized what it was about Indian fighting I didn't like. It wasn't the danger. That was something I'd accepted the day Judge Blackthorne swore me in and I'd never questioned it. Rather, it was the waiting, the long periods of inactivity while something was brewing beyond my control. I'm not talking about tension, although there was plenty of that as vague movements here and there in the grass told me Lame Horse's braves were deploying themselves for the coming attack. What it was was boring as hell. A man can starve for weeks and still have enough fight left in him to give you a run for your money. By the same token, you can deprive him of water until you're sure he's long since dried up and blown away and yet have him slash your throat from ear to ear when you show up to view the remains. Bore him long enough, however, and his reflexes will slow and his brain begin to rot away. I'd felt this same way during the war when I was laid up in the army hospital, following the progress of the fighting in bits and pieces from the newspapers and, when I wanted accuracy, stories told by incoming wounded from Atlanta, Gettysburg and finally Appomattox. Even now, as much in the thick of things as back then I was out of it, I felt the same sense of stagnation and uselessness, as if I were missing something important.

The hell of it was that I wasn't. Unlike the Montana high

country, where night falls with the unexpected abruptness of a guillotine blade, dusk seeped in over the prairie interminably through the pores in the vermillion and blue-black streaks that were smeared across the western sky on the heels of the departing sun, casting layer upon layer of gray wash over the landscape until the features bled together, and that's when the scenery we had been watching for hours began to move. They rose from the grass like shadows up a wall when the lamp is turned up, indistinct gray shapes scarcely darker than the charcoal sky that stretched behind them. The wind had died, but that didn't matter because they moved noiselessly, high-stepping deer fashion through the grass without so much as a rustle. It was eerie, unreal. I was almost afraid to shoot for fear that the dream would then become a reality. I shrugged it off—literally, for something cold had begun to inch its way up my spine—drew a bead on the shape nearest me with the Spencer, and fired. It advanced without faltering. The only explanation I could come up with for that was that they looked bigger than they were and I had missed. It was like fighting ghosts.

I was getting set to fire again when there was a movement to my right, Jac was on his feet, starlight glittered on something metallic in his right hand, he made a lunging motion, there was a solid sound like an axe biting into wood, and the shape I had been about to shoot at staggered backward three steps, doubled over, and sank almost gracefully into the grass. At that moment another shape that had been walking behind the first wheeled and swung the silhouette of something long and deadly in the métis' direction. Before it could squeeze the trigger I snapped off a shot, aiming low this time. The figure spun halfway around, dropped its rifle, and fell.

Having shot his wad when he threw the knife, Jac now

was unarmed. I tossed him the Spencer and he caught it just in time to thrust the muzzle into the belly of a brave who had abandoned stealth to charge him with tomahawk raised, and blew him inside out.

That turned it from a ghost watch into a good old-fashioned Indian fight. They were charging on foot along a front twenty yards wide, those who had guns popping away at targets they couldn't see any better than we could ours, those who hadn't swinging tomahawks and clubs and trade axes and bows and lances and singing the war songs their grandfathers had sung when they went to fight the Pawnee and Crow. Hudspeth snapped off two shots in rapid succession, dropped one warrior and wounded another so that he released his lance and had to get down on all fours to grope for it in the tall grass, then swung left and splintered the bow of a third just as he was drawing back to let fly with an arrow.

"Cut out that goddamned circus shooting!" I shouted, for the gunshots were deafening.

"What circus shooting?" he demanded. "I was aiming for his head!" Then a bullet splattered the top of the log over which he was peering. He cried out and rocked back on his heels, rubbing his sleeve across his eyes.

"Hit?" I had to blurt it out the side of my mouth as I fired the Deanc-Adams into the bulk of a shape coming up on me hard. It ran a few more steps and collapsed at the foot of the woodpile. I angled the revolver downward and put a second bullet in it for good measure. Playing 'possum is as old a trick as Indians have.

"Bark in my eyes." He rubbed them with the heels of his hands, the Smith & Wesson dangling by its butt from his right.

An Indian armed with an eight-foot lance stopped

running, struck an athletic pose with his legs spread apart, and took aim with the steel-pointed weapon at the helpless marshal. I sighted in on him carefully and squeezed. The hammer snapped hollowly against an empty shell. I squeezed twice more. Same story. The brave's throwing arm was in motion when Jac caught him with a bullet from the Spencer. The lance left his hand before he sank, whistled through the air, stuck point-first in the top log just below the marshal's face, drooped, and fell. By this time Hudspeth had the bark cleared from his eyes and fired at a brave who had gotten down on one knee to draw a bead with his rifle. He missed, but the redskin flattened out in self-defense.

I punched my last cartridge into the chamber of my revolver. We were all scraping bottom now. There were more Indians out there than I'd expected after they had been playing it so cautious. If we all got lucky and claimed one for each round, that left a good half dozen to battle with our bare hands. I fancied my thoughts were much the same as those that had gone through Custer's head during his last moments. It was strange how often he had been on my mind of late. Or maybe it wasn't so strange.

My first shot after reloading spoiled my figuring when it sailed clear over the head of a befeathered brave near the center of the advancing line. As I picked him off with the second I was wondering if it might be possible to line a pair of them up and make one bullet do the work of two so I could get back on track. You might say I was a little off my feed by this time.

Then I heard something that made me regret all those church services I'd missed since I was five years old.

It was a godawful noise, shrill and deep at the same time, raucous and distinctly unpleasant, a wail of agony and yet a roar of triumph, like all the damned souls of Hell letting go at once. It had no comparison. Once you heard it you never forgot it, and when you heard it again, no matter where or under what circumstances, you didn't have to stop and think to identify it. You just knew it was a steam whistle.

It climbed to a scream, paused, and climbed again, finishing the second time on a growl. It might have been miles away and it might have been right on top of us. Owing to the nature of the sound and the warping quality of the dry night air, there was no way of telling just how close it was. For an instant while it was blasting I thought I spotted an orange flash on the distant horizon that might have been flames spouting from the stack of the engine, but it could just as well have been sheet lightning of my imagination. In any case, the effect of the noise upon the Indians was immediate and devastating.

In earlier days, before the Union and the Western Pacific had bisected the great buffalo herds and the iron horse was a thing unknown on the prairie, its cry might merely have made the braves curious, much as the rattle of pots and pans on a frontier where man had never before set foot might attract inquisitive deer. But just as a deer once shot at while investigating such a noise will react in the opposite fashion when he hears it again, so the Indians who had learned the hard way that the great flame-snorting beasts brought only death and misfortune to their tribes. For all they knew, this train might be carrying more troops from the seemingly inexhaustible store of fighting men that the Great White Father struck out like arrowheads in his eastern lodge to send against the nations. They stopped fighting suddenly and melted away before the harsh noise like tallow before a hearth. One minute we were going at it fang and claw, and the next we were alone in the midst of a silent prairie. After a few moments we heard the drumming sound of retreating hoofs, then silence again. Where the braves had picketed their ponies so that we hadn't seen them remains a mystery to this day.

As if to taunt them, at that moment the whistle blew again. This time for sure I saw flames on the horizon.

"Now, what made 'em break it off so quick?" Hudspeth wanted to know. We were standing now. Faintly I could feel the buzzing vibration of the distant train's wheels through the soles of my boots. "It's still a good five miles off. They had enough time to settle our hash and take a few souvenirs besides."

"Indians have no concept of time. Have you got anything in that gun besides air?"

He was still holding the S & W. Suddenly reminded of it, he glanced down, then returned it sheepishly to the pocket inside his vest. "No. But they didn't know that."

"Still breathing?" I called to the métis, who was standing with his captured Spencer in both hands. He assured me that he was.

The whistle sounded again, perceptibly closer this time. I handed my gun to the marshal. He stared at it, then at me.

"What's this for?"

"Protection in case they come back. Get this wood burning while Jac and I fetch the Indian. Jac, give him your matches. I hope you've got more in that rifle than Hudspeth left himself."

"One round," he said.

"Good enough." We left Hudspeth gathering dry grass for tinder and headed on up the slight rise that led to camp.

"That was fair shooting for a man who believes in turning the other cheek," I told the breed, who was walking behind me.

"A little religion is a good thing," he said. "In its place."

I could tell by the way he said it that he was smiling, although it was too dark to see. "I have said that I will fight for what is mine."

The wallow looked naked now that the trees were gone. A spatter of starlight reflected off the surface of the puddles in its muddy bottom. I was wondering if it might be a good idea to water the horses now so that they wouldn't try to drink on their own after we turned them loose and get themselves mired down, when a flash of red and yellow flame splintered the darkness, a shot crashed, and something tugged at the left flap of my jacket, which was swinging free of my rib cage. Later I found a hole in it where the bullet had passed within an inch of my hide.

Pere Jac wasn't so lucky. He gave a little sigh, sank to the ground, and never got up this side of Purgatory.

# CHAPTER 16

I t's surprising how much your eyes can see in an infini-
tesimal amount of time, even though it takes your brain
five times as long to comprehend it. In the instant the shot
was fired, I saw in the brief illumination of the explosion
our prisoner swaying at the top of the grassy knoll, his feet
still bound together, my Winchester braced horizontally
across his back in his manacled hands, the muzzle pointed
in our direction. The fight at the railroad had given him
time enough to struggle upright and make his way over to
the horses in order to get his hands on the carbine in my
saddle scabbard. Likely he had fallen a few times and
dropped the weapon more than once while freeing it from
its holder and getting it into position, but those were minor
setbacks for the Scourge of the Northwest.

I said that the brain is a lot slower than the eyes. Even so,
I had all this put together between the time the bullet pierced
my jacket and Jac hit the ground. By that time reflex had
taken over and I was already moving. Meanwhile Ghost
Shirt was struggling frantically to manipulate the Winchester's lever behind his back and rack in another shell,
muttering curses beneath his breath in English, there being
no equivalents in the Cheyenne tongue. He was succeeding
when I launched myself at him in a tremendous leap—I
paced it off absent-mindedly on my way back later, it was

twenty feet, not bad for a middle-aged peace officer—and piled into him, locking my arms about his waist. But before we connected time seemed to freeze, and I felt as if I were suspended while the carbine's lever clicked home and the young chief's finger closed on the trigger. In the instant of collision there was a roar so deafening it seemed to be inside my skull and the left side of my face caught fire.

We came together then, with an impact that tore the Indian off his feet and sent the Winchester flying from his hands. The horses, although picketed, had been milling around nervously as far as their tethers permitted ever since the first shot, and now were between us and the wallow. We landed right under the feet of my gray. It whinnied and did a quick dance to avoid us. One of its hoofs stamped dust out of the ground a couple of inches shy of my right ear.

The jar had knocked the wind out of the Indian momentarily, but before I could press my advantage he squirmed out of my grip. Bound though he was, he fought like a sack full of badgers. Every time I tried to straddle him and pin him down he kicked at me with his lashed-together legs or arched his back and rolled out of my reach. I was just grateful that his dog was still off somewhere hunting and unable to join in. The second time he got away I reached for my gun and grabbed a handful of prairie air. I'd forgotten giving it to the marshal. Angry at myself, I flung an arm out longer than it was designed to go and snatched hold of something that tore when I pulled at it. Ghost Shirt's collar.

He tried to squirm away again, but I had a piece of his throat as well and held on. His windpipe throbbed in my hand, struggling for air. I pulled myself closer and got a leg over him before he could put a knee where women and savages instinctively aim. Even then he pinned one of my ankles beneath his body and threw himself over on one hip, and I would have gone over had I not thrown out a hand to brace myself. My injured wrist all but buckled beneath the shock. By then, though, I'd felt something that sent new strength coursing through my strained muscles. I'd reached for the ground, but my fingers closed over something hard, cold and familiar. The Winchester. Holding him down between contracted thighs, I swung the carbine over my head by its barrel and braced myself for the downswing. He wouldn't live to see the train, let alone the scaffold in Bismarck.

I nearly wrenched my shoulder out of its socket when I swung and the carbine didn't move. Someone had clamped a hand around the stock. I blinked and looked back over my shoulder at Hudspeth's bulk standing over me.

His feet were planted apart the length of an axe handle, which made him about as flexible as an adobe wall. To hedge his bet, he had drawn my Deane-Adams and clamped it to my right temple when I turned my head. The barrel was still warm from firing. It struck me then that of late this particular firearm had not done me a whole lot of good.

"He's whipped, Page." His voice was tired and hollow, the dull note of a gong muffled in rags.

"Jac," I said.

"Jac's dead."

I released my grip on the Winchester slowly. Beneath me Ghost Shirt's eyes gleamed dully in the starlight. I got up.

At the base of the hill, the woodpile blazed brightly, exposing a twenty-foot section of track. Here and there the upturned face of a dead Indian reflected the reddish glow. Closer now, the approaching locomotive's whistle took on added depth against a background of chuffs and clangs and humming rails. I went over to where the métis lay stretched out with the Spencer across his stomach.

"Match," I said, holding out a hand toward Hudspeth.

He hesitated. "There ain't but three left. We might—"

"Match!" I barked it this time. He handed one over without another word. I struck it on the seat of my pants, bent, and held it over the still figure's face, cupping my other hand around the flame to shield it from the wind. In its glow I saw that Jac had retained his perennial half-smile even in death. His eyes glittered between half-open lids. The seams in his face looked deeper than ever now that there was nothing to distract my attention from them. I suddenly realized that he was a good five to ten years older than my extreme earlier estimate. On the edge of the illumination a neat round hole four inches down from his collarbone showed how lucky the Indian's shot had been. A couple of inches this way or that and in six months it would have been just another scar.

The flame was burning my fingers. I shook it out and dropped the charred remnant into the pocket of my jacket. Force of habit. Fires were as hazardous in my native Montana with all its forests as in the grassy plains of Dakota.

The engine was only a mile off now. In two minutes it would be on top of us.

The same thoughts must have been going through the marshal's head, because he said, "No time to bury him." I ignored him and strode past him to the horses. I had my cinch undone when he realized what I was up to and stepped in to give me a hand. In a few seconds we had all four of them unrigged. As they wandered off to graze we gathered up our saddles and bridles, leaving behind Jac's McClellan, and started back down. I took the time to spread the métis' saddle blanket over his corpse, not that it would afford any protection against the coyotes and magpies once they scented fresh meat. I then took charge of Hudspeth's gear while he loosened the cord that bound Ghost Shirt's ankles, heaved him to his feet, and pushed him stumbling ahead of him down the slope. At the bottom the marshal gave him a brutal shove that sent him pitching headlong into the grass. Then his ankles were drawn together once again.

By now the engineer had spotted the flames, slowed down, and was hanging on the whistle as if he thought the escaping steam might blow the obstruction off the tracks. I saw him in the glow of the flames belching out of the broad black stack, a smear of crimson face beneath a tall hat made of striped pillow ticking leaning out the window of the cab over an arm crooked at the elbow, sparks from the stack swirling about him like fireflies on their way to the cinder bed. Below him the steel driving arm flashed as it cranked at the wheels, at times seeming to come within two or three inches of his sleeve at the top of its cycle. Behind the engine, oily black in the darkness, rumbled the wood car, baggage carrier, and two passenger coaches followed by the caboose, the windows of all three illuminated in yellow. The smoke pouring from the stack was a gray streamer trailing a mile behind the red lantern that swung from the railing of the caboose.

At any time that speeding behemoth could have rammed our flimsy barricade and sent it flying in blazing fragments all over the prairie, but the engineer didn't know that. When it became apparent that the offending substance would not go away, he hauled on the brakes. A jet of white steam erupted from beneath the boiler. Sparks sprayed from the shrieking wheels. Wood groaned, steel screamed against steel in a grotesque parody of human anguish. The driving arm reversed itself without pausing and the entire mass of metal ground to a shuddering halt three feet short of the pile of burning logs.

While all this was going on I had left our gear with Hud-speth and crossed over to stroll among the bodies scattered south of the tracks. I had my revolver, which the marshal had returned to me, fully loaded now from the cartridges in my saddle bags, in my hand in case any of the corpses should still be breathing. But none of them was, nor was any of them Lame Horse, which was what I had come to deter-mine. All were Cheyenne. I left them and approached the engine, which was snorting and blowing like a stallion im-patient to be on its way.

"Mister, you better start explaining." The engineer's de-mand was delivered over the breech of a pre–Civil War Walker Colt, for God's sake, a cap-and-ball six-shooter as long as a man's arm from elbow to fingertips. I smiled re-spectfully.

"You wouldn't want to use that," I assured him. "I'm law."

He thought that over. He was a wasted strip of leather with a wind-burned face cracked at the corners of his eyes and mouth and a perpetual squint. His side-whiskers were gray tipped with white and the hairs were long enough to curl in upon themselves. A smudge of soot stained his moist right cheek. He was sweating, but not from the tension of the moment. The heat inside the cab from the open firebox was withering. I kept my eyes on him and on the fireman standing behind his shoulder, a big man whose short-cropped black hair reminded me of greasy wool. At first I'd thought his face was blackened from his exertions be-fore the flames, but now I realized he was a Negro. He was naked to the waist, and his slabbed chest glistened like new iron beneath a sheen of sweat and a sparse covering of coiled hair that ran in a thin line down his stomach into the damp waistband of his pinstriped pants. At the moment he was trying without success to get the engineer's attention by tugging at his sleeve and calling him "Boss" in a voice as deep and clear as the echo from the bottom of a barrel.

"So you're law." It wasn't the most clever thing the engineer could have said, especially after he'd had all that time to think up a good retort. But a friend of mine was dead and I was in no mood to render him senseless with my wit, so I let him go on to the obvious. "Let's see some proof."

"This proof enough?"

Hudspeth's growl, coming from the other side of the cab, took all the sand out of the man with the Walker. He didn't even bother to turn around and confirm the fact that the marshal was standing on the step plate with his freshly loaded Smith & Wesson pointed at his back. He just sighed and laid the relic in the palm of my free hand, the one that wasn't holding the five-shot.

"That's what I was atryin' to tell you before," the Negro informed him.

They were convinced, of course, that they were being held up. I couldn't blame them. I hadn't seen a mirror for some time, but looking at Hudspeth—dirty, unshaven, his clothes wrinkled and torn—I got a fair idea about how much I looked like a lawman after all this time on the trail. I don't suppose I smelled like one either, but whether that made any difference amid the occupational scents of wood smoke and oiled steel and their own perspiration was open to debate. Whatever the case, I was climbing aboard to display the badge and lay their fears to rest when the fireman released the brake.

The locomotive jolted forward, throwing me off balance and wrenching the handrail on the other side out of Hudspeth's grasp. His gun went off into the ceiling and he dropped out of sight. As I threw my arm out to catch myself, the Deane-Adams struck the wall of the cab, jarred loose from my grip, and clattered to the steel floor. I fell four feet and landed on my back on the ground, the Walker bouncing from my left hand as if propelled by a spring. When my wind returned I found myself staring down, or rather up, the bore of my own weapon in the black man's hand. I spent more time on the wrong end of that piece. There was no doubt about what he had in mind. The cylinder was already turning when I clawed my badge out of my pocket and thrust it at him.

For an agonizing moment I wondered if it would mean anything to him at all. Everything depended upon how he had been treated by lawmen in the past. Then the cylinder rolled back to its original position and he backed off without lowering the gun.

"What's going on, Gus? Why aren't we moving?"

The newcomer had appeared from the darkness at the rear of the train. Round and cherubic, he carried a lantern and wore a baggy blue uniform with brass buttons and a black-visored cap set square on his shaggy head. With him was a taller man whose erect carriage and squared shoulders made me think he was more accustomed to a uniform than the well-tailored suit and vest he was wearing, but a uniform far different from his companion's. His reddish hair was graying at the temples and had a windblown look. Like myself when in civilization, he was clean-shaven, a rare enough thing in that bewhiskered era, his spare cheeks and firm jaw shadowed in blue where the razor had scraped them without missing a stubble. While the conductor appeared to have eyes only for the railroad personnel present, the tall man took everything in with cool eyes under brows so pale they were visible only because of their contrast to his deep tan, which had only recently begun to fade. I figured him for cavalry.

Gus, it seemed, was the engineer. He had alighted from the cab to reclaim his ancient revolver. When it was safely in his belt he rattled off his version of the events, gesticulating at the flaming woodpile, now past its peak and burning spottily where the logs were not already charred, at the marshal, who had recovered himself and was standing on the top step of the cab, his gun trained on the Negro's back and his badge gleaming ostentatiously on his lapel, and finally at me where I sat on the ground eyeing the muzzle of the Deane-Adams in the fireman's hand.

"Well, what more proof do you want?" This from the tall man, addressing my guard. He had a raspy voice—roughened, I supposed, from years of barking orders under fire—but with an undercurrent of smoothness that suggested breeding beyond that offered by the manual of protocol.

Still the Negro hesitated. A glance passed from the tall man to the conductor, from the conductor to the engineer, and finally from him to the fireman, whereupon the last sighed and returned the gun to me. I holstered it and got to my feet with a helping hand from the tall man. A ridge of calluses ran across his palm and between his thumb and forefinger where the reins are held.

"Cavalry?" I asked, just to confirm what I already knew.

He laughed, white teeth gleaming against his burned skin. "Lord, no! Horses are for racing and drawing buggies. Lieutenant Colonel Andrew Locke, 16th Engineers, retired."

I grinned in spite of myself. "You're the first ex-military man I've met since the war who didn't claim to be a full colonel."

"There aren't many of us left. I wish you'd introduce yourself. Old soldiers are always being pumped for colorful stories, and I'll need a name to go with this one." He indicated the bodies of the slain Indians, almost invisible now that the fire was dying. He seemed to be the first to notice them, judging by the way the others suddenly forgot all about us and stared at the carnage. At first glance the corpses did look like discarded railroad ties scattered over the right-of-way.

I gave him our names and told him that we had fought the Indians over a prisoner trussed up on the other side of the tracks. "We're commandeering this train to take him to Bismarck," I finished.

The engineer and conductor raised their voices in protest. The colonel, however, merely rubbed his chin thoughtfully.

"I don't think I can let you do that," he said finally.

"You don't have any choice." I turned to the engineer. "Get up steam."

"You don't understand." Locke remained calm. "This is a private express."

"Yours?"

He shook his head, then looked thoughtful again. "Perhaps I can work it out. Will you come with me?"

"Where and why?"

"The last car. A few minutes now might save you an hour."

He sounded sincere, which added to my distrust. But time was running short. At any minute Lame Horse and his Cheyenne might overcome their fear of trains, and I had no illusions about the ability of six men to stand them off with only (so far as I knew) four guns and a museum piece among them. Ignoring Gus's protests, I yanked the Walker from his belt and handed it up to Hudspeth. "See that the fireman stokes the box, and put Gus to work clearing the tracks. I'll be back in five minutes."

"Someone's got to watch the pressure gauge," the engineer snarled.

"The conductor's not doing anything."

Colonel Locke and I mounted the steps to the platform of the second coach, where we stopped before the door that led inside. He turned to me and his voice dropped below a murmur.

"I have to whisper," he said. "The old man has ears like a cat. Just keep quiet and agree with everything that's said."

Before I could question him he rapped softly on the door. Immediately a voice that had to belong to either an orator or a wounded moose boomed an invitation from within. We entered.

It was just as well that my companion had advised me to keep silent, because I was struck dumb by my first glimpse of the coach's interior. I had expected an ordinary day carrier, narrow and cramped with a double row of hard seats facing each other in pairs on either side of a bare aisle. I wasn't prepared for a palace.

The dominant color was wine red. It covered the two easy chairs in plush velvet, tickled my ankles where I stood on the carpet, threw off a sheen from the curtains on the windows and from the drapes that concealed all but the brass lion's paws that were the feet of a huge four-poster bed in the far corner from view. A chandelier the size of a bull buffalo's head dangled from the paneled vault of the ceiling, its crystal pendants sparkling in the light of two globe lamps, one of which stood on the bar—a bar, by God, of polished oak with a decanter of what looked like burgundy and two long-stemmed glasses atop it—the other on a reading table beside the larger chair, overstuffed with a winged back and arms of curved walnut. The man at the bar pouring amber liquid from a second decanter into a glass was also overstuffed, but unlike Judge Flood, whose excess tonnage hung out everywhere, this one's was all up front in a solid, rounded globe of belly that started at his collar and swelled out so far that I doubted he could clasp his hands over it without straining his arms, then swept back to balance between his normal-size thighs like a hot-air balloon supported upon a pair of uprights. He was in shirtsleeves and vest, the obligatory gold watch chain describing a grand arc across the biggest part of the bulge. Upon it were strung ornaments representing various guilds and lodges the way an Indian might display scalps on a thong.

"A brandy man, I'll wager," he announced over his precise operation with the decanter and glass. His voice was not a bellow like Flood's, nor a rumbling bass like that of the black fireman, but its resonance carried the best qualities of both. It was a voice trained to ring in the rafters of a great marble hall. He spoke as if he'd been expecting me and as if we'd already been introduced. "I trust this cognac will cut the dust to your satisfaction. It's not Napoleon, but with the country just emerging from a depression it's inadvisable to flaunt one's affluence. That is the phrase you Westerners use, is it not? 'Cut the dust?' Or perhaps I should say *we* Westerners, since I am to be one henceforth."

"I'm partial to rotgut," I said, but accepted the proffered glass from a strong, stout hand with a thick gold band around the wedding finger.

His eyes twinkled at what I suppose he considered a prime example of frontier wit. They were the kind of eyes that twinkled easily or flared hot with anger or grew soft and gentle, all at a moment's notice and upon command. Like those of Major Harms they were brown, but with a dash of yellow, like the cognac. His face was round but not bloated, the dewlaps folded neatly on either side of a fleshless beak and darting immediately into the cover of his whiskers, which, beginning at the tops of his cheekbones, grew into a magnificent noose-shaped mass that concealed his vest as far as the second button. He had started growing them before I was born. They were a shade darker than the iron gray of his hair, thinning now but in the best way, retreating in twin horns of pinkish scalp to the left and right of a healthy widow's peak that topped the bulge of his forehead in the style of a Crow pompadour. He would never be as bald as Judge Flood. I looked to the colonel for an introduction.

He, too, had been extended a glass of cognac. He sipped at it, then touched his lips with the corner of a silk handkerchief and returned the latter to his breast pocket.

"Sir," he said, addressing the host, "this is Page Murdock, deputy marshal for the federal court of Judge Harlan Blackthorne at Helena, Montana Territory. Deputy Murdock, allow me to present Senator Harold Firestone, late of the United States Congress and former Governor of the State of Illinois." He paused, then added, for the other's benefit, "Deputy Murdock is sympathetic."

# CHAPTER 17

I sipped at the cognac while my host studied me with new interest. I could tell it was good liquor because it didn't have much taste. The ideal spirit, I imagine, has no flavor at all. But that wasn't what concerned me at the moment. I was wondering what a politician was doing away out here in the middle of nowhere and just what it was that I was supposed to be sympathetic with. Out of the corner of my eye I caught a subtle signal from Colonel Locke reminding me of his earlier admonition. I decided to trust him for the time being and kept my mouth shut.

"Tell me, Mr. Murdock," said the senator. "What is it about this country that you despise? The greed for territorial expansion or the corruption in lofty government circles? Or is it something else? Something personal, perhaps? I am curious to know."

I was glad I wasn't supposed to say anything. I stood there like a plaster Cupid while he waited for an answer. He was a couple of inches shorter than I and had to cock his bearded chin upward to engage my gaze. There was a hard glint in his eyes now, one of suspicion. Or maybe I was reading something into them that wasn't there. The silence was growing threadbare when Locke plunged in.

"Deputy Murdock is a frontiersman, Senator. He feels

that civilization is encroaching upon his world and blames Washington City for its systematic destruction."

Firestone kept looking at me. "And how did you learn of our mission? It is supposed to be a secret." This time I caught a genuine trace of distrust in his tone. The colonel had his work cut out for him.

"Deputy Murdock is a friend of a friend," he said cryptically.

To my surprise that bit of nonsense seemed to satisfy the senator. I got the impression that he was eager to place his trust in me and was prepared to meet me more than halfway. "Very well," he said. "I caution you to remain silent. As far as anyone else is concerned, I have retired from politics and am on my way to assume the supervision of my cattle herd in Montana." Then he softened again, visibly, and smiled, crinkling the skin around his eyes. "I knew that you were in sympathy when I looked out the window and saw you boarding this coach. I said to myself, 'Here is a man who will not accept abuse lying down.' I assure you that you are not alone, and that when we reach our destination you will find many others who feel as you do."

"He has a partner," Locke put in. "A marshal named Hudspeth."

He seemed unruffled. "He, too, is sympathetic?"

"He's my partner," I said. Now I was doing it. Five more minutes with these two and I'd be speaking in riddles for the rest of my life.

"Then he is welcome also." He turned to Locke. "Place their belongings in the baggage car and see that they are made comfortable in the other coach." Back to me. "We will talk more later, after we have both rested. Travel exhausts me. I am afraid that I am no longer the campaigner I was in my youth." His eyes clouded over and I could see that he really was played out, as much as a man can get in this life. His complexion was sallow and the whites of his eyes were turning an unhealthy ivory around the edges. If he wasn't dying I had never seen it before.

Locke kept silent until we were back outside and beyond earshot of the rolling palace. Then he produced a metal flask from an inside breast pocket and tipped it up, letting the contents gurgle twice before he lowered it and replaced the cork. He looked as if he needed it, so I didn't blame him for not offering me a swig. He and Hudspeth would get along.

"When did he snap?" I asked then.

"A year and a half ago, when he lost his bid for a third term in the Senate." He returned the flask to his pocket. I noticed a similar bulge on the other side of his coat, but not from another flask. I wondered if this was some new style I hadn't heard about, or if it was just that a man whose drinking habits required a portable supply found it necessary to carry a hideout gun as well. "He was planning to go for President in eighteen eighty, and had his eye on that election. When a thirty-two-year-old war veteran knocked him out of the seat he'd held for twelve years it was too much for him. Ostensibly, he's on his way to take over the ranch he owns south of Medicine Hat. He thinks he's going there to meet up with his private army and prepare to cleave off Idaho, Washington, and Oregon and start his own country."

He paused to let that sink in. It didn't take as long as he expected. I said, "When a politician loses his grip he doesn't fool around, does he?"

"It's really not so farfetched when you think about it. Every politician harbors a secret desire to be king of something."

"I wouldn't know. I stopped voting after the last election."

He smiled without mirth. "The Hayes steal. That little

stunt did more to undermine popular confidence in the democratic system than four years of civil war."

"Is there an army?"

"Forty men in army surplus, armed with war-issue Springfields. No ammunition. He'll finish out his life in that lonely spot, drilling his tin soldiers and strutting around like a Mexican general in the uniform he designed for himself. He'll be out of the way and harmless."

"Who's paying the soldiers?"

"He is. You don't spend half your life in public office in this country without becoming a millionaire. The bank draft he's carrying in his vest pocket would feed a family of ten for thirty years."

"Is that why you're armed?" He started. I smiled. "Next time you have a suit made, tell your tailor to leave more room around the left shoulder. What is it, a shoulder rig or a pocket like Hudspeth's?"

He swung open the left side of his coat to reveal a glossy leather holster beneath his armpit, tilted forward to bring the ivory-handled butt of a small Remington within easy reach. The rigging was concealed beneath his vest.

"What are you, his bodyguard?"

He shrugged. "Bodyguard, adviser, companion—"

"And keeper?"

That didn't bother him. Not much did, I guessed. "It pays well."

"Better than the army? Why'd you leave?"

"You can only go so far in the service, unless you've distinguished yourself in battle, in which case the White House is the logical next step. I don't like politics. Besides, men who erect privies for generals' wives don't get their names on the front pages of newspapers."

I didn't ask him why he felt riding herd on a madman had

any more future than service in the 16th Engineers. At best it would just make him angry, and I didn't know how much reserve he had or how good he was at getting that Remington out of its nook, and didn't care to find out at this point. That was one thing about life in the West. With everyone packing a weapon you had to be careful what you said or did. I reversed directions.

"What's a friend of a friend?"

His face cleared at the question. He was glad of the change. "Conspirators in high places," he explained. "Firestone is convinced that the country is rife with them west of the Mississippi. Not that it isn't, and on the other side as well, but not the kind he thinks. He hopes to strike the first blow for revolution."

"Oh, Christ, not another one."

He laughed, a trifle too heartily. "There's small danger of that happening outside the twisted confines of the senator's skull. Let's go see if we're ready to push on." He almost threw an arm around my shoulders as we struck out toward the other end of the train, there was that much politician—and liquor—in him. But there was enough soldier in him to refrain, and to change the sweeping gesture at the last moment into a tug on the back of his collar as if it had become twisted.

"How do you plan to explain the Indian?" I asked.

"Don't worry about that. The old man never leaves his car. Just to be safe, though, you might consider locking your prisoner in with the baggage."

"No good. I'm keeping him in sight to end of track."

"Then lock yourself in with him."

"Not without windows." We had reached the engine, where the fireman was busy chucking wood into the box while the engineer, having cleared the debris off the tracks, leaned against the wall of the cab with an eye on the pressure gauge. The conductor stood about studying his watch and looking impatient. Hudspeth glared at them from the ground. Jac's Spencer was in his hands, my own Winchester lying at his feet with our gear, which he had carted from the other side of the tracks. Ghost Shirt, who had accompanied it, lay propped up on one elbow nearby, in as comfortable a position as he could manage considering his trusses. The steady throb of the boiler drowned out whatever conversation there might have been.

"You're entitled to the truth," I told Locke in a voice too low to carry past him. "The Indian is Ghost Shirt, chief of the northern Cheyenne. His medicine man is the leader of the braves who are out to bust him loose. I don't know how many he's got with him, but it can't be a lot or they would have rushed us in a body hours ago. That doesn't count for much, though, because they're used to being outnumbered. In any case I doubt that we've got any such edge. I thought you should know what you're letting yourself in for before we set out."

He turned that over for a while, inspecting it from every angle. He didn't look alarmed, but then it was hard to say how he looked when he was. For him, the deadpan he showed me may have been the way he expressed fear.

"Tell me," he said at length, "would it make any difference if I said no?"

"At most it might cost Hudspeth and me some ammunition. One way or another we're taking the train."

"That's what I thought. So why tell me at all?"

"Maybe I was touched by that little speech you made about the democratic system."

I don't know if he heard the answer. He was busy studying Ghost Shirt, who was busy studying him back, although

ot quite as clinically. It looked as if the Cheyenne was eye-
ng Locke's throat where the blood bubbled close to the
urface. The links joining the manacles jingled ominously
ehind his back.

"Let's not tell the others," the colonel advised. "Gus is
oo contrary and Ephraim, the black, is too smart. They're
etter off not knowing."

"You're the colonel."

"Go to hell."

At last the locomotive was ready to go, snorting power
and straining at its leash. Hudspeth stood guard over our
prisoner while Locke and I loaded the saddles and parapher-
nalia into the baggage car (minus the rifles, which Hudspeth and I retained), then, after I had cut loose the bonds
on the Indian's ankles and hoisted him to his feet, mounted
the cab to keep temptation from Ephraim and Gus during
the long journey west. That must have taken some heavy soul-
searching on his part, considering how much he hated train
travel. The conductor, for whom the colonel vouched, was
allowed to return to his caboose with a strongly worded
admonition—mine—not to speak to Firestone about the
Indian. Madmen make me nervous, because you never know
how they're going to react. To preserve his ignorance we
elected to escort Ghost Shirt to the empty coach through
the baggage car. We were entering the latter, Locke in front,
me in the rear, the Indian sandwiched between us, when the
car rocked beneath a sudden weight and something the
color of tobacco spit swept past us into the interior, whirled
about, and stood in the middle of the darkened aisle, legs
spread and showing its teeth in a grin of warning. A growl
rippled from deep in its throat. The colonel slid a hand onto
the butt of the gun beneath his arm. I reached past our prisoner and placed a hand on his shoulder, stopping him.

"Don't risk the shot. He belongs to the Indian. As long as you don't threaten his master he's sweet as a drugged rattlesnake."

"You'd better be right." He advanced a cautious step. The dog went for his leg with a bellowing snarl. He leaped back tearing his pants leg on a fang.

"Good advice, Murdock," he said acidly, drawing the Remington. The mongrel hunkered down growling, its hackles bristling.

"Call him off!" I rasped in Ghost Shirt's ear.

He shrugged. "I am not sure that I can. He hates soldiers."

"How can he tell?" demanded Locke. "For that matter how can you? I'm not wearing a uniform."

"A snake is a snake, with or without his skin."

"Call him off or you'll lose him," I snapped.

The Indian spoke to the dog in soothing Cheyenne. The animal appeared to be listening. After a moment its hackles flattened and it lowered itself the rest of the way to the floor. Only the warning growl remained.

"Walk," said Ghost Shirt.

Locke grunted and stepped forward reluctantly, gun in hand. The growling increased in pitch as he circled around the animal, but it kept its position, one eye peeling back, until Ghost Shirt and I had passed, when it got up and fell into step behind us. At the last moment I ducked through the connecting door on the Indian's heels and pushed it shut on the dog's snout. It yammered savagely, I caught a glimpse of bared yellow fangs in the space between the door and the jamb, and then, with a double thump, the dog was separated from us by a barrier an inch and a half thick. It whooped and the door bounced when the weight of its forepaws slammed against it, but held. Claws scraped frantically at the wood. I hoped for the colonel's sake that there were

nough walls between his employer and the animal to muf-
le its angry yelps.

While the bodyguard went on to resume his duties in the
private car, I pushed Ghost Shirt into a seat of the more conventional first coach with his back to the rear of the train so
hat I could sit opposite him and watch the connecting door,
committed the Winchester to the overhead rack, and unlocked one of the cuffs. Then I brought the wrist that was
still manacled around in front of him and secured the empty
iron to the wooden arm of the seat. He bore it all without
complaint. From the way he placed his free hand to his ban-
daged head I figured it had begun to ache again, but that
could just have been a ploy to throw me off guard. With a
prisoner as crafty as he was, having to watch him every
minute was enough to give a man a headache of his own.

With the thought, I suddenly realized how desperately
tired I was and dropped into the seat facing him as if my
knees were operated by hydraulic pressure and all the water
had suddenly drained out. I was getting old. I had lost count
of the days I'd spent on the trail, but I knew I'd been out
longer than this in the past, gone through at least as much,
and still had enough sand left to rack up points in Purgatory by visiting certain establishments on Helena's east
side. Now I didn't think I could stand the walk. The West
had sucked out my youth and left me a brittle shell. For the
first time I understood how Hudspeth felt, and it scared
me. Mine was no profession to age in.

The train started forward, taking up the slack between
the cars with a lurch that rocked us in our seats. I sneaked
a look at the Indian to see how he reacted, but from his stoic
expression I gathered that a train ride was nothing new to
him. I kept forgetting his eastern sabbatical. The scenery
outside began to roll past, slowly at first, then picking up

speed until my own reflection was all I could make ou
against the night-backed glass. But before it did, I saw the
corpses of the slain Indians scattered beside the cinde
bed, dim but unmistakable in the light of the smoldering
fragments of wood the engineer had tossed off the track.
wondered how Locke was going to explain them away to
the senator, or if he had contrived some way to keep him
from the windows until the danger was past. Given his spe
cial talents, either was possible.

At twenty-five miles per hour the whistle sounded
hoarsely, sending vibrations tingling through my boot soles
It was a hoot of derision for the pioneers whose wagons and
oxen had crawled over the same ground at the rate of five
miles per day only a few years back. In four hours we would
cover more territory than Hudspeth, Jac and I had covered
in as many days. Every minute we kept rolling was another
half mile between us and the surviving Cheyenne. Still, I
felt no relief. One of our number was dead, and one hundred miles separated the rest of us from absolute safety. I
didn't think Lame Horse's medicine could resist odds like
those.

# CHAPTER 18

I hadn't been sitting there ten minutes when the train's motion and my own exhaustion combined with the delayed effects of the senator's cognac and I fell asleep. How long I slept I couldn't begin to guess, but when I awoke with my forehead clammy against the window I had a stiff neck and the inside of my mouth tasted like the water in a buffalo wallow. It couldn't have been too long, because the first thing I saw when my eyes opened was my prisoner watching me with a predatory alertness. When I stirred, his eyes darted to the dusty floor and the stoic expression returned like a trained hawk recalled to its master's arm. I determined not to fall asleep again, but just to curb his ambition I slid over, trapping the gun in my holster between my hip and the wall, removed the key to the manacles from my left hip pocket, and transferred it out of his reach to my right. The Indian observed all this, but you wouldn't have known it from the bored look on his face. I watched him in silence for some time.

"Is there any special reason you hate the whites so much, or is it just the usual?" I asked finally. A little salty conversation seemed like just the thing to clear away the fog.

There was another long silence during which I gathered that he wasn't in the mood to answer. That came as no surprise. He hadn't said ten words to me in English or any other language since we'd met. I had given up on him and was trying to make some tune out of the noise the wheels made as they chuckled over the rails when he spoke. The sound of his voice made me jump.

"How does one describe a snake to a man who has never seen one?" He spoke low for an Indian, eschewing the high-pitched oratory by which his people set such store. "If you say that he slithers, that he speaks with a sibilant, and that he spits venom, do you convey his worst qualities adequately? Or is it better that you show the wounds where his fangs have struck?"

On "struck," he tore open his faded shirt with his free hand and yanked it down over his shoulders, twisting as he did so to show me his back. I winced. In the coal-oil light the scars stood out like long white worms against his burnished skin. One of them curled up over his left shoulder to the base of his neck. I could picture the man who wielded the whip letting the tasseled end slide of its own weight down across the torn flesh after the blow had landed.

"Who did that?" I fought to keep the grimace from my tone.

"My white schoolmaster in Iowa." He sat back, shrugging the shirt back over his shoulders. The muscles in his chest rippled with the movement. "I made the mistake of letting him see me talking to a white girl before class. He was a big man, and I was not yet grown. He lashed me to a tree in front of the school with his belt and horsewhipped me in front of my classmates. All the time he was beating me he quoted passages from an article he'd read that compared the American Indian to the Negro and said that each was incapable of learning anything but the most rudimentary rules of survival. A month later his house burned down."

"What took you so long?"

"He had a strong arm. It was three weeks before I stopped passing blood."

"What happened after the fire?"

"Nothing. I stole a horse and left that night to return to my people."

"And you base your hatred for an entire race on that one incident?"

He shook his head. He had the bearing of a proud animal, despite the irons. "That was only the climax. You are not Cheyenne. How can you know what it is like to be told all of your life that your people are the finest that has ever lived, and then find yourself surrounded by strangers to whom you are lower than a maggot in a buffalo chip? Strangers who lack the courage to tell you so to your face but whisper among themselves when they think you cannot hear? Among the People, if one brave is angered by another he does not gossip like a squaw behind the other's back, but calls him out to settle the matter by contest of arms. I have more respect for the man who whipped me than for these others, for he at least was man enough to make his feelings known. You can fight an insult, strike back after a blow, but what can you do against a thought? An Indian is nothing if not direct."

"Is that how you felt when you sneaked back and fired his house?"

That one caught him off guard. For all his reputation, he was still a spoiled boy, unaccustomed to having his word questioned. I pressed on before he could reply.

"Everywhere I go I keep hearing about the Noble Red Man who neither lies nor cheats," I said. "I haven't caught up with him yet, but when I do I'm going to tell him he's spreading a false impression. The greatest liar I ever knew is summering in the Bitterroot Mountains right now, along with five or six hundred of his Flathead followers. He'll pass you the pipe with one hand and lift your scalp with the other. Yet not a drop of white blood flows in his veins. Explain that."

"If he shows two faces it is the white man who taught him how."

"Then he learned his lesson well. Don't put me down as an Indian hater. I think you have a legitimate beef. But why can't you face the fact that you're no better than anyone else? That you're just different?"

"Does it not shame you to think that you are stealing our land?"

"I never stole an acre."

"But you did not try to stop those who did?"

"For the simple reason that it was none of my business. I believe in letting a man fight his own battles. Who spoke for the Comanche when your own people drove them out of the Black Hills into the desert? Or for the peaceful tribes they forced out generations earlier? Or for the Cheyenne when the Sioux pushed their way in from Canada? You're not complaining because we're not as good as you are but because we're not better. You're a hard man to please."

"You use words like a weapon, white skin."

I sighed. "I didn't expect to win you over. After twenty-two years, though, I thought it was time you heard the other side." I paused. "You know that Lame Horse is after your job."

If I'd expected that to surprise him, I was disappointed. He went on studying the floor between his feet as if his future could be read in the patterns his moccasins had made in the dust. "Some of my warriors have told me this. They are wrong. He knows his place."

"The problem is you don't agree on where it is. I saw that

argument you had with him back at the mission. I didn't
have to understand Cheyenne to know he's got ambitions."

He met my gaze then. A faint smile played over his lips.
"At last you have become tangled in your own net of words.
Have you not already said that it is Lame Horse who tried
to free me tonight?"

"Naturally. There's no guarantee that you'll hang soon
even if we get you to Bismarck. With all the publicity you've
been getting it's a real possibility that the sob sisters back
East will pressure the President into commuting your sentence to life in the penitentiary. As long as you live you pose
a threat to your successor. Dead, you're a martyr and powerful medicine, nothing more. The best thing that can happen to Lame Horse is that you get killed in the confusion
while he's trying to break you loose."

"Only a white would think such thoughts."

There we were, back at the beginning. Nothing brings out
the stubbornness in an Indian like cold logic. I changed the
subject.

"Where'd you get the dog?" I nodded in the direction of
the baggage car, where the mongrel could be heard whim-
pering frustratedly and digging splinters out of the door.
Like its master, it never gave up.

"Why do white men place so much value in owning
things? He is my companion, not my property. I got him
nowhere."

"Meet him, then."

He ran the fingers of his free hand over his plaits—
searching, most likely, for lice. He found none. He was
cleaner than most Indians, a condition ingrained in him during his stay with the whites, whether he liked it or not. "We
met in the Black Hills, in your year eighteen seventy-two.
We have been together ever since."

"Who bobbed his tail?"

"The white trader who claimed to own him. I cut off one of his ears to show him how it felt."

He watched me out of the corner of his eye for some reaction. It was his turn to be disappointed. I have a high threshold of shock. "Why did you name him Custer?"

"Their hair is the same color." He toed the dust. "Was the same color."

I stared at him, but he didn't add anything. "It really goes deep, doesn't it?" I asked him. "The hate."

"Before I was born," he said, eyes still on the floor, "when still in my mother's womb, I saw the plight of my people as clearly as others see it now. The spirits sent me this vision so that I would be prepared to take up the reins and lead the People to their rightful destiny. I knew before I took my first breath that the way would be hard and my enemies many. Still I did not turn away. I have seen our braves slain and our women and children defiled. Always I held to my course. While a single Cheyenne breathes I will not lay down my arms in defeat, not if it means the death of my people and the end of our way of life for a thousand generations."

It was a sad speech. Sad not because of the certain doom it carried, but because he didn't believe it, not one word of it, any more than I did. His exposure to our culture had ruined him for his own beliefs. I might have felt sorry for him if the memory of Pere Jac's death weren't so fresh.

I was about to pursue a different line when Colonel Locke came in bearing two glasses filled nearly to the brim with cognac. I sat back as if caught whispering in class.

"I thought you might be getting thirsty back here." He held out one of the glasses.

I didn't take it. "There's one missing."

He stared at me for a moment, uncomprehending. Then his eyes slid toward the Indian and understanding clouded his features.

"Keep your liquor," snapped Ghost Shirt, before the colonel could say anything. "It is one of the main reasons for our troubles. The Comanche do not touch it and they are still a great people."

"Next time offer him one." I accepted the glass.

Locke made a nonchalant gesture of concession with his free hand and lowered himself onto the edge of the seat across the aisle. He did all this on board a moving train without spilling a drop from a full glass. I wondered how much it would take to get him drunk enough to lose his natural poise. He took a sip and frowned at the glass as if its contents weren't strong enough.

" 'It's not Napoleon,' " he said, swallowing his voice in imitation of the senator's stentorian tones, " 'but with the country just emerging from a depression it's inadvisable to flaunt one's affluence.' "

Pleased with his impersonation, he smiled and crossed his legs, holding the long-stemmed vessel delicately between thumb and forefinger. I noticed that his socks were handwoven and bore a tiny gold monogram. So his job did pay better than the army. I didn't look close enough to see if the initials were his or if he wore Firestone's brand.

"Is it worth it?" I asked.

He looked at me, still smiling, and raised his brows. Tiny threads of blood gave the whites of his eyes a pinkish cast.

"The money," I said.

He glanced down at his glass and saw in it what I was talking about. Then he sipped again. "Is it any of your business?"

"It is if trouble comes and you're too soaked to remember one end of that shoulder gun from the other."

"In my valise are three sharpshooter medals I won during my last hitch. I was so blind drunk when I took two of them they tell me I couldn't see my group when it was shown to me."

"What about the third?"

"I couldn't locate a bottle in time. Worst score I ever made. But I won just the same."

"You're having fun with me, aren't you?"

"My valise is in the baggage car. Shall I fetch it?"

I didn't bother to answer, which for him was answer enough. Relieved, he started to sit back, then remembered that the way he was perched left nothing behind him for support, and straightened again. "Good. I didn't want to have to shoot that damn dog."

"How's the senator?"

"Sleeping, thank God. I gave him enough laudanum to keep a horse happy for a week. Diluted, of course. Like his reason."

Again I said nothing. If he insisted on acting like a supercilious ass it was no business of mine. He was good at it, though. I almost believed him.

At length I had to give in and say something. If I hadn't, the monotonous sway and rumble of the coach would have taken me under for sure. "I was just asking Ghost Shirt why he named his dog Custer."

"No surprise. I met the man in Washington when he was testifying against Secretary Belknap. A mutual friend introduced us in a restaurant. I was with a young lady at the time. The way the Boy General preened himself in her presence you would have thought he was a pup in its first heat. I don't think he even knew I was there after we shook hands. And him with that vision of a wife of his sitting right across from him. I proposed a toast to him in Chicago when the news came in about the Little Big Horn. They were still talking about it when I left."

"The Little Big Horn?"

"No, the toast."

I said Locke was poised. I'll add that he was charmed to boot. How else explain his timing in having just drained the last drop from his glass when Gus hit the brake?

As if shoved violently from behind, Ghost Shirt pitched out of his seat so hard he sprained his wrist when the manacles binding him drew taut and the seat's wooden arm split down the middle with a sharp report. Later I found that even the steel links between the cuffs had been stretched out of shape. Colonel Locke slammed shoulder-first into the back of his own seat, but caught hold of it before the backlash could throw him into the one opposite. Seated as I was facing the rear, I was spared the first trauma as my seat back absorbed most of the concussion, so that I did no more than spill what was left of my drink over my shirt and lap, but when the coach bounced back I duplicated the Cheyenne's headlong dive. There was no chain to stop me, and only a last-minute twist to the right saved me from a broken neck when I came into contact with the seat opposite. A sound like walnuts being crushed in another room filled my ears as my shoulder struck the wooden framework. I hoped it was the polished hickory giving away and not my shoulder, but I doubted it because an instant later the pain came and my brain cells began to blink out in clusters. All around me oaken pegs groaned beneath the pressure of a well-built coach tearing itself apart, and a screech like half a dozen eagles being castrated all at once burned a red-hot hole through my eardrums.

Then it was all over and the car had settled and my brain cells opened up one by one, allowing me a rare view of a cobweb sagging hammock-like an inch from my eyes in the corner I had somehow managed to jam myself into. It wasn't what you expected to see first thing upon coming back from the dead. Even so I could have kissed it. My left shoulder, numb now, gave up on me when I tried to push myself up off the floor where I was kneeling, but with the help of my right hand on the window sill I was able to hoist myself back into my own seat. My knees tingled sharply. I looked down and saw that they were bleeding through my trousers. Six months later the last sliver from my shattered glass would work its way out of my flesh.

I was sitting at an angle, or rather the coach was, the curtains on the windows dangling at a forty-five-degree tilt from the rods. Across from me, Ghost Shirt had slid back into a sitting position and was busy testing his fettered wrist between thumb and forefinger for breaks. It wasn't broken, but it was beginning to darken and swell. Locke, across the aisle, picked his glass up from the floor, still intact, and set it on the seat facing him. Of the three of us, he alone had emerged unscathed from the upheaval. Fools and drunkards.

The silence parted when a window at the other end of the coach, jarred loose from its frame, fell forward, executed a complete flip, and crashed to the floor. Then the quiet closed back over it, swallowing the last tinkle so effectively that after a moment it seemed as if there had been no such disturbance. We stared at each other like mourners on all-night watch over a corpse. At length:

"This is getting to be a habit," said Locke.

That did it as far as the tension was concerned. I got up, swaying to catch my balance on the tilted floor. Pain blazed through my left shoulder when I grabbed at the back of the seat for support. I stifled a curse.

"I'm going up front," I told Locke before he could ask

questions. "You'd better see to the senator." I pulled my carbine down from the rack and headed toward the door without waiting for an answer.

The locomotive was perched at a crazy angle, its stack heeled away over to the left and pouring smoke out of it at a tilt that suggested a strong wind, although there was none. Steam rolled out through the spaces between the wheels and swirled in the yellow beam of the lantern mounted over the boiler. In it I saw the twisted ends of the rails pointing heavenward at an even sharper angle only a few yards ahead. Someone or something had torn them up and given them enough English to derail a train whose engineer had not been as alert as Gus. That individual was climbing down from the cab as I approached. He spotted me and, out of instinct, snatched for the Walker Colt that was no longer in his belt. I held up my hands, palms forward, to show that I was friendly.

"How come you were able to stop in time?" I asked him.

"Two-mile grade up ahead." His southwestern twang held a sharper note than usual. "I was slowing down some to take it when I seen the ends of them rails glint in the lantern beam. I didn't have to see no more. Holdup men done the same thing down in Colorado when I was with the U.P. in seventy-one. We keeled over then, and I lost one of the best firemen I ever had. Not this time, though. This time I got her stopped quick enough. Quicker'n I expected, truth to tell." He hooked a finger inside his mouth. He was bareheaded, and in the reflection of the light coming off the bent irons I saw a thin trickle of blood leaking out of a split lip and down his chin. It mixed with the smudge on his cheek when he rubbed it, so that I couldn't tell what was blood and what was soot. Like the rest of us, he had kept moving when the train stopped.

"Are you all right?"

"I've lost teeth before. Forget it. Worry about getting them rails fixed before any holdup men come around. That's what I thought you was when you come up on me so sudden."

"I wish that's all it was," I muttered.

"What's that?"

"Can't you put her in reverse and take her back to Fargo?"

"Not enough wood."

"We've got three cars and a caboose. If you've got a fire axe we're in business."

"Nothing doing. I got retirement coming up and I ain't about to tell James J. Hill that I burned up four of his cars, one of 'em a private Pullman. No, sir."

"Would you rather face whoever tore up the rails?"

"Same difference."

"What if I told you it was Indians did it?"

He squinted at me through the gloom. Suspicion glittered in the slits of his eyes. "You know something you ain't telling?"

"It would take too much explaining. What about it? Hill or the Cheyenne?"

He turned that over, frowning. Then he shook his head curtly. "No, by God! Hill's got nothing to do with it. I ain't never run from no fight before and I ain't about to start now. We're staying and fixing the rails."

I was in no position to fight reasoning like that, especially since I had made much the same speech to Hudspeth on the east bank of the James River when I was younger and more foolish. I sighed. "All right, I guess I can't make you. You're the only one who can run the train. Have you got the tools?"

"A crowbar and a pair of sledges in the cab. No spikes,

but we can use the ones what's there if they ain't been busted or throwed away. Might be we can get it done before morning, if the irons ain't too bad twisted and we don't get jumped first."

"That's a hell of a lot of ifs."

He shrugged.

"How are the others?"

"Ep's burned some, not bad. You better see to your friend, though. His head damn near busted the throttle when we stopped." He went ahead to inspect the damage to the rails while I mounted the cab.

I announced myself first and was glad I had. Ephraim, the fireman, was waiting for me at the top with the aforementioned crowbar raised over his woolly head. The light of the flames crackling in the open box turned his skin from iron to bronze and made the burned flesh on his right breast and cheek look worse than it was. His hair was singed where it met his forehead. He must have stuck his head right into the box when the wheels stopped rolling. His eyes had a hunted animal look. When I got close enough for him to see me clearly he relaxed and dropped the bar clanging to the floor.

"How bad?" I asked, indicating his burns.

"I done had worse, I 'spect." His dungeon-depth voice was soothing. There was a church choir in Helena that would have given anything to have that bass in its ranks, if he weren't black. "I'd sho' feel better, though, if'n you'd ask your friend there please don't open no holes in this child's hide with them there cannons he's aholdin'."

I looked in the direction he had nodded, where Hudspeth was sitting on the floor with his back propped up against the opposite wall of the cab, his Smith & Wesson in one hand, the obsolete Colt in the other. He had the Spencer pinned beneath his not inconsiderable bulk. His forehead was smeared dark with blood, but I could tell by his heavy breathing that he was conscious.

"It's me," I told him. "Murdock."

"I knew that." He spoke laboriously. "It's the nigger I was watching. He tried to take the Walker a minute ago."

"To pertect us," flared the fireman. "I heerd footsteps acomin' and thought it was them holdups come to shoot us. He was gonna put one in this child's belly when I backed off," he added.

"Give him the Colt," I told Hudspeth.

He stared at me, his barrel torso heaving. His breath was coming regularly now. I decided he wasn't hurt badly. "You must of thunked your head harder than me," he said at last.

"I don't know how you feel about it, but I prefer to fight one enemy at a time. You and I aren't going to stand off the Cheyenne all alone. Give him the Colt."

"Injuns, sho' 'nuff?" Ephraim rolled his eyes at me, the whites showing in the light of the fire. He sounded more eager than frightened. Black or white, they were all the same, these Easterners, coming out here thinking the West was something put on for their own entertainment. I ignored him. Hudspeth took nine, then handed over the Walker as I'd known he would all along. We had gotten to know each other pretty well during the time we'd spent together.

"I hope you know what you're doing," he growled.

"So do I." I gave the revolver to the fireman. He accepted it enthusiastically, checked the cap beneath the hammer, thrust it into his belt.

"Lame Horse isn't as impulsive as I thought," I said. "The way I figure it, he put his braves to work tearing up the track with their lances and trade axes on their way to where they met us, just in case we made it on board. We've got till dawn before he catches up to us, maybe less. If we don't get those rails fixed by then we'll have to fort up and hope for the best. Does it hurt?"

Hudspeth rubbed the bloody spot above his eye with the heel of a hand. It was congealing now over a jagged gash an inch and a half long. "Not so much that a belt of good whiskey couldn't cure it," he said.

I grinned. "We'll see about that after I check up on our prisoner."

Custer was whooping it up fit to be tied as I mounted the platform between the baggage car and the coach, whining piteously and doing his best to turn the door into kindling. He reminded me of an old hound I'd once had who would set all the other dogs to howling for miles around every time I stepped outside without him.

It struck me then. Drawing my belt gun, I propped the Winchester against the wall, kicked open the door of the coach, and threw myself into the first seat on my left, landing hard on my hurt shoulder.

That was a mistake. Somewhere someone crushed a fresh batch of walnuts and sparks of white-hot pain swirled before my eyes. For an instant I was blinded. Through sheer act of will I forced myself to see through the swimming red haze. Gun in hand, I scrambled over to the opposite seat and peered cautiously over the back.

I hadn't missed much. Ghost Shirt was gone, along with my handcuffs and six inches off the arm of the seat he had occupied.

# CHAPTER 19

The door opened at the other end of the coach as I was getting up from between the seats. I raised my revolver to the level of the handle and thumbed back the hammer. My injured shoulder throbbed a half-beat off from the rapid banging of my heart. Colonel Locke came in and closed the door gently behind him.

"Sleeping like a baby," he said, turning. "I must have given him a stronger dose than I thought. Did you—" He stopped when he saw the gun.

"Ghost Shirt," I barked. "Did you see him?"

"Why, no, I—" He realized the implication of my words and glanced at the seat in which he had last seen the Indian.

While it was still dawning on his sodden consciousness I retrieved my carbine and pushed past him roughly, heading for the door through which he had just passed. Outside I leaped to the ground and looked up and down the length of the train as if expecting the fugitive to be standing there waiting for me. He wasn't. I did find the piece of wood he had taken with him when he finished the job the sudden halt had started, lying on the ground south of the tracks, but that was no clue at all, as he might have flung it there to throw me off while he lit a shuck north.

The first thing Locke and I did was search the train from top to bottom. I had learned my lesson the time a defendant on trial for murder in Judge Blackthorne's court made a run for it while court was in session and officers scoured Helena for two hours without result, only to have the janitor stumble upon him crouched in the rear of a cloakroom down the hall from the judge's chambers. We divided the train down the middle—or nearly so, Locke wanting nothing to do with the baggage car and its fanged occupant—me taking the front as far back as the coach, the colonel seeing to the caboose and the senator's car just in case our quarry had slipped inside after his own exit. We checked under the carriage and up on the roofs. I even risked my skin looking through baggage, where I knew he couldn't be from the way the dog was acting. The third time it went for my leg I should have shot it, but I didn't. I'm like that sometimes. I considered letting it out to see if it would lead us to its master, but gave that up because there was no way of telling whom it might attack when it did. Besides, the dog was Cheyenne. Silly as that sounds, I've seen horses brought up on Indian tradition throw their new riders when tracking down members of the same tribe for unfriendly purposes, and it was just possible that this mongrel would lead us into God knows what rather than betray the whereabouts of the man who took care of it. We didn't have time to find out. So when I left the car I made sure Custer was still inside.

I met Locke outside the coach. He was carrying the lantern I had seen the conductor with earlier.

"Anything?" I demanded.

"Just the conductor."

"What did he see?"

"I didn't ask. He's dead."

"Ghost Shirt?" I snatched his sleeve.

He shook his head. "Not unless he rammed the poor

man's skull into the steel railing on the back of the caboose. That stop splattered his brains all over the platform. I dragged his body inside."

"Well, that's that." I put away the Deane-Adams. "He's either taken off on his own or gone to meet Lame Horse. I hope he decided to go it alone."

"Why?"

"Lame Horse doesn't know our firepower since we came on board. He may hold off attacking until dawn just to play it safe. If Ghost Shirt gets to him with what he knows, they'll hit us right away. What are we, twenty miles from where you picked us up?"

He calculated. "More like fifteen."

"Two hours, then." I had him hold up his lantern and looked at my watch in the yellow light. "Seven if they wait till morning. With luck we'll have the repairs done by then. How much have you got in that flask?"

He had produced the item in question and helped himself to a swig. He touched his lips with the back of his hand, held up the vessel, shook it and listened to the contents sloshing around inside, frowned.

"Two swallows."

"Not enough." I held out my hand. When he gave it to me I tipped it up and finished what was left in one long draught. As the warmth of it spread through my system: "Mind if I borrow this?"

"Be my guest."

I climbed to the platform of Firestone's car. Since Locke was his bodyguard I paused outside the door and shot him a questioning glance. Although perplexed, he nodded his permission. I entered the sanctum.

The lamp on the bar was still burning. Fortunately it was bolted down or the entire structure would have gone up in flames after that last stop. Even the chandelier, its chain clamped securely to the ceiling, was still intact. In the corner, the curtains on the great four-poster had been left open just enough for me to see Senator Firestone's mountainous belly quivering beneath the counterpane as he slept in the grip of his opium-induced dreams.

Someone, probably the colonel, had had the foresight to place both decanters in the cabinet beneath the bar after his last visit, and neither was damaged. I uncorked the flask and poured into it what was left of the cognac. Locke had been hitting it hard, but there was more than enough to fill the pint container. The colonel was standing in the doorway as I turned to leave.

"This must be a first," he observed. "A reverse conversion."

"It's not for me."

"I've heard that before."

"Nobody likes a drunk with a sense of humor." I put the flask in my hip pocket and accompanied him outside. "I don't suppose you've any firepower aside from that Remington," I said when we were back on the platform.

He shook his head. If I hadn't known how much he'd consumed already that night I might have sworn he was dead sober. He changed roles as often as a repertory company.

"How about ammunition?"

"Under the bar. Two boxes."

"Get them." I stepped down and struck out toward the engine.

Hudspeth, on his feet beside the locomotive as I approached, wasn't surprised to learn that our prisoner had escaped. "Figured as much, the way you two was scrambling all over the train a while ago." He patted his forehead from time to time with a bloodstained handkerchief.

"Course you know if he gets to Lame Horse we're dead as rocks."

"Maybe not. Maybe they'll leave us alone once they have him."

"You said yourself they won't."

"It doesn't cost us anything to hope."

The engineer appeared from the front of the train. As he crossed the beam of the powerful mounted lantern I saw that his lower lip, although no longer bleeding, had swollen to nearly twice its normal size.

"Give Gus the Spencer," I directed the marshal. "We need as many hands as we can get. You can't fire two guns at once, and you've got enough ammunition to stop a war with just that Smith." I indicated the cartridge belt he had liberated from one of the troopers at the Missouri, strapped around his waist.

"Got me a gun." Gus patted the butt of the Walker Colt sticking up above the waistband of his pants.

"I give it to him," announced Ephraim, descending from the cab. "It's his'n anyways."

"From now on you're a rifleman." I took the Spencer from Hudspeth and gave it to the fireman.

"She's loaded up tight," said the former, as Ephraim inspected the breech. "Used all the shells there was left. What was that you said before about bringing whiskey?" His eyes shone eagerly as he looked at me.

"Sorry. All out."

His shoulders sank.

"Will brandy do?" I held out the flask.

He seized it with a noise a hungry St. Bernard might make accepting a raw steak. Suddenly his jaw tightened. He lowered the flask and rammed the cork back in with the heel of his hand.

"Reckon not." He thrust it back at me.

We stared at each other for some time in silence. Then I felt a slow grin spread over my face. I was a father watching his son take his first step unaided. "Keep it," I said. "For later."

Ephraim cleared his throat loudly enough to drown out the ticking of the boiler as it cooled. We all looked at him. "Seems a shame to just put it away like that," he ventured.

It might have been that my eyes played tricks on me in that poor light, but just then it looked as if the ends of Hudspeth's handlebar moustache twisted upward in the first smile I had seen on his face since we met. He turned the flask over to the fireman, who held it out in front of him for a moment, admiring it. Then he yanked the stopper and did for a quarter of the vessel's contents in one healthy pull. Drawing the back of his hand across his mouth, he returned the flask with a grateful nod to the marshal, who offered it to Gus.

The engineer shook his head. "I'm a man of temperance," he explained. "When I ain't, I don't do a lick of work for days, and from the looks of them tracks that's one thing we can't afford."

"Can they be fixed?"

"Won't know that till we try." He walked around Colonel Locke, who had just joined us bearing the two boxes of cartridges for his shoulder gun, and came back from the cab a minute later carrying a heavy sledge in each hand. "Who's first?" He held out one of them.

I stepped forward without thinking and took the hammer in my left hand, the right still holding the Winchester. The weight of the instrument when he let go sent a bolt of lightning straight up my arm to the shoulder. I dropped it and was following it to the ground when Hudspeth caught me in both arms.

"Let's have a look at that there arm," he said, lowering me to the prairie. I lay on my stomach while his powerful fingers poked and probed my shoulder in the light of Colonel Locke's lantern. The little shocks I felt as he did so were bearable after the big one I'd just experienced. His whistle of surprise was long and low and faintly reminiscent of the train's throaty blast.

"Iron-butt Murdock," he snarled finally. "Waltzing around with a dislocated shoulder like it's a stubbed toe. Here." He thrust something in front of my face. After a beat I recognized it as the knife I had given Pere Jac after capturing it from the Cheyenne back at the Big Muddy.

"What am I supposed to do with that?"

"You'll figure it out. Open up."

I did as directed. He jammed the hidebound handle into my mouth. I bit down on it. It tasted of leather and old sweat. He took my left hand in his own left, got himself set amid a general rustle of clothing, and then I felt the weight of his boot against the lump of displaced bone behind my shoulder. Realization came to me in a rush of panic. I tried to get up, but the pain and his boot held me down. I was wobbling the knife handle around in my mouth to find voice enough to protest when he pulled the arm tight and threw all his weight forward onto his foot.

Multicolored lights danced and exploded behind my eyelids. My blood sang in my ears. I bit down hard. My teeth ground through the rock-hard leather and into the wood beneath, dislodging splinters into the pocket beneath my tongue. Hudspeth's grip tightened crushingly on my hand and he heaved every ounce of his two hundred-plus pounds

against the stubborn knob. It fell into place with an audible pop.

He was still panting from the effort a moment later as I
pushed myself to my knees with my good arm and then got
up, swaying on willowy legs. It took me a while to spit out
the last of the splinters. "You bastard!"

He snorted. "That's the thanks I get. Back in Bismarck
you'd pay a doc two dollars to do the same thing and be
grateful to him afterwards."

"Where'd you learn to do that?"

"I didn't. Just thought I'd give it a whirl. It worked, didn't
it?" he added, reading the expression on my face.

"Maybe I can do the same for you someday."

"No thanks. You done enough to me this trip." He accepted one of the sledges from Gus. "You won't be swinging no hammers for a spell. Which works out, us needing
someone to look after the long guns just in case that injun's
still around."

The engineer set the other hammer down on its head and
turned toward the cab. "Come on, Ep, let's fire her up and
back her down onto the level."

"No," said Hudspeth.

Gus stopped, turned back. "You want her to flop over
whilst we're working?"

"We'll need all the weight we can get on them rails to
hold 'em down. Think you can take her forward all the way
to the end?"

"The end is right! Hell, all she needs right now is a stiff
breeze to turn her into scrap. I ain't about to go back and
tell James J. Hill—"

At this point the marshal interrupted with a suggestion
as to what he could tell James J. Hill that I won't repeat.

What he said next was more significant. "All right, if you won't do it I'll get someone who will. What about it, Ep?"

The engineer made a nasty sound in his nose. "He don't know the first thing about it! He's just a—"

"Sho' can, Marshal," the fireman broke in. "Can and will. Mr. Gus, he been trainin' me to be an engineer."

"You won't never make it now, boy!" He spat the words. "I'll sure as hell see to that!"

"Shut up."

Hudspeth was mostly bluster, but when he said that, people generally obliged him. His gaze lashed from the engineer back to the fireman. "Get up steam and take her as far up on them bent irons as she'll go."

Ephraim double-timed it back to the cab.

"Just don't forget that I didn't have nothing to do with it," Gus insisted.

Hudspeth beat me to it. "Who the hell cares?" He hoisted his sledge over his shoulder—making the engineer duck—and strode off in the direction of the damaged rails.

Locke, hefting the other hammer, smiled at his retreating back. "Not bad for a man who doesn't drink."

I kept my mouth shut.

At length Gus unbent enough to go back and release the private car and caboose from the rest of the train so that if it did go over it wouldn't take one of our more distinguished citizens with it. Meanwhile, Hudspeth and the colonel put the sledges and crowbar to work straightening out the worst kinks in the irons as Ep performed double duty as engineer and fireman, going back and forth between the box, the wood supply, and the throttle, all the time maintaining a vigil on the gauge to keep the boiler from doing the Indians' job for them. All this time I stood over the rifles watching everything and feeling useless. My shoulder felt worse than

it had before the marshal had put it right, but at least it was
in a position where I could depend upon it in a pinch. When
at last the engine was ready, Ep gave two blasts on the
whistle to clear everyone out of the way, released the
brake with a sigh of escaping steam, and gave the throttle a
nudge that started the engine rolling forward.

The rails, or perhaps it was the train itself, groaned ominously as the incline was scaled. The wheels found traction
only every third revolution, spinning in between with an unearthly squeal, and the twisted steel rails bent downward
beneath the creeping weight. Not enough, however, to keep
the top-heavy engine from swaying like an Indian medicine
man in a deep trance. I wiped that image out of my thoughts
the instant it occurred. Indians and medicine men were on
my mind too much of late.

A yard short of the irons' uprooted ends, the cab began
to tip. I cringed in anticipation of the inevitable.

"Back up!" Hudspeth bellowed, drowning out the engine's snuffling wheeze.

The driving arm stopped, then began cranking backward
even as the wheels on the far side were leaving the track.
They fell back with a bang as the train lurched into reverse.
As soon as the danger zone was past the marshal signaled
stop by waving the lantern. The boiler exhaled its pent-up
breath.

Ephraim alighted carefully, negotiating the extra couple
of inches between the damaged rail and the ground in a
smooth striding motion. He whooped his relief.

"You folks nearly had crushed nigger for dinner, and
that's a fact," he said.

Gus, more active now that his own moral crisis was over,
used the crowbar as a lever to take the twist out of each rail,
holding it taut while Locke and Hudspeth secured it by

pounding home the spikes first in one, then the other. The engineer then resumed his place at the throttle and backed up the locomotive a step at a time to make room for the repairs as they progressed. Ep spelled Locke to free him for crowbar duty, his great black muscles writhing with each swing of the sledge. The noise of steel on steel rang out over the prairie for the first time in five years.

It was back-breaking work, as the corkscrewed track had to be held straight while each spike was being driven, and the vibration of all that pounding made the hands holding the bar tingle until they grew numb and slipped off, and the end of the bar bounced up like a snake striking for the arm or skull that was not pulled out of the way fast enough. The second time that happened it caught Locke high on the right temple with a solid thump, stunning him. Hudspeth handed his sledge to Gus and took the colonel's place until he had recovered himself enough to resume his task. In this manner the labor went on into the early morning hours.

Standing out of the way watching them, shifting my weight from one foot to the other, I had grown so drowsy by about three o'clock that the first owl hoot didn't register. I perked up at the second one. Hollow and echoless, it sounded very far away. A pause, then a third. It would have been soothing but for my knowledge that it wasn't far away, and wasn't made by anything that remotely resembled an owl.

## CHAPTER 20

**N**or did it stop at the owl. A moment later there was an answering hoot from another quarter, and then, farther off, the complicated scan of a mockingbird. Closer—too close—a mourning dove's sad refrain tooted like air passing through a pipe. We might have been in an aviary.

They weren't fooling anyone, not out there in the middle of a lonely prairie with no place for a bird to roost, and they knew it. They were just reporting their positions to each other in the only way they knew how, a highly efficient form of field communication that went back some two thousand years. More important, they were trying to scare us. Fright is the strongest medicine there is, and no one ever used it to greater advantage than the war-loving Cheyenne.

At the first calls Hudspeth and the others had stopped working and gone for their arms.

"Go on working." I spoke loudly enough to be heard over the engine without shouting. "If they don't know how many men we have, acting scared is the quickest way of telling them."

"And if they knows?" said Ephraim.

"Then we'll die no matter what we do."

"I'd heaps rather die fighting." This from the marshal.

"Either way you end up a handful of bloody hair. Go back to work."

There was a pause while they bounced glances around
among themselves. Slowly they returned their guns to their
proper places and took up their tools. Steel clanged.

Time crawled after that. I figured that if Lame Horse
knew our strength he'd attack within half an hour of his arrival. I spent every minute tight as a coiled rattler. As the
half hour drew to a close and minute piled laboriously upon
minute without a bullet in my back, I began to relax by degrees. If they were planning to hit us before dawn we'd be
five minutes dead.

A metallic glimmering over the eastern horizon foretold
that event some three hours later. "Break it off," I snapped,
surprised at the sound of my own voice after all those hours
of silence.

The others looked up from their labors. Aside from that
nobody moved.

"Ain't finished yet," Gus protested. "Next train comes
down this track, without no warning—"

"That's their lookout. If you're really worried about it you
can leave behind that red lantern on the caboose as a signal. Don't forget to couple those last two cars. Locke, Hudspeth, put the tools away and join me in the coach. No
hurrying. We don't want them to know we're leaving just
yet. Start stoking, Ep."

"Just who made you ramrod of this here outfit?" demanded the marshal.

"A sore shoulder. Get moving." I picked up the Winchester and threw the Spencer to the fireman, who caught
it in one hand. The first bullet found him in that position.
He spun and fell, spread-eagled with the rifle flung out to
the side. Another one clanged against the boiler, then another and another, whistling off the base of the stack.
More kicked up dirt all around us. At that moment, a line

of shadowy riders spilled up out of a cleft between the rolling swells to the south like ants from a kicked hill. They were snapping off wild shots and yammering at the top of their lungs.

"Get on board!" I shouted, backing up and firing the Winchester from my hip as I went. I nearly tripped over Ep, who was still kicking with a hole the size of a man's fist over his left breast. Tossing the carbine to Hudspeth, I called for him to cover me as I gathered up the Spencer and a handful of the fireman's belt and dragged him to the coach. My shoulder was forgotten.

"I need a fireman!" Gus shouted from the cab.

"Locke!"

The colonel waved his understanding and ran a zigzag pattern between flying bullets toward the engine. His Remington bucked twice in his hand, its muzzle flashing. An Indian who had been galloping up on him shrieked and back-flipped over his horse's rump. Whinnying, the animal lost its momentum, executed a wide, clawing turn to the right, and took off bucking for the open prairie, narrowly missing Hudspeth as it brushed between us.

A Cheyenne slug splattered the corner of the coach an inch above my hat as I hoisted Ep's limp, heavy body onto the platform and bounded up behind him. Either their marksmanship was improving or God was on their side. Hudspeth, hammering away with the Winchester at every target that presented itself, swung aboard directly behind me.

Indians were clattering all over the place now. Crouched on the platform, I fired the Deane-Adams at an occasional flash of horse and rider in the light of the lamps still burning inside, without visible result. I heard the snapping of a light gun in the direction of the engine, and once the deeper roar of the Walker, and hoped Gus wouldn't forget to pick

400 LOREN D. ESTLEMAN

us up. Ghost Shirt's dog was going wild in the baggage car, which was no longer connected to ours.

The grayness to the east had given way to dirty pink. I had enough light to shoot by, but if there had been a friend among the riders harassing the train I wouldn't have known him from the others. I figured there was little chance of that and kept popping away at the fleeting forms.

Over everything, the panting of the engine grew loud and rapid. I was relieved to see for the first time that the rear of the baggage car was looming near, and threw out a hand to brace myself against the railing just as we made contact with a smashing jolt that threw me sideways into the marshal, pinning him between my shoulder and the wall. The couplings caught and held. We began rolling forward at a painfully slow pace, but picking up speed as we went.

I placed a hand over the gaping mass of gore that was the fireman's breast to see if his heart was still beating. Warm blood squirted between my fingers. At that moment his great chest swelled with air and expelled it in a long, drawn-out sigh. I waited, but it didn't fill again and no more blood came. Gus was right. He would never be an engineer.

Hudspeth had ducked inside the coach to see to the other side of the tracks. After a space I felt the platform rock beneath me and figured it was him returning. At the same time, a solitary rider sitting a black and white pony drew abreast of the coach and swung the muzzle of a Spencer in my direction. It was Lame Horse.

Hudspeth had extinguished the lights inside the car, but there was enough natural illumination now for me to recognize the shiny, ebony-painted face with the jagged streak of yellow lightning slashing from his right temple to the left corner of his jaw. The necklace of shrunken human fingers bounced on his breast as he galloped to keep up with the accelerating train, slapping his reins one-handed back and forth across the animal's withers. You had to hand it to him for spunk. Hitting a moving target from the back of a horse in full gallop is next door to impossible, yet here he was fixing to do just that. He set a lot of store by the medicine in that necklace. Using it as a guide, I was steadying the foresight of my revolver on the top of the vulnerable arch below his breastbone when something burst behind my eyes and the lights went out.

The blackout lasted less than a second, but by the time my senses came swimming back I found myself sprawled on the platform, my head humming and my right leg swinging over the edge where the wind of our passage set my pants cuff to flapping. The Deane-Adams was nowhere to be seen. My first thought was that Lame Horse got lucky, but then I realized that the blow had come from behind. I looked up to see a familiar figure crouching over me.

My handcuffs dangled glittering from the swollen wrist of the hand holding the engineer's Colt by its long barrel like a club. That meant that he had been inside the cab, which in turn meant that he had been hiding in the one place I had given only a cursory search, the wood car. He had sprung from beneath a layer of camouflage, dispatched Gus and likely Colonel Locke, and scrambled over the roof of the baggage car to do for me. All this came to me in the instant of awakening. The moment he saw me lying helpless at his feet, Ghost Shirt let out a whoop and, swinging the revolver over his head as if it were a tomahawk, leaped up to hail Lame Horse.

The medicine man was ready for him. Within arm's length of the platform now, he thrust the bore of his rifle into his chief's midsection and blew him into history.

The force of the bullet slammed him against the door of

the adjacent car, where he sank down with surprise on his face and both hands buried in what remained of his stomach, his feet still on the platform of the coach so that he formed a human coupling between the cars. Behind the baggage door an animal throat let go with a howl that made my scalp crawl.

Lame Horse was losing ground now to the train, which although it had begun to lose momentum with no hand at the throttle was still traveling too fast for a horse to keep up, but he had time enough to turn the heavy rifle on me. Before he could pull the trigger I snatched up the Spencer that was lying beside Ep's corpse and slammed an ounce of lead into the middle of his war paint. The yellow slash dissolved behind a cloud of red. He clutched at his face with one hand, but it was just his nerves reacting. I didn't see him topple. By then both horse and rider had slid out of sight behind the corner of the coach.

The train was moving perceptibly slower now. Hudspeth emerged from the coach carrying my Winchester in one hand and his own Smith & Wesson in the other. He helped me to my feet.

"What the hell happened?" he wanted to know. "I leave you alone for one minute—"

I ignored him. Ghost Shirt was still breathing. I stepped across to the other platform, where he lay with his mouth working soundlessly. Planting a finger in one ear to close out the noise of the train, I bent over him and placed the other ear so close to his lips that they almost touched. For a moment I froze in that position, straddling two cars and leaning against the door of baggage to maintain my balance. Then the Indian's neck muscles let go and his head rolled of its own weight to one side. The hypnotic light drained slowly from his half-open eyes. I straightened.

"What did he say?" The marshal's voice was so hushed I may only have guessed at his words.

"Something about Lame Horse," I said. "It wasn't, 'Forgive them, for they know not what they do.'"

When the train had rolled almost to a stop we sprang down and made our way to the locomotive. There were no Indians in sight. In the cab we found the engineer slumped over the throttle, the back of his head a pulpy mass covered with matted hair. Locke was leaning against the wood supply busily tying his handkerchief around his right wrist. A dark stain was spreading over the fine silk.

"He hit Gus with a chunk of wood the size of a man's thigh," he explained as we mounted the cab. "The damn fool was too busy replacing the one bullet he'd fired from that cap-and-ball to notice him. I had just put away my gun. Ghost Shirt searched me, but I guess he didn't know about shoulder holsters. I went for it while he was picking up Gus's revolver. I wasn't fast enough. The Remington went over the side and I played dead. Did you see which way he went?"

I nodded. "He isn't playing."

"This one's skull must be near as thick as yours, Murdock," said Hudspeth, examining the engineer. "He's still breathing."

"How bad is the wrist?" I asked Locke.

"Just a graze. I would've given anything for one like it when I was in the service. The wound pension would have served me in good stead."

"Trouble." The marshal hefted the Spencer, which I had exchanged for the return of my carbine. I turned in the direction of his gaze.

A dozen Indians were approaching slowly on horseback from the east. Some of them led other horses, across the backs of which were slung their dead. The brave mounted at the point, powerfully built like Ghost Shirt but several years his senior, wore his hair in a pair of plaits that hung almost to his belt, the ends tied with bright red ribbon, and had his face painted black on one side, red on the other, with a white line the width of a finger separating them down the middle. Across his chest he sported a breastplate made of bones fitted together by a squaw's patient hands. The Cheyenne at his left carried a rifle upright with its butt resting upon his thigh. A scrap of white cloth swung from its bore.

"It's a trick," said Hudspeth.

"If it is they're taking an awful chance. We'll let them come."

They stopped a few yards away. The silence that ensued was broken only by the occasional shuddering snort of an exhausted mount. Finally the man holding the flag of truce spoke. A young brave with a pouting expression beneath his dead black paint, he had the high, thin voice of a born Indian orator.

"This man is Broken Jaw, of the Cheyenne nation." He indicated the breastplated warrior, whose hard eyes remained fixed on a point somewhere above our heads. "He wishes to say that the white men fought bravely and well this day, and that he is not angry with them because of this."

I said nothing. Indians take a long time to get to the point.

"He wishes also to say that while there was one among the Cheyenne who did not behave this day as a Cheyenne should, and whose soul will wander forever the Place of the Dead in disgrace because of this, the black white man who died this day will take his place beside Heammawihio, the Wise One Above."

I perked up at that. Broken Jaw had witnessed the medicine man's treachery as well as Ephraim's death. In that tribe, the worst thing you can say about a fellow warrior is to accuse him of not behaving "as a Cheyenne should." I wanted to hurry the spokesman along, to find out what he was getting at, but if I tried I'd only be butting my head against twenty centuries of tradition.

"But there was a great sadness this day as well. Tomorrow the heavens will weep and the sun will hide its head."

At last we were making some progress.

"Broken Jaw has come to claim the pod in which dwelled the soul of Ghost Shirt so that he may prepare it for its final great journey in a manner befitting a great warrior of the Cheyenne."

"Tell him his wish is granted," I said, after I had translated that into plain English.

The spokesman told him nothing, but then he didn't have to. It was obvious Broken Jaw understood most of what had been said. I told Locke and Hudspeth to wait there and turned my back on their protests as I led the party back to the baggage car. There, the head warrior dismounted to gather up the body.

"One moment," I said. He watched in silence as I produced the key to Ghost Shirt's handcuffs and removed them from his lifeless wrist. "So his soul will not wander in chains."

There is no word for thanks in the Indian languages, because none is needed. I saw the gratitude in Broken Jaw's eyes as he nodded at me.

The renegades had come away from the fight at the Missouri with no lodge poles with which to construct a travois, and so the pod in which Ghost Shirt's soul had dwelled was committed to the indignity of being draped over the back of an empty horse. Then Broken Jaw and the Indians who had helped him mounted up and left without a word. They didn't break into their death chant until they were almost out of sight on the eastern horizon. By then it was hard to distinguish the toneless dirge from the morning breeze that had just begun to stir the grasses on the prairie. Sometimes, when I'm alone and the wind comes humming beneath the cornices outside the window in gusts that rise and fall with no recognizable pattern, I hear it still.

# CHAPTER 21

**G**us sat on the floor of the cab with his turbaned head in his hands, his legs dangling over the side. When he spoke he lisped wetly through the space where his bottom two front teeth had been before the train's sudden stop had rammed a healthy share of the ironwork into his mouth. That stop seemed a week old now. It was midmorning. Taking turns with a shovel they had found in the cab, Locke and Hudspeth had just finished burying Ephraim and the conductor deep enough to keep the wolves and coyotes from scratching them up for a day or two.

"Can you run the train?" I slipped my arms into the sleeves of my jacket, which I had taken off to clean the wound, apply the bandage and a liberal dose of cognac from the community flask. The left one went on carefully. My shoulder was beginning to set up.

"I need me another fireman. Lately I been going through 'em like cigars."

"I can still stoke wood." Locke returned from the rear of the train, where he had gone to check on the senator. A fresh shine in his eyes told me he'd made a stop at the bar, where burgundy was still available. "I'm learning to enjoy physical labor all over again."

"We'll cure that soon enough," said Gus.

"How's His Lordship?" I asked the colonel.

"Happily ignorant. I gave him a drop more laudanum. He'll sleep the rest of the trip."

"Is that how you usually handle him?"

He shrugged. "It can't do him any harm. His doctors say he has a stomach cancer. He won't see winter."

"Does he know?"

"If he didn't, do you think he'd be in such a hurry to make a name for himself in history?"

"All right, then, get her up." I turned toward the passenger coach, where Hudspeth was waiting.

"What time is it?" the engineer demanded.

I hauled out my watch. "Quarter of nine."

He swore, scrambled to his feet, got dizzy, grabbed the side of the cab for support, swore again. "There's a freighter due in Bismarck at noon. If it's nine she's an hour late now. We got to get moving."

The rest of us had managed to keep up a head of steam without a crash course in locomotive operation. Gus released the brake and the train was churning at a stiff clip by the time I reached the coach. I grabbed hold of the platform railing with my good arm and swung aboard.

"Figure on keeping a pet?" Hudspeth was sitting in the first seat facing the door on the right, Locke's flask in hand. His nose was flushed and all was right with the world.

When I raised my eyebrows he gestured with the flask in the direction of the baggage car, where Custer was barking up a storm.

"Damn!" I plunked into the vacant space beside the marshal. "I got so used to his racket I forgot to turn him loose when the Indians left. Gus won't stop now, not with several hundred tons of freight breathing down his neck."

"Shoot him when we get to Bismarck."

"I suppose we'll have to." I sighed.

"What do you mean, we? I ain't no dog killer!"

We stared at each other. For no reason at all we burst out laughing. We hadn't forgotten Pere Jac or Ep the fireman or Ghost Shirt and all our wasted efforts. It was just that after everything that had happened to us since we'd made this trip in the other direction, we had either to laugh or shoot each other, and we'd both done enough shooting to last us for a while. We roared until our sides ached, and for the next four hours we didn't dare look at each other for fear of starting it all over again.

The usual curiosity seekers were gathered on the platform in Bismarck as we eased into the station. I felt a pang, not of remorse at the end of a mission that should never have been undertaken in the first place, but for the trouble ahead. Curiously, my chief concern was for my partner. I wondered what would happen to him when Judge Flood learned we had failed to deliver his stepping-stone to the Congress. I got up, took down my carbine, and handed him the Spencer—his by inheritance.

"We'll let the local law take charge of the mongrel," I told him. "Pick up our gear afterwards."

"Suits me." He heaved himself to his feet. He really was a big man, six foot one and solid as two hundred and fifty pounds of salt pork. I let him go ahead of me down the aisle.

I was behind him on the coach platform when something exploded and his chest was enveloped in smoke. I was forced to let go of the Winchester as he fell backward into my arms, losing his own rifle. Mine clattered on the railing and dropped through the slot between the cars before I could catch it.

"You son of a bitch, this is for the fire."

I scarcely recognized the voice rising above the hubbub of panic-stricken spectators, because I'd heard it only once

before. Dry and whispery, like sand sifting through a screen,
it went with the man it belonged to, whom I placed right
away. Sergeant Burdett, his shiny rain cape thrown open to
expose his gun belt, stood alone in what was now a cleared
space on the station platform, a heavy Army Colt smoking
in his gloved right hand, its muzzle pointing at me. His good
eye was cocked in my direction, its dead mate and the
powder-burned cheek in shadow beneath the shiny black vi-
sor of his Yankee cap. He gave everything time to sink in
before his finger tensed on the trigger.

Senator Firestone chose that moment to come waddling
along the station platform from the direction of his private
car, leaning backward to balance the forward pull of his
enormous belly. He'd just awakened. Pink scalp showed in
patches where his hair stuck up in tousled spikes and his
eyes were still puffed from sleep. He walked right up to Burdett as if he were approaching the Senate podium.

"What do you think you're doing, soldier?" he demanded
in his trumpeting baritone. "You're upsetting everything!
Early, much too—"

The Colt roared twice. I heard both slugs slap his great
mound. He staggered backward, puffing and blowing
through his whiskers, and sat down on a packing crate beside the station door. He died in that position, looking like
a passenger who had fallen asleep waiting for the train. By
that time Burdett had forgotten all about him, and swung
the revolver back to me.

I reached over and tore open the door of the baggage car.
Eighty pounds of crazed animal bounded out through the
opening, hesitated on the car's platform for half a heartbeat,
then leaped eight feet for the first uniform it saw. Surprise
and fear kindled in the sergeant's eye. He fired, blowing a
hole through the bellowing monster, but not in time to stop

its spring. The bellow soared to a shriek and it piled into its killer, bearing him down to the platform. Burdett's own roar was nearly as bestial as he shoved the lifeless weight from his chest, but before he could raise his Colt, Hudspeth, propped up on his left elbow where he had fallen after the first shot, pumped six bullets from his Smith & Wesson into the sergeant's heart as fast as the cylinder would turn.

The sigh of steam exhaling from beneath the boiler was the loudest sound when the marshal reached inside his still-smoldering coat and drew out Colonel Locke's steel flask. A thumb-sized hole was punched in it near the base.

"Bastard," he grumbled as he shook the last drops out of the aperture. Burdett's bullet rattled inside. "Wish I could do it all over again."

Judge Blackthorne was in a foul mood when he came back from court. His false teeth were clamped so tight they creaked and his robes, cut for a man an inch taller, made an angry noise as the hem scuffed the floor. He didn't look at me seated in the chair before his desk as he undid the cord behind his neck and spiked the sober black garment on its peg.

"Rough session?" I asked.

"Damn Philadelphia lawyers." He shrugged into a shiny black coat with beaverskin facing on the lapels and sank heavily into the high-backed leather chair behind his desk, where he sat working his porcelains for some time in silence. Then he pounced.

"Why in the name of sweet Jesus did it have to be Harold Firestone? Have you any idea how many friends that man had in the Congress? Have you any idea how hot they've been making things for me since the news got out?"

"It wasn't my choice. And stop acting like I'm the one

who pulled the trigger. You got my report." Written in our own special code, it had run to eleven pages and cost more to send out collect over the wire than I would have paid for two good horses, saddles included. His reply, not in code, had been much more brief and, I suspected, considerably toned down by cooler heads at Western Union. Now I went over it again, filling in the blank spots. The words came easily since I had repeated the story several times at the top of my lungs for Judge Flood's benefit. Refusing to speak until we saw him had cost Hudspeth and me two hours in the Bismarck jail. Local law and the marshal had not gotten along for years. Following our report—received in stony silence—Hudspeth had bought a ticket on the next train to Fargo, where he planned to rent a horse and pay a visit to the métis camp to inform Pere Jac's widow and family of their loss. Blackthorne listened with his short beard on his chest and his fingers laced across his spare middle. He was proud of that trim waistline, although he did nothing whatever to maintain it.

"It fits with what I was told by the commanding officer at Fort Ransom," he grunted, when I had finished. "The slant was different. That man doesn't like you much."

"I got that impression."

"You know, of course, that the papers are calling the incident at the station a planned assassination."

"The papers are always good for an afternoon's entertainment."

"In this case we're encouraging it. It's better for all concerned if the public thinks the killing of ex-Senator Firestone was carried out with malice aforethought by a demented army deserter. Which is technically correct. Sergeant Burdett had orders to return to camp if he was unable to prevent you from reaching the railroad. He went on alone after the others turned back."

"Except that it was Firestone who was demented, and that Burdett didn't know him from Adam when he put him under. He just got in the way. He took one look at that uniform and thought it was one of his own toy soldiers jumping the whistle on his grand revolution. Where does that leave Hudspeth and me?"

"Nowhere. Officially, you weren't there. As the senator's bodyguard, Andrew Locke was the one who shot the assassin. The earlier reports will be forgotten eventually for lack of substantiation." He tried out his diabolic smile, but it wasn't the same with his teeth in. "I'm sorry, Page, but there's no glory in it for you this time. In the long run, though, it can only help your reputation to leave the public ignorant of your part in the thing. It really was a wasted trip, with nothing to show for it."

Nothing but a pile of corpses, I thought. Aloud I said, "Sorry to disappoint you."

He shrugged. "Don't apologize to me. I'm ahead of the game. I had a debt to pay and now it's square. Now I don't owe Abel Flood a damned thing, the hypocritical bastard."

"I wish you'd told me he was a hypocritical bastard before I left," I snapped.

"I figured you'd find out soon enough. Have you put in a voucher yet for that lost gun?"

I patted the new Colt in my holster. "This will do until I find another Deane-Adams."

"Not much chance of that, here in Colt country. Where are you going?"

I had gotten up and put on my hat, a new one to go with my first bath and shave in many days. "To get as close to dead drunk as my credit at the Belmont will take me." I took a step toward the door.

"No need for that." He opened his bottom drawer and tossed me a full bottle of the expensive Bourbon he had shipped in quarterly by the case from Kentucky. I caught it in one hand.

"Don't turn cow eyes on me," he snarled. "It's coming out of your salary."

I said something a man doesn't usually say to his boss and expect to remain employed, and left.

Don't look for anything like an ending to this, because no such thing exists, not in real life. Too many details overlap, and offshoots of one incident go on to weave themselves into something else that sprang out of something else before that, just as the Civil War never ended but went on in Mexico with much of the original cast. For me the Dakota episode was over. I don't know about the others.

Colonel Andrew Locke dropped out of sight after we had parted in Bismarck and I never heard from him again. If he found the upward mobility he was looking for when he left the army, it wasn't in any profession that got headlines or I would have caught wind of it one way or another. I doubt that he stuck with what he'd been doing. There isn't a lot of call for bodyguards who let their charges get killed, no matter what the papers said about their quickness on the trigger after the fact. The best guards never get their names in print.

Speaking of names, Abel Flood's didn't appear on the ballot during the 1880 presidential election because he died on the bench late in '79. He succumbed quietly to a stroke while court was in session, and all the parties involved with the case under consideration went on screaming and yelling the way they always did so he could hear them until someone noticed that he hadn't moved or blinked for ten minutes. The next day the Bismarck *Tribune* devoted eight columns to his three decades of service and the territorial governor decreed that flags throughout Dakota be flown at half-mast for thirty days in his memory. A street was eventually named after him, then dropped in favor of another after local law enforcement reminded the mayor that every major cathouse in the city was located along the original.

I was told by a friend that Major Quincy Harms had issued an order to place me under arrest the next time I entered Dakota following the death of Sergeant Burdett, but I don't know that for certain because I never found reason to go back. In the winter of 1882 he and two of his officers were separated from the rest of the command by a sudden blizzard during a raid on a camp of renegade Sioux. His body and that of his adjutant were found in a cleft between two buttes after the spring thaw, but they never recovered the third, which led to some ugly rumors about the others that persist to this day.

Whether he retired, quit, or was sacked, A. C. Hudspeth left Bismarck within a year of our adventure and rode for a time with a Wild West show operating out of Chicago. I know that because I saw his name on a poster in Rock Springs, Wyoming, while escorting a prisoner back to Helena for trial. According to the date on it I had missed him by a day. After that I scanned the newspapers fairly regularly in the hopes the show might come to my neighborhood, but I never heard of it again and it's likely it folded along with the dozens of others that couldn't hope to compete against a name like Buffalo Bill. Sometime around '85, an old girlfriend who knew more about my past than I preferred wrote me from the home she was sharing with her new husband in St. Paul that a candidate named Hudspeth had just made a bid for public office there on a law and order ticket. That didn't sound much like the marshal, unless he had caught the bug from his employer, but then I suppose if it weren't contagious we wouldn't have politicians at all. Whatever the case, he lost by a landslide. That must have been particularly hard to take for a man who didn't like the taste of dregs.

Everyone knows what happened to the Indians. The railroads resumed building the following year, settlers poured westward, and no man, primitive or otherwise, stands in the way of progress for long. Many Ponies, the Miniconjou chief who was more interested in pleasing his new squaw than fighting the white man, died doing both at what the official military histories would one day christen the Battle of the Missouri, while sharing a buffalo robe with his eighteen-year-old bride in their tipi. His fellow tribesman Tall Dog was captured and taken under heavy guard to Fort Abraham Lincoln, where, according to the report, he hanged himself in the guardhouse with a lace from one of his moccasins. Broken Jaw buried his dead in state on the west bank of the James and was leading his decimated band back to the Mormon stronghold when the reinforcement troops General Sherman had promised Fort Ransom fell upon them and cut them to pieces. In so doing, they lost three troopers to every brave. If you flip through a recent book entitled *Conquest of the Frontier* you'll see a picture of Broken Jaw's bullet-riddled corpse propped up on a door alongside those of two of his warriors, taken by a New York photographer while on a visit to the fort.

And last month in Washington City, the Smithsonian Institution opened a new exhibit centered around a glass jar containing a gray something said to be a piece of Ghost Shirt's brain.

Read on for a preview of

# THE
# SUNDOWN
# SPEECH

## · LOREN D. ESTLEMAN ·

*Available from Tom Doherty Associates*
*in November 2015*

A FORGE BOOK

# CHAPTER 1

Roll the clock back a dozen years, maybe more; Michael Jackson was still alive, Iris, too. I could walk all day without limping. Tweet was bird talk, the chain bookstore was the greatest threat to civilization since ragtime music, and the only time you saw a black president was in a sci-fi film. Going back is always a crapshoot.

Downtown Ann Arbor was draining into Zingerman's Deli at 11:00 A.M. A chirpy Bohemian girl with her cranberry-colored hair wrapped in a bandanna snood fashion worked her way down the hungry line, taking orders and offering cubes of cheese and curls of lunchmeat impaled on toothpicks, and feet ground away at the black-and-white tiles in dirty sneakers, glossy Florsheims, cork sandals, and nothing at all. In the town that invented the five-dollar fine for possession of marijuana, "no shirt, no shoes, no service" was just a quaint suggestion. In those days you could even smoke tobacco if you didn't mind being glared at.

I'm used to it. I paid for my order and took my receipt outside, to a picnic table to light a cigarette and wait. It was a bright warm day and there were plenty of halter tops and navel piercings to admire.

In a little while an employee carrying a tray with a side of pork pressed between thick slabs of sourdough asked me politely to put out the butt. I did that. My clients had arrived, anyway. I got up to meet them.

They fit the description I'd gotten over the telephone, the woman straight-haired and graying, no makeup, wearing a dress of some unbleached material that hung from straps on her shoulders like a sandwich board, the man trailing a couple of steps behind in corduroys and a soft shirt with the collar spread, gray at the temples, with the pinched expression of an actor in an aspirin commercial. They wore identical glasses with no rims.

The indigenous local species: *Homo Arboritis.*

"Amos Walker? My goodness, you *look* like a detective. I'm Heloise Gunnar. This is Dante."

No other identification, i.e. *Dante, my husband.* It was no business of mine.

Her grip was firm, the hand corded with muscle. His hand fluttered in mine and was gone. I let the detective crack go and we sat facing each other on opposite benches.

"What do you think of Zingerman's?" Heloise Gunnar said. "We thought as long as you were coming out from the city, you might as well sample a native institution. It's always being written up in travel magazines."

"I thought maybe you picked it because it's on Detroit Street. Make me feel at home." The place looked as far away from the Motor City as Morocco. You only saw open-air crowds like that in the Farmers Market, where there's strength in numbers.

"Is it? We're hardly aware of street names anymore. Dante was born right here in town, and I came out after I graduated Berkeley."

"That would be in the sixties?"

The skin whitened a shade around her nostrils. She had some vanity after all under the patchouli. "Seventy-four. I majored in English Lit. I don't get to use as much of it as you'd think managing a bookstore."

After football and stoplights, Ann Arbor majors in bookstores. Managing one is no more a topic of dinner conversation there than pouring steel in Gary.

"What do you do, Mr.—?" I asked. So far he hadn't said a word.

"Gunnar." He lifted his brows. "Didn't you hear my wife?"

So they were married; or as good as. I said something about not every wife taking her husband's surname.

"I work for the U of M." He made it sound as if there was no alternative other than shelving books. "Information Services."

That meant exactly nothing to me. I'd only asked out of politeness. It was that stage of the relationship.

Our meals came, borne by a left tackle with a block M tattooed on one forearm. I had rare roast beef and cheddar on an onion roll, Heloise Gunnar portabello mushrooms on whole wheat, Dante something that looked like sphagnum moss between coarse slices of unleavened bread. His eyes followed my red meat like a dog's. There's no reason for all this detail other than I've made a habit of it. You can tell a lot about a client from what he eats, and even more from what he doesn't.

We made dents in the bill of fare and washed everything down with our drinks of choice. I had black coffee, the Gunnars mineral water with no fizz. I wondered if they flew this close to type when they weren't in public.

"You were recommended to us by Dr. Albierti." Heloise dabbed at the corners of her wide unpainted mouth with a brown paper napkin. "He's a professor emeritus with thirty years in Romance Languages. You freed his daughter from a cult."

"She joined the Young Republicans," I said. "I found her living in Saline with a professional lobbyist. I told her to call home; that was the job. Did she?"

"Yes. He sent her money. She's married to a yoga instructor here in town. So we know you get results. Missing persons, that's your specialty, right?"

The roast beef was fidgeting uneasily in my stomach. I'd begun to suspect a practical joke. It had Barry Stackpole all over it. If she said she was Wiccan I was going to pull the plug on the interview.

"Who's missing?"

"Jerry Marcus." A bit of moss clung to Dante's lower lip. He flinched when Heloise reached out and swept it away with her napkin.

"Jerry Marcus," she said, as if he hadn't spoken. "He's an *auteur*. Do you know the term?"

"It's a film director who reads subtitles. Does anyone in your circle operate a forklift?"

"I don't know what that is. Jerry's an independent. One of the new breed: digital. He does most of it on a computer. We met him at a party in the Michigan Union, where he was raising money for his first commercial project. Do you know much about science fiction, Mr. Walker?"

"I get a lot of it from clients. But you tell it, Mrs. Gunnar. You're covering the meal."

"Dante and I prefer *Ms.* I almost didn't take his name; you were right about that. It was never a legal requirement. But when you're born Gilhooley, you make certain concessions. Jerry's script, which he wrote himself, is about aliens from a planet run by a totalitarian regime come to earth to clone both front-runners for the office of President of the United States. He's filming every last foot here in town and in the suburbs. He brought along a disc of what he'd shot and showed it to us on his laptop. He's made a very effective use of the smash cut. Do you know what that is?"

I said I didn't; I had to throw her one. She got animated then; up to that point she'd been Wednesday Addams.

"A smash cut is a quick camera transition to a new scene, punctuated by a sudden loud noise, designed to shock the audience. You know, like when a quiet scene is pierced by a phone ringing shrilly. The sound effect belongs to the next scene, but you hear it while the first is still on screen. It wakes people up."

"Maybe if the quiet scene was cut, they wouldn't fall asleep. How much did you invest?"

"How did you—? Oh, yes, I suppose it's obvious. Fifteen thousand; fifty percent of the budget, with millions to be made if the film opens. *Opens,* that's what they say when it's a success right off the bat. These days, if it isn't, it's as if it was never released in the first place. *The Blair Witch Project,* that opened and how. It was shot on a shoestring and outstripped everything the studios pumped millions into that year, including *Fight Club,* starring Brad Pitt. We made the check out on the spot and signed a contract that required him to provide an accounting in six months. That was nine months ago."

"He took a powder."

She glanced down at the front of her dress, looking for powder. "Disappeared," I said. "You should watch a movie sometime without a little green man in it. Did you try to get in touch with him?"

She glared at me through her glasses. The lenses were thick; it was like looking at two angry planets through an electron telescope. She hadn't liked that last crack.

"If we hadn't, would we be meeting with you?"

"I can probably find him, if he isn't in a landfill. I can almost guarantee that when I do it won't include the fifteen grand. Not all of it anyway."

"Any portion would be welcome. At the very least, if he's absconded with our money, we'll have the satisfaction of seeing him prosecuted. Do you carry a firearm, Mr. Walker?"

"The governor says I can. Do you think it's that kind of a job?"

"Definitely not. Dante and I are major contributors to the gun control lobby in Washington. You must promise us that your gun will remain locked up at home, or wherever you keep it, throughout the investigation. We can't have someone's death on our conscience."

"No dice. Call Greenpeace."

"In that case, this interview is over. What do we owe you for the consultation?" She jerked open a handbag made of burlap fastened with a drawstring.

"Damn it, Hel!"

She jumped. I almost did. I'd had Dante down for some throat operation that prevented him from raising his voice above a murmur. He'd taken another nervous bite of his sandwich, and the spot of green against the color of his face looked like Christmas.

"Do you know how many press releases I have to write in order to make fifteen thousand dollars? It isn't as if you make commissions on those books you sell. You could do better in tips working in this restaurant."

If his wife's eyes were suns instead of planets they'd set him on fire through those heavy-duty lenses. But she said nothing.

That clinched it for me. "I get five hundred a day," I said. "Three days in advance, to cover the cost of ammo."

I'd tossed that in to see if she'd balk. She didn't, although when her gaze shifted to mine I almost ducked back into the anthill. I finished my sandwich while she made out the check. They really know how to make beef sing at Zingerman's.